STORM

Books by Bonnie S. Calhoun

STONE BRAIDE CHRONICLES

Tremors (ebook)

Thunder

Aftershock (ebook)

Lightning

Surge (ebook)

Storm

STONE BRAIDE CHRONICLES △ 3

STORM

A NOVEL

BONNIE S. CALHOUN

Revell

a division of Baker Publishing Group
Grand Rapids, Michigan

© 2016 by Bonnie S. Calhoun

Published by Revell
a division of Baker Publishing Group
P.O. Box 6287, Grand Rapids, MI 49516-6287
www.revellbooks.com

Printed in the United States of America

Library of Congress Cataloging-in-Publication Data
Names: Calhoun, Bonnie S., author.
Title: Storm : a novel / Bonnie S. Calhoun.
Description: Grand Rapids, MI : Revell, a division of Baker Publishing Group, [2016]
    | Series: Stone braide chronicles ; #3
Identifiers: LCCN 2016027390 | ISBN 9780800723781 (softcover)
Subjects: LCSH: Regression (Civilization)—Fiction. | Survival—Fiction. | GSAFD:
    Science fiction. | Dystopias.
Classification: LCC PS3603.A4387 S76 2016 | DDC 813/.6—dc23
LC record available at https://lccn.loc.gov/2016027390

16   17   18   19   20   21   22   7   6   5   4   3   2   1

1

September 25

Selah launched herself from the back of the AirWagon and landed with catlike grace in a crouch behind it. Her long, dark brown ponytail swung across her shoulders as she inspected the area side to side. Her breathing played catch-up to her runaway heartbeat. She had no fear for herself but was scared for her mother and Dane as they hid inside the vehicle.

She slowed her breathing and concentrated on the directions of the shots. The serenity of the sun-drenched morning fled with the departing songbirds.

A barrage of weapons fire lit up the side of a nearby boulder, bathing it in starbursts and scarring its surface with white streaks as it propelled bits of chiseled stone in her direction. She ducked around the back of the AirWagon and pressed herself against the side.

The sound was unmistakable. Bullets. They'd been worried about another ambush on the way back to TicCity from

WoodHaven since they hadn't made contact with Taraji yet. Selah was just beginning to relax as they reached the final mile into town.

A bullet ricocheted off a tree stump, bit the dirt in front of her feet, and sent up a burst of dust. She flinched. "Somebody tell me where they are!" Her energy-thrusting skills were great for physical combat but lousy against lasers and bullets.

When their caravan cleared the forested bend in the road, Selah stood to survey the area. Gunfire slammed into her weapon, jerking it from her hands. Selah spun away and over the side of the AirWagon to get out of the line of fire. The pulse rifle's demise saved her body from serious injury, but that full body twist was going to haunt her backside later on.

Mari slid a crossbow over the side of the AirWagon. "Here. I've got your mom and Dane secured."

Selah slid the quiver over her shoulder and nocked an arrow. Mari slid down beside her with her own crossbow, and they worked their way around the thrusters and to the front. A metal shot sliced the side of the vehicle. They pulled back.

Multiple shots zipped by from at least two directions in front of them, pinning down the vehicle. Shots echoed behind the AirWagon where Bodhi and Mojica were defending the back side. They were surrounded.

Selah lay flat on the ground and edged around the landing wells and away from the shooting. She watched behind her where Bodhi and Mojica fought the bullets with laser shots. Elongated bursts of rapid fire belched from two guns hidden in the tree line.

She listened to the echoes from the shots and took aim at deep foliage beside a wide oak tree across the road. Selah sucked in a breath to steady her shot, and let it fly. The arrow sliced silently through the greenery and rewarded her with a solid thunk.

Mari sank a second shot into the bushes on the other side of the tree. Silence followed from the foliage. Selah released her breath. Her heart thudded. There was still hope.

She turned to the other end of the vehicle, listening for more gunshots to home in on their direction. The shots petered out. Bodhi and Mojica had taken care of the back assault.

Bodhi low-crawled along the back and down the side to reach Selah. "I knew I should have demanded you keep Mojica up here. There are more splinters up here, almost as though they know where you are," Bodhi said, his laser dart at the ready.

Selah, trying to distinguish between two different gun sounds, patted his arm and ignored his scolding. "Mari and I have taken out the two on our left, and before you distracted me, I was about to get the other one. Excuse me a second." Selah rolled away from Bodhi and peered out between the air-lift mechanisms. She could see the flash from the other shooter. These weapons confused her. They fired much faster than the old-fashioned guns she was used to.

Her hands started to shake, so she gripped her crossbow. She watched a half minute longer than normal when spotting, but she had to be sure. She nocked the arrow.

A huge weight slammed her to the ground, and her crossbow skittered several feet away. She changed her center of gravity and flipped the direction of the arrow in her hand. *Bodhi, where are you?*

She swung back hard, stabbing the assailant's leg with her

arrow. He roared in pain as she propelled him from her back. He flipped over, slamming his back and head into a tree.

Bodhi dove into fist-to-fist combat with another dark-clad figure. Bullets peppered the dirt on the far side of the vehicle. Selah clawed at the dirt to reach Bodhi's laser dart. She rolled over and pulled the trigger before it registered that she wasn't its authorized user. Nothing. She scrambled to her feet and gripped the barrel like a club.

Selah raised the laser dart to hit Bodhi's attacker. The weapon jerked from her hands. She gasped and pivoted to face her new assailant.

He swung the weapon at her. Selah threw up her arms to shield her head. The others were too close for her to use an energy thrust on the man. She went into a fighting stance.

Mari fired an arrow, striking the man's hand. The weapon jerked from his hand and skidded across the road to land behind Selah. She tackled the man below center, propelling them both against a boulder. He came up swinging and his gloved fist clipped her in the chin. Her increased strength absorbed the shock, but it still spun her to the ground face-first.

The assailant she had stabbed in the leg grabbed Mari from behind. She stomped on his foot, drove her elbow into his ribs, and head-butted him. He let go.

Tiny stones ripped at Selah's palms. Her hands clutched at the dirt and sparkles invaded her vision. She rolled away to avoid another blow. Bodhi grabbed her attacker and spun him around into his waiting fist. Selah scrambled toward Mari.

An ear-piercing squeal.

Selah drew her chin to her chest and wrapped her arms around her head to shield her ears. The pain in her head weakened her knees. She stumbled a few steps into Mari and dropped to the ground along with everyone else. The brain-numbing sound ended, and TicCity security forces wearing sound-canceling headgear rushed to surround the group.

As the splinters rose with hands raised to their heads, the one closest to Selah made a break for the woods. Selah realized her new endurance would be tested. Five fast steps and she tackled him. Two of the TicCity security force rushed to her aid and took the splinter into custody.

Bodhi displayed his TicCity credentials to the security force. He hauled up the splinter he'd been fighting by the back of his collar and deposited him in a security vehicle.

Selah sat on the ground with elbows planted on her bent knees. Mari reached out a hand to help her up.

"That didn't seem to affect you as bad as it did us." Selah took Mari's hand and sprang to her feet.

"It felt like the technology we use in WoodHaven. My appliance shielded me from some of it." Mari held up her wrist.

"Let's keep that to ourselves."

Mari nodded and brushed her sleeve down over the appliance. "You go be Glade's daughter. I'd rather not show my face too much in case we run into someone who could recognize me. I wouldn't want WoodHaven to suffer because of my choices. I'll check on Pasha and Dane." She hurried through the crowd to the AirWagon.

Mojica marched around the AirWagon, escorting the two they'd fought at the rear. She reached Bodhi with her captives, and the security forces took possession of them. She and Bodhi strolled toward Selah.

Bodhi slid his arm around her waist and hugged her close. "Are you all right? Some days you really worry me, firefly."

Selah rested her head on his shoulder, her nose pressed to the coarse fibers of his jacket. Everything he owned was infused with the gentle musk of his shaving scrub. It had become a soothing aroma to her, giving the illusion of safety even in the face of full-scale chaos. If only they had enough time to explore a life together. "We've come through once again, right? So it's not yet the day to worry."

Selah gave him a playful wink and disengaged from his warm embrace. It was becoming a common occurrence for her to go from a life-threatening battle one minute to joking around the next. At first she had thought this behavior a symptom of a mental break of some kind. But Glade had told her it would become a sanity-saving ability to leave the battle behind and still see the joy in every minute of life. She suddenly missed Glade and his wisdom.

Bodhi's brows drew together. "You need to stop batting those green eyes and being flippant about such dangerous situations. Take them seriously or you could—"

"What? Fracture in nine months? I promise I do take these seriously, but if I don't add some levity, the weight of the situation is going to crush me." Selah instantly felt sorry for her snappy tone. She touched her fingertips to her lips and then to Bodhi's. She'd feel a lot better when the transport got here. She was just not willing to accept that Taraji had been defeated or killed.

He tipped his head at just the right angle, and she glanced past his ocean-blue eyes to his head marking. She hadn't seen it for a few weeks. *It looks different.* She reached up and brushed back his blond curls. *But what's different?* She couldn't put a finger to it. "Have you noticed any difference in your head marking?"

"No, I never pay any attention to it," Bodhi said as he surveyed the activity around them.

"It figures," Selah said, shaking her head. "You'd have to comb this curly mess to notice your forehead."

Bodhi grinned. "I've got to see if anyone in TicCity security knows this bunch." He strolled off in the direction of the command unit.

"Yeah, go on. We'll talk about the haircut later," Selah yelled after him. She watched his confident stride. Her heart ached with love . . . love that at this moment didn't have a future.

"Hmm, this does not look good." Mari sidled up to Selah and Mojica. "What I remember of TicCity politics from the times I came here with Glade is that the head of Council security never goes out on an operation. Her job is a ceremonial assignment."

"They warned us at the last stop that we might find resistance from more splinter cells trying to capture me. Being the novarium and the hope of the world—whatever that means—coupled with my nine-month expiration date, and these hordes of men trying to capture me at every turn and I don't even know what for—"

"Selah," Mari said.

"What?"

Mari cracked a smile and shook her head. "You're rambling again. Focus. The TicCity Council woman."

Selah sucked in a breath. Every move she made had consequences for so many people, and at the moment they didn't

11

know if Taraji had succeeded. She squeezed her eyes then exhaled slowly. This would all work out. Her family could rest in peace in TicCity and figure out a careful plan to the West before she fractured. "I guess whatever the reason, it was fortunate to have TicCity security meet us on the road when we needed to be rescued."

The tall, solidly built Council woman removed her head gear, letting long red hair spill from her helmet as she strolled toward Selah. She glanced at Mojica and offered a wry smile. "Well, finding you together saves me a trip."

Mojica furrowed her brow and opened her mouth to reply. Selah shot her a look to cut her off. She understood what was going on. The Council woman thought Mojica was Taraji. Their Amazon-like stature and long dark hair made them almost resemble twins if you weren't acquainted with either of them. It was easy to see how they came from the same clan. Selah decided she might need this mistaken identity to work in her favor.

"Thank you for coming to our assistance. My father would be pleased at your level of support," Selah said. She didn't like this woman. Glade had faced opposition from her at every Council meeting, but she had just saved the day, so gratitude was in order.

The woman pursed her bright red lips, which seemed out of place with the tan-colored uniforms, and looked down her nose at Selah. "Yes, well, it was purely circumstantial luck at best. We got word of Glade's demise from the convoy of your survivors that arrived. This will be the last assistance you get from the Council security. With Glade's passing, the regime has finally and permanently changed in TicCity."

"Congratulations on your new job, but the fact remains that I'm still the novarium and the legends have finally been proven true. We're going west in search of the Third Protocol," Selah said, hoping Treva was with the survivors.

"Good, then you won't be upset at my announcement," the woman said.

Selah watched the security forces gathering up the assailants into TicCity Council transports. "What announcement is that?"

A bored expression spread across the woman's face. "Out of respect for Glade Rishon, I'm giving you forty-eight hours to clear out of TicCity or be sold to the highest bidder."

2

Selah spent the last mile into TicCity staring out the front screen, trying to avoid talking to her mother. This road ran to the sandy shore beside her Lander quarters, which were in a sprawling U-shaped building that housed the Repository, the Institute for Higher Learning, and Glade's offices. Even though she had to leave right away, there were still files she needed from the Repository, and she wanted to go through Glade's office—

A hand rested on her shoulder. "Did you hear what I said, darling?"

Selah tensed. "No, Mother. I'm sorry. I've been told I have to get out of town, and I'm a little overwhelmed at the moment."

"We needed to head out right away anyhow. But you must listen. We've been reading the journals and book from the leather bag—"

"Mother," Selah interrupted. She thought about Amaryllis. "You can tell me about the books when we start west. I expected to have more time to get this all together. Having only forty-eight hours creates opportunities for error, so I can't think of anything else right now."

Pasha seemed ready to protest but pressed her lips together and turned away. Selah instantly felt bad for snapping.

The AirWagon lowered to the ground next to her building. With too many other things to worry about, Selah felt relieved to be able to stall opening another bag—a leather bag—of more problems to worm their way into her waking hours. Glade had mentioned at one time that there were things he hoped Selah wouldn't find out until he was gone. There were probably things in Glade's files that she and Mari would want to know, but they would have to wait their turn.

Selah climbed down and helped Dane and Pasha down. As she passed by, Pasha touched her palm to Selah's cheek. Selah hugged her mother in apology, then readjusted her neckline to be sure the mark below her collarbone didn't show. It had taken only a few unpleasant encounters for her to learn it was better to hide the fact she was the novarium . . . even among other Landers.

From the corner of her eye, Selah saw movement. She turned quickly—right into Treva's excited embrace.

"I'm glad you're safe. I was so worried," Treva said, out of breath from running.

"Me too. Were you with Taraji? Is she here with the transport?"

Treva shook her head. "No. She sent me on ahead with the wounded. Word is the Council's only giving you forty-eight hours to leave TicCity. There must be something we can do. Glade has friends on the sitting Council."

"The Council woman who brought security to our rescue outside town told me in no uncertain terms that I'm a part of the past they're trying to eliminate from their *civilized* society," Selah said.

Treva gasped. "But I need more time—you need more time." Her words came out broken, as though she were trying to say them between sobs.

Selah understood her fear of remaining here alone, yet Treva refused to join them on the trip west. She took Treva's arm, motioned the others to follow, and led her around the building and toward the elevator to their quarters. "Look at you! All worried about me and you traveled all the way here taking care of the wounded. You look worn out. You have to keep your strength up for the trip."

"I'm not going. I can't leave Cleon. He's not dead." Treva's voice quivered as they got in the elevator.

Treva's grief over Cleon's death had seemed to debilitate her. Selah too mourned the loss of her stepbrother, but the love Treva and Cleon had shared was special.

Selah leaned on the door and asked the others to take the next car so she could be alone with Treva. The doors closed around them.

Selah choked out her words. "Honey, Cleon is gone."

Treva shook her head. Loose strands of dark hair fell across her eyes and gave her a glazed expression. "No! I'd know if he was gone. He's not. I have to wait here for him."

"You heard what Glade said. The Mountain is sealed forever. We even tried to find Glade, but all the openings collapsed. There's no way in or out," Selah said. It occurred to her that even if Cleon was alive, he would be trapped in that forsaken Mountain forever. She shivered thinking of that fate for anyone, let alone her brother. It was the stuff night terrors were made of.

The door opened on Treva's floor. She inhaled deeply and straightened as she exited. She turned and smiled at Selah. "In any case, I have to keep working on the cure for the novarium fracture in case you get over the mountain range and have to turn back."

Selah frowned. "I hadn't thought about getting delayed. I only worried about fighting splinters. If we're blocked, I'm afraid we'd never make it back here. It's going to be winter in a couple months, and we don't know what we'll find."

"But if I discover the cure—or whatever it is the Third Protocol provides to the process—and it works on a novarium here, *all* Landers will change. Remember, the Keeper in the Mountain told us that. So it means you would also change." Treva's lip quivered. "I could be the one to save you."

Selah felt Treva's pain at not being able to save Cleon, but his chest wound had been too great to survive. Working on the cure at least gave Treva purpose, and one day Selah was sure she would heal from her grief. Selah hugged her again, knowing her friend's mind was set on staying in TicCity. She hadn't been banished like Selah, and her degrees in microbiology and genetics made her a valuable commodity TicCity wouldn't want to lose.

The doors opened, and Selah watched Treva walk down the sky-blue hall probably for the last time. So many people had left her life in the last few months. She felt numb to the sadness. Then again, that could be a degraded response due to her condition. Sometimes she felt unsure of herself, while at other times she felt like she could defeat the world. Regardless, she had a little less than nine months to connect with the Third Protocol or her enhanced body structure would break down and she would fracture.

The elevator arrived at her floor. Selah stepped out and strolled to the large expanse of glass that coated a whole side of the building. It gave a glorious view of the Atlantic Ocean, and the color scheme of the hallways perfectly matched the blue of the sky and surf. This view was one of the things she would miss most. She'd never see her beloved ocean again.

Selah keyed open the door to her living quarters as the second elevator arrived with the rest of her family and crew. Pasha, Dane, and Mari got out, but no one else.

"Where's Bodhi and Mojica?" Selah ushered them into the safety of her quarters and closed the door. She wanted to savor these moments of security that would be few and far between in the next nine months.

"Mojica went with Bodhi to get the equipment we'll need, and I think she said something jokingly about hijacking a military transport. Then Bodhi is going to gather his belongings and come back here," Pasha said.

"I didn't think he'd stay too far from where I am," Selah said.

Pasha knitted her brows. "That's just what he said. I hope you don't mind, but I took it upon myself to suggest that he take Treva's quarters for the night, and she can come up and spend time with you until we leave."

Selah smiled. "He didn't demand to sleep in the hall in front of my door, did he?"

Pasha seated herself on a long couch against the photo-plate wall depicting the ocean lapping at a sandy shore. "He did, but I exerted 'mother' pressure to change his mind. It seems like he loves you very much. But since he was the one who transitioned you, how much more of his abilities will he lose?"

"I'm hoping he tapped out a while back. He hasn't had any weakening other than a loss of brain activity like mind-jumping and a slight decrease of physical strength. And yes, I love him too." Selah smiled. She pulled Dane down on the couch with her and messed up his hair. He acted thoroughly embarrassed. It felt normal, and that suited Selah fine.

"If any of you are hungry, help yourself to whatever you find in the kitchen, and if you want to rest, use my room or spread out here—"

The chirping sound of the vid-phone on her desk drifted across the long expanse. Selah moved to answer the machine in her office area.

She tapped the sensor. Treva's halo-image popped up, floating in midair. "You've got problems. I just read the latest Council briefing, and you're locked out of the Repository and Glade's offices. They consider you a security risk now."

Selah muttered under her breath. "I had files I needed from the Repository. I found a link that points to the West, but I corrupted the download and lost a lot of the data."

"I can't get you in the Repository, but I need to show you something else before it's too late."

Treva avoided her eyes.

Selah moved closer to the halo-image. She didn't like when Treva did that. "What's that look for? What do you have?" Her chest tightened and her mouth went dry. Why did she have a bad feeling about this?

"I have to let you see what a fracture looks like before they ship him out," Treva said.

"Wait. What? A fracture? There's a fracture in TicCity and you didn't tell me?" Selah's heart slammed against her chest as though trying to escape. Fear of the unknown, anxiety about whether she could handle being confronted by what she could easily become—the past three days had been a deluge of emotions, and they seemed to be getting worse.

"I didn't have access to the patient before, but suddenly he's part of my caseload. When I couldn't get you to him before, I didn't want you to be tortured knowing a fracture was close by, so that's why I didn't say anything. Sorry," Treva said.

"When can I see him?"

"We have to go to the MedTech Unit now. It looks like he's getting transferred out this evening."

Selah slapped the button to close the connection. She bolted for the front door and past her family. "I've got to meet Treva."

"You need security." Mari hopped up, blocking the doorway. "Wait for Bodhi."

"No time." Selah tried to dart around her. "I've always been safe in TicCity."

Mari put out a hand. "That Council woman on the road flat-out said she was going to sell you to the highest bidder. That doesn't sound safe to me."

"Please, Selah," Pasha chimed in. "At least take Mari with you."

Selah set her jaw. They reminded her of the way Glade had annoyed her when he set out to protect her. There was no arguing with all of them. "Mari, we have to go now. This could be the only chance I have to see a fracture before it happens to me."

Pasha pointed a finger at Selah. "Don't talk that way. It's not going to happen to you. I'm reading every scrap of paper in the leather bag that Glade and the Keeper thought was important. We'll find the Third Protocol in time." Her eyes started to tear up.

Dane looked from her to Selah. His lip started to quiver. Pasha pulled him into her arms.

He looked up at her. "What's going to happen to Selah? What's a fracture?"

3

Selah and Mari left before Pasha launched into her age-appropriate answer to Dane about Selah's condition. No matter how gently it was said, Selah didn't want to hear again how she was going to die or go mad—or both—in less than nine months if they didn't find the Third Protocol.

The elevator opened. Selah and Mari started to exit on Treva's floor, but she rushed out of her door and into the car. "We need to get there now while shifts are changing. They'll be too busy to give us much grief. But Mari, you'll have to wait outside. I don't have any kind of clearance for you."

Mari started to protest. Selah touched her arm. "We'll be in the MedTech Unit. It's a fortress. I'll be safe. We won't be long."

They hurried out the living quarters' main entrance and crossed the courtyard.

Selah marveled at how normal the day seemed out here, with the sun shining, people milling about the courtyard between classes at the Institute for Higher Learning . . .

She stopped and turned toward the sea.

Waves lapped at the shore, and off in the distance, almost to the horizon, sat the geodesic dome housing Petrol City. She had never gone out there to visit Treva when she was teaching classes, but she was drawn to it by a strange feeling of familiarity.

Mari slid her hand onto Selah's shoulder. "Are you all right? You look far away."

Selah smiled and patted Mari's hand, then pulled away from the comfort of her sister's touch and turned back to the business at hand. Her insides tensed. Her whole world was about to change—again.

"Mari, you've got your communicator with you, right?" Treva led them up the stairs to the MTU, stopped at the entrance, and looked back over her shoulder before yanking on the heavy oak door.

"Yes. Do I need to call someone?"

Treva ushered them inside. "Tell Bodhi to meet us, and we'll be out by the time he gets here."

"Why are you calling Bodhi when we're only a dozen yards or so from our quarters?" Selah asked.

"Hopefully it's just cautionary. I guess we should be mindful of everything we see or hear," Treva said.

Selah took her by the arm. "What's the matter?"

"I think we're being followed."

Selah and Mari rushed to the door and peered out the glass panels.

"What did you see?" Selah asked. Mari keyed her communicator to Bodhi and spoke in hushed tones.

"There are three men seated on the benches around the tree. I've never seen them before, and their boots are caked with mud," Treva said.

Mari closed her communicator and rejoined the girls. "Bodhi will be here in a few minutes. What's wrong with having dirty boots?"

"No one who has a reason to be in the Quadrant would be caught dead with dirty shoes, let alone ones caked with mud," Selah said.

"Let's finish and get out of here. Mari, stay here by the door, and if anyone asks, tell them you're waiting for me." Treva motioned Selah down the cavernous hall.

Selah shrugged off a chill and hurried behind her. The temperature inside the old stone building was at least ten degrees cooler than outside. Unlike her part of the building on the front of the complex, which had been washed away by the tsunami during the Sorrows and then replaced by high-tech glass, these cavernous halls were part of the original stone structure. The only daytime illumination was a floor-to-ceiling window far down at the other end. Their footsteps echoed down the hall.

Selah quivered again, and without warning a starburst flashed before her eyes. She stumbled, grabbing Treva's sleeve in the process.

Treva moved to steady her. Selah blinked and stretched her eyes open to refocus.

At that moment, a screech filled the space, echoing the length of the hall. The hair stood up on Selah's arms and at the nape of her neck.

"Now, that's someone who is *not* fine. It's crazy they're letting him suffer like that." Selah's words rushed out as she felt the blood drain from her face.

"In here." Treva motioned her to a white door on the left. "We can get permission from the healer for access to him."

The girls stepped into the lab, which was brightly lit by large luminescent panels in the ceiling. The majority of the room contained individual work areas and medical equipment Selah couldn't identify, so she hoped Treva would take notes.

"Hello, Treva, what can I do for you today?" Brejian, the lead healer, had an imposing six-foot frame, with black hair standing several inches tall like the bristles of a horsehair brush. She had a scar that started at her scalp, moved down the left side of her face, and ended at the corner of her mouth, which caused her lips to barely move when she spoke.

Treva put on her best smile. "Good day, Brejian. We'd like a few minutes with the unfortunate young man before he's transferred—"

"That is not possible." Corel, the assistant dressed in a white lab coat like Brejian's, looked up from his bio-computer and rose so quickly his long legs tangled in the chair. He nearly flung himself across the desk, but recovered quickly and darted to where they stood. Selah bit her lips, stifling a smirk.

"Why can't we see him? He's now on my caseload." Treva, hands on hips, looked at Corel as though she were ready to do battle.

"Because it's simply not allowed. He has to be prepped

for the transfer, and it takes time. Besides, I don't know why he'd be on your caseload. You're not even a real doctor." Corel towered over Treva by a good seven inches or so, his long dark hair tied in an unkempt ponytail at the nape of his neck.

"Easy, Corel." Brejian glared and raised a hand.

"I assure you I am a medical professional with several bio-engineering degrees from the Mountain, including micro-biology and genetics, and I'd be glad to recite them if you have about a half hour." Treva glared at Corel then turned toward Brejian.

"I will vouch for Treva's credentials. She is the person single-handedly responsible for Glade's recovery at the Mountain." Selah spoke lightly so it didn't appear as though she was trying to intimidate Brejian by mentioning her father's name.

Brejian turned to Treva. "We need to talk after you've seen him. Hurry. The transport squad will be here in an hour." She tightened her already thin lips. "Corel, take them down to his unit." She turned to Treva. "Be mindful, he's very fragile at this juncture."

Corel stormed to a wall hanger and grabbed a large, old-fashioned key ring. "I think it's quite useless to waste time when—"

"Corel!" Brejian began to tremble. "No one wants your opinion!"

Corel's nostrils flared. He stared at Brejian as though they were having a silent conversation, but Selah couldn't sense any streaming or mind-jumping, and she didn't know if they were Landers or not.

Corel turned to the door and slapped it with his palm. "Follow me!"

"And wait there with them," Brejian added.

Selah exchanged grins with Treva as they followed Corel down the hall. Seeing him so perturbed and haughty was amusing.

The rapid pace set by his long legs made them trot to keep up. He loped down the wide corridor to a distant door and fiddled with the metal ring until he found the right key. They traveled through another hall and another door. Selah's hands grew moist. This maze of hollow-sounding halls brought back memories of the Mountain.

Corel stopped at a metal door and slid open a small rectangular panel to expose a wire mesh–covered glass.

Selah wondered at the extreme nature of the thick metal dressing the door like a lock. Her laugh came out as a nervous croak. "Is this door heavy enough to hold back the boy?"

Corel's face was blank, but his glaring eyes spoke volumes. "He broke through the last two, so we're hoping this one holds until they get him out of here tonight." He peeked in then unlocked the door and motioned them inside.

Selah sucked in a breath and stepped forward but paused at the open door. She had to know what the road ahead could possibly look like.

Corel gestured. "Go on in. The light hurts his . . . um . . . eyes, so we keep it low."

Subdued lighting created foreboding shadows, and the air smelled sour with sweat. Selah glanced at Treva and shrugged. She wasn't about to let low light keep her from observing. But was she happier with just wondering about rather than outright knowing the affliction that could become her reality—or, better stated, loss of reality?

They shuffled into the cell. The door slammed shut behind them.

Selah jumped. A surge of lightning zipped through her body. In the last few months she had come to realize her adrenaline rushes caused the lightning. More worrisome, though, was the fact that the surges didn't seem to bring the same kinetic responses as they did in the beginning. She seemed to get less from each surge.

The key scraped in the lock. It felt final. Her emotions jumbled again.

Selah breathed harder. She couldn't tell if it was due to the lightning surge or fear of being locked in. At this moment in time they both produced the same effect. When her eyes adjusted to the dimness, she saw a young man curled in a fetal position on a small, thin mattress substituting for a bed.

Treva moved closer to Selah. "Should we try to mind-jump?"

"No. We don't know if touching minds with him in this condition will push him into the abyss or not." Selah pursed her lips. "Maybe try a stream?"

A dense coat bound the young man from his neck to his hips. The sleeves covered his hands and ended in leather straps that wrapped around his body and cinched at the back, thus keeping his arms tightly crossed over his chest. His head rocked back and forth and occasionally banged into a darkened, dried blotch on the wall at the back of the bed.

Treva stumbled back a step. "I tried streaming his thoughts, but they're so chaotic. He's gone . . . for good."

Selah squeezed her eyes shut. She didn't want to accept that she might become like this if they didn't find the Third Protocol before her novarium year ended. She moved forward a step at a time. "Hello, my name is Selah." She turned to Treva. "Did you see his name anywhere?"

Treva looked around the bare room. "Nothing here to identify him. There was no name on my case sheet either, just his designation and a number."

Selah turned away and slapped her hand on the door several times. "Corel, what is the boy's name?"

"Katlo," the muffled response said. "His name is Katlo Seston."

The boy moaned loudly. Treva backed away from the bed.

"Katlo, can you hear me?" Selah bent over, moving to eye level with the bobbing head. There had to be a part of him they could reach . . . a part of her that would live.

He rocked faster. Treva touched Selah's shoulder. "Maybe you shouldn't get so close. He could be dangerous."

Selah wondered if people would think the same thing about her several months from now.

The rocking turned into a wail. Selah straightened up as the boy's head rose. A string of drool snaked from the right side of his mouth and lazily stretched into a clear thread to the bed. With eyes closed and mouth stretched wide, Katlo continued the high-pitched wail.

Selah only flinched, but Treva covered her ears.

She tried again. "Katlo, we've come to he—" How could she say *help*? There was nothing they could do for him. "Can you hear me?"

His eyes flew open—bloodshot with large star-shaped cataracts covering the lenses. Selah gasped and stumbled back. Treva moved in for a closer look.

"This is indicative of a lightning strike. I've never seen anything this bad before. But his chart says this is a hematogenic condition." Treva tried to get a better look. Her movement agitated the boy and he squirmed with renewed vigor.

"This is no time for big words." Selah backed farther away, trying to pull Treva with her.

Treva wrestled free. "They say he's got symptoms of a blood disorder. I think I can—"

The boy launched himself off the bed at Treva, knocking her to her knees. She grabbed the leather strap at his waist as he pounced on top of her.

Selah screamed. "Corel! Help!" She grabbed Katlo by the other side of the strap, and the two girls flipped him onto his side.

From the corner of her eye, Selah saw the small panel on the door open and close. Her heart raced as she helped Treva scramble to her feet.

Katlo grunted and rammed Treva headfirst like a charging bull. She threw her arms out to ward him off. Selah tried to throw herself between them, but Katlo back-shouldered her to the mattress. The edge of the metal frame dug into her backside. She winced at the white-hot pain and watched, frozen, as Katlo dislocated his shoulder and wretched his arms up over his head.

He tried to stretch the strap connecting the sleeves around Treva's neck. Treva grabbed his shoulder and twisted, pulling him down to the floor. They rolled. He pinned her down.

Selah seized the back jacket straps and yanked. Her leg muscles tightened as she tried using her body as leverage to dislodge Katlo from Treva. She was breathing hard now. His strength seemed superhuman, and even Selah with her novarium abilities struggled to control his violent weight.

With his legs free, he kept using his body as a battering ram, continuing to pummel Treva and drag Selah along with him. She sucked in a breath and pulled.

The door crashed open and Corel rushed in. With one hand, he lifted the struggling boy off Treva, bounced him back to the mattress, and jammed a hypo-pen into the side of his neck.

Katlo seemed no worse for wear. He continued to wail, thrashing about and banging his head on the wall, then suddenly went limp.

"I told you it was no use. Now I think you two ought to get out of here before he does serious damage to you. It's a good thing there was a tranquil dart hypo-pen on the next station or you'd have been in serious trouble." Corel spit out the words with unmasked contempt.

Selah stared at him, disturbed by his body-speak. *He let it happen on purpose. He could have stopped it at the onset, but he wanted to teach us a lesson.* She grabbed Treva by the arm and helped her hurry from the room. "Are you all right?"

Treva smoothed her tunic. "More fear than pain. He just knocked the wind out of me."

Residual fear pressed in on her. Selah felt numb at the hardcore reality staring her in the face—what she would become if they failed. Treva also remained quiet for the length of the first hallway. They clutched each other tightly.

Going through the second door and out into the main hall,

Selah sighed, tears in her eyes. She'd never be able to pretend she hadn't seen that poor boy whose reality would only get worse.

Treva ran a sleeve across her eyes, lifted her head high, and smoothed her tunic with shaky hands as they approached the lab door. She turned to Corel. "Thank you for coming to our aid."

Corel mumbled something and entered the lab, leaving them alone in the hall.

Selah looked at the ceiling, high and dark above her, and felt that darkness pressing in. "Eliminate them from civilized society. That's what the Council woman said." She turned to Treva with a pained expression. "They're locking them away, hidden from society."

"There's not much that can be done until I—or you—find the cure," Treva said.

Resigned, Selah hugged her. "We'd better get on the road west or else that will be me." A shudder skittered up her back.

Treva seemed to regain her composure. "I've got someplace to start working. I've only ever seen that kind of cataract going a full 360 degrees around the eye lens after a lightning strike, and I know this boy was nowhere near lightning when the fracture started."

"So are you saying it was an energy surge?" Selah turned to look at the lab door.

"I think so. At least I know where to start," Treva said.

"Are you sure I can't talk you into coming with us? We could set up a traveling lab for you to work from."

Treva patted her hand. "I know you don't believe me, but

33

I would feel it if Cleon was dead. And I don't. I loved your brother more than life itself, and I will wait here until my dying day for him to find a way to come back to me."

Selah wanted to gently remind her that Cleon couldn't have survived the catastrophic extent of his injuries.

"Besides," Treva added with a soft smile, "my uncle was still alive . . ."

Selah pulled her lips tight. She just couldn't bear to cause Treva any more pain by trying to convince her otherwise.

Selah had lost her hair tie in the scuffle, and unlike Treva's hair, which remained firmly twisted in a knot despite everything, Selah's disheveled hair hung around her shoulders and in her eyes. She pushed it back behind her ears and then wrapped her arms around Treva's shoulders. She was feeling worse every minute because she was going to miss this dear friend very much. They'd likely never see each other again.

Treva nodded. "You go on and get ready to leave this place. I'm not so sure Corel helped us as fast as he could have. I want to talk to Brejian."

Selah gave her a sideways look. "Do you think you could ask her to let me into the Repository for a few minutes?"

The door to the lab opened. Brejian charged toward them.

Selah backed away. Her senses heightened. Had Bodhi gotten to the building yet?

"Are you all right? Corel told me what happened." Brejian's concern appeared genuine.

Treva stepped forward. "No thanks to Corel. I'd say you people have some explaining to do about why you'd allow the novarium to come to harm."

Selah moved up beside her. "I saw Corel look in the viewer. It was a good minute before he came in."

Brejian shoved her hands into her lab coat pockets. "There is no telling what that idiot was thinking, but I want to make you a proposition."

4

Treva held up a hand. "I've heard about some of your antics here in TicCity. Let me guess. A proposition with you includes Selah giving up a blood sample."

"I think what I have *for* Selah is more important than what I want *from* her," Brejian said.

"From Selah? You realize she's leaving in a matter of hours," Treva said. "I don't think there's anything she could do for you, considering her current status."

Brejian glared at Treva. "Yes, I read the daily bulletins. I know her status—"

Selah crossed her arms over her chest. "What do you want from me?"

Brejian turned to Selah. "I want to leave here with you." She pulled them to the other side of the hall. "I seem to have stumbled on some very damaging information about the present administration and their dealings with novarium. I'm

37

relatively sure they will eliminate me when they find out what I know."

Selah straightened. Was this some kind of trap? She glanced down the length of the long hall for Bodhi. He stood with Mari at the doorway. She relaxed. "What kind of information?"

Brejian shook her head. "I'm not saying anything until I'm safely out of here."

"Why should Selah believe you?" Treva pressed her fists to her hips. "You could just be exaggerating to get a ride, and then have nothing to back up your proposition."

"That information is not part of my proposition," Brejian said.

"Then what are you offering her?" Treva moved closer, invading Brejian's space.

Selah stretched out an arm to hold Treva back. "What are you offering?" she echoed.

Brejian lowered her voice. "The Repository."

"What? Access to the Repository? What's your angle? You're smart enough to know if you give me access to Repository files, you can't be sure I'd follow through and take you with us."

"You misunderstand me," Brejian said. "I'm not offering *access* to the Repository. I'm offering you *the* Repository."

Selah's brows drew together. She could feel the woman's sincerity, but she still wasn't sure if she could believe her.

"Selah doesn't have a lot of time, and you're talking in circles. Either tell her in plain words what you mean or we're out of here." Treva motioned Selah toward the front doors.

Brejian grabbed Treva's arm. "I've been compiling the files on data cubes. I have a complete copy of the Repository, and

I will trade it for passage out of this place and into someplace safe in the West."

Selah stared at Treva and then at Brejian. Her thoughts jumbled. She needed this mental storm to pass. "You have *everything* from the Repository, and you're willing to tell us what you found about this Council and the novarium?"

"Yes—wait! I didn't include the Council actions in the deal." Brejian looked nervous.

"If you've actually got the Repository, then I would definitely consider letting you travel with us." Selah heard the familiar clomp of Bodhi's boots coming up the hall. He slowed and stopped behind her. Even without hearing him, she'd have known it was him by the smell of his shaving scrub.

"Is there some kind of problem?" Bodhi leaned in, and Selah felt his breath on her neck as he spoke. She shivered.

Selah stared at Brejian but answered Bodhi. "We have now brought on a healer for our trip west."

Treva frowned. "But—"

"No buts," Selah said as she turned to Treva. "I've made a decision. You've already made your decision to stay here."

Treva winced.

Bodhi moved between the two. "What's going on here? And when did the healer join us? I have strict limits on our supplies—"

"Are you taking a food processor?" Brejian asked. "I have a year of food packs set aside. I will supply my own."

Bodhi pulled Selah to the side. "Are you crazy? What if she's some kind of plant from the Council just to keep tabs on you?"

"She said she has a copy of the Repository. I consider that

more important than worrying about the Council. When we leave here they'll be the least of our worries, but if I can get the files in an uncorrupted form, I may be able to find a cure for your problem," Selah said.

"My 'problem' has plateaued. It's *your* problem that is ongoing, so if it's not going to help *you*, I think it would be better to leave her here. We know nothing about her," Bodhi said.

"She says there's information about this Council and something to do with novarium," Selah said. "I wouldn't be so willing to trust a stranger, but this is our last chance to get *anything* from those records, and we know Glade inputted the majority of the Repository. Can we afford to leave it behind?"

Bodhi walked back and forth a few times and ran a hand through his blond curls. "I don't know. We don't know this woman at all, other than as a healer."

The front door opened and muffled voices drew their attention. Bright light streaming from the windows in the doors cast a halo around the approaching shadow in the dark hall. Mojica emerged into the light and strolled to Brejian. They clasped each other's arms above the wrist.

"This woman wants to come with us to the West. She says she has the Repository and she's willing to trade it for passage. What would you say about that?" Selah said to Mojica.

A broad grin spread across Mojica's face and she clapped Brejian on the back. "You've done it! Outstanding timing."

"Is there something I should know?" Selah glanced between the two.

Mojica tipped her head. "I thought you'd have noticed by now. We're of the same clan."

Bodhi stepped closer as if to protect Selah from an unseen predator while Mojica and Brejian bared their right arms. Each woman had a tattoo of an exotic bird with long tail feathers that began at the back of their right hand and snaked up their arm to their shoulder.

Treva's mouth dropped open. She motioned to Selah. "We saw this tattoo in the Mountain on that young man and his crew who saved us from the gang."

Selah looked at each arm in turn. "I don't understand. Why am I beginning to see so many of these? What does this mean?"

"It means there's always been someone watching over you as the novarium. We are of the Kinship," Mojica said.

Treva stumbled back. "But that group is like the Blood Hunters. They're splinters!"

"Ladies, we've known Mojica from the beginning, and then Taraji, so if Brejian is of the same clan, I guess she's fine with me," Bodhi said, raising both hands in mock surrender. "I came over because Mari called, but I've got a lot to finish. I've set our departure for tomorrow noon whether Taraji is back or not." He looked at Brejian. "Have you heard anything about Taraji yet?"

The healer shook her head. "Not a thing. It's total communications silence."

"See! We need to wait another day for her," Selah said. "And I have so many things to gather. I need to see Amaryllis."

Mojica shook her head. "I don't think that's a good idea. I don't like the looks of some of the men I've seen congregating in the courtyard, and I doubt TicCity Council will give us help if there's trouble."

"Mojica, you stay with Selah, and I'll finish the arrangements. We'll meet at your quarters in two hours." Bodhi strode down the hall and out the door.

Selah watched him go. Even in his weakened state Bodhi remained clearheaded and sure about his decisions, while she felt a growing apprehension at the confusion that assaulted her, sometimes lasting several minutes or more. "You know he left you here to deal with me and my insistence on seeing Amaryllis," she said to Mojica.

Mojica screwed up her lips. "Yep, I saw that caged-animal look in his eyes when you said her name."

"Excuse me. Does anyone remember that I'm still waiting for an answer?" Brejian looked annoyed, though more confident than she had ten minutes ago.

Mojica's communicator went off, and she turned away to answer it.

"Yes, you can come with us. You can help me with the files," Selah said. "Be ready to go by noon tomorrow. Treva will help you get ready. She knows how we—"

"Selah, we have a problem. We put an auto-relay on Glade's communicator until we left here. A message just came in to Glade's estate from the Bantors. They heard of Glade's passing and want a larger payment to keep Amaryllis," Mojica said.

"The East Creek Bantors?" Brejian asked. "They've gained quite a reputation lately as smugglers." Her face flushed and she lowered her eyes. "I've bought several black market compounds from them. And word has it the Blood Hunters are using their property as a way station."

Selah stiffened. "I don't know about any payments Glade

was making. But if they're doing anything illegal I don't want Amaryllis near them." She threw her hand up. "Blood Hunters! This is crazy. I have to go get her." Would Amaryllis hate her for forcing her to leave? She dreaded taking the girl from people she had bonded with so well over the last few months, but for her own peace of mind, Selah couldn't leave her there.

She charged toward the doors, but Mojica grabbed her arm. "It's not safe. Just like in the Mountain, if they're that much into contraband, they've got a pulse on Council activity so they know where enforcement is at all times. They may know about your new status, and this could be a trap to catch you."

Selah tried to pull away. Mojica didn't let go. Selah stared down at the hand clamped on her arm, then glanced up at Mojica. "Are we really going to come to blows on this?"

Mojica pressed her lips into a scowl but released Selah's arm. "Selah, you can't go alone."

Selah marched toward the doors again but yelled over her shoulder, "Then you'd better come with me because I'm going to get her right now."

5

Selah, Mari, and Mojica traveled northwest out of Tic-City to where the river branched into three waterways. Then they followed the stream called East Creek into the Bantors' family lands. Selah felt confident with Mari and Mojica as her backup. It would have been nice to have Bodhi along too, but he wouldn't be thrilled about her interference with the happiness Amaryllis had found, especially with Selah's life being so uncertain. She hoped Amaryllis would forgive her for separating her from her parents.

Selah's head had cleared, and she spent the half-hour trip running through scenarios where they might have to fight to get Amaryllis back. She hoped the fact that there would be no more payments might make the Bantors more agreeable to letting her leave.

Mari came to the front of the AirWagon carrying a new pulse rifle she had unpackaged and inspected. "Here, use your trigger finger to set the code."

Selah hefted the new weapon in her hands, and the signal set chirped. "How many weapons were you able to get?" she asked Mojica.

"Taraji had shared the codes with us to get all the equipment from her second squad. It was fueled with discretionary funds that Glade made available many years ago. The Council can't trace it, so it doesn't exist. We got four more pulse rifles and a couple laser darts, and a transport if we want it."

"How many can that carry?" She handed the weapon back to Mari.

"They're made for sixteen," Mojica said as she navigated the AirWagon between trees.

Mari peered at the forest around them, hurried to the back of the AirWagon, and returned with three laser darts. "I think we need to stay armed." She checked the charge chamber on each weapon as she handed them out, then scanned the trees on either side. "Mojica, you've got movement at one o'clock."

"I see it," Mojica said as she dialed back the throttle. "Ten o'clock also." She slowed the AirWagon into a hover.

Five men dressed like farm boys rushed from the trees on either side and stood in front of them, pointing antiquated rifles that fired bullets. All three women rose and pointed their laser darts.

Mojica spoke with the confidence of a high commander. "Gentlemen, if you will, please note this AirWagon is equipped with the latest in projectile shield protection. Your metal bullets will be attracted to the shield and not to us. But we, on the other hand, are using energy pulses that will pass through the shield and broil your butter." To accentuate her point, Mojica shot at a tree branch over two of the men, and it crashed to the ground between them, shattering their tough-guy façade as they scurried out of the way.

One of the men on the far side of the road spoke. "What do you want?"

"I came to see the Bantors. They have charge of a child who was in my care, and they want to see me," Selah said. One of the men ran off up the lane. She searched the other men's body-speak. None appeared overly hostile. It was all posturing.

A shrill whistle sounded. The four remaining men disappeared back into the trees.

Selah checked to the right, Mari checked to the left. No one.

"I guess that means we're free to go," Mojica said and cycled up the AirWagon.

"I didn't know we had that kind of technology. It would have made me feel safer around splinters," Selah said. She plopped onto the seat across from Mojica, and Mari sat behind her.

"We don't have that kind of technology," Mojica said with a grin.

Selah and Mari chuckled and slapped Mojica on the back.

"There you go." Mojica nodded to the left as she cycled down the AirWagon.

Amaryllis sat on the porch with a man and woman whom Selah had met only once—the Bantors. Mojica angled up beside them and Selah stepped down.

Amaryllis ran to Selah and launched into her arms. She laughed with delight as Selah swung her off the ground and hugged her for all she was worth.

Selah laughed. "You must have gained twenty pounds in the last couple—"

"Miss Rishon, we have some important business to attend, and the child need not be present," Bantor said.

Mojica called Amaryllis up into the AirWagon, and Selah strolled up onto the porch.

The man leaned on the turned wooden railing. "We've found ourselves in some unusual circumstances, and we need a larger payment by at least fifty percent—"

"Let me stop you right there. I didn't know my father was making any payments to you—that was his business. But he is dead and there is no money, so there won't be any more payments whether the amount was raised or stayed the same," Selah said.

"Well then, you'll have to take the kid with you. I'm not prepared to feed any charity cases around here," he said.

Selah looked between the two. No expression of remorse from either husband or wife.

Momentarily stunned by their callousness, she dreaded what she now had to do—tell Amaryllis that the parents she loved didn't want her. "Fine. If that's the way you want it." Selah's knees shook as she descended the porch stairs and climbed into the AirWagon.

She motioned to Mojica and Mari to let them talk alone. As the two women moved away, Selah sat down beside Amaryllis and wrapped her in her arms. "I've missed you a lot, little one," she said.

Amaryllis smiled broadly and sat up straight. "I'm not little. I've grown a whole two inches. Natalia said if I grow much taller my dresses will be shirts."

Selah released the girl and searched for strength to say her next words. "How . . . how would you feel if I asked you to

48

come to the West with me? We would never be coming back this way, so you wouldn't be able to see your new parents." Selah squeezed her eyes shut, waiting for the child's anguished sobs. Nothing. She opened her eyes.

Amaryllis stared at her. "I thought you didn't want me."

"I thought you loved the woman who looked like your real mother." Selah's heart tapped a staccato beat.

Amaryllis frowned and pushed out a big sigh. "She doesn't look anything like my real mother. I just said that to make you feel better about leaving me here."

Selah's hands shook. "My sweet girl, why would you think I wanted to get rid of you?"

"Because your father said that it would be a big burden on you as the novarium to be saddled with taking care of an orphan." Amaryllis dropped her head.

"I would never want to be rid of you. It has broken my heart these last few months without you." Selah pulled the child into her arms again.

Amaryllis lifted her eyes. "So you don't want to get rid of me?"

"No."

"I can come with you?"

"Yes, as soon as you grab your things." Selah smiled.

"I told you I've outgrown everything. Nothing to take." She shrugged and they started to laugh. "And please don't call me Amaryllis anymore. I'm grown-up now. I want to be Rylla."

Selah nodded. It felt good to have something to laugh about. But the feeling was short-lived.

Mari and Mojica scrambled to the front of the vehicle carrying pulse rifles. Selah jerked her head up from Rylla's and saw that the AirWagon was surrounded by at least ten men. She snatched up her pulse rifle and pushed Rylla to the floor near the fortified compartment where they often stashed weapons.

"What's going on here?" Selah shouted.

"Well, you owe me some payments, and since you say Glade didn't leave any funds, I figure we're just going to have to take *you*, since you're the *novarium*." Bantor leaned against the porch railing and smirked. With a look of horror on her face, his wife hurried into the house and slammed the door.

Selah stiffened. This had been a trap, and now Rylla was going to be in danger because of her foolish move. She calculated every possible scenario, then put her weapon down and slowly raised both hands.

"I think it would be profitable if we discuss this without weapons," Selah said to Bantor as she walked toward the AirWagon steps. "May I?" She motioned to the porch. Mojica and Mari balked, but Selah backed them off with a sideways glance.

Bantor grinned, showing a missing front tooth that Selah hadn't noticed before, probably because he hadn't smiled. She stepped onto the porch, remaining stone-faced. Mojica and Mari had caught her drift and moved to the far side of the Air-Wagon. The men around it were so confident of their position that no one moved away from the group to guard the ladies.

Selah angled herself toward Bantor so a majority of the men were in close proximity on the other side of the railing. She stopped advancing when she had her maximum range figured.

Bantor stared at her. "Well, what do you have to say for

yourself, *novarium*?" He made *novarium* sound like a curse word, the way he spit it out.

She gathered her anger constructively. "I would say you're probably a splinter, or you're being paid by the splinters." She sensed the charge building.

Bantor yelled over his shoulder to the men standing around the AirWagon, "Well, look at this, boys. The little gal isn't as stupid as some say she is."

Selah's hands began to shake. She balled them into fists and set her jaw. "Are you Blood Hunters?"

Bantor sat on the railing and propped his boot on a large box. Resting an elbow on his raised knee, he picked his teeth with a wooden needle and chuckled.

Selah saw the charge signature floating in her vision—blue and purple waves. She thrust both hands in his direction.

The collective power of her thrusts had gained twice as much force in the last week. Bantor flew over the railing backwards with feet flailing in the air. The nexus of the thrust continued to the first two men near the AirWagon. They slammed into the next three, and pandemonium broke out.

Selah leaped from the third step of the porch into the Air-Wagon. "Get us out of here!"

Mojica had already cycled up the machine, and they shot off through the rest of the group, knocking a couple down as they passed. The men recovered and began shooting at the AirWagon.

Mari crouched in the back with her pulse rifle. Selah grabbed her own pulse rifle and fired at the men who had mounted Sand Runs to chase them. The large, knobby tires of the four-wheeled dune buggies gave the men good traction on the slippery grass.

One of the men wore a helmet control for a big gun mounted on his Sand Run. It fired a whole barrage of bullets wherever he turned his head. Every once in a while one would reach the composite AirWagon hull, and Selah flinched when metal whined against metal.

"We need backup," Selah yelled to Mojica. Another Sand Run with a mounted gun joined the chase. Mojica tapped her communicator and spoke in short, fast sentences.

Mari fired on a Sand Run. The energy pulse shorted the machine and blew the rider into the air, and the machine coasted to a stop. The air hung ripe with weapon discharges.

A shot whizzed by Selah's right ear. Rylla screamed. Selah spun to see the child huddled near the corner in a fetal position and the spot on the floor where the bullet had lodged.

Selah yanked open the fortified compartment. She pointed at the door. "Get in," she yelled to Rylla. The girl shook her head.

A small explosion rocked the AirWagon, jolting them from side to side. Rylla squealed and scurried into the compartment. Selah slammed the door and dove back to Mari's position. "What was that?"

"Some kind of hand charge. They pulled a pin and threw it. That guy rode on a charged-up Sand Run, but I think I disabled it because he dropped back and I don't see him coming." Mari drew aim and fired on another Sand Run.

Selah disabled one of the big guns by pulsing exactly where the gun joined the Sand Run. Unfortunately for the driver, he was sitting in front of the connection. He flew one way and the big gun went the other.

"I could hear Bodhi trying to answer me, but the signal is

garbled in here. The Blood Hunters must be jamming communications," Mojica yelled as she fought to keep them at top speed for the terrain.

"Got it. We're on our own." Selah didn't take her eyes off the target. She fired another pulse. A Sand Run went airborne and flipped twice after expelling its driver. Selah didn't want to believe what she was seeing. The more attackers they disabled, the more showed up, like cockroaches disturbed by light.

Mojica wrestled to keep the AirWagon on a straight path on the narrow country road. The trees on the left and the stream on the right kept the Blood Hunters behind rather than surrounding them, but soon they'd come out of the forest into the flat lands.

Selah nudged Mari and pointed up the hill. "They're coming in AirStreams now."

Mari looked at the small bullet-style hovercrafts exiting from the woods. "How fast do they go?" She fired on and disabled the second gun mounted on a Sand Run, but the open spots in their assault were swiftly being filled by the new aboveground pursuers.

"Up to forty miles an hour, from my experience," Selah said over the sound of the weapons barrage. "The higher from the ground they climb, the slower they get. If they stay close to the ground they go faster."

"That's not good," Mojica said. "Forty is our top speed. We can't lose them, but I hope to keep them at bay. And I hope Bodhi gets here."

"Try to keep us above rocky ground. They'll have to go higher like we do, and it will slow them down," Selah said. She took aim at an AirStream. It rose and slowed at the same time she fired. The pulse deflected across its bow and into the woods, snapping a treetop.

A Sand Run charged from the woods, and a man hanging on the back of it leaped onto the side of the AirWagon and hung there like a tree frog. By the time Selah got to that corner, he was climbing over the side. Selah whacked him with the butt of her pulse rifle, and he fell backwards from the AirWagon, landing on an AirStream and its surprised driver. They skidded off the road, hit the embankment on the forest side, and caught fire as they flipped into the trees.

Selah felt more focused than she had in quite a while. The feeling exhilarated her and her hands trembled. She reined herself in and carefully drew a bead on the closest AirStream. It dipped off to the right and disappeared around their vehicle as the trees ended and the fields spread out before them.

Mari stopped another Sand Run. "Where do they keep coming from?"

"They're stationed all along this route. I can see their tracks, looking at the grass from this angle," Mojica said. She slapped on her communicator. An errant shot ricocheted off the side shield near her. Mojica ducked, swerving the AirWagon.

Mari and Selah groped for a hold but slid to the side. Selah lost her grip on her pulse rifle, and the feed chamber wedged between two partitions. She yanked to get it free as Mari fired on an AirStream delivering another climber.

An advancing Sand Run shot at Mari. She dodged it at the same time the next attacker crawled over the side. With her hands busy trying to free her weapon, Selah kicked at him, delivering an unexpectedly powerful blow to his midsection. It threw him against the side of the AirWagon. He gasped like a floundering fish and scrambled toward her. Selah let go of her weapon and bounced to a crouching position, fists ready to fight. The attacker pounced.

Another AirStream fired on Mari, drawing her away from where Selah struggled. Mojica couldn't turn to help without letting the AirWagon slow down enough to be overrun.

Selah threw up a side kick. Her foot connected with ribs, resulting in a crunching sound. She'd have rather thrust the man over the side, but the energy from such a burst in close quarters could hurt Mari and Mojica. A bullet whizzed by her head and glanced off the fortified compartment door.

Inside the closed space, Rylla screamed.

Selah punched her attacker with a solid right. She heard the compartment rattling. The attacker lunged at her. Another Blood Hunter scrambled over the side.

Mari turned to fight him, and yet another assailant scaled the side and attacked her from behind.

Selah watched the compartment peek open. Rylla would get hurt. She pushed her assailant in that direction and slammed him against the side, effectively closing the compartment door. The Blood Hunter wrestled to keep hold of her. The smell of his rancid breath soured her stomach as they struggled. Her foot slipped and she slammed her head into the same compartment door.

Suddenly, cold metal pressed to her neck. "I'd rather keep your head attached to the rest of you, but it's your choice," the man whispered in her ear.

Her stomach threatened to revolt. Selah went limp as he slipped a band over her wrist and jerked it tight. The knife nicked her throat. Selah gasped as he jerked her wrists together.

Mari quickly subdued her first attacker with a right jab to the throat, and the man fell to the deck gasping and clutching at his throat. The next man over the side whacked Mari in the head with a hand weapon. She went down.

The AirWagon cycled to a stop as one of the Blood Hunters pressed a rifle to Mojica's spine.

Selah, her hands bound, peered around the assailants to find her sister. A Blood Hunter dragged Mari to a seat in the far corner where he bound her hands. A trickle of blood oozed down the right side of her head. She looked up and spotted Selah.

"Are you all right? Your head is bleeding," they said at the same time. Both lifted tied hands to search their head.

Selah felt her spot. Her fingers came away sticky with blood, but no deep crease, just a mushy spot. "It's only a scratch." She gave an apprehensive smile as she pressed her fingers to the stinging spot on her neck. Would Bodhi find her in time?

The Blood Hunter watching her jerked on the lead attached to her restraints. She jerked back harder, almost pulling him off his feet, then glared at him, daring him to do it again. He charged at Selah but another man stopped him. "They'd all better be in good condition when the boss gets here." The man added something she couldn't hear. All she could make out was the word *novarium*. Obviously he knew *what* the target was but not *who*. She filed that observation for future reference.

Mari opened her mouth to speak, but her eyes rolled up and her lids closed as she passed out. Selah cried out and tried to reach for her sister, causing a rush of men to tackle her.

Mojica backhanded the guard holding the weapon on her,

then gave a sweeping kick that knocked his legs out from under him. His rifle skittered off under the forward seats and he scrambled away from Mojica to chase it. Two other Blood Hunters corralled Mojica in the close quarters. The AirWagon quickly swarmed with the men and their boss.

Then the sky went dark.

A shadow moved from the nearby ridge and settled over the AirWagon, blocking out the light.

Selah looked up at the underside of a projectile-shaped airship transport large enough to be military grade. A patterned system of thick conduits on the transport's almost flat underside began to glow a brilliant green, then a low hum vibrated the surface of the AirWagon. Selah couldn't contain her surprise or her enjoyment at the look of dismay on the Blood Hunters' faces when their weapons were snatched from their hands by the magnetic current. If the situation hadn't been so dire, she might have actually laughed.

Blood Hunters darted over the sides, vacating the Air-Wagon and moving off a good distance toward their assembled posse. But they didn't leave. They just waited. For what?

Mojica scrambled to untie Selah and they both darted to Mari, who was waking up. She propped herself up as Mojica untied her, and Selah checked her head wound.

Mari shook her head several times. "I need to get rid of this fog. Let's get out of here. Don't waste time fussing with me. Navigate."

Mojica helped her stand. "We'll be safer in the transport. Bodhi's going to land so we can—"

A loud volley of explosions rocked the ground, vibrating through the AirWagon. Selah stumbled sideways and slammed into the compartment door. She snatched open the door and grabbed Rylla in her arms. They headed for the steps.

Another volley. The transport took a hit broadside with a brilliant flash and a stream of sparks. It veered sharply away to the south and dropped back behind the ridge. The Blood Hunters began a new advance on the AirWagon.

Selah kicked at her pulse rifle and dislodged it from the side plates. She checked the load. "Can we get out of here?"

Mojica tried to power up the controls. "Magnetic mislock! It shut down too fast and the thrusters won't engage."

Selah watched the Blood Hunters advance. They moved slowly at first, but when their advance was met with no resistance, they rushed forward, shooting.

"Should I fire to keep them back?" Selah followed their movement.

"Let them get close enough to do real damage. Scare shots are just a waste of the energy pack," Mojica said as she punched different combinations and complained to the inanimate control panel.

"Here they come!" Selah tried to push Rylla back into the compartment, but she refused to go. "Go sit by Mari and help her get her bearings," Selah ordered. She regretted coming here and putting the girl in danger. The men could just as easily shoot her as they could any of the others.

Rylla scrambled to Mari's side. Two Sand Runs revved their engines. Selah could hear the AirWagon thrusters trying to engage. She remembered the time her stepbrother Cleon overcame a mislock. She was sure Mojica would get the thrusters to kick in any second.

The Sand Runs now drove within shooting range. Selah

ran through the scenario. She couldn't protect them alone. Mari was in no shape, and she didn't want Rylla handling a weapon.

She picked a target, leveled her breathing, and took aim.

A wall came down in front of her.

6

Selah jerked back. Her mind tried to digest what she saw—patterns of rectangles and squares, raised and sunken, fitting together in a dark gray wall that went up as far as she could see. No warning, no sound. Her mouth dropped open at the same time Mojica swung around from her navigator seat, snatched up the pulse rifles, and lifted Mari to her feet.

It wasn't a wall. It was an up-close side of the airship transport. She could barely make out the impressions on the side facing her, where the propulsion and maneuvering wings had retracted below the plates as the transport magnetically hovered mere inches from the side of the AirWagon. An elongated crack appeared from the side of the wall, and a ramp came to rest on the top edge of the AirWagon. Taraji appeared in the opening, motioning them in.

Selah grabbed Rylla by the hand and hurried behind Mojica, who was acting as Mari's crutch. They climbed on a seat to step onto the ramp. Taraji directed them in at the top and the ramp rose behind them.

The fear drained from Selah's throat, taking the lump with it. She pulled Rylla down on the bench that lined one side of the narrow, elongated chamber. The dark curved composite wall felt like a safe cocoon. She hugged Rylla with trembling arms, and Rylla clung to her.

Mojica guided Mari toward the infirmary as Taraji finished punching in the code to the panel next to the ramp opening.

Taraji turned to Mojica. "Bodhi could use you on the command deck. We weren't quite sure which defense combinations to use against the charges they're firing using Mountain technology."

"I'd hoped to get calmer circumstances to calibrate this transport for Mountain tech, but you've done well." Mojica turned and bolted from the chamber.

Taraji stared at Selah without speaking. Selah lowered her head. "I'm sorry."

"For what?" Taraji set her jaw and leaned against the wall.

Selah knew she'd hear about this episode from both her mother and Bodhi, but apparently Taraji was the prelude to her soon-to-be tongue lashing. "For coming out here to get Amaryllis. I know it was foolish, but I would never be able to live with myself if I'd left her behind."

Taraji's jaw muscles worked and she crossed her arms. "They're only being cautious for your protection. You could have been captured by a very powerful faction of Blood Hunters, and everything we've gone through to get here would have been for—"

The muffled sound of an explosion accompanied a sudden

jolt of the transport. Selah's muscles quivered with fear and anticipation of another battle. Would her selfishness be their undoing? Her heart raced as she gripped the seat against the violent shake.

Bodhi veered the transport to the left. He tried to gain altitude and speed with the large vessel while wrestling the controls at each new volley of bombs raining on them. He glanced at one of the side screens on the control panel in time to see a guy on a Sand Run fire a bomb from a tube mounted on his shoulder.

Mojica charged onto the command deck and slid into the seat beside Bodhi. He looked at her with a scowl. "She talked you into coming out here, didn't she?"

Mojica strapped on her harness and slipped her boots into the foot straps on the control grid. Their seating units were connected to the transport on gimbals that kept them floating straight up no matter the angle of the transport. "What did you really expect her to do? Leave the kid here? Selah may be dying, and for sure is never coming back to this place." She pressed her thumb into a depression on her chair arm, and a control panel cantilevered out of the dash in front of her. "Loosen the reins." She lowered a VR visor and punched in her access. "I've got control."

The ship rocked to the right. Mojica shifted the joystick to the left and stomped on the right stabilizer pedal.

"How long can they fire on us?" Bodhi momentarily forgot about being angry at Selah. He watched the distance increase, but shells continued to reach them.

"Not much longer, my friend." Using her left hand, Mojica

manipulated combinations of colored pads on the keyboard in front of her. The percussions stopped, but Bodhi could still hear the shells exploding. His attention jerked to Mojica. "How'd you do that?"

"New shield technology." Mojica grinned. "The magnetic shields are up, and unless someone walks where we're sitting, they won't even see us, because the construction of this vessel has the ability to bend light and make us blend into the scenery. But it's only good when we're out in the open. The system is still glitchy and the magnetics can interfere with other systems. The ship isn't seen, but the interference is evident, which can effectively give away our position. That's your next lesson. So how 'bout we run through TicCity and get on our way before they follow us that far."

"But we weren't planning on leaving until tomorrow," Bodhi said. He didn't like hearing they'd soon have to confront this gang again.

Mojica shook her head. "Those plans have disappeared like throwing sand in the ocean. The Blood Hunters won't stop now that they've seen Selah. They know this is their last chance to catch her."

"So that message you relayed to me from the adoptive parents—it was their ploy to get Selah into their territory." Bodhi's chest tightened. He should have suspected and had guards with her.

No. Mojica and Mari were more than adequate.

Bodhi inhaled sharply. He had to stop second-guessing himself, but he couldn't afford mistakes. He'd promised Glade he'd protect Selah with his life. "I'm calling the Council. They should at least give us protection until we leave."

Mojica accelerated the vessel. "I wouldn't bother. That woman looked like *she* was ready to swoop in and take Selah's—"

"TicCity Council Chambers. What is your business today?" The hologram woman smiled pleasantly on the command deck screen.

Mojica rolled her eyes.

"I'd like to speak to the Council woman," Bodhi said. He was sure she'd offer help.

The screen went black, then immediately he was looking at the same woman with black eyes who had met them on the road. She pulled a covering on over her arms. Her look displayed guilt. What was she hiding?

"Madame Council woman, I'd like to ask your assistance with the adoptive child that Glade Rishon placed. We encountered Blood Hunters when visiting the child's adoptive parents—"

"You had an AirWagon when you came to town. What vehicle is this with video capabilities?" The Council woman scowled.

"It's a private vehicle," Mojica said to the monitor.

"Well, we as Council should—"

"I'm asking if you could give us added protection for Selah until tomorrow." Bodhi leaned forward and raised his voice.

The Council woman lowered her chin so her eyes looked larger when she looked at the screen. "The only reason you've been safe so far is out of courtesy to Glade's memory. I was quite smitten with him when we first came out of the Mountain. But I was not the one he wanted." The woman looked almost wistful for a moment. Then she snapped back to the present. "That was then. This is now. Glade is gone, and you had better be too . . . soon."

Bodhi tried to itemize the tasks he still had to complete. "We need until tomorrow."

The Council woman shrugged. "That's up to you. We offer no protection. With Glade gone, our sector's last allegiance to the cause has ended. We moved beyond it when Glade originally sacrificed himself to the Mountain, thinking he'd never be back. Come to think of it, we have you to thank for that debacle."

Bodhi recoiled. "How can you be so callous? After all he accomplished for the cause over the years, Glade died in that place, and Selah is now trying her hardest to complete the Third Protocol. When she does, all Landers will be changed." Bodhi stared at the woman, trying to understand how anyone could be this depraved about protecting human life.

"Yeah, well, we don't know if that will be a good thing or a bad thing, now do we?" The Council woman looked as though she'd suddenly let her pretense fall.

Bodhi decided to probe. "Do you really think it would harm us?"

"We don't know what variances have been added over the last 150 years . . . possible contaminants. We could demolecularize to common dust in an instant and it would all be over. Most folks have voted to press for another cycle rather than take the chance." The Council woman shifted in her seat.

Selah pushed her way between Bodhi's and Mojica's stations and turned the monitor to face her. "So you all voted to let me fracture and, from what I've seen in the last few hours, essentially go mad, just so you continue your lives uninter-rupted? Now I get it! All those novarium who have fractured and you've sent away—you purposely kept them from at-tempting to find the Third Protocol," she said in disgust.

Bodhi wanted to reach out and pull her close. He would not let that happen to her. He would find the Third Protocol or die trying.

"Well, hello, Selah. Can't say I'm glad to see you're well." The Council woman sat back in her seat and drummed the arms of her chair.

"Glade told me about you." Selah leaned into the screen. "He told me the only reason you all left me alone as a no-varium was because he was my father." She pointed at the screen. "And the only reason he lived to see me become the novarium—since all the other novarium parents in this sec-tor mysteriously died before their child transitioned—was because he was in the Mountain my whole life, where you couldn't get at him."

"Yes, well, that was a mistake on the Council's part that should be rectified with the Blood Hunters' compact." All pretense gone, the Council woman tented her fingers and stared defiantly at Selah.

Bodhi pulled the screen back to him. "So you'd let her be drained for blood samples and then killed?"

The Council woman didn't answer.

"Answer the question," Selah said. "Tell me to my face you'd let me die."

The Council woman shrugged. "You're the last novarium we'll have to deal with for 150 years. Maybe after that long the remaining Landers will be willing to let the cycle end. But at the moment people are getting agitated, and you have to leave. I don't dare get in the middle. I have to live here, and either way you'll be gone shortly." She hesitated. "I guess after my past history with Glade, I owe you something. The parting advice I have for you is . . . your only hope is to find the old woman." She slapped the connection closed.

Selah looked between Bodhi and Mojica. "The old woman? What does that mean? This is the second time I've heard about her."

"No idea. Maybe Pasha and Mari will find a clue in the documents," Mojica said. "I called Treva while you were talking. Brejian will be ready to go in a half hour."

"I'll finish the other transactions from here and order the supplies from the depot for us to pick up," Bodhi said. The Council woman's callous disregard for Selah's life furthered his determination.

Selah leaned against the side of Bodhi's command chair. "It just hit me. All these people have died just to keep their sector from being changed. How many other sectors have done this?"

"Their excuse is the change could be something bad," Bodhi said.

Selah pointed at the blank monitor. "I don't believe that! The Council woman was from the same original group as Glade. She originated in the Mountain. She knows the project goal, and she's hiding some very important information. I could read that in her body-speak."

Bodhi nodded. "Glade knew about the change. Although he never said why, I don't think he'd have chosen it for you if the final results were bad." Bodhi was certain Glade would not choose to have something harmful befall the daughter he loved so much.

"Folks, I think we have a problem." Mojica pushed back her VR visor. "I was trying to alert Pasha that we're coming in hot to snatch them up, but I'm getting no connection at the living units."

"How far away are we?" Selah paled as she sat in the navigator seat behind Mojica.

Bodhi stared at her while Mojica had her attention. Her eyes looked tired. He needed to encourage her to rest more often. She worried about everyone else more than herself, but that was one of the reasons he loved her.

"About ten clicks." Mojica pulled up a pair of joysticks and worked them with both hands.

Taraji and Mari entered the command deck. Bodhi was encouraged to see that Mari looked a lot better now.

"Perfect timing. Mari, take a seat next to Selah, and Taraji, you change places with me. We have to go into TicCity, and you know the landscape." Mojica unstrapped and swiveled out of the command chair, and Taraji swiftly replaced her.

"Everybody strap in. We need to do this right now," Taraji said.

Mojica seated herself at the tactical station behind Bodhi while Mari grabbed the second navigator seat beside Selah and swung it around from the console to face forward.

"Where are we going?" Mari asked.

"The living units. The Council threatened my life, and now my mother isn't answering," Selah said

"Mojica, I need you to issue us weapons," Taraji said. "You know this style transport. Our armory is in the same place.

69

Configure the pulse rifles to match your military X11B. Use the same configuration on laser darts for personal protection and issue communicator bands. I want everyone tagged so we've got instant communications at all times." She strategically maneuvered the large air vessel over TicCity and onto the shoreline, then followed it northward in the direction of the U-shaped complex containing the living quarters.

"That configuration was never tested in the Mountain, mainly because there were no magnetic fields to shoot through." Mojica tipped her head. "What kind of resistance did you run into saving the transport from the Blood Hunters?"

"They were a lot more sophisticated with their weapons than I expected. I lost several good men," Taraji said. "Glade left specific orders for weaponry specs and upgrades to security that I previously thought were overkill to battle Blood Hunters. But after the fight I just lived through, I think his orders could have been more robust."

Mojica motioned to Mari and they hurried from the command deck.

"Will we get resistance from TicCity when they see this vehicle?" Bodhi strapped in and brought down his VR visor. He pressed his thumb into the depression in his chair's arm to bring up his control panel.

"Most definitely. I was hoping to ferry everyone out of town in the AirWagon we just left behind," Taraji said.

Selah bit her lip. "I'm sorry I caused—"

"Stop! Own it," Taraji said as she slowed their approach. "Are you sorry you got Amaryllis?"

"No," Selah said. "But I'm sorry we lost the AirWagon."

"It was a necessary loss," Taraji said. "I need you to evaluate each situation from now on, not with emotions but with logical outcomes in mind. We are entering an unknown world and our logic may be the only thing that saves us."

"Is it necessary to be so hard on Selah?" Bodhi asked.

"Bodhi, even though you look like a twenty-year-old, you're 150. You've experienced these hard lessons. Selah is eighteen and doesn't have the luxury of time."

"I thought when Glade died your service to him ended," Selah said softly.

"We are Kinship. Since the time of our ancestors, our service has been for the success of the novarium, and this time we have a good chance of completing the Third Protocol—"

Selah gasped and pointed past Taraji to the command deck window. "Look!"

7

S elah's stomach knotted with fear. She could clearly see numerous TicCity security vehicles ringing the living units.

"Look where? What do you see?" Bodhi stared out the wide window that wrapped around the conical front of the transport.

"In front of our living quarters, there are a lot of security vehicles," Selah said.

Bodhi's jaw dropped. He looked down at his data stream. "That's more than a click. It's at least three quarters of a mile up the road. How can you see that?"

"I don't know, but I can see the building as well as if I were standing in front of it," Selah said. She hadn't noticed any lightning surges accompanying her farsighted vision. While fighting at East Creek, this kind of clarity hadn't manifested, so the ability must have come about in the last hour. Selah shivered at the thought of more unknown things happening to her mind and body.

Taraji cycled down the transport and drifted to a stop, hovering thirty feet above the ground. "We'd better come up with a plan before we storm in there. As soon as they see the transport, the Council is going to attempt to commandeer it."

"Is there a way to sneak in and get my family?" Selah watched the crowd for any sign of her mother or Dane.

"If they haven't been detained, yes. But I wouldn't know how to reach them if they get picked up. I'd never get past Council security. I'm sure they've been alerted to whose side I'm on," Taraji said.

Selah spotted her young brother being dragged to a security transport. As usual, Dane struggled with the security agent. Twice he almost got away but was dragged back by the collar.

"They've got Dane." Selah's knees weakened. She watched as he broke free and started to run. Her breath quickened. The guard snatched him by the collar, literally lifting him off the ground. Anger welled in her chest. "Help him!"

Bodhi pressed on the joystick. The transport slid forward.

"No." Taraji pulled back the control. "We need to sit it out."

"That's my brother being hauled away!" Selah's voice rose. She knew Bodhi and Mari were on her side, but would that be enough to move Taraji to action?

"Tell me when security has both of them," Taraji said.

Selah stared at the vehicles surrounding the living units. She scanned the scene for her mother. Just as she was about to change her focus, Pasha came into view. Selah's heart pounded in her ears. The guard had her in restraints.

Selah drew her brows together. "They've got both of them."

Taraji punched in a couple commands and veered off to the right, avoiding the rest of the beach and obscuring Selah's view.

Selah panicked. She tried to keep her family in sight by running down the side of the command deck and peering out the portals, but they moved out of range. "Wait! You have to go back. We need to get them out of there."

Taraji continued on her route. "And how do you propose we do that?"

"Well, I don't know—"

"And neither do I at the moment. But I *do* know we've worn out our welcome here, and when we free them we'd better be on the fast track out of TicCity," Taraji said.

"We should get the supplies and Brejian, then grab them up," Bodhi said.

"Can we be sure they won't hurt my family?" Selah returned to the navigator chair.

"Nothing is certain." Taraji slowed as they approached the depot. "But I think they're doing this to draw you out, so they won't hurt them right away."

"You're telling me they might decide to torture my family to force me to expose myself?" Selah ground her teeth together. Would there ever be a time when she wasn't hunted or responsible for others around her being hurt?

"I don't think they'd be that dramatic, but they might put them on public display to determine how resolved the people are about stopping you from reaching the Third Protocol," Bodhi said. He tapped his earpiece. "Yes, can you bring them in with AirStreams? We're overhead now."

Taraji lowered the transport onto the depot parking area, keeping it in a steady hover, and Bodhi brought down the left-side ramps. Selah watched out the portal as at least a half dozen of the smaller hovercrafts delivered large crates and cases of supplies, making at least three trips each.

Mojica entered the command deck carrying laser darts and leg holsters. "I've been monitoring security communications. If we're not out of here in the next hour, we may never leave. They're amassing firepower we can't beat even with the X11B technology we've got below." She passed out the weapons.

Mari clutched a case of communication bands and earpieces. "I tried to contact Treva but I'm getting interference. I can hear the artificial modulating harmonics. We're being blocked."

"I've been trying too. If we can't contact her in the next few minutes we may have to leave Brejian behind," Taraji said.

"No. We can't abandon Brejian. She has the Repository files I need, and she's only willing to trade them for passage out of here." Selah readjusted the strap on her laser dart and glanced out a portal. She didn't want to lose the one bright light of hope that might help Bodhi.

Running men brandishing weapons caught her attention as the last AirStream approached the open ramp. Taraji muttered under her breath and tapped her panel to close the ramp. The AirStream veered off.

"Time to leave," Taraji said. She shifted the joysticks, lifting and pivoting the transport at the same time. She tapped her earpiece twice and motioned for Bodhi to listen in. "Treva Gilani."

Taraji maneuvered the transport opposite the side where

TicCity security was stationed at the moment. "Tell Brejian to come out the back . . . What do you mean you're not here? Why are you there? The two of you could be caught. Don't—"

Bodhi slammed his fist into the chair arm and turned to Selah. "I don't believe this. Treva and Brejian heard about Pasha and Dane through their status report and went to the security unit to rescue them."

Taraji mumbled under her breath again and sharply turned the transport to the west of the complex. "I know what she's trying to do. Brejian's clearance will get her in to see them, but there's going to be too much manpower for them to get back out. I think this is the best break we're going to get. You'll have to go in for the rescue and hope luck is on our side. I don't like not being on the ground, but our best chance to get away with this is if I'm at the helm, so I'm staying here. Bodhi, you and Mojica have to do this one."

Selah jumped to her feet. "No! I'm going too. That's my mother and brother."

"They would have a feeding frenzy if they spotted you down there," Bodhi said, rising from his seat.

"At this moment, I can see better, fight better, and move faster than any of you, and I'm *not* going to sit on my hands when I could be an asset to my family's survival." Selah sucked in a breath and set her jaw.

Bodhi looked to Taraji. "Tell her she can't go."

Taraji pursed her lips then grimaced. "I have to admit, she's right."

Bodhi's voice deepened. "This puts her in too much danger."

Selah stepped up to him and placed her hand gently on his chest. "Danger is going to be around every corner. The more I learn to use my new abilities, the more I may be able to fight the breakdown as it affects my body." Her confident smile didn't betray the knocking in her knees.

Bodhi covered her hand with his and brought her palm up to his lips. He kissed it softly. "My sweet firefly, I love you. I can only hope that one day we'll live in a world where we're always safe. But since today isn't that day, I'll settle for being at your side."

"Oh no you won't," Taraji said. "Mojica is going with Selah."

"I don't want her going down there without me," Bodhi said.

Mojica stepped between them. "Bodhi, I am Kinship. I think I proved my abilities rescuing the child. If you think you could best me in battle, I will allow you to take my place."

Bodhi pressed his lips tightly together.

"Will you please retake your position at the helm and help pilot this monster of a craft, which you have proven to be exceptionally skilled at," Mojica said.

Bodhi gritted his teeth then nodded. "You keep her safe or you'll answer to me." He kissed Selah on the cheek.

Mojica smiled and patted him on the shoulder as he slid back into his seat.

"Okay, you two, I'm ready to drop you in. I've keyed your communicators to see both Treva and Brejian on your screens. You find them and they'll find Pasha and Dane," Taraji said.

Mari helped strap on Selah's communicator. "I wish I were well enough to go, but I'd just slow you down."

"That's okay. You rest. You suffered quite a blow to the

head, and I don't want to risk more injury to another member of my family," Selah said.

Rylla hurried through the chamber entrance and threw her arms around Selah's waist. "I was listening at the door. You can't go down there. They'll try to kill you again." She tightened her hold.

Selah gently pried Rylla from her. "Honey, I have to go. My mother and my little brother Dane are down there."

"Your mother and brother? When did they come to Tic-City?" Rylla tried to take Selah's hand.

Selah transferred the girl's hand to Mari's. "We haven't had a chance to talk about everything that's happened. But we're leaving here and going west as soon as I rescue them."

Rylla squirmed to get her hand free of Mari's grip. "I'll help. I know the way! The Bantors brought me to the security offices all the time while they were conducting business."

"Figures they'd be friendly with the Council," Selah said. "But you're staying here. We'll be back shortly." She buckled on a utility belt and checked the charge on her laser dart again.

"That's not fair. I want to go." Rylla wrenched free of Mari and ran out through the command deck entrance.

"I'll go down and make her something to eat, and hopefully by the time I've soothed her ruffles, you'll be back. Stay safe, sis." Mari hugged Selah and headed for the quarters below.

Selah followed Mojica through a side entrance. It would be good for Rylla to have a younger brother. She thought about introducing Rylla to her mother and Dane. She hadn't really had time to bring up the subject of the girl.

Mojica stopped in front of a vertical silver tube with a

circumference of about six feet. The shimmering length disappeared up into the ceiling and down through the floor. A hum radiated through the floor and vibrated Selah's spine.

She stopped. "What is that?"

"A magnetic stairway. What you see isn't a solid. It's a wave." Mojica stuck her hand through what Selah had thought was a solid tube.

Selah gasped. "How does it work?"

"As we go through the wall, a magnetic floor panel will develop below you. After we're completely inside, touch your hands to the wall in front of you. Anywhere you put them, hand holds will appear. Anywhere your feet touch will be a step. Like this." Mojica went first to demonstrate.

Selah ran her hand through the beam. It was fluid like water running between her fingers. But when she clenched her fist, the energy became solid. The smooth texture felt like transparent plascine. Her heart pounded with anticipation as she followed Mojica. When she concentrated and didn't overthink moving through a void with no discernable floor beneath her, the motion of climbing down the energy beam resembled descending a ladder. The tube extended with them. When they stepped onto the ground, the tube silently retreated into the vessel.

Mojica sprinted to the back entrance of the security center and flung open the door.

Selah glanced back toward the transport and gasped.

8

Bodhi ran through the views on each of his exterior monitors, watching for security guards. His back stiffened. He rotated the monitor view to get a full shot of the hull. A small figure crawled from a partially opened ramp and used the utility guides to lower herself to the ground. Rylla!

How did the girl find access to the control panel? "No, no, no!" Bodhi yelled.

Taraji jerked her head in his direction. "What now?"

He pointed. "Rylla. She got the number four ramp open and squeezed her way out. She's following Selah." Bodhi wasn't sure what to do. This could compromise the whole operation and put Selah's life in jeopardy.

Taraji shook her head. "Nothing we can do now. It'll be providence if we get out of here in one piece. Lucky for us, they haven't discovered my security code back door. I still have a little video leverage. I tapped the interior cameras."

"Do you see Selah and Mojica yet?" Bodhi felt the tendons

in his neck tightening. He needed visuals, as though seeing her would provide her safety. Glade had given him the lifetime honor of protecting her, and here he sat in an impenetrable transport while she risked her life once again.

He ran clammy hands along the legs of his tactical suit, then toggled through the camera angles again. His rapid movements almost missed the two guards coming around the side of the structure.

Suddenly Bodhi felt the transport rising. "Stop! What are you doing? We can't leave them vulnerable."

"We have to move above where the guards could reach if they shoot a grapple," Taraji said. She wore her VR headset and flipped through the camera feeds by blinking her left eye.

Bodhi rose from his seat.

"Where do you think you're going?" Taraji said. "Sit down. I need you to man the secondary weapons plateau."

Bodhi spun to face her. "Weapons? TicCity transports don't have weapons."

"This transport is a special design by Glade himself. His affiliation with the Kinship provided more than enough funds to facilitate the upgrades. Sit." Taraji waved a hand over the arm of her chair, activating a virtual screen that scrolled out between them. She reached for a rectangular box of controls on the screen and swiped them to the left, sending the box sliding toward Bodhi's end of the screen.

Bodhi slowly sank into his command chair. "What do I do?"

"Lower your VR screen."

Bodhi reached up and moved the clear band over his face. The controls came alive. Screens of indoor and outdoor cameras rolled along the top and bottom of his vision.

"Weapons control is your right eye, screens use the left. Please don't mix them up. We don't have the luxury of training time." Taraji maneuvered the transport around to face the scene.

Bodhi watched helplessly as the two guards reached the corner. His heart raced. There was no way to warn Selah or Rylla.

Selah turned when she heard the transport move. Fear rose to a gasp as she watched Rylla scurrying across the open expanse.

Rapid footsteps sounded on the gravel behind Selah. Guards would be coming around the building at any second. She whistled Rylla's birdcall. The girl's head jerked in the direction where Selah pointed. Rylla ducked out of sight behind some bushes and dashed around the other side of the structure. Selah retreated inside and closed the door behind her.

She leaned against the inside wall for a moment, heart pounding in her ears. Why didn't the child ever listen? Hopefully she would be smart enough to stay hidden until they came back out.

Selah pushed off the wall and ran to catch up to Mojica, who was moving carefully down the wide, unadorned corridor. How to find her mother and Dane? She tried to focus her hearing. She mentally begged Dane to make a racket so she could home in on a direction. Nothing.

"Taraji gave me the security layout on my communicator, but we need to decide which way to go. None of these areas are marked," Mojica said as she transferred the map to Selah's communicator.

Selah didn't hesitate. She pointed at the map. "We need to go right. That's where the building gets congested. They wouldn't keep prisoners on the fringe of the complex."

Mojica agreed. They turned at the next corner and worked their way down the hall, checking doors and unlocked cross-passages as they went. Halfway down the light gray corridor, a door behind them slid open and two security guards strolled into the hall.

"Hey, what are you two doing in this part of the complex with no escort?" One of the guards charged toward them.

Mojica fired her laser dart in the guards' direction. Both men dodged the pulse and fired back. One shot went wild, singeing a black streak on the ceiling. The other blasted between Mojica and Selah. Mojica returned fire, pinning the men in a side corridor.

With not enough time between laser bursts, Selah didn't have the opportunity to use a hand thrust, and she couldn't see the guards well enough to focus the ability. She studied the map and raced to each of the corridor entrances. The last one opened. She tapped her headset and alerted Mojica, who worked her way toward the opening while returning fire.

They tumbled inside the new corridor. The door slid closed and Mojica fried the access panel with two quick shots. "That ought to keep them busy for a few minutes." She checked the charge on her weapon and redialed her load dispersal for the closer parameters.

Selah did the same. She walked along each side of the hall with her fingertips to the walls. Even though her heartbeat had returned to its normal cadence, her fingers vibrated with different rhythms depending on the depth of the area on the other side of the wall. She marveled at the feeling of sensory radar.

"Where to now?" Mojica asked.

Selah stopped. Familiar warmth on the north wall. Strong. "It's this way to the north."

Mojica looked at her map. "The north corridor is up this hall."

They both raced to the new opening. Selah slapped the access and it opened. Mojica checked all directions. They weren't being followed. She raised her weapon to target the panel after they were inside.

Selah stopped her. "No one saw where we went. We might need to come back this way."

"Perhaps, but we've already blasted the first entrance to keep them from following, so we could only get back so far without seeking a new way out. There's a maze of corridors, and the map doesn't indicate which have exterior doors other than the one we came in."

Selah pinched the bridge of her nose. She felt a momentary flash like a tremor of thunder or a surge of lightning. Whatever it was, she could feel it building to a perfect storm.

Mojica stared at her. "You all right? You look a little flushed."

Selah shook her head. "I'm okay. We have to keep going. Each conversion I go through changes in scope and intensity, and it's starting to feel like all the variations are happening at once."

Mojica led the way. It calmed Selah to actually feel that she was getting closer to her family, but at the same time it was a new sensation she'd not experienced before. They walked past a side hall, and the feeling faded.

"Wait. We have to go this way." Selah turned back to the hall. She had a flashback of Bethany holding her family hostage. She jolted to a stop. "This is a trap."

"I think we already assumed that," Mojica said.

"No, it feels different, more convoluted than just capturing me. I'm getting strange sensations." Selah shook her head.

"Well, this is your family. Do you want to go back?"

Selah balked. "No! I'd never leave them behind."

Mojica started down the new corridor. They passed a door on the other side of the hall, and Selah felt the urge to run. She jerked to a stop, startled by a flurry of unfamiliar feelings.

She signaled Mojica and pointed to the suspicious door. Mojica nodded and took aim.

Selah clenched her fists. She knew it was a trap, but there was no choice. She swung the door wide.

Pasha and Dane sat in the corner. Relief at their safety bolstered her as she turned from her family to face their captors.

The Council woman sat behind a wide black plascine desk, flanked by two security guards.

Selah pressed her hands to her hips and started the mental process to use her thrusts. "What is the purpose of dragging my family from my quarters and detaining them?"

The Council woman sat back. "You are just as belligerent as your father—"

"Then I'm in good company. I've asked you a question and I would appreciate an answer. Why are you holding my family?" Selah's fingers began to tingle.

"To catch you, of course, and apparently you've made it very easy for me to accomplish." The Council woman smiled.

"I wouldn't say it was quite that easy." Mojica moved into the room with her laser dart drawn.

The guards raised their weapons.

"Hold it!" The Council woman lifted a hand. Her men looked at each other and lowered their weapons.

"Selah, are you prepared to get all of these other people killed with you?" The Council woman sat rigidly and didn't appear ready to back down.

"I don't want anyone to die. I just want to leave in peace." Selah felt the pulse building in her hands.

"But if I let you leave in peace, *I* will have no peace. You see, the First Protocol still living in this area don't want any kind of change to come. Your transformation of all Landers is what they fear and have fought so hard against for the last 150 years. Although I have to admit you've gotten much farther than the rest."

Selah squeezed her fists. "Don't you think I've earned the chance to complete this? Because of me the way to the West is open. Nothing will ever be the same because of that fact alone."

The Council woman nodded. "And just maybe that means you were the last novarium and we can put this behind us for another 150-year cycle, or maybe forever." The Council woman smiled and motioned to her guards. They raised their weapons.

Selah thrust out her hands. "Noo!" The guards and the Council woman jerked back and slammed against the wall five feet behind them. They fell into a heap at the base of the wall.

"Run!" Selah snatched Dane by the hand and they piled

out of the room with Mojica in front. The hall lights suddenly turned red and a siren roared to life. Dane struggled to cover his ears with his hands, but Selah wasn't letting go.

They turned two corridors, and at the next junction Mojica hovered by an opening door. A guard came rushing out. Mojica whacked him in the head with her weapon, knocking him unconscious. She then closed and lasered the keypad for the corridor.

Selah felt resistance. "Slow down," she yelled to Mojica over the siren. "It feels like the next corridor is an ambush."

Mojica motioned them against the wall and Selah peeked around the corner. Fifty feet down the hall she could see the corridor filling with guards headed their way.

"We have to go back the other way. That's too many." Selah ran to the other end of the hall and peered around the corner in the only direction left to go. Several soldiers had burst into that hallway far down on the left and were also headed this way.

Selah pulled back. They were trapped. She ran back to Mojica. "We have nowhere to go. I'm going to have to give myself up to get you out of here. I wish I knew where Treva and Brejian were. Reinforcements would help."

"No, Selah," Dane cried as he grabbed her hand. Pasha ran her hand across Selah's hair and embraced her.

"Ack!" Pasha jumped away from Selah and the wall.

Selah and Mojica spun to train their weapons on the moving wall panel. It fell away and Rylla peeked out. "Hurry! We have to get through the ventilation system before they shut it down."

"Don't think this excuses you for disobeying me about

staying on the transport," Selah said. But she secretly beamed with pride and relief. The child always amazed her.

"Yes, ma'am." Rylla grinned from ear to ear.

Selah knew that was Rylla's contrite way of asking for forgiveness. She smiled but inwardly cringed at the things Rylla might show Dane.

Mojica went first to check the passage, then Pasha with Dane following behind. He stopped next to Rylla and glared at her. A pout crossed his face and his brows furrowed. Selah wanted to laugh, but she knew it would just make him angrier. Pasha came back, grabbed him by the hand, and marched him away through the narrow space.

Selah and Rylla closed the panel and hurried to catch up. Mojica slowed as she came to a T in the shaft. Rylla scurried past her and to the right. They walked quietly, single file.

Five minutes later Rylla signaled to Mojica that the outside door was up ahead. Rylla leaned on the panel but it didn't push out.

Selah moved forward past her scowling brother. "What's the problem?"

"It won't move. It shouldn't be hard to push at all," Rylla said.

Mojica moved up beside Selah and they both put their shoulders to the panel. They got it to move a sliver—enough to see a vehicle had pulled up outside and its left wheel was against the vent.

Selah hung her head. *So close.* "We have to go back to the last junction you know of that has an exit."

Rylla thought a minute. "I know. The Bantors had to go to the MedTech Unit, and they left us five kids in the adjoining section for three hours. We went all through the vent work in there. Come on, this way." Rylla hurried off through another narrow silver plascine vent that ended at a wall.

Selah helped Rylla remove the clips holding the panel to the wall. Everyone filtered out into an area not directly connected to the security section. The sound of the blaring security siren was muted here.

Selah's shoulders loosened. Freedom was close.

They hurried through the entrance portal for the building and turned the corner—into two guards with pulse rifles. Selah bit her lip. Laser darts were no match for pulse rifles, even Mojica knew that. Both women raised their hands.

"I'll give up. Just let my family go," Selah said.

"My orders are to bring in any of you I catch," the guard yelled.

"Well, if all of us rush you two, there's going to be a tussle and someone might get hurt," Selah said.

The guard closest to her raised his pulse rifle toward her head. "We could have an accident."

Rylla, Dane, and Pasha started to argue loudly with the guard. The second guard blew a shrill whistle for order.

From the corner of her eye, Selah saw Treva moving up beside the wall unit on the right, and Brejian had worked her way up on the left. Selah eye-signaled Mojica, and their count ended just as the guard opened his mouth to yell again. He stopped when he saw that four people had weapons trained on him. Selah and Mojica pushed the guards into a storage room and scorched the access panel.

The group followed Treva and Brejian out of the unit. The transport lowered beside them with a ramp levering to the ground. Everyone moved to race aboard as the ramp touched down.

Treva stopped.

9

Selah hurried to Treva's side as the others ran up the walkway. "What's the matter? We have to go. They'll be coming after us any minute."

Treva shook her head. "No, I told you I can't leave. I won't abandon Cleon—"

"Cleon is gone!" Selah bit her lip to quiet her outburst. She closed her eyes at the fresh pain of losing her stepbrother. "I love you." She hugged Treva tight and felt the shiver in her friend's shoulders.

Treva's eyes glistened with tears. "I love you like a sister and I'll miss our friendship terribly."

"Yours was the first friendship that felt like a sisterhood." Selah could barely talk around the lump forming in her throat.

Treva tried to smile. "See, I got you ready for the real thing with Mari. I'm sorry, but I can't bring myself to leave. Be safe, and make me proud," Treva said with a hitch in her voice.

Selah decided to try one more time. "Are you sure?"

Treva nodded. "Your mom has a package for you." With a smile, she handed Selah the pulse rifle and took off across the lot at a jog.

Selah's heart clenched as she watched until her friend disappeared among the trees. Her shoulders slumped and she pressed her lips together. *No. Don't try calling her back. Her heart would never find peace anywhere else.* She turned and hurried up the walkway. Mojica closed the ramp behind her.

The transport lifted off. A feeling of floating hit Selah. Was it from the elevation or simply relief? Either way she would remember this day. The twenty-fifth day of September, her family was finally together and free.

A violent percussion rocked the transport, shaking them from side to side.

Selah smashed her shoulder into the outer wall. The next jolt whacked her head into the hull. She grimaced and regained her footing. Could TicCity have gotten reinforcements that fast?

"Mother, keep the kids down here." Selah and Mojica dashed for the command deck, leaving Brejian, Mari, and Pasha with two startled children. They burst onto the deck as Bodhi and Taraji traded commands.

"Swing wide and give me a starburst," Bodhi shouted as he swung a VR screen into place and lined up his sights.

Another jolt and a large vibrating boom echoed through the chambers. Selah grabbed for a wall handle. Bodhi and Taraji clicked on their seat restraints, but Mojica armed the tactical console and stayed on her feet, balanced perfectly for riding the jolts as Selah once road the waves of the sea on a board.

Another jarring percussion.

Selah's heart thudded hard against her ribs, making her arm pulse. She worked her way to the navigator chair.

"Fire your aft cannons on my mark," Taraji barked. "Five, four, three . . ."

Port-side thrusters discharged, swinging the rear of the transport to the right.

"Fire!"

Bodhi released a barrage of pulse cannon fire in the direction of the hovering TicCity security transports. They were smaller and more maneuverable, but no match for this super transport. Selah's fear subsided as the enemy transports dropped their pursuit one by one. They tried spreading out, but Taraji set the transport to sweep the general area and Bodhi laid down several tracks of fire.

Selah watched the crosshairs on Bodhi's VR screen following every minute move by the targets, and in some cases he led their movements by laying down a trail of fire that they eventually ran through. He also eliminated two units that had evaded the first firing cadence. The remaining three in that group broke off pursuit and turned back to TicCity.

"They're leaving now, but will they come back?" Selah peered out at empty airspace.

"Doesn't matter. We can outrun them. They'd have to turn back sooner or later because of low power cells," Taraji said.

"Is there any damage from their pulse charges?" Selah tried to spot damage out her portal.

"That's not possible either. We have magnetic shielding that creates an impenetrable field around us, especially since we're now calibrated for the frequency they're emitting from their Mountain technology," Bodhi said as he lifted a VR screen from his vision. "Those jolts were just the shield absorbing the charges."

Mojica leaned over to the command chair and slapped Bodhi on the back. "Well done."

"Outstanding!" Taraji increased their altitude and speed until they were cruising at about fifty miles an hour.

Bodhi accepted the praise but looked a little embarrassed and bewildered. Selah knew he didn't remember enough of his past to decide whether having these abilities was a good or bad thing, and that uncertainty sometimes bothered him.

"I knew he had to be former military from the way he slung on gear in the Mountain. But now we can definitely say it's aeronautics," Mojica said.

"Not necessarily. The hand-eye coordination could be ground combat," Taraji added.

"Not true. They wouldn't learn leading edge—"

"Hello! You two are acting like he's not in the room." Selah planted her hands on her hips.

Mojica and Taraji stared at her as though she had spoken an unknown language.

Bodhi shrugged. "Don't look at me. I don't remember anything about an occupation, just flashes of my temperament."

"Along with Glade, we as the Kinship planned this day for many decades," Mojica said. "Our functions in the plan were designed with Taraji as pilot, myself as tactical, and Brejian as navigation. But we were never supplied with a stationary armaments specialist, which in itself was daunting because these systems are far more advanced than what even I'm used to." She shook her head. "I must confess. For many years I considered that a major oversight, but Glade proved true. He did indeed provide for this through Bodhi."

"What is a stationary armaments specialist?" Selah asked.

Mojica and Taraji both shrugged and said in tandem, "The shooter."

"Even if that *was* true, how could Bodhi know how to use systems so technical that TicCity doesn't have anything even close in comparison?" Bodhi? A shooter? Selah didn't want to believe that had been part of Glade's plan all along. The whole idea made her feel like a long-stringed puppet, which caused doubt about her own decision-making abilities to creep in.

"The technology is actually very old. The government was experimenting with it before the Sorrows. We've just built up enough infrastructures to be able to use and duplicate it again."

Selah frowned. "There's got to be some other explanation. Glade didn't know anything about Bodhi before we rescued him in—"

"May I enter the command deck?" Pasha stood in the doorway.

Taraji remained focused on the console but motioned her in.

Pasha moved to stand beside Selah. "I've been trying to tell you what I've read in Glade's documents. I think he knew Bodhi was the one coming to transition you."

Selah's eyes widened. "Well, there's apparently a few other things you haven't told me either."

Pasha's smile always disarmed Selah, and this time was no exception.

Selah suddenly remembered the bag of documents in her quarters. "Oh no! We left Glade's papers behind."

"No we didn't," Bodhi said. "I picked up the gear at your quarters before we took the transport out for a shakedown run. I figured it would save time later."

Selah sighed with relief. "You're wonderful!" She threw her arms around Bodhi's neck and kissed him. Then her eyes flew open and she dropped her arms. She glanced in her mom's direction as her face warmed. She'd never kissed a guy in front of her mother before.

She lowered her eyes and stepped back. "I—I'm sorry . . . I was just so happy that . . ."

She snuck a glance at Bodhi. He looked rather pleased—flushed but pleased.

Pasha moved between Selah and Bodhi and wrapped an arm around each of them. "Glade made it very clear in his writings that he gave his blessing to you two."

"*If* we survive!" Selah said. "Then why did he give us such a hard time? He only seemed to relent at the end."

Pasha gave a slight smile and hugged Selah. "He was a father reluctant to give up his daughter to another man. After all, he had just found you. I think he was a little jealous of not being able to command all of your attention. He did believe Bodhi loved you."

"How did he know?" Bodhi said.

"He knew your character before the Sorrows," Pasha said. "You were a hotshot Air Force pilot for the newest configuration fighter transport. Glade said that your passion for Selah was more obvious than your love for your former job."

Selah lifted her head from her mother's shoulder. "How do you know that?"

Pasha raised a hand. "I saw Glade's notes about Bodhi in reference to piloting this craft. But that's not our problem right now. We've calculated this vehicle's specifications and mass, and we can't go fast enough or high enough with the present weight to make our destination in time."

Taraji turned to the group. "I've worked that through already. This vehicle was originally made to carry forty troops, but there are only nine of us. That's why it took me slightly longer than expected to get here. We modulated sleeping quarters for ten and created larger open work areas and left all the extra panels behind. The power units will last for three years at the new weight, and I was also working on several innovations for security that might come in handy."

"That helps me to understand more of what was written." Pasha turned to Selah. "You have to see the mountain of pearls I discovered—"

"Well, I've helped her fight bad—"

"I don't care. She's *my* sister—"

The arguing children poured onto the command deck. Selah stepped between. "Whoa, you two need to step into opposite corners for this duel."

Rylla wrinkled her nose. "What kind of duel are we going to have? You won't let me play with real swords anymore."

"Because the last time you swung a long blade, you sliced one of Glade's maps clean in half. I was the one who heard the rant every time Glade thought about it," Selah said. "Besides, I only used the word as a figure of speech."

Dane narrowed his eyes to slits. "She played with a real sword? Why haven't you ever let me play with a long blade?"

Selah's mind flashed with thoughts of things a twelve-year-old mischievous girl could teach a nine-year-old curious boy. She squeezed the bridge of her nose with her thumb and forefinger. "Mother, please help." Selah knew her limits, and managing two children definitely fell beyond her outer edge.

Pasha herded the children from the command deck.

Tension released from Selah's neck. "How's Mari?"

Pasha pressed her thumb to the nearby panel for identification, then called the lift to send the children below. "She's fine. She may have a concussion, so we'll have to watch her through the night. But the way she dove into helping us decipher the data, we may wind up needing to force her to take a rest."

"I'm almost afraid to ask, but have Brejian's records helped?" Selah didn't want to pin her hopes on a hunch, but that was exactly what she was doing. Glade had spent an inordinate amount of time in the Repository, and she was convinced that would lead to the West.

Pasha turned back. "So far, she's directed me to several areas of Glade's files that were enhanced by the data cubes she brought from the Repository. She and Mari are scampering about like mice evading a broom. Do you want a report from her? I know the value of her data should be at least equal to you getting her out of there and to someplace safe."

Selah stood slightly behind Bodhi's command chair with her hand resting on his shoulder. His touch supplied her with strength while fear robbed her of it. "No, but I want to talk to you, so I'll be coming down to see what you figured out."

"We found the tactical room and began laying out the

records. There is a surprising order to the way things fit together. It's starting to look like a 3-D map." Pasha called the lift back up and followed the children below.

Selah looked at Taraji and Mojica. "Can we land to have a meal and discuss all this?"

Mojica leaned over and extended a fist between the two command chairs. Bodhi put his fist on top of hers, and Taraji put hers on his. They gave a three-second count and broke apart. "How about we three keep this mammoth transport in the air and moving forward while you work with Brejian on where we're going?" Mojica said.

"How soon do you need a course correction?" Selah headed toward the door. Pasha had piqued her curiosity about Glade. It stirred a new measure of excitement in her.

"It will take four hours of straight flying for us to get back to the Mountain, then we divert to the open pass. So about that time we'll need a direction or we're traveling blind," Taraji said.

After setting a time marker on her communicator, Selah turned to follow her mother.

Selah grabbed up a slice of Mari's summer sausage and a hunk of crusty bread from the feast Pasha had laid out for a late afternoon meal. She wandered into the tactical area looking for her mother.

She strolled to Pasha's side. "So what are these pearls of wisdom you have to share with me?" She savored the spicy meat as she looked at stacks of old papers.

Pasha tipped her head. "What are you talking about?"

Selah frowned. "You wanted to share some pearls of something?"

Pasha's expression brightened and she chuckled. "I wanted to share the mountain of pearls we discovered." She turned and pointed to the tactical layout table in the center of the room.

The back of Selah's neck prickled with excitement as she moved toward the 3-D wonder spread out on the table, showing mountains and trees, lakes and rolling hills. The flat areas were laced with little mounds that looked like drops of dew resting on blades of grass—like the dome of Petrol City, but without the metal latticework shell supporting the exterior.

Brejian worked at setting up a series of data cube halo-projectors on the topographical map they'd created of the old West. At the lower edge of the Great Lakes and extending to the West Coast lay a single line of circular domes resembling a string of pearls draped across the mountains.

"This is wonderful, but how do we know it's accurate?" Selah slowly worked her way around the table. The most she had ever seen of the rest of the country was a colorful wall map of the United States that was preserved in the Borough building back home in Dominion. It had been published in the ancient year of 1995, and the flat map hadn't done justice to the mountain ranges she could see here.

"Pasha started the discovery by reading Glade's journals," Mari said. "He left instructions for building this model from his data glass. We've been working with a small model since we left the Mountain, but once we got here all these appliances were adaptable to this huge model." She used a digital distance meter to test a mountain height according to the written data on that location.

"So you didn't think it was important enough to tell me this?" Selah noticed that places labeled "Cleveland, Ohio" and "Chicago, Illinois" had huge, glistening pearly domes. "What are those domes made from?"

"As far as we can tell it's magnetic energy." Pasha raised a hand. "And excuse me, young lady. I tried to tell you about this several times, but you were always too busy with other things."

"Well, you tried to tell me some stories about a woman and a bear, and birds with red wings and such," Selah said.

"I was asking you why they put such a premium on a collection of children's stories," Pasha said.

"Mother, I still don't know what we're talking about."

"The Stone Braide Chronicles. The book with the symbol on it. It's a collection of fairy tales," Pasha said. "A beautifully bound book of such quality, and they've protected it for so many years, but it's only children's stories. Well, at least Rylla and Dane are enjoying them. But with every new discovery we find, I've come to you. You are just too busy."

Selah wanted to protest, but some of those moments flashed in her mind, showing just how she had dismissed her mother. She frowned. "I'm sorry. I was rude."

"You weren't rude, my darling." Pasha wrapped her arms around Selah's shoulders. "You're just trying to respond to all the situations thrust upon you. Some of them have carried you beyond your youthful innocence, so an outburst once in a while is understandable as long as you are truly sorry about it afterward."

Selah lowered her voice and turned her face toward Pasha's ear. "I'm truly sorry that I was rude to you." Selah kissed her on the cheek.

Pasha smiled and patted Selah's hand. "We'll have plenty of travel time to talk, but right now we need our destination plotted as accurately as possible. It will mean the difference between you living or dying." She moved back to the table and worked on setting up two more data cubes.

Her mother had now become the next version of her father. Selah knew that tone. "Are you avoiding me?"

"Yes." Pasha slowly shook her head. "You remind me so much of your father, even down to the way you tip your head when you're perturbed. It's distracting, and my mind wanders back to our younger days. At the moment all I see when I look at you is Glade telling me to complete this project and save our daughter. So we can discuss my mistakes at another time."

Selah felt a rush of love for her mother that overwhelmed any anger she had for being kept in the dark about her additional Lander heritage. "Okay, but I'm counting on us getting to talk."

"I promise. Now come and look at this. We plugged in Glade's data, but wound up with huge holes in the landscape in these spots." Pasha pointed out slightly different-colored areas. Selah surmised it was because the data cubes filling in those areas were much older and getting low in their energy charge.

"The Repository had hidden records of the First Protocol recorded way back at the beginning, including the original plans for the novarium." Brejian worked on filling in details to the map. "So that supplied us with the lay of the land and major domes."

"In the package from Treva was the Keeper of the Stone journals from her parents. Those helped fill in some of the minor gaps and two good connections. Oh, and here, Treva left this for you." Pasha handed Selah a small folded parcel tied with a leather lace.

Selah accepted the package with both hands and held it to her heart. They were too far away now. She couldn't feel Treva anymore. She said a silent goodbye.

"But we got the greatest break from the Mountain documents that Pasha said came from a Keeper in a cave," Brejian said. "He chronicled the building of the trail from Chicago to the West Coast. They lost three novarium before it was completed, and he never recorded what happened afterward."

"Obviously it never worked or we wouldn't be here," Selah said. "What are all the domes for?"

Mari walked in carrying a disorganized stack of curling yellowed pages. "As far as I can tell the domes were the only way they had breathable air at the time. It took many years for the dust to leave the atmosphere from the super volcano."

"The domes are big enough for whole cities?" Selah's insides fluttered. "Are they original cities from before the Sorrows?" She stared at the clear drops. First wonder, then fear. Why was she feeling this way?

"Yes and yes," Mari said as she deposited the sheets on a long table covered with other stacks of yellowed papers. "The fact that they are original cities and part of our trail west led me to search until I uncovered this." She leafed through a stack of the pages.

Selah moved from the table to give Mari her full attention as she stopped flipping pages and held one out. Selah's jaw dropped. She ran her eyes over every detail. Her knees weakened as her fingertips turned cold. The clan crest for the dome at Cleveland was the exotic bird of the Kinship, but the crest for the dome at Chicago was the sword and lightning bolt of the Blood Hunters. There was no getting away from them.

Mari dropped the paper back on the stack. "These two camps have been at this battle since way before the Sorrows. They built competing dome communities to highlight their developments in the company."

"So why didn't they contact our side of the country? I've never known anyone who thought others were alive in the West." The markings concerned her, but there was much more she needed to know about this situation. Staring at the map increased her agitation.

"That was the way it was supposed to be. Apparently these were the people that *caused* the Sorrows, and the bio-domes were part of the preparations." Mari pulled over a chair on rollers and sat in front of her latest pile of papers.

Selah fingered a couple of the piles. Yellowed pages of words that could fit together to save her life. But at the moment, her existence felt as fragile as the curled and cracked pages. "These people created the Sorrows? What kind of insane purpose was that supposed to accomplish?"

"Greed," Mari said. "The Repository files are very old and very enlightening. Volume one of the First Protocol says the Kinship are the primary owners of and research team for a company that had a contract with the United States government. They found out that the government wanted to use their research for some dictatorial purpose, while the Kinship wanted to use it to create a disease-free world."

"What was the government's purpose?" Selah glanced over a section of pages about magnetic variances.

"We don't know. It was redacted from the documents," Brejian said without looking up.

Selah lay the pages down. She didn't understand anything about magnetics. "Who was the company?"

"That was redacted too," Brejian said. She got another cube working and it filled in an empty area. "Why do you care?"

"I wanted to know the name of the company that ruined the world we're living in while they had these bio-domes and a cozy future." Selah stared at the shiny bubbles and could almost make out buildings, but that had to be her imagination playing tricks.

"With the way to the East blocked, do you think there is anyone left who cares about it 150 years later? Like back in TicCity, no one really cared, and they even knew about novarium," Mari said with a shrug.

Selah looked back and forth between them. "I don't know why I asked." She put her hand to her head. She could hear sounds that seemed like voices. Her head cleared.

"That's all right. We've been able to figure out that the Blood Hunters were the equally powerful other half of the company. They were on board with the government contract, but they also wanted to become wealthy selling their product to any country that wanted it," Mari said. "A captured memo says they planned for a small suitcase nuclear device to explode in Washington, DC, so they could swoop in with their technology. With one pill they would relieve everyone of the harmful effects of the radiation and restore people to perfect health."

"Only another, smaller group felt the country was too corrupt and didn't deserve the technology, and they were in the process of hacking the company servers. They inadvertently rerouted the activation message about setting off the nuke, and it went to three operatives instead of one. With none of them having prior knowledge of the other, and each having a valid activation code . . ." Pasha shrugged. "All three nukes exploded, and the resulting harmonics caused the dramatic plate shifts."

Selah held up a hand. "So these domes weren't built to create new atmospheres. They were made to resist nuclear fallout."

Mari nodded. "Exactly! I think this was an end plan for a very long time. No biochemical company would have nuclear devices lying around on a whim, especially three of them. So these explosions were to be planned events. The domes were basically a force field, but the rest of the things that happened just cascaded, and there were no options to stop any of it once it started."

"Wait! You just said 'biochemical company.'" Selah swung to face Mari. "Where did you find that information?" Her personal search for help with Bodhi's lost abilities would have to involve something chemical in nature.

"I didn't see it in any one place, but it was just the overall talk about compounds and chemicals I've worked with in the past. Most chemical talk was redacted, with huge spaces of file corruption," Brejian said.

"I'm glad we've learned a little about this strange world, but what information do we have that's new? We reach the Mountain pass in very short order, and we need a direction to travel."

"Folks, I think we have a problem." Pasha's face went ashen.

10

S elah bolted to her mother's side. Pasha waved her off
but patted her hand.

"I wanted to get a better picture of our history so I
attempted to line up the sets of documents according to time
periods." Pasha pointed to piles from Glade, the Keeper, and
Treva. "I compared these to the Repository file because that
was supposed to be the original edition . . . but it's not."

Selah looked at each of the three women. They wavered in
her vision as she grew light-headed for a second. The transport must have turned. She dismissed the feeling. "You said
Glade did most of the data keeping for the Repository, so
how could it not be the original copy?"

Mari marked her place and turned to join the conversation.
"As I look at the places where differences show up, it seems
like Glade purposely deleted information from Repository
files that was critical to identifying what the project was about
or how the parts interacted with one another. And as far as

I can see he deleted all references to the Third Protocol. The only place we find those references is in the individual documents from Treva, the Keeper, and Glade."

"So Glade must have known what it would take to accomplish the Third Protocol. Why would he hide that and not tell us?" Selah's lips went dry as sudden doubts about her father rose.

Brejian looked up only long enough to speak. "I gather Glade was doing it to prevent the other factions from finding enough information to copy the novarium process."

"They took a good amount of my blood when we were in the Mountain. We're sure they were trying to accomplish the same thing," Selah said.

"It can't be that easy," Brejian said. "He wouldn't have purposely deleted this much information if the process could be duplicated with just a couple vials of your blood. Something changed the process or destroyed it. I couldn't get enough data to figure out which."

"All I want to know is what happens at the *end* of the process?" Prickles of fear slithered up Selah's spine. Her knees trembled. She'd been trying to deny it, but fear had dug in like a tick that wanted to suck her dry.

"That's the problem," Pasha said. "His deletions keep us from following any more leads. All this time Glade had been working on the clues to the West, but he didn't leave any further points to aim at." She made a sweeping gesture with her arms. "The leads end here with this map and the mountain of pearls."

The air left Selah's chest like she'd been punched in the stomach. "Why did the old man give us this bag of journals and papers if they weren't going to help us? What's the point? What are we missing?" She ran her gaze over the piles of data and felt like sweeping it all onto the floor.

"We've gone over the collection more than once. It gave us this full layout with that string of habitats, but that's it. The clues stop here. All that's left is a bunch of personal observations and the children's stories," Mari said.

Brejian raised a finger. "Or they changed format and we need to look for some other common denominator. Or . . . maybe we're supposed to find that in the communities along the way."

"The build line of the habitats runs to the West," Pasha said. "We want to go west, so that's where we'll start. We need a discussion with Taraji and Mojica on how to gather information from the locals without giving away why we need it. Glade went to extreme lengths to mask the rest of the route."

"Didn't you notice? They *all* started hiding it. After the mountain-of-pearls data from each dome, there's nothing left but personal stories. Considering those were written in different time periods, it definitely feels planned," Mari added.

Selah tried to get her jitters under control. "We don't need to be guessing now." She began to pace in front of the tactical layout. "We need to go . . . We need to . . . ." Her head felt like it was floating, lighter than air, as a starburst popped and flashed multiple times before her eyes . . .

"That one had the deer with big antlers," a girl's voice said. Rylla?

Selah tried to focus on the voice, but it changed to a boy's. "Well, I like the rabbit story 'cause Selah likes rabbits." Dane.

"The bear claw one was scary," the voices agreed.

Focus.

"Hey, look. Selah's eyes are fluttering."

"Go get my mom."

"No, you go!"

Selah struggled to open her heavy eyelids. "S-stop arguing. Dane, get Mother." She ran her tongue across parched lips. Her throat throbbed when she swallowed. "Rylla, water, please."

She forced her eyes open and raised her head. *What happened?* She looked around. Where was she? The room was narrow and long, with two beds built into a pale blue composite wall and a storage area along another wall. Lights snaked from the bulkhead on bendable wands. Selah laid her heavy head back to the pillow but forced her eyes to stay open.

"Well, welcome back, sleepyhead," Pasha said as she entered the room with Dane in tow. Rylla followed behind with a water bottle and cup. "Now that you children see she's awake, it's your bedtime. Good night to both of you."

The children obediently kissed Selah on the forehead and went off to bed.

Selah edged into a sitting position. "What happened?" Her head still felt fuzzy and mentally misshapen, and the room blurred in and out with swirling colors.

"We're fortunate to have a healer on board. Brejian checked your core temperature and verified you've transitioned into the next phase," Pasha said. Her face registered concern.

Selah swung her legs over the side of the bed and sat up

straight, fighting the nausea threatening to overwhelm her. "What are the symptoms?"

"The cycles are noted in three-degree increments," Pasha said. "Brejian said in the three months this cycle takes to complete, your internal temperature will increase by three degrees and your senses will also increase. You may manifest new skills that you haven't discovered yet, but at the end of this cycle you will peak, and from then on you will decrease by three degrees per cycle. At the end of six months—"

Selah raised a hand to cut her off. The harder she tried to forget the fractured novarium, the more his haunting eyes drilled into her subconscious.

"I didn't want you to think I was keeping anything else from you—"

"Wait! Mother, what time is it? They needed directions—"

"Take it easy. We've set down for the night. There's no moon tonight, and Taraji and Bodhi didn't think we should travel in unknown territory when we couldn't see what the landscape looks like," Pasha said.

"Are we safe here?" Selah put weight on her feet and stood. Her head cleared like wind blowing away the morning mist. She felt better than she had in quite a while.

"Yes, they've got the magnetic shields activated," Pasha said.

Bodhi entered the room. "Pasha, do you want—" He grinned when he saw Selah standing. "Hey, firefly! You're awake. We're starting a strategy session. I was coming to get Pasha. Do you feel well enough to join us?"

Selah nodded. She followed behind Pasha into the tactical room and took a seat at the large topographical map table.

Bodhi sat beside her. She leaned her head against his shoulder. Not so much from weariness but from a sudden need to feel him close.

"We need to come up with a strategy about why we're in town, where we came from, and what our business is," Pasha said. "I imagine there isn't much travel around these parts."

"Hmm, probably not that easy," Taraji said. "We're coming to town with a vehicle that is probably larger than anything they've ever seen. And we know absolutely nothing about these domed societies. For all we know everyone could be bio-marked, and we have no way of compensating."

"Like in the Mountain," Selah said.

Mojica nodded. "I have to admit, I'm leery of drawing up in front of that dome in the transport. Maybe there's a way to hide it and go in on foot. Or maybe we should go in at night or at least do a recon job to get an idea of what we're dealing with."

"Night recon sounds like a better plan. We need to wait until daylight to get an idea of the terrain," Taraji said.

"How far did we travel before you stopped for the night?" Selah looked at the map that mimicked their travels.

"We're right here." Bodhi pointed to the mouth of the pass. The distance looked so small on the table, but they had figured the first dome was at least four hundred miles away.

"What does the terrain look like on the other side?" Selah peered at the 3-D model that had trees and foliage-covered mountains. She wondered if the terrain looked like that now. Her impression of the other side had always been an ocean's worth of gray, volcanic dirt.

"It was dark before we stopped, but I pushed it this far because we wanted to cross over in light," Taraji said. "Besides, I didn't think any splinters would follow us this far away from their base."

Selah looked across the table at Mari. "You're awfully quiet. What do you think?"

Mari sat forward in her chair and ran her fingers through the emitter beams, disrupting the visual signals. "We're acting like this is just another trip to a neighboring jurisdiction, but we're leaving our known world and we're never coming back. I think it's just hitting me."

"Do you regret coming along?" Selah's chest tightened. She had never imagined being without Treva, or without her sister.

Mari hesitated. The room went quiet. She rested her elbows on the table and interlocked her fingers. "I haven't known you very long, but you *are* my sister, and you were directly responsible for me getting to see my father one last time." She looked down at the table.

It felt like the air had been sucked from the room. Selah gulped, trying to get ahead of the tears threatening to form. She tipped her head to look into her sister's eyes. "Mari?"

Mari lifted her head. "I couldn't imagine this world without you now that I found you, and I can see Father in your eyes. It makes me feel closer to him to be near you." She shook her head. "Father raised me to be a brave leader. But at the moment I don't feel very brave. I feel scared, and I'd just like to go home and hide my head in a hole and wish all of this was a dream."

Selah's hands started to shake.

Mari studied the expression on Selah's face. "You look like I feel."

"You made me stop to think about all that you gave up to come with me. I've only ever had brothers, and I cherish having a big sister. I don't want you to have regrets."

Mari smiled. "I'll only have regrets if you don't make it."

11

Selah stood behind Bodhi's command chair, staring out at the landscape. The sun came up behind them, spreading the transport's ominous long shadow across the barren landscape. At first it seemed like an exaggerated pointer leading the way, but as the sun rose, the shadow shortened until it was trailing them. From Study Square she remembered seeing vintage images of the moon's pockmarked landscape. Those could have been pictures of the terrain in front of her.

"Are you too busy for a visit?" Mari strolled onto the command deck and wrapped her arm around Selah's shoulders.

Selah leaned her head to touch her sister's. "No, nothing to do until we reach the first dome. How are the kids behaving for my mother this morning?"

"They've both had their noses stuck in that storybook. Actually being able to touch the paper and turn the pages

119

has them enchanted. I bet they'll know those hundred pages by heart." Mari laughed.

"I'm glad they're behaving. I worry about Rylla teaching Dane some of the things she learned when she was his age." Selah moved to sit at one of the navigator stations.

Mari sat at the second station. "She's a hard-shell little girl. I'd pit her survival skills against any ten grown men. I hope she does teach him." She pointed toward the front shield. "Have you seen any signs of life yet?"

"Not one. When we first crossed through the pass this morning it had been scrubbed clean by the torrential rains. The flood did a good job of clearing a noticeable trench for quite a few miles. If we'd come by land it would have been the opening we needed." Selah paused. "If the events at the Mountain hadn't triggered the flood, could we have flown over it?" She wondered if sealing the Mountain might have been avoided. She felt guilty about trapping that society—for the rest of their lives.

"Even if *we* didn't need the flood to fly through the pass, everyone who comes after us will now have the ability to pass to the West. I guess this was the method of setting society free again once the novarium had come," Taraji said from her console.

"I can see why land travel would have been impossible before now, but why did no one ever fly?" Selah stared out the front of the transport.

"Because the earthquakes and volcanic explosion changed the landscape, pushed up new mountains, made new sink-holes, and moved water sources. There were stories that back at the beginning airplanes tried going west, but communications with them were lost and they never returned. After a while no one else tried, and since the majority of aeronautic technology came from the West, eventually civilian flying ceased altogether," Mojica said.

Taraji turned from her console. "Truthfully, the farther we've come, the less ash there is. The majority of it drifted against this side of the mountain range. But as far as the eye could see from the highest point on our side of the Mountain, there was nothing but ash and barrenness. If they'd have known . . . ."

That didn't make Selah feel better. She trained her sights on the horizon as they flew toward Cleveland and the first dome. What did she *expect* to see—a gray desert with a half-moon dot? What would she *like* to see—people, buildings, trees? She thought about home. She'd like to see forests of trees. Her eyes strained to see farther. Her heart fluttered. No! Was it wishful thinking? She saw sticks like the bristles of a brush. A hint of color.

A grin crept across her face. "Don't laugh at me, but I think I see a tree, an evergreen."

Bodhi spun around in shock. "I'm not even going to ask you the distance you're seeing that at because there is nothing in front of us. Where are you seeing a tree?"

"The horizon, maybe twenty miles."

Taraji and Bodhi stared at each other.

"Twenty miles?" Bodhi said. "Do you realize how fast that change came about? How do you feel?"

Selah concentrated on the tree. "I see the top of another one!"

"I'll spread the word below so they can turn on screens to follow along." Mari darted from the command deck.

"Can we go any faster?" Selah's hope blossomed for the first time since the sun had risen, shedding light on this world of emptiness. At first she'd seen just gray, petrified tree trunks splintered to their dead cores, surrounded by the bleak landscape of yard-deep gritty ash from 150 years of no disturbances—no signs it had been subjected to any kind of weather.

But now she could see life.

"Not at the moment. I'm getting some strange readings from transport integration. Ideally this system should have been field tested before we took it across the country, but we didn't have the luxury, so we may have a few kinks," Taraji said.

"This problem seems a little different," Bodhi said as he ran his hands across several sensors in the halo-control. "The power variations are tacking up on several systems at the same time, and none of the systems are related, but then the surge vanishes—"

"Like now!" Taraji threw up her hands as the monitor's hot lights each cycled down to normal. "This is going to drive me to distraction."

Selah didn't understand the control problem, so she remained fixated on what she did understand—the growing size of the tree. "How close to Cleveland are we?" They approached the edge of a ridge.

"About twenty miles," Bodhi said as he concentrated on monitoring the other systems.

The transport moved to the end of the ridge, hovering over the sloping valley leading toward the waters of the southern edge of Lake Erie.

Selah stared out over the barren gray landscape sloping

toward the waters. Her mouth opened in awe and disbelief. Was it a mirage? She squinted and refocused her eyes. The sloping gray turned to an oasis of green spreading out in all directions. On this side grew a forest that had expanded out of the valley and up the ridge. Those were the evergreen treetops Selah had seen.

Her gaze traveled along the tree-lined slope and into the valley where the green rolled on for at least ten miles. At the far end of this oasis sat the shimmering pearl-colored dome. Selah felt something, not a flash or tremor, but a feeling of familiarity that welcomed her with a shiver of anticipation.

"That is nothing like what I expected," Bodhi said. He keyed the scanners, looking for any military-type intervention. "Nothing hot in the area."

"Good, then we'll skim into the valley." Taraji maneuvered the transport into a slow glide into the valley. "I agree about the looks. I expected the domes to be small like Petrol City."

Selah was still in awe. "It has to be five or six miles across. It looks like solid material. Is that really just energy?"

Mojica strode onto the command deck. "It's a pure energy field, and the harmonics are so strong that we can't use the shielding technology to camouflage our look without the risk of burning out the cylinders."

"Is that so bad? We could just hide the transport in the woods," Selah said.

Taraji nodded to Bodhi and he spoke. "Even if we can hide in the woods, we have to get to the area of the dome. The transport is too large to travel that far through the woods."

Selah heard the whoosh of the rising lift. Brejian exited

and stopped in the doorway of the command deck. "May I come onto the floor?"

"Please, join us," Selah said, smiling at her formality.

"I've been watching on the smaller screens below and I wanted to see the dome in real time. I've waited for this for a very long time. I would like to view it on approach since I don't intend to come outside again," Brejian said.

"We're going to be a moving target for quite a while until we find out if we're welcome," Taraji said, "and we can still make the transport impenetrable. If it's far enough in the woods no one may notice it."

"I don't think we need to worry about all that. Try this." Brejian held out a slender eight-sided crystal.

Taraji took the tube and looked it over before sliding it into an identically shaped receptacle in the security panel. "You've had a security beacon all this time, and you let us worry about having the children in harm's way—"

"I'm sure Brejian has a logical reason for the omission." Selah tried to hide her sarcasm as she pulled the woman from Taraji's line of sight.

Brejian stared at Selah. "I'm sorry, I didn't know if you'd be as trustworthy if you had access to the keys ahead of time." She blushed and lowered her head. "That eight-sided purple one slides into the security—"

"Yes, we know where it goes, but how did you get it, and what other ones do you have?" Mojica asked.

"The Cleveland dome was founded by my ancestors before the Sorrows," Brejian said. "Each of us was given a mandate and the means to return someday."

Selah pushed her way into the conversation. Why had

Brejian kept her relationship to the dome a secret? "So you're coming home," she said. "I can understand you not trusting me, but you didn't trust Mojica and Taraji enough to let them know the dome was your home?"

"I regret that now," Brejian said.

Taraji and Mojica exchanged worried glances.

"So do I," Taraji said. "We are of the same clan. I wouldn't have expected you to hold back important details about this dome. What are you trying to hide?"

Brejian pressed her lips together. "I'm not hiding anything. I haven't been to the dome since before the Sorrows. I didn't even know if it would still be here, and you surely don't expect me to know anything about the present internal society. Details from 150 years ago are not going to be of much use."

Bodhi's brows drew together. "I don't care if you're Kinship, with this omission you've proven to be untrustworthy as far as I'm concerned."

"No Kinship would dishonor our clan by causing harm to a novarium," Mojica said.

Selah looked from Mojica to Brejian. She trusted Taraji and Mojica and would have to give Brejian the benefit of the doubt . . . until something changed her mind.

"You said there were *keys*. What are the others for?" Taraji steered the transport over the rolling slopes and around several stands of evergreens.

Selah watched out the front shield as they slid lower into the lush green valley extending northward from the edge of the volcanic ash.

"One is the magnetic lock that will give us admittance into the dome," Brejian said.

"Activating this security beacon will ensure Selah's family's safety in here while we're inside," Mojica said.

"Are we're sure that this is all legitimate?" Bodhi asked as he turned to Selah.

Selah shrugged in resignation. "We're out of other options. We have to trust Mojica and Taraji."

"You have to find the Keeper," Brejian said. "He will guide you through the pearls to find the Third Protocol."

"You know who we're supposed to see? Do you know how we can find this Keeper?" Selah planted her hands on her hips.

Brejian's eyes darted back and forth. Selah tried to read her body-speak, but there was no noticeable impression. "I don't know anything about the present Keeper or how he or she operates." Brejian shrugged. "I don't even know if they still have a Keeper. I'm repeating what I once knew."

"Information about the pearls would have helped while we were looking for clues in Glade's documents." Growing anger flushed Selah's face. Taraji and Mojica couldn't have known about this—or did they? She tried to read their body-speak, but there was nothing. Was this lack of impression new, or had she never been able to read Kinship? "We could've been better prepared if you'd let us know this was your home."

"Waiting until we actually saw the dome intact became the next objective," Brejian said. "My information would have been useless if the dome had been destroyed."

"Our enemies have tried diligently to thwart the novarium process, so we may run into a dead end," Mojica said. "That could even be the reason no one else has completed the process. It was designed for only a true novarium to be able to decipher. So your information could have relieved some of the anxiety we felt about the trip without compromising the outcome."

"As I said before, I'm sorry. I won't make that mistake again," Brejian said.

"I don't know anything about this process. How can I decipher anything?" Selah chewed on her lip in frustration.

Taraji turned from her console to face Selah. "There will be things that only you can understand."

"What if I've broken down by the time those things come about?" Selah rubbed her fingers across her forehead. "What will become of my family and all of you?"

"I'll keep you safe," Bodhi said softly.

Selah spun around and planted a kiss on his cheek. "I like that you feel that way, but I'd rather you tell me that you'll keep Mother, Dane, and Mari safe."

"Let's not think that far ahead. We have a clear-cut objective with this dome in front of us," Taraji said.

"We're leaving Pasha and Mari here with the kids while we're inside," Mojica said.

"I'll be staying when you continue on," Brejian said. She turned to Selah. "Your mother has all of the records from the Repository, and we've verified the data points of this dome and the Chicago dome with the other information from Glade's bag."

Selah was excited about seeing the inside of the dome but apprehensive about Brejian's connection to it. The new uncertainty made her eager to continue west. She worried about the Chicago dome. It was considered home to the Blood Hunters.

She turned to Mojica. "Should we carry weapons?"

"I think we could holster laser darts, and if they won't

allow weapons we can leave them at the entrance," Mojica said.

Selah heard the familiar whoosh of the lift as it rose. The door slid open to admit Mari carrying a large box of devices and laser dart sidearms.

Mojica took the sidearms to pass out while Taraji and Bodhi took turns navigating and strapping on equipment.

"Everybody gets their own scrambler. I've keyed units from WoodHaven to each one of your biological frequencies to cancel any type of audio or microwave energy aimed at you," Mari said. She laid the box on the console and handed out devices.

"Do we have communication through this one?" Mojica asked. She strapped on her laser dart and wrapped the scrambler strap around her arm.

"Yes, I transferred our present frequencies into these sets, and I think you'll be happy with the increased range," Mari said. She grabbed the handful of earpieces. "I've calibrated these communicators to sync with the scramblers. They should reach anywhere inside the perimeter of the dome."

"We're pairing up *my* way. Do you hear me, Selah?" Taraji glanced over her shoulder.

Selah rolled her eyes in mock disgust. "What have you decided?"

Taraji smiled. "Bodhi's traveling with Mojica, you're with me, and Brejian will separate from us once we get inside."

"Why can't I pair with Bodhi?" Selah wanted to be close to him. They hadn't spent any quality time together since they'd entered the transport, and she felt disconnected from him. With Bodhi at her side, Selah's fierceness strengthened.

Taraji lowered her head but raised her eyes, making them look larger. "Are you going to press me on this issue? I'm pretty sure you'll agree that Mojica and I are the most capable combat fighters here. So it doesn't make much sense for us to have most of the experience on just one team."

Selah ran through the logic, and as much as she wanted to argue, there wasn't anything she could say other than, "No, I'm not going to press you. Are we ready to find the Keeper?"

12

Selah walked down the ramp beside Taraji with Brejian following behind. Bodhi and Mojica scouted out the area first and stood alert at the bottom of the ramp. As they stepped off, Taraji remoted the ramp back into the transport.

She'd thought Bodhi was ridiculous for insisting she wear a heavier jacket, but as she inhaled the cool crisp air, she understood. *Remember to thank him later.* She glanced around the foreign landscape. Her breath caught as she viewed the beauty of the changing seasons. Most of the surviving trees were evergreens, but dotted among the dark green background, like the splashes of color on one of her mother's loom patterns, were the vibrant fall colors of maples, elms, oaks, and chestnuts.

Off across the field, maybe a half mile away, Selah spied an enormously overgrown apple tree laden with golden-yellow fruit. Many of the overburdened branches were bent to the ground, where a mature doe and two fawns grazed in the massive litter of apples. Food and game . . . this wasn't a wasteland.

The ground turned uneven. Selah threw her hands out for balance and shifted her gaze back in the direction they were walking. Mojica led them toward the dome. Selah tried to take it all in at once. The shimmering wavy lines of energy—the iridescent green, pink, and yellow swirling colors of the dome—were like oil dispersing over water. The sight made her giddy with excitement. Maybe it was just because she was getting a respite from people trying to capture or kill her.

Her hands grew moist, and she wiped them down her pant legs. Her heart started to race, and she inhaled deeply to calm it. Both instances were explainable—she was wearing a heavier jacket and traveling at a faster rate than normal. Besides, she felt great.

The closer they moved toward the dome, the better she felt. Selah thought about that as she walked. Should she say something? No. They still had Brejian with them. She might want to send Selah back to the transport. And there was no way she was going to be kept from seeing this wonder.

They slowed as they got within five feet of the dome. Selah wanted to touch it. She reached out a hand. Brejian pulled her back. "You don't want to do that."

Selah lowered her arm. "Is it dangerous? Why are there no signs?"

Brejian smirked. "Do you normally have to tell adults not to stick their hands in the fire?"

"Well, no, but this is different. There aren't even danger signs telling people not to touch."

"No, this isn't different. The dome has been around more

than 150 years. Magnetoelectric current was in wide use before the Sorrows, so I'm sure people know not to touch the dome, and there's no need for signs because I doubt things have changed that much. There were no societies outside the domes. It's not safe."

Bodhi glanced around. "Are you sure we can enter at this spot? I don't see a door."

Brejian moved forward. "This is where I directed Mojica to come. There are no tracks because people don't come outside."

"This is like the Mountain society, except it's not underground, and hopefully there's no one like Bethany Everling in charge." The thought drew a chill up Selah's spine. "How much do we know about this person we need to find?"

"I'm well acquainted with the integrity of the Keepers here in this dome. I would like to hope that they haven't succumbed to greed like the evil people in the Mountain," Brejian said.

"I'm sorry. I didn't mean literally, I was just thinking of the closed-in space. I was never a fan of the Mountain."

"I've never thought of it that way. Yes, they're similar," Brejian said. "Unfortunately, staying inside is a matter of survival here. It is not the friendliest weather." She snapped open the cover on her bag, grabbed a red four-sided stick crystal, and jammed it in a blackened area on the shimmering dome.

Selah's eyes widened and Mojica stumbled back from the instant opening. The area in front of them evaporated like a mist, and the group stepped into a bustling crowd of people dressed in brightly colored clothing. Taraji spun around, but the opening had disappeared.

Selah was distracted by the smell and covered her nose. It

reminded her of the odor in the Mountain. But no one else seemed to notice. She leaned over to Brejian. "Do you smell that?"

Brejian shook her head. "What does it smell like? Maybe someone is cooking."

"I hope that's not food. It's hard to describe, some kind of chemical odor," Selah said.

Brejian tipped her head to the side. "Very curious. I didn't think you'd be able to pull that out of the—"

"Does anyone notice we're drawing a crowd?" Bodhi positioned himself in front of Selah. The mass of people closed in around them, sweeping them along with a sign-waving throng.

Mojica worked her way to Selah's side. But she didn't feel threatened. It was quite the opposite. The group had energy.

The crowd took up a chant. "Storm for all! Storm for all! No more death squads! Storm for all!"

Taraji pushed her way to Brejian. "What's going on? How do we get out of this?"

Brejian looked around and continued forward. "It seems nothing ever changes. There wasn't enough STORM for the population 150 years ago, and as much as things have changed here, the basics remain the same—the Keepers are still controlling life and death," she said.

"What's STORM?" Selah asked.

"I'll explain later. In the middle of this craziness isn't the place," Brejian said.

The crowd jostled them along. There was no way to avoid it. People swarmed forward, packing the street between the echoing canyon and the tall stone buildings. Selah figured the mob was at least three hundred strong.

"You should have warned us," Taraji said as they hurried along. "We could have brought better weapons."

"Weapons won't do you any good in here. They aren't allowed in the dome," Brejian said.

"We have our sidearms." Taraji patted her laser dart.

Brejian smiled. "They won't work in here."

Taraji's expression froze. She pulled out her laser dart and checked it. "There's no charge." A look of panic spread across her face. "Check your weapons." Bodhi and Mojica did so and acknowledged their weapons were also offline.

Selah pulled hers out. "No charge." She turned to Brejian. "One more thing you conveniently forgot to tell us."

"Sorry," Brejian said. "I've forgotten a lot about this society."

Selah felt the answer was too convenient, but the crowd distracted her with their body-speak sensations. They didn't feel hostile, just hopeful.

The crowd slowed in front of a multistory carved stone building. With their signs bouncing up and down, they continued the chant. Selah stared up at the building's stonework. It reminded her of the buildings in an ancient town she had passed that had been reduced to rubble, except here the windows weren't broken and kudzu hadn't taken over, and the building was scrubbed shiny and clean until the beige sandstone gleamed.

Mojica grabbed Brejian. "What are you leading us into? I'm getting tired of hearing you say that you *forgot* another important detail."

Taraji muscled her way in between them and pried Mojica's fingers from Brejian's jacket. "Stop! We need to know what we're here to find, and like it or not, only Brejian can direct us to the Keeper."

"I'm tired of this sixty-questions game. We're in the middle of a mob of strangers who could lash out at Selah any minute, and we have no way of protecting her," Mojica said to Taraji. "I know many of these people are Kinship, but I don't know their intentions and neither do you."

"You believe me, don't you?" Taraji faced off with her. "We've been waiting for this for a hundred years. You need to trust in all we've ever been taught—"

A light shone down on Selah's head. She and Bodhi looked skyward. A bearded old man appeared next to Selah.

He smiled.

She smiled.

They disappeared.

13

Selah backed away from the old man. The noisy crowd disappeared, but so had Bodhi and the rest of her team. Yet she didn't feel panic, which was concerning in itself. "Where am I?"

Her eyes jerked back and forth. She was in an office, with long polished wooden tables to the right, a heavy ornate wooden desk to the left, and waist-high bookcases topped by a glass-lined wall in front of her. The other side of the glass was dark, but she was pretty sure it wasn't the outside. She turned to see a blank wall behind her.

The old man looked amused. "You are where you wanted to be." His eyes twinkled above a beard resembling a mound of snow. Riddles. Just like the Keeper in the Mountain cave.

"I didn't ask to come here, wherever *here* is," Selah said. She needed to get her information and keep moving, especially with her family waiting in the transport.

"No, but you are looking for me." The old man seated himself in a wooden rocking chair behind the desk.

Selah relaxed and moved toward his desk. She had only ever seen old people sitting in overstuffed chairs, but this man preferred hard wood. Curious.

"Wait! You're the Keeper." She hadn't met too many people who actually looked old. Most of them were like Glade, remaining whatever physical age they'd been when the change happened.

He smiled. His cheeks dimpled. "See, you're a smart girl."

"I figure anyone who could create and maintain magnetic dome technology could also whip up transport tech—you know, the light over my head and all. So I know how I got here. But where am I and where are my friends?"

"Your friends are down below on the street. See for yourself." He pointed behind her. Tall, oblong windows appeared in the smooth wall.

Selah ran to one and peered out. "Bodhi! Up here!" She banged on the glass to no effect. She tapped the communicator pad on her scrambler then touched her earpiece. "Bodhi, can you hear me?"

"You are ten stories up. I know with your enhanced vision they appear close, but they can't hear you down there. And I also control the communications in and out of this building and this dome." The Keeper leaned forward and rested his folded hands on the desk.

Selah thought she should be fearful around this stranger, but she wasn't. Her heartbeat remained steady and she wasn't tense. Was this Keeper able to manipulate her body chemistry somehow? "Why have you kidnapped me when you're supposed to help me?"

"I haven't kidnapped you, just moved you to a location

where we can become acquainted with one another without interruption. I've waited a very long time to meet the novarium."

"How do you know I'm the novarium?"

The Keeper pointed. "You mean other than the marking below your collarbone there?"

Selah glanced down. With her coat open, her knit shirt was pulled to the side, giving an almost full view of her mark. "Outside the dome it's chilly. In here it's sweltering, and I was about to shed my coat when you so rudely snatched me up." Selah took off the coat and yanked on her knitted shirt. The mark disappeared underneath the fabric. "I suspect you're using bio-scanning and you had something to do with our weapons not working."

The Keeper nodded. "Yes, you would be correct on both counts. But I scanned you as you approached the dome, so I was well aware of your makeup—actually, *all* of your party's makeup—before you entered. And having three Kinship with you who haven't been here in more than a hundred years was a good sign of the novarium's presence."

"Great. I'm glad you understand, but we don't have time to get to know each other. I have to find the directions for traveling west and move on." More words stuck in her throat. Should she be telling him this? Her team hadn't discussed how much information to share.

The Keeper looked at her with kind eyes. "You may call me the Keeper, but I don't have directions to the West."

"You may call me Selah, and my father's data said you would help us."

The Keeper leaned back in the rocker. He stared at her

for several seconds. Selah wondered if she should sit in one of the chairs by his desk or lean back against one of the tables—something, anything, to not be standing in the middle of the room.

"Yes, I will help you, but it is my job to pass on just the next step. No one station was ever given more than a single progression as a responsibility. If one stop became compromised it wouldn't lead directly to the Third Protocol."

"Well, great. Give us whatever it is that I'm supposed to get from you and we'll be on our way," Selah said. This was working out better than she'd thought.

"I'm afraid it's not going to be that easy." His face suddenly grew serious.

Bodhi pushed his way past Mojica for the second time. How did this happen? How did four grown people lose Selah? "Where could she have gone? We've all gone three yards out. How could she disappear?"

Taraji returned to the group. "Nothing. She's gone."

Brejian remained at the spot where Selah had disappeared. "You're not listening to me. I'm telling you, she was bio-ported."

Mojica circled back and grabbed Brejian by her jacket again. "You didn't tell us this would happen. How could you let her get separated from us?"

Bodhi felt sweat running down his back. His heart thumped against his rib cage, and the more he thought of losing Selah, the faster it pounded, resounding in his head. Not when they'd come this far! Not now! He stripped off his coat and threw it at the wall beside them.

Everyone scattered from his vicinity.

"What happened? Where did she disappear to?" Bodhi backed Brejian into the brick wall and stared her down. "If anything happens to her, you will answer to me." Why had Selah trusted this healer?

Brejian's eyes darted like she was searching for an escape route. Bodhi took a breath.

"Wait a minute." Taraji nudged her way between the two. "I trust both of you. So let's get a hold on this. Brejian looks like a roach trying to run from the light because you just crawled down her throat for no good reason. So loosen up your bootlaces, lover boy."

Bodhi's cheeks warmed. He lowered his head and ran his hands through his hair. "I'm not buying her lack of explanations. I didn't trust her before we left TicCity, and I really don't trust her after these missteps. It's all too convenient." He slammed his fist into the wall. Pinpricks of pain radiated up his arm. "It's my fault for being lax."

"It's no one's fault," Brejian said as she reached down and grabbed Bodhi's coat from the ground. "The Keeper's in control of the dome. I didn't know what to expect, but I can assure you that Selah is safe and we will hear from her soon. Let's find a way station and she'll find us." She handed the coat to Bodhi and started to walk away.

Bodhi put a hand out to stop her. He leaned back against the wall. "Not so fast. What's a way station, and how will she find us?"

"The same key that let us into the dome will unlock a temporary residence for the holder. The Keeper will know where we are." Brejian brushed aside his hand and worked her way through the crowd and down the long city street, heading toward the center of the dome.

Mojica looked like she wasn't sure what to do while Taraji shrugged, but they both followed Brejian.

Bodhi turned his attention from the immediate problem, and the noise around them came back into focus. The people were strangely jovial for such a large crowd. He wasn't about to trust Brejian, but maybe he could get more out of her using Selah's honey-coated tactics.

He leaned away from the wall and trotted to catch up to Brejian. "What are they marching about?"

Brejian looked around. "The same thing as usual—STORM."

"Storm? They're marching about the weather?" Bodhi chuckled as he followed Brejian into an ornate stone building on the right side of the street. "I guess having all this nice weather could make you testy once in a while."

Brejian drew up to her full six-foot height. "STORM is the acronym for Singular Transition Oral Regiment Method."

Bodhi assumed the pride in her voice meant she'd had something to do with the project somewhere along the line. "I'm sure it was a very important project, but I don't know what that means," he said. Diplomacy wasn't a skill he practiced often, but at the moment Brejian was the only one who knew of Selah's whereabouts.

Brejian crooked a finger in Bodhi's direction and led the group back outside. "Do you see any old people?" She put her hands on her hips.

Bodhi looked around at the throng as they milled about the building up the street. He glanced at Mojica and Taraji, who shrugged. "No. Why?"

Selah glared at the Keeper. "You just told me you were going to help me and now you tell me it's not going to be easy. What's your game? Are you going to tell me the next station or not?"

"I'll decide when you are ready to know the next station."

"So I was right. You are holding me hostage to further your purpose," Selah said. These people always had a reason, no matter how bizarre.

"You might have a difficult time leaving. There is a storm system coming in that will last quite a while, and the magnetic interference will prevent your leaving here." The Keeper began to rock in his chair.

Selah thought for a second. Magnetic interference was already becoming problematic for the transport. "I have family in our transport. Can they come inside? How do I get to them?"

"I will have a vehicle suitable for the weather at your disposal to ferry them back here." The Keeper continued to rock. He seemed unconcerned about whether Selah left or not, and that intrigued her.

"You know I would stay if I could," Selah said. She hoped she sounded contrite enough.

"Young people are always in such a hurry," the Keeper said. "You forget to absorb life."

"Forgive me for not agreeing with you, but my clock is ticking. I have roughly nine months before I fracture into teeny-tiny patches of brain cells that no longer know how to talk to each other. I need to find the Third Protocol."

"Go and rescue your family while there is still time to bring them inside, and we will talk." He handed her a four-sided translucent blue crystal. "This will get you back to me no matter where I am in the dome."

Selah shoved the crystal in her pocket. What kind of storm was coming? It didn't matter. She didn't have an ability that could overcome weather. "How do I get to my friends so they can help rescue my family?"

"I will send you to them. I've opened outside communications. Call your family and tell them not to hesitate or all will be lost."

Selah appeared in the middle of Brejian pointing at the crowd. "Help me! Brejian, show me how to get back to where we came into the dome. A vehicle will be there to rescue my family."

Bodhi pulled her into his arms. "Hey, where've you been? We were worried—"

"There's no time! The Keeper said a magnetic storm is coming and we need to get Mother, Mari, and the kids in here," Selah said as she pulled away. "Taraji, call my mother and tell them to be ready to leave there in five minutes."

Taraji keyed her communicator. Selah swallowed the lump in her throat.

Brejian jumped into action. "Follow me! We have to hurry before it's too late." She sprinted back through the crowd with everyone following.

"Where are we going?" Bodhi yelled as he raced up the street beside Selah.

"There's a vehicle waiting where we entered the dome. It will ferry Mother, Mari, and the kids here to ride out the storm," Selah said.

"I'm sorry you'll be trapped here that long," Brejian said.

Selah turned. "What?"

"There's the vehicle," Taraji said.

Selah looked at Brejian. "What do you mean?"

"I'm going." Taraji jumped in beside the driver. The gull wing lowered and the dome wall in front of the vehicle vaporized.

Whirling gusts of winds roared like the herds of horses Selah had seen thundering across the southern plains. The force pushed her backward. Bodhi steadied her. She raised her hands in front of her face to keep the pelting rain that felt like needles of ice from hitting her. The vehicle rose.

Gale-force winds pushed the small vehicle farther away from the opening, rocking it back and forth. Even with the wind howling, Selah heard the engines on the vehicle cycle up. It shot forward as the rain turned to blowing snow. The dome shimmered until the magnetism became so thick that the opening closed.

Selah slumped to the floor with Bodhi at her side. Mojica helped up Brejian, who had been propelled by the wind into some crates stacked in a nearby shipping area. They came toward Selah.

"What is going on? How long will this last?" Selah asked. Brejian's words "that long" kept playing through her head.

Brejian shook her head. Selah grabbed her arm. "How long?"

"It could be months." Brejian seemed to recoil at her own words.

Selah gasped and sagged against Bodhi's shoulder. She refused to panic even though her insides were screaming.

One thing at a time. After her family was safely inside there would be time to figure the rest out.

Time felt like a rubber string. It stretched out and seemed like hours. Then it snapped back and it had only been minutes. Selah gripped Bodhi's hand tightly. She knew she was cutting off his circulation. She relaxed her hold. Bodhi, his lips pressed together, offered a slight smile.

"The Keeper will supply your family with suitable quarters while you are here," Brejian said to Selah.

Bodhi looked between Selah and Brejian, realization spreading across his face. "Quarters? I thought you were exaggerating to be funny. What kind of snowstorm would take that long to pass?"

"This is a magnetic snowstorm," Brejian said. "Since the super volcano during the Time of Sorrows, the magnetic lines in this part of the country have been shifted north. When solar flares pass through earth's atmosphere and magnetic snowstorms happen at the exact same time . . . well, that's why people don't live outside the dome. There can be as much as ten feet of snow for as long as three months before it's melted enough to get to the next dome."

"How do you know this? You haven't been here in over a hundred years. It could've changed," Bodhi said.

"Nothing here changes." Brejian pointed up. "Do you see that lit red band extending in either direction around the dome? It's ten feet above the ground—where the snow reached the first winter after the Sorrows. It also means Level Five weather. That's as high as the line can go for danger. It was blue for Level Two—just cooling temperatures—when we came in."

"How long will it take to bring my family back?" Selah asked.

"The storm looked like it was picking up rather quickly. They've been gone ten minutes. I'd say at least another ten."

"What if something happens to the rescue? Bodhi, call Taraji. I want to know if she has them yet."

Bodhi keyed his communicator and tapped his earpiece. He listened. "Nothing. I don't have a signal."

They each tried. Selah was the last to shake her head. "Did Taraji reach them when she called?" No one could verify if there had been a two-way conversation.

Selah looked up at the lit red line pulsing around the dome. The weather above it, visible through the clear dome, was hauntingly beautiful. In her travels north, she had once held a snow globe and watched the storm inside the globular dome. Now she was in the dome and the storm was outside.

She looked at her scrambler for the time. Fifteen minutes gone.

Bodhi moved to look over the control panel the vehicle had activated to leave the dome. "I spotted the communications signal, but it's at zero." He walked back to stand behind Selah and placed his hand on her shoulder.

Selah felt better knowing he was close. She still didn't fear this place, but she wasn't entirely comfortable here either. She looked at Brejian. "Are you sure we're safe here?"

"I guarantee that the quarters they give you will be safe because of the Keeper, but I have to check around to determine if there are any disagreeable factions," Brejian said.

Selah looked at her scrambler again. It had been twenty minutes. They should be coming any time now. She started to pace but was careful to stay off the flight path the vehicle would come in on. She looked up again. The sky was growing dark with heavier snow. Her knees began to tremble, so she sat on a crate, her mind whirling with crazy thoughts. It wouldn't be fair for her to have come this far and then have her family taken away.

Selah inhaled and blew out a series of short breaths. *This shouldn't be happening.* Why was she safe and they weren't? She glanced at the scrambler. Twenty-five minutes. They should have been here by now. Something had happened.

I need to go find my family. Selah sprang to her feet, searching for a vehicle to take her outside.

There was nothing. Even if there was a vehicle, how would she find her family in this weather? She could collide with the rescue vehicle and kill everyone. And that would be her fault.

She sat back down, then stood up again. Tears silently slid down her cheeks. She was helpless to do anything on her own. The feeling was foreign and unsettling.

Selah looked down at her scrambler. Bodhi covered her wrist with his hand and shook his head. "Stop. You're making yourself crazy."

A single tear slipped to her chin. "I can't lose them." Bodhi let his hand drop away. She looked down. Thirty minutes. Selah sat down and rested her head in her hands. *Please don't take them away.* She hadn't even had time to enjoy her family all together because she'd been so preoccupied about herself. She promised to change and spend more time with them.

It had been too long now. *Something's wrong.* More tears dripped down her cheeks.

The entrance dissolved, blowing snow raced through, and the vehicle flew in like a slingshot. The pelting snow ceased as the opening closed.

Selah ran to the right side as Taraji opened the gull wing.

The two laughing kids poured out into Selah's arms. "You should have seen it. We spun right around in the air. All the way around," Dane said. Rylla nodded in happy agreement.

Pasha and Mari climbed out the side. "Oh yes, it was wonderful fun having my snack roll around in my stomach like that, but at least we're safe," Pasha said.

Brejian looked relieved, as though any misfortune that could have come to Selah's family would have been her fault. "Come on, let me get you to the way station to see where the Keeper is housing you." She hurried ahead but looked back often to judge their progress down the street.

Taraji stayed in front while Mojica brought up the rear. Bodhi glued himself to Selah's side while Pasha walked beside Mari.

"That was enough air turbulence for a whole month. What's going on? Why were we summoned into this place?" Pasha asked. She glanced around at the congregating crowd that was getting thicker the farther they moved down the street. Selah could guess her thoughts.

"The snowstorm might last three months, and the snow could get ten feet tall," Selah said. "We're safer in here."

"We were safer in our own environment in the transport," Pasha said, looking around hesitantly at the chanting people.

Brejian called back, "This is also a dangerous magnetic storm that could disrupt systems on the transport. Remember, we were having problems with it yesterday. If you were trapped there in ten feet of snow with no power, we'd have found your frozen corpses a couple months from now."

Pasha made a face. "Don't talk like that in front of the children."

"They're back there with Mojica. They can't hear us, and besides, Rylla has seen a lot worse," Selah said.

"I just don't like to see folks tormented by unpleasant things," Pasha said. She gestured back at the crowd they had just worked their way through. "What's the matter with them? Why are they protesting the storm?"

"It's not actually the weather they're protesting. Brejian was just starting to tell us about that," Bodhi said.

Brejian directed them to the way station where Selah had reappeared earlier.

Selah inhaled a sharp breath at the beauty. They walked the polished marble floor to a large rotunda with a gilded ceiling composed of numerous large paintings. A glass light fixture with hundreds of sparkling prisms hung from it.

"The word STORM is an acronym," Bodhi said.

Brejian raised a hand. "Let's talk about that only in private." Bodhi nodded, but Selah didn't know why. They waited quietly while Brejian checked them in and then followed her along a bright, colorful corridor.

Mojica and Taraji moved the group closer while Brejian opened the housing unit. "Are we getting into more covert stuff that we have no business being part of?" Taraji asked as they followed behind Selah into a vast great room that opened to an outdoor garden with a seating area.

Selah hurried to the glass doors to look out on the beautiful flowers. The smell from them was wonderful—such peace in the midst of a storm. She turned back to the group.

Mojica glanced around the large family area. "It wouldn't surprise me if Selah's in—"

14

Selah spun around. This time she was standing in the grass of a large flower garden. A warm radiance gave light as though the sun was shining, but when she looked up she could see the blizzard raging outside the dome. The Keeper sat at a wrought-iron table and chairs underneath a trellis covered in grapevines and hanging fruit clusters. He gestured her over as he poured hot amber liquid into two cups.

She approached the table. "Thank you for rescuing my family, but you have *got* to stop whizzing me out of rooms when I'm in the middle of a conversation."

She took a seat at the table and studied her cup. It was a fine white glass or ceramic. The old lady in the Mountain had cups like this in her dining room. Selah carefully slid her finger into the handle and lifted the cup to sniff the liquid. She looked up and saw the Keeper smiling softly as he watched her.

"What? Why are you looking at me like that?" She took a sip. The drink was tangy like an orange but sweet like honey.

"You seem less agitated now that your family is safe. So I thought we could talk." The Keeper sat back and picked up his cup.

"I hope you don't take this wrong, but if you only want to *talk*, I'd much rather be with my family," Selah said.

The Keeper chuckled. "Fair enough. I thought you would want to know that with the size of the storm, we've estimated you'll be here at least ninety days."

Selah frowned. She'd have to trust in Mojica and Taraji's confidence that she'd be safe here. "That would have us leaving here sometime in December. Do you think we'll miss being hit by another storm on the way west?" It occurred to her that she'd reach her six-month peak around the time they left here, leaving them only six months to find the Third Protocol.

"We typically have a break in between major events, so it looks favorable. But it will take everything your team has to prepare for the six months of trials after you leave here."

"I'm not happy to be stuck here for so long, but we'd appreciate any help you can offer."

The Keeper sat forward. "You will spend the next three months here, relatively safe, as your strength builds and your mental capacity heightens, but when you leave your strength will start to drain. You will need people with highly trained skills of combat and survival to navigate what is left of the world out there."

"Our transport doesn't have the ability to take additional people," Selah said. Besides, her trust only went so far, and taking strangers with her was not part of the plan.

"I'm not talking about more people. I'm talking about better people. You have two Kinship traveling with you. They will benefit from training on our systems, which are compatible with their DNA," the Keeper said.

"I have three people. Bodhi Locke is—"

"Bodhi Locke is useless. He is the Second Protocol who transitioned you. Why is he even with you?" The Keeper looked disgusted.

Selah hesitated, not wanting to be rude. "How do you know that?"

She caught the small, almost unperceivable movement of the Keeper's eyes darting from side to side. "Remember, I scanned all of you before you came into the dome."

Even without his body-speak she knew that was a lie. She bristled. "I don't know or have a say in how you run this place, and I appreciate that the dome's purpose is to protect me, but you do not get to dictate who travels with me."

One side of the Keeper's mouth raised in a sarcastic smile. "You're in a relationship with that Lander. Well, that's nothing new. I've seen it before. What a waste."

Selah's face contorted with anger. "You don't get to make that call. Bodhi gets the training too, or none of us will participate."

He ignored her words. "I scanned your transport when you came in. We have halo-trainers in our archives for commanding the systems in that vehicle. Mojica and Taraji could gain an advantage by being trained daily," he said as he made a selection from a gilded box.

Selah balked. "Don't change the subject! Does Bodhi get the training?"

The Keeper frowned but waved a hand. "Yes, he can have the training."

"Good." Her anger began to subside. "The only other thing that would make this a fruitful discussion would be you telling me about the next station."

The Keeper furrowed his brow and looked at her hard, then shrugged and sighed. "Your survival has always been our ultimate goal, so information comes on a need-to-know basis, but in this extended situation I guess it can't hurt to tell. You will be traveling next to the dome at Chicago, Illinois, to find the Seeker."

Relief poured over her, but then she thought that seemed too easy. "What is a Seeker? Are they different from you?"

The Keeper sat back. "At one time long before the Sorrows, we were all one company with one goal to help mankind. Then greed and personalities tore that goal asunder."

Selah recoiled at the thought of Blood Hunters being humanitarians. "But the Chicago dome is home to the Blood Hunters. How did they wind up being so much different from you?"

"Greed drives a man to do strange things. Instead of wanting to help the world, they decided they wanted to make obscene amounts of money, and if the world benefited in the long run it would be a plus. They took the name *Seekers* to make it sound like they had a higher purpose."

Selah frowned. "Their higher purpose disintegrated into evil. They've been trying to kill me for the last few months."

"An unfortunate by-product of greed. It's hard to take the humanity out of the equation." He held out a multifaceted purple prism with a star shape at the end. "This will allow you admittance to the Chicago dome."

She snatched up the crystal. "You could've saved me a lot of angst by telling me the first time. We could have gone on our way." Just holding the prism made her antsy to leave.

"You would have been caught in the magnetic part of the storm halfway between here and Chicago, and that is probably where your party would have died."

Selah sat back as the thought sank in. How easily they all could have died. Her sense of responsibility pressed in like a crushing weight on her chest. For a moment it was hard to breathe, but she shook off the feeling and jumped to her feet, jostling the table. "You said you wouldn't tell me till I was ready, and now a couple hours later you're telling me. Do you really think I'm ready? What kind of game are you playing?" She tightened her hand around the crystal. The sharp edges pressed into her flesh. She tried not to wince, refusing to appear weak.

"You will be ready by the time you're able to leave," the Keeper said calmly.

Selah relaxed her fist. Lightning flashes crossed her vision. Anger and fear rose and prickled across her chest, then subsided, leaving her drained. What was that? Was it a normal flash, or had the Keeper put something in her drink? She lowered back to the seat and fingered the rim of her cup. The disturbance in her head cleared like a breeze pushing away the morning fog. It felt like her new normal after such an event.

She still didn't trust this Keeper or this place, but Mother had taught her as a child that she could catch more flies with honey than with vinegar. She needed these people a lot more than they needed her.

"Speaking of the storm, what is the STORM those people

are protesting?" Selah pushed the cup away with the tips of her fingers.

"STORM is the acronym for Singular Transition Oral Regiment Method," he said.

"Those are big words. What does it mean?"

"Do you mind if we discuss this in my office?" The Keeper rose.

"Yes, I do—"

Selah put her hands out to steady herself as she found herself in the Keeper's office. "I wish you'd warn me when you're going to do that."

"Sorry. You will soon tune into the frequency and feel when it's coming. The others did," the Keeper said as he walked past his desk to the low bookcase.

"Are you talking about other novarium?" Selah walked beside him.

"Yes, of course the other novarium."

Selah stopped. "How many others?"

"Oh, I don't know. Over the years . . . probably fifty-five or sixty." He waved his palm over the top of the bookcase and a control panel rose from the surface.

"You mean there were up to sixty others and none of them made it?" The staggering implication accompanied another lightning surge. This time she was confident that it was part of her new normal. Selah leaned against the bookcase. That number was far beyond what she had been told.

"Do you want to know about STORM? Or lost novarium?" The Keeper lifted his hand from the panel.

Selah stared at him, sparkles dotting her vision. "Yes, I want to know about STORM, but at the same time I think I deserve a minute to understand just how hard this process is to accomplish. Sixty other people have failed. Why should I be the one who makes it?" Selah leaned her back to the bookcase and looked at the floor till the lightning passed. She wanted to be confident, but all these things kept chipping at her resolve.

The Keeper turned from the glass to face Selah. "I guess it depends on whether you have the fire inside you to make it."

She wanted to say that after all the lightning charges she felt full of fire, but she didn't want to tell him more about her condition than she had to. "Well, it looks like you haven't picked a winner so far," she said wryly.

"I'm a total stranger to you, as you are to me. If I told you I knew you could make it, that would be a lie. I would like to *hope* you could make it, but that outcome belongs to something much bigger than me." The Keeper raised a finger and an eyebrow. "If you could complete the Third Protocol, then our application of STORM would no longer be necessary." The Keeper gestured back toward the glass.

The lights came on, and a cylinder five feet in diameter rose from the floor until it reached the ceiling of the two-story room. The covering on the side of the cylinder slid back to display a pulsing multicolor shade of blue.

Selah stepped closer to the glass. Her vision had cleared, but this time the sparkles came from within the tube. "What is that?"

"They call it the *mother*," the Keeper said.

"You mean like the starter my mother uses for her sourdough, or the mother in apple cider vinegar?" Selah said.

The Keeper nodded. "You are one of only a few who understand the concept. There may be hope for you yet."

"Well, that's a first. A vote of confidence." Selah did want to learn about what she was, and if this guy was willing to teach her, she'd have to show him a little trust. Besides, they'd be stuck here a few months whether she interacted with him or not.

"First, I have to impress upon you that this is for your knowledge only. It can never be shared with another living soul. It would destroy our society before its time."

Selah smirked. "Isn't that a little dramatic? Someone besides you and me must know the secret."

"No one, and at the moment I'm the only one who knows unless you agree to never repeat the information," the Keeper said.

Selah thought for a second. He had already afforded her the trust of handing over the next key. "I will never repeat the information."

"The formulary in that receptacle—"

"Wait! You're going to believe me just like that?" Selah's eyes widened as she threw up her hands. She hadn't believed *him* that easily.

"Well, of course. You wouldn't lie to me, would you?" The Keeper stared at her.

"No . . . no, I wouldn't lie to you." Selah picked up an odd sensation from the old man. Strange, but she knew he was telling the truth. Either he was extremely trusting or he was setting her up for something.

"Okay then, the formulary in that receptacle has been dispensing pills for the last 150 years. We have kept sample results over the years for each batch, and in the last twenty years the produced batches have become weaker. Between births and deaths the population is remaining steady. So we've tried to hide the weakness by dispensing pills later and making people think the aging is coming from the delay rather than alarming them about weaker batches." The Keeper closed down the tube and it returned to the floor.

"Why can't you just tell them the truth?" Selah didn't know the people, but telling them the truth seemed like the only way to let them be part of their own destiny.

"Because there would be only a small minority who would understand the situation. Then there would be the group that would figure out how to cheat the system and start a black market of stealing others' pills to increase their own dosage, and society would break down and not be here for the . . . next novarium." The Keeper looked down. "I'm sorry I had to say that, but it is our reality if you do not succeed."

Selah's shoulders slumped as she frowned and shut her eyes tight. Then her eyes flew open. "Wait, what does STORM's quality have to do with me succeeding?"

"When you connect with the Third Protocol, all Landers will be changed, but so will all parts of this project. They are all interconnected," the Keeper said.

"What do you mean by 'all parts'? What other parts are there besides the Protocols?"

The Keeper shrugged. "The Kinship, the Blood Hunters, the Keepers here in this dome, the Seekers in the next—we all employ some variation of the same building blocks. Therefore everyone involved in this project will change in some way. But meanwhile we must persevere as we are." The Keeper returned to his rocker. Selah followed and sat in one of the heavy wooden chairs next to his desk.

"My success is tied to more lives than I ever understood." Selah leaned forward and rested her elbows on her knees. "What happens if I don't—" The word stuck in her throat. "What happens if I don't succeed?"

"You are the last novarium in this first cycle. We will wind down until this society has died out to a population of approximately twenty people, which will allow the mother enough time to regenerate to multiply pill production and build the society for another 150-year cycle," the Keeper said.

"What about the dome? Will it survive with that few people?" This was the first place she'd been to on the other side of her mountains, and she found it to be lovely. Knowing his society was headed for extinction because a novarium didn't succeed must be a heavy burden. She was gaining more respect for the Keeper's responsibility.

"We expanded the dome at the beginning to be self-regenerating. We've become an established safety point between the storms, but that is not our immediate problem." The tone of his last few words became deeper.

Selah lifted her head. "Why do I know that tone of voice— and not like it?"

"Because I've been given new information. One of the groups I worried would get a foothold in the unrest has massaged an old theory. Early in the last century someone told a variegated story rather than the true purpose of the novarium in the Protocol. Therefore the truth was lost, replaced by speculation and a whole society that wants nothing better than to experiment with your DNA in hopes of creating a permanent formula."

Selah heaved a great sigh as she stared at the ornate tin ceiling. "There's always someone who wants my blood. I've lived that way for the last three months." She lowered her gaze and looked square at the Keeper. "So what is the immediate problem?"

Bodhi had traced his steps across the great room and into the garden four times already. All he could concentrate on was Selah's disappearance. She said it would need to happen for her to meet with the Keeper, but Bodhi still didn't like it. He strolled back into the great room. Mojica was explaining the situation to Mari and Pasha, with the two kids stretched out on the floor beside them, quietly reading stories from the Stone Braide Chronicles.

"There are no old folks, or at least no old-*looking* folks. People still age, but *old-looking* age is just a disease," Brejian said to Taraji. Bodhi stopped pacing to listen.

"So you're telling me people here take a pill once a year and never get any kind of sickness or disease. How can I believe such a thing? There would be people coming from far and wide to steal and duplicate the technology," Taraji said.

And Selah was the target of such misguided thieves, who thought her blood was a fountain of youth.

"Each pill is especially coded for the recipient so there can be no theft, and the only recipients are original descendants of the founding families. But lately those dosages are given farther and farther apart, which is causing visible aging that people aren't happy with. That's why they're protesting," Brejian said.

Taraji shook her head. "Nothing ever changes. People are the same everywhere. There will always be something the masses are unhappy about even when they live in a paradise like this."

Brejian stood. "Yes, you're right, so I hope you'll take the information my people have provided. Selah is in danger here. There is a group of rogue scientists who think adding novarium DNA to STORM can create a perpetual pill that doesn't need yearly renewal."

Bodhi strode across the room. "That's similar to what the Mountain people tried to do with her blood. Where is the Keeper holding Selah? We need eyes on her at all times until we leave here."

"We can go out to the console and request a message be sent to Selah. I don't know if the Keeper has restrictions on communications when she's with him," Brejian said.

Bodhi motioned her from the seat. "Come on then, please. We need Selah back here now. She needs to hear this." He nodded to Mojica and led Brejian out of the housing unit and down the hall.

As they turned the corner a tall, mustached man entered the marble-floored lobby with a loud, determined stride. Brejian stopped short and Bodhi almost plowed into her. The tall man paused as well. Bodhi turned to Brejian, but she had shoved her hands into her jacket pockets and displayed the biggest smile Bodhi had ever seen on her. He turned to look at the man. He was giving the same all-teeth grin. It annoyed Bodhi when people smiled like that. It seemed to be exaggerated for effect.

Bodhi stepped out of the way as the two people rushed to each other. He frowned. Brejian had been back in the dome for a matter of hours, yet she already had access to a whole information network and, apparently, a man now coming to renew an acquaintance. He hadn't missed her presence for more than a few seconds all day. How was she doing it?

"I'm sorry to be so rude. Bodhi, this is Healer Cinanji. Cinanji, this is Bodhi Locke. He's a member of the party I arrived with, and unfortunately, they will need to remain here until the storm has passed."

Cinanji smiled graciously at Bodhi. "Thank you for bringing my first love back to her home. I'm sure I will see you around the dome for the next few months, so enjoy our hospitality. What is ours is yours." He bowed at the waist, kissed Brejian's hand, and went on his way.

Bodhi watched him go. He didn't believe a word the man said, and he already didn't trust Brejian, so to think they were conspiring together was only logical. He needed to keep the enemy close. "Where would he be going here in a way station?"

"Oh, I don't know. Why do you want to know?" Brejian gazed in the direction the healer had gone.

Bodhi turned and stared her down. "Because we're worried about people infiltrating our system to grab Selah, and he appears to be a perfect example. All he has to do is see that light in your eyes, and I bet you'd tell him our whole itinerary."

Brejian glared at him. "Listen, you haven't liked me from the start—"

"You're right, and that's because you've lied. I've seen you snickering behind Mojica's back, and I'm not sure how you've gotten all your information since being in the dome, but it's making me nervous."

Brejian pursed her lips and held up her hands in surrender. "All right. Enough. I guess you have a right to know. I was one of the ones sent out early on. We were supplied with implants that always register an active dome frequency. I re-activated it once we came inside, and now I'm reconnected to my network."

Bodhi grinned. She had given in too easily, but he'd play along. "So you rekindled a relationship too?"

Brejian's mouth opened. "Oh, no, no. I didn't do that. It was a perfect accident, us coming into the lobby at the same time."

Bodhi nodded but continued to watch the healer while Brejian sent a message to Selah by way of the Keeper.

He didn't like this. There was something wrong and he was missing it.

They walked back toward the housing unit. Bodhi quick-ened his steps, barged ahead of Brejian, and flung open the door.

His eyes widened.

Selah stood in the middle of the great area, Mari beside her, as Mojica and Taraji relayed what Brejian had learned. She turned as Bodhi rushed to her and scooped her up in a bear hug. She started to laugh at the fierceness in his hug but quickly stilled as she felt the tremor in his embrace. He was afraid.

Bodhi set her back on the floor. His face reddened. Selah's heart dissolved into mush at the love and concern radiating from him. She decided to make light of it so he didn't feel more embarrassed.

"You're going to have your hands full. I'm the prey of the

century and we're trapped here in a blizzard. It sounds like one of those stories Rylla and Dane have been telling me about."

Bodhi tipped his head and looked down at her. "Do you feel all right? This isn't a joke. You're in danger."

She blinked. "And how would you prefer I act? Do you want me to be cowering in the corner? This is now a fact of my life. I have to learn to adapt or perish. There have to be malcontents in a population this large, but if I worried about danger around every corner it would drive me crazy before the fracture does. I'm choosing to live on a level of trust."

Bodhi planted his feet. "I'd rather you took your security more seriously—"

"Easy! Easy, you two," Pasha said. "Be glad that Selah's returned. It looks like we're going to be here for quite a long time."

"I was trying to wait until we'd settled in, but here's serious for you," Selah said to Bodhi. "Mojica, Taraji, and *you* will start training. The Keeper has combat halo-trainers for our transport in their archives," Selah said. "So he was willing to trust us enough to offer combat training, which we desperately need."

A smile spread across Bodhi's face. "I can deal with that."

"Brejian, would you help me set up the training sessions since you know how to interface with the system?" Taraji said. She ushered Brejian to the outer door.

"Can you also show me where to find provisions to stock this kitchen so I can feed the children?" Pasha followed behind Taraji and Brejian and closed the door on her way out.

Mari directed the kids back to their reading of the Stone Braide Chronicles. Only Bodhi and Mojica remained with Selah.

"Everyone else knows what we're going to share. We were trying to get Brejian out of the way because I don't trust her," Bodhi said.

Selah pinched her brows together. "What has she done wrong? She's Kinship and Taraji's pick. Her information was critical to us getting here. The fact that she had the crystal to open the dome, and the Repository files . . . well, I've found her very helpful." Selah had pored over the Repository data on Bodhi's condition, but since talking to the Keeper she knew if she completed the Protocols, Bodhi would be restored like everyone else.

"She's not telling the truth about something, but I can't put my finger on it," Bodhi said.

"Well, I'll promise not to be alone with her until you figure it out. In the meantime, I've found that there've been at least sixty novarium. We know none of them made it to the end, and until we make it to the next station we don't know how many of them actually made it away from here," Selah said.

Mojica crossed her arms. "So the info Brejian heard must be true. It's ironic that we're trapped for three months with the Kinship sworn to protect the novarium. Meanwhile the residents' super health pill, which allows them to live long enough to help the novarium, is getting weak. But the kicker is they've decided that novarium DNA *added* to STORM can create a perpetual pill. How many things can you find wrong with that theory?"

Selah soaked in the irony that every one of the lost or captured novarium could have been the answer for all. That would have saved her from needing to be the novarium—but it also would have prevented her from meeting her real father . . . and Bodhi.

A ruckus grew louder on the other side of the outer door. Mojica dragged furniture in front of the door, and Bodhi pushed Selah into one of the back rooms. Mari herded the children in with her.

Selah trained her hearing on the shouting voices. She knew Taraji's and her mother's voices. She also heard two strange voices. Heavy tones. They must be large men.

Someone screamed. There was a scuffle.

Selah tried to push past Bodhi. "My mother's in that hall. Let me go."

A body slammed into the door.

"Stay here!" Bodhi shouted as he and Mojica rushed the door and jerked it open. Taraji kicked a beefy man through the doorway. He flew into the living unit and landed in a heap but came up swinging. Mojica delivered a knockout blow while Taraji subdued the second man and Bodhi ran out of the unit.

"Keep the kids back here," Selah said to Mari before she darted out the bedroom door and into the great room. She glanced at the man as she ran by. He had a bird tattoo.

Where was Mother? She ran to the curve in the hallway. In the lobby ahead Bodhi swung at a man. He blocked the man's returning punch and connected with his chin. The man gave a hard blow and Bodhi flew against the corridor wall.

Selah cried out a warning. Bodhi looked toward her, and the man struck him again. Bodhi stumbled back. Selah charged up the long hall as anger welled inside her.

Bodhi drew back and slammed his fist into the man's stomach. He doubled over. Selah was at full charge as she broke from the hall into the lobby, and just as she was about to launch a thrust at the man, Brejian came running into the lobby, followed by a half dozen security agents.

"Arrest that one there," Brejian yelled as she pointed.

"There's two more down in our unit," Selah shouted.

Brejian pointed at the other agents. "Down the hall that way. Unit three. Get the other two." The agents hurried off with the first prisoner in tow.

Selah looked around. Pasha sat against the wall near the opening to the hall. Selah's hands grew moist. She ran to her. "Are you all right?" She wiped one hand on her slacks and stretched it out to help her mother up.

Pasha rose to her feet, unsteady at first. Her long hair, pulled back loosely in a low ponytail, had several escaped tendrils framing her face. "I must confess I'm not used to all this violence."

Selah hugged her. "Sadly, it's become a normal and expected part of my day, but the farther west we get, the closer we are to the end of it."

Bodhi joined them after a heated discussion with Brejian. Anger etched his face. "I wanted to know why she wasn't with Taraji and Pasha. She said she was but broke away when the three men were bringing them back to the unit so they could grab Selah."

"That's what happened," Pasha said. "The first man Taraji kicked into the unit was holding on to Brejian as we came up the street. She forced him to his knees out on the sidewalk. That's how she got away."

"We need weapons," Bodhi said. They walked back to the room and passed the three captured men as they were hauled away by the agents.

"I'll talk to the Keeper," Selah said. She needed to practice her abilities. She should have moved faster and been ready to thrust sooner.

A shimmering heat wave passed in front of her as she entered the open doorway to their unit. She pressed her lips together, turned around, and glared at the Keeper standing there, both fists pressed to her hips.

"I wanted to know that you hadn't sustained injury," the Keeper said.

"Next time use a communicator. We need weapons. Now!" Selah said.

"Why?"

"To protect ourselves!"

"Did the other men have weapons?"

"No, but—"

"But what? The others didn't have weapons because it is against the law to have them here. Should I break the law for you? Do you not know how to protect yourself without using a weapon?"

Selah gritted her teeth. "Yes, I know how to protect myself, and so do the others. I am asking you for additional help."

"How will that serve you when you leave here?"

She huffed. "Well, at least it will give us a chance to get out of this place alive rather than turn us into staked prey for these animals wanting to drain my blood."

"You are perfectly prepared to handle anyone who comes against you," the Keeper said in a calm voice.

Selah stared at him closely. Did he know who was going to come against her? Had she misjudged the trust she had begrudgingly placed in him? "Are you going to help us?"

15

October 30

Selah walked around the great room picking up her training gear and bag, late for a training session again. Mojica and Taraji would be coming to find her any minute.

A stampede of children's feet filled the hallway and spilled into the great room. Rylla thundered through with Dane behind her. They both fell on top of Selah, laughing and giggling.

"Aren't you two supposed to be in classes?" Selah tickled Rylla under the arms. The child rolled away in laughter. She reached for Dane next, who became a mass of wriggling arms and legs, trying to avoid tickles.

"Mother has appointments to nurse indignant people," Dane said as he squealed and squirmed from Selah's grasp.

"No, you dumb boy." Rylla smacked her forehead with the heel of her hand. "I've told you before. The word is *indigent*, not *indignant*. They are poor people, not angry people." She wrinkled her nose and flipped a hand back and forth. "Well, they may be angry because they're poor, but that's not the point. Right now they're just poor."

"Hey! I don't want you calling Dane names. He isn't dumb, and neither are you, Miss Vocabulary Word Star," Selah said as she hugged them close. Both children had blossomed despite the circumstances and become quite adept at spotting people who could be dangerous to Selah. Pasha had been vocal in her reservations, but both children were being trained in self-defense by Mojica and Taraji in case they ever got separated from the family.

"Selah, how can there be poor people in a place like this?" Rylla snuggled into Selah's right side while Dane burrowed in on the left.

"I don't know. I've never thought about it."

Late. The indictment flashed at her like an ancient road sign. The kids were just another pleasant diversion to keep her from the fruitless training sessions. Selah disentangled herself from the snuggle session, shoved the gear in her bag, and slung it over her shoulder.

Dane snickered. "Mother says they are *really* poor people, like sleeping-in-straw poor—"

"Dane! It's not nice to laugh at people down on their luck."

The boy lowered his head. His eyes darted around, searching for an escape route. "Yes, ma'am. I'm sorry, ma'am." A smile played at the corners of his mouth.

Selah sauntered to the door without another good reason to hesitate. She grabbed the old-fashioned silver door handle. "Be sure to get your assignments done, and stop calling me ma'am—that would be *my* mother." She laughed and blew kisses as she closed the door behind her.

A man hurrying up the hall bumped into her gear bag, forcing her to sidestep. She grunted as she whacked the wall.

The guy turned back. "Sorry."

Selah turned to face him. "So—"

A burlap feed sack slid down over her head and arms. Selah scrambled to force her way out as the musty cloth released a cloud of seed dust that choked off her air and caused her eyes to water. Tears slid down her cheeks, offering a blurry vision of the outside through the loose weave.

Selah shouted for help but stopped mid-yell. Screaming would draw the kids out here, where they could get hurt. A pair of large muscular arms corralled her flailing hands and clamped her arms to her sides even with her gear bag still strapped to her back. She struggled for air, coughing, panicking. She tried shallow gulps but breathing fast made her dizzy.

She leaned forward and jerked up, propelling herself backward and running the assailant into the wall. He grunted as she forced air from his chest, but he held tight. She tried to kick out backwards, but her boot only glanced across his shin and her foot slid between his legs. The guy grunted and trapped her foot between his knees. She untangled her foot and pretended to fall in the process.

Her captor held tight. For a moment he was bent at the waist, balancing her weight with her feet off the floor. They were near the wall. If she could get a foot on it, she could walk up it and flip over his head. She had broken one of Taraji's holds using that move once.

The man who had first bumped into her charged back toward her and grabbed for her legs. Through the loose bag weave Selah made out the man's features. A purple scar on his right cheek, scraggly facial hair. Selah kicked out, aiming for his vital organs. She made contact with a satisfying thud. He stumbled back. The man restraining her lifted her feet off the ground, giving her better leverage to kick the other man. This time her boot connected with his face. A spray of blood and saliva flew from his mouth. The man slammed into the wall, smearing the liquids as he slumped to the floor.

The captor yanked Selah back from the fallen man. He slammed her feet to the floor, sending shooting charges through her ankles. *Ignore the pain.* Selah flexed and pulled the guy forward. She stomped on his instep then jerked up and head-butted him with all her strength.

Selah heard his nose crack, followed by a muffled moan. The arms holding her dropped away and Selah darted off, flipping the feed sack from her head as she ran. She slid open the panic switch on her scrambler and pressed it. Nothing happened.

She looked down and pressed the button again as she ran. The pounding footsteps of her pursuers echoed in the long hallway. Where to go? Not back to the children. She shot through the lobby and into the next corridor. There was an open hallway on the right. She ran through and locked the door behind her, then navigated the long, twisting hallway.

At a cross hall, she stopped and leaned against the wall, huffing to catch her breath and coughing to rid her lungs of the seed dust. She peeled off her scrambler and held it up to the light, trying to figure out why it wouldn't work. Had it been damaged in the scuffle? She examined the surface. The cover slid easily and the button seemed unmarred.

She gulped and coughed again. For the first time in a month

she had no connection to a Keeper. She had been indignant—yes, Dane's word was a good choice—at the requirement that she remain tethered to the Keeper like a child. Now she was scared that she wasn't. She strapped the scrambler back on and started to walk.

Nothing looked familiar, but at least there were no footsteps following her. She could alert Mojica or Taraji—then she'd hear this was her fault because she was delinquent for practice. If she called Bodhi, it'd be the same thing because he was waiting with them. That left her to take care of herself. She'd never call the rest and put them in harm's way. She didn't want them called to fight for her sake.

Selah bit down on her lip. Where was she?

A door stood ajar on the right. She glanced around and snuck in. Shelves and bookcases of clear and colored data cubes ringed the wall behind a desk with a woven basket sitting on the edge. The basket held some five-sided tokens with purple centers and numbers stamped on them.

Muffled voices filtered through the wall from an unknown direction.

Selah knew better than to let herself be trapped in a room. Fear made her heart pound. Why had she stopped here? She tried to connect with the Keeper again . . . Nothing.

The corridors resembled a maze. Hallways, a door, and another turn. She saw outdoor light.

Selah ran to the door and palmed the exit screen. The door released and she stepped outside, leaning against the building in relief. The radiant sunshine warmed her face. She fingered her scrambler and slid back the cover. Her finger rested above the button. Maybe something inside had been blocking the signal.

She pushed the button. A heat wave passed in front of her face and her upper lip tingled.

Selah straightened her top and threw her workout bag in the corner by the Keeper's desk. "What happened? Did you do that to shut me up about having privacy?"

He pulled back, a blank expression on his face. "I will be glad to help you when I know the nature of the problem."

Selah paced in front of the desk. "You drive me crazy, for one thing. Your answers are all so clinical and exact, and you show no emotional attachment when you talk about almost sixty novarium not making it. This is my life we're talking about here. I was assaulted when I left my family's quarters."

"I'm sorry my demeanor doesn't meet your expectations. After 150 years of watching people die needlessly because a few folks couldn't settle their internal differences, I've become quite calloused to the situation. And next, I leave contact up to you when I don't have matters of importance. You said you didn't wish to have your bio-signs monitored." The Keeper leaned back in his rocker.

Selah skidded to a stop. "It didn't work!" She held up her arm, slid back the lid, and pressed the button. She felt the familiar sensation of the heat wave as her upper lip tingled.

Selah was standing back in front of the Keeper when she opened her eyes. Feeling stupid for pushing the button, she gritted her teeth and charged toward the Keeper's desk. "Well, it didn't work the first or the second time I pushed it."

The Keeper swung toward his mobile command panel. "I

don't see any system interruptions. When and where were you at the time?"

"The way station outside my quarters sometime in the last half hour, and even as I was running through the lobby I couldn't reach you." Selah's hands started to shake. Tremors ran up her arms and down her legs. She had to lower herself to the heavy wooden seat to keep her legs from betraying her. Using the bio-system to transfer here had increased the frequency of her tremors, but after the shaking was over her muscles always seemed stronger, so she figured it was amplifying the lightning surges. But she didn't want to share that information with the Keeper yet.

The Keeper peered over his spectacles. "Are you operating within normal parameters?"

Selah smirked. "Yes, I am in normal parameters, but I don't think the system is. Would you please send security agents to my quarters to be sure the children are okay until my mother returns?"

"Already done. I would say this was preventable. If you had been on time to your training session a half hour ago, you wouldn't have been in the hallway to be attacked," the Keeper said.

"If it wasn't today, it would have been tomorrow. There's something going on though. It didn't seem all that difficult to get away from them. I wonder if they're not trying to capture me but test me for some reason." This was her offhand announcement in case the Keeper was involved. Her trust of him only went so far, and right now it encompassed him protecting her family.

The Keeper motioned her to his desk. A video panel rose

from the surface. "I pulled the feed to see what you were up against. Look."

Selah swung the panel around. Her jaw went slack. The "easy" time had in reality been an all-out fight of technique and speed with two men about three hundred pounds each. Watching a playback of her speed on a digi-screen and experiencing it were two separate things. She was moving twice as fast as she'd thought.

She turned to the Keeper. "Is this normal? I mean, for me to be moving that fast and fighting that hard?" She stared at her hands, turning them over. "I don't look or feel different."

"Yes, it is very normal. You will reach your peak in two months, so until then you must train to stretch the new muscle abilities and tensions. There is much knowledge here that will be easy for you to assimilate in your accelerated growing stage. Mojica, Taraji, and even Bodhi are working very hard and—"

"And I need to face it." She winced. "I've come to the end of the training I can do with them. I've even been holding punches so I don't hurt any of them." Selah felt her cheeks warming. She had told him more about her strength than she wanted to.

The Keeper looked over his glasses. "I wondered when you'd ask to move beyond your friends in training. Very well, the earliest I can set up an all-day combat session will be the day after tomorrow."

Selah swiped up her gear bag and moved toward the wall. "Great. Then I'll see you in a couple days. My brain needs a rest from learning." She offered her most delicate one-handed wave while her brain raced with the step forward she had just taken. It did feel logical at the moment. If she didn't offer the Keeper more trust, she wouldn't be able to learn the training that would serve her in the future.

The Keeper swiped over the signal to send her back.

Selah entered the great room out of thin air. The kids enjoyed seeing her appear that way, but her mother, not so much. Lucky for Selah the only occupant at the moment was Mari.

"You've got to let me try that one of these days." Mari sat on the long seating area with her legs tucked up under her.

"I don't know if the Keeper would appreciate riders, but I'll ask," Selah said as she strolled over to the seating unit and dropped her bag beside it. "The kids said you and Mother are taking care of the indigent. How does someone become indigent in the dome?"

Mari leaned a leg up on the seat cushion so she could turn to face Selah. "They're the people who have sick family members."

"But they get yearly doses of STORM. They shouldn't be getting sick."

"That's the dirty little secret of this place. Years ago the pills used to keep all disease and sickness away, but not now. The pill strength is going down, and they are adding weeks to each handout period. People are aging and disease is getting a foothold."

Selah knew the same story, but the Keeper had acted like it was a secret. "How did you find out?"

Mari jerked around. "Find out? So you knew? You knew this was happening and you didn't say anything to us?"

Selah held up both hands. "I have enough to worry about with getting us all out of here safely. Besides, I'm still not sure how far we can trust the Keeper I'm working with. Sometimes he seems helpful but at other times I worry if he's part of the problem."

"But there's a bunch of talk at the clinic that these Keepers are corrupt," Mari said.

Selah sat next to her sister. "Give me a reason why Keepers would do anything like this."

"There's talk that life in Brook Heights is very expensive, and the elite folks are willing to pay for more STORM. So the Keepers are stealing it from the poor and selling it to the rich."

Selah sat back on the seat. She could see that happening. If she didn't succeed to the Third Protocol, this society would become almost extinct. She wondered how many Keepers were here and how far they'd go to keep themselves alive. "We don't know anything about this world. What you're saying could be possible, but on just hearsay, you're asking me to lock horns with the only person who has the ability to get us out of here safely. I'd need solid evidence before I could act, and then I don't know what we could do about it."

"Well, to hear those at the clinic talk about it, there's all kinds of evidence. They say Keepers have sold novarium to Blood Hunters. That's why so many have disappeared and none have ever made it."

Selah frowned. "How many novarium disappeared?" She knew from the Keeper how many had passed through, but he hadn't said anything about disappearances.

"Dozens!" Mari spread her hands. "Multiple dozens. And

I hate to tell you, sister, but when we're talking wealth and power among Keepers, the one you got is the king Keeper!"

"So then who do we trust here? Brejian is not on my top favorites list. But please don't tell Bodhi. I don't want to deal with his 'I told you so's.'" Selah's head swirled with the list of uncertainties just in this one place.

The front door opened and Bodhi strolled in looking none too happy. Selah knew it was because she hadn't shown up for training.

He walked across the room and sat in front of Selah with arms crossed. "We waited for you, but when you didn't show we finished the second part of the exercise. You'll need to play catch-up tomorrow."

Selah didn't want to face him. She tried to laugh it off. "The Keeper wants me to try a new program to test some emerging abilities. So yay! He gave me a couple days off until it starts. I bet this training is going to be brutal." She pretended to roll her eyes and frown. With this new information from Mari, was it a good idea to let the Keeper segregate her to private training?

Bodhi pressed his lips together and lowered his head. "I guess we've become inadequate at teaching you." Selah could see the hurt in his eyes.

"No, that's not it," Selah lied. "He just thinks I know all of your moves and need someone I can't second-guess." Her face warmed. She always blushed when she told stories.

The need to get away from Bodhi grew stronger. Selah started to rise from her seat.

The front door opened and Brejian hurried in. "I'm sorry I'm late." She appeared disheveled. Half of her shirt hung loose at the waist. Selah gestured to it, and Brejian used nervous hands to tuck everything in and smooth her hair.

Selah wasn't all that friendly with the woman, but she was a distraction from Bodhi's angry gaze. She leaned over the arm of the chair so she could look around Bodhi. "Since they moved you out of the way station and into permanent quarters, you've been getter later every day. I think you need to get in earlier at night or start sharing the fun."

"You both need to take this more seriously," Bodhi said, glaring at Selah and Brejian. "We're only here for a few months, and every minute counts for getting Selah prepared."

Brejian jerked a glance in his direction. "Excuse me, *sir*, but my job was supplying you with the Repository files in return for a ride. Selah got the files and I am here. End of discussion."

"Then why are you here around us?" Bodhi asked.

"Pasha asked me to research some information, and despite your rude demeanor I agreed to help her." Brejian glared back at Bodhi.

"Easy, you two," Selah said, raising her hands.

Bodhi stabbed a finger at Brejian. "In plain language, I don't trust you." Selah watched the thunder gather behind his eyes.

"Well, the feeling is mutual," Brejian said. She planted her feet and looked like she was ready for a fight.

"Mother!" Selah yelled. "Brejian is here."

Pasha hurried from the kitchen, wiping her hands on her apron. "What did you find?"

Brejian shook her head. "No one has seen her since last night."

"What am I going to do? The daughter needs someone to change her dressings," Pasha said.

Selah leaned forward, suddenly wondering where Rylla and Dane were. "Who are we talking about?"

"It's one of the families we help at the free clinic," Mari said. "The mother disappeared after the lottery and—"

"Whoa!" Bodhi threw up his hands. "Why are you mingling with those people?"

"What do you mean by 'those people'? Do you think you're too good to mix with the poor?" Brejian put her hands on her hips.

"I mean mixing with *any* of the people in this dome." Bodhi moved his hand around in a circle. "You seem to forget they keep attacking Selah."

"Which seems bizarre on its own because they just seem to be testing my strength and not actually trying to grab me," Selah said.

"Oh, and it's so much better that they haven't been successful at kidnapping you," Bodhi said. He smirked. "Maybe you're getting to be just that good."

Selah could see the pride in his eyes.

"I don't mean to break up the lovefest, but I've got a missing mother, and her child is in serious need of medical assistance," Pasha said. "I don't know how much longer we can supplement her care."

"Doesn't she have any relatives?" Bodhi turned away from Selah, which she didn't mind at all.

"She has an aunt and uncle who will take her, but only if she's well. All their kids work on their farm," Pasha said. "They'll leave a sick kid with us at the clinic. She's not their responsibility."

"That's what I mean. We'll be leaving in a couple months,

and we're never coming back. Why are you involving yourself with these people?" Bodhi looked annoyed.

"Because Mari and I have nothing else to do here except watch you train for combat and teach the children," Pasha said. "We wanted a little more interaction with the world."

"I'm worried that someone might use your involvement with these people as a way to get to Selah," Bodhi said.

"All of our relevant research is securely stored in the transport, where we can't get at it." Mari shrugged. "We needed something to do, to at least feel useful. No one has mentioned Selah or the novarium."

"Sometimes the key to helping ourselves is in helping others," Pasha said.

Selah could see Bodhi cave at their generous hearts. "Well, just don't get Selah involved," he mumbled. He sniffed the air. "Is that fresh bread I smell?"

"In the kitchen," Pasha said, crooking her finger at Bodhi. He followed her into the kitchen.

"Explain to me what you've gotten yourself into," Selah said to Mari. She wasn't worried about the people they associated with, just what kind of situations they could get into.

Mari sat up. "Here's the short version—because of the reduced strength of STORM, some people with weaker immune systems are developing diseases—"

"And the diseases could be stopped if the Keepers gave these sick people more doses of STORM, but because they don't, the diseases are starting to spread," Brejian said.

Selah instantly understood the Keeper's reasoning. There weren't any extra pills anymore, but the people weren't allowed to know. Her mind fast-forwarded and saw how the colony would die out if she didn't succeed with the Third Protocol. Another world of people depending on her . . .

"And the desperation has led to a black market for STORM." Brejian frowned and shook her head. "I can't believe this is going on in the dome. Gambling with your health and selling your heritage are crazy things. There have to be Keepers involved. They control the coding of STORM. So if someone is selling their STORM, the coding has to be changed to the new person."

Selah appreciated that Brejian trusted her enough to discuss a problem the Keeper said was secret. With the implications, the graft looked to involve at least some of the Keepers. "It has to be a Keeper changing the coding."

Brejian nodded.

"How can people sell their health?" Selah wondered what kind of circumstances would cause people to knowingly risk their health.

"If they're healthy, they can become very wealthy in auctioning off their yearly dose of STORM," Brejian said. "The momentary wealth is followed, in many cases, by a compromised immune system that draws every germ it can find and increases the population of disease in the dome."

Selah looked around. "So what am I missing? How can anyone auction off STORM? Its manufacture dictates one activation code per person."

Brejian blinked. "You know more about the process than I would have expected. Where are you getting this information?"

Selah pressed her lips together. The Keeper had sworn her to secrecy about the source of the pills but not about the black market that he defined as the immediate problem. "The Keeper told me about the lottery and the black market."

"The Keeper shared that information?" Brejian's jaw flexed like she was grinding her teeth. "I'm surprised he'd be that open with an outsider."

"I'm not really an outsider. The Keeper felt it necessary to raise my angst by telling me just how many more people were dependent on my satisfactory outcome." Selah hated how sarcastic she was becoming, but the heightened awareness that came with the lightning flashes made her cranky.

Brejian diverted her eyes. "I've just never known him to be that open with strangers."

Selah calmed some. "Apparently things have changed dramatically since you were home last, and the biggest change seems to be this black market of STORM."

Brejian sighed. "Someone has hacked the program and can change the activation code of a STORM dose to another recipient."

"That's impossible. That code is tamperproof and set by the Keepers . . ." Selah's voice trailed off. She had just given credibility to Mari's claim of corrupt Keepers.

Brejian lowered her head as though she were fearful of looking at Selah.

Mari joined the discussion again. "The going consensus is that there's a group of Keepers siphoning off pill strength to sell extra protection to the elite dome populations. That's why people play the lottery—for a chance at an additional dose."

Selah jerked her gaze in Mari's direction. "You two are describing different problems, but both of them could involve the Keepers." If the Keeper had been truthful, the dose strength was a problem of degradation, not subversion . . . but could she believe him?

"Not all Keepers." Brejian narrowed her eyes. "There are honest, dedicated Keepers."

Pasha returned from the kitchen. "This doesn't solve my present problem though. The sick child's mother is still missing. They told me the area down by the docks where she was last seen—"

"Oh no you don't!" Selah rubbed her fingertip back and forth across her forehead. "Mother, you are *not* going down to any docks."

16

November 15

Selah hadn't seen much of her mother for the last couple weeks. Not since the first disagreement about that woman who played Joli. Besides STORM, Joli was the only other dome vice that nearly everyone participated in. A caustic game involving cards, dice, and figurines, it ruined every life it touched, including that of this woman who played it constantly, to the detriment of her sick child.

"Selah, over here!" Mari waved from the other side of the gymnasium, near a stack of crates labeled *food*.

Selah worked her way along the rows of empty cots toward Mari, where two dozen patients were spread out along the back rows. As Selah got closer, the smell of antiseptic mixed with body fluids assaulted her nose.

"What's going on here? What happened to the clinic at the bottom of the hill?" Selah looked around at the numerous neatly placed rows covering the polished wooden floor. There had to be a hundred cots set up.

"There's been an outbreak of plague. We have at least fifteen patients coming in from different parts of the dome," Mari said. "They're expecting it to escalate quickly among the compromised. The Cleveland School Center has the only building big enough."

Selah started to worry about passing something to Rylla or Dane. "Maybe we shouldn't be so close."

"Apparently living in a germy world all our lives has had an inoculating effect. We're not susceptible to any of the disease strains plaguing them." Mari carried over another case of antiseptic.

"Can we help them at all?"

Mari frowned. "It's pretty much a lost cause. Their immune systems are literally crashing by the day. I'd say in ten years they should just about all be gone."

Selah couldn't understand where her mother got so much compassion or the stamina to do this day after day. It had become almost an obsession for her, and Selah wondered how she would handle it when they were ready to leave.

"Where's Mother?" Selah wanted to cover her nose, but she didn't want Mari to chastise her.

"She's trying to console the girl," Mari said. "Her mother is gone again." The child also happened to be the only girl patient, and Mother would have spirited her away from the dome if it was at all possible.

Selah had always managed to avoid coming here when the Joli-addicted woman was missing. She knew what would come next. Pasha would compel her to help them find the woman. Maybe she could get away before her mother spotted her.

She turned. Too late. Pasha scurried between the cots.

"I'm so glad you're here. You came at just the right time. We need to go to the wharf."

"Mother, have you lost—that place is dangerous," Selah said.

"But it's not dangerous for you. Do you see that boy over there?" Pasha pointed to the far left corner. "He just came from the wharf and he saw the girl's mother getting beat up."

"That's what he said last time." Mari pressed her lips tight.

"He said it looked bad this time." Pasha wiped her shaking hands on her slacks.

"She keeps telling people she won the lottery. People around there will kill you for that kind of prize." Mari shook her head. "No, I don't want to go there either."

"Then it's settled. We're not going," Selah said as she glanced to her right. Brejian worked her way between the rows as though she were walking through a field of prickly thorns.

"What are you doing here?" Selah strolled toward Brejian, moving closer to the door.

"Pasha called me to draw her directions to somewhere," Brejian said. She seemed concerned that Selah would be displeased.

Selah frowned. "Oh no. Get out of here fast. She wants you to—"

"Brejian, I'm glad you're here. Now we can go." Pasha hurried over.

"No! You're not going to the wharf. I refuse to go, and I refuse to let you go," Selah said.

Pasha put her hand on her hip. "Listen, young lady. You might get away with bossing others around because they're captivated by the fact that you're the novarium. But I'm your mother. It doesn't impress me. You don't have to go. I'll go myself." Pasha snatched Brejian by the hand and dragged her off between the rows of empty cots.

The irony was not lost on Selah that the ramshackle abodes and everyday world of the dockworkers was located directly below Brook Heights, the only exclusive conclave of the Keepers.

They walked down the hill toward the dome's portion of Lake Erie as the sun set. Strange angular rays of sun shot into the dome over the frosted sides that delineated the snow lines. Eight feet to go and they could leave here. Checking the lines to see the progress had become Selah's daily ritual.

"Where's the place we're supposed to look for this woman? Some of these businesses look sketchy as far as safety goes," Selah said to Brejian. She had successfully evaded running into Mojica and Taraji when they stopped by the housing unit, so she was able to change into her boots and drop off her scrambler so the Keeper couldn't track her. Everyone else still wore theirs, and now she felt a little twitchy having Pasha and Mari in a situation where she needed to trust Brejian for their safety. She didn't want others to suffer if she was making a mistake. Why had she let her mother talk her into this crazy search?

Brook Heights was at the top of the only hill in Cleveland and was the center location in the dome, making Selah wonder if the dome was generated from there. At the top, the streets were smooth rocrete roads with fusion lighting, pristine passages, and well-kept stone masonry buildings. But down here at the bottom where the lanes were populated with questionable business enterprises and the smell of rotting fish from the wharf outdoor market, the roads morphed into worn cobblestone streets, with garbage everywhere and liquid-propellant flame lights on wrought-iron posts. High tech clashed with ancient.

Despite the danger, Selah envisioned living a fantasy life like she'd seen in one of the ancient paintings in the Borough building back in Dominion, with a parasol, a hooped skirt, and a horse and buggy traveling over these cobblestone streets.

Brejian jumped at a loud bang as they stopped at the last cross street. The wharf lay straight ahead.

Loud music and raucous conversations drifted from the left while screams and breaking glass filtered from the right.

"Why would this woman come down here?" Selah gestured to the left and tried to imagine the desperation that would bring a woman here. They worked their way down the street searching between buildings.

"She was probably trying to make more money for a shot at the next lottery. Apparently she was quite a roller with the Joli game," Brejian said.

"Why didn't she just use the Joli winnings to buy STORM?" Selah asked.

"It would take ten years of Joli winnings to pay the black market price of STORM," Brejian said.

"This is a small and closed environment. I don't understand why the Keepers can't get control of the black market operation." Selah stopped and searched behind a railing leading to a belowground shop.

Brejian checked both directions as they stood there. "I guess that's a good indication there are corrupt Keepers in the system."

"Wait! Explain to me how you get to be a Keeper and how many there are." Selah was still trying to figure out if the Keeper mentoring her could be involved, but she didn't want to come out and ask because Brejian seemed to have a connection to him.

"Keepers are the original members of the team who developed the Protocols. They and their ancestors have kept the designation. It's now an honored title almost like royalty. They continue to maintain the dome and its purpose," Brejian said almost reverently.

Mari stepped closer to listen. "How many are there?"

Brejian shrugged. "Most of the people living in Brook Heights."

"The rich section." Pasha shook her head. "Absolute power corrupts absolutely."

"So I guess that explains the black market and why it isn't shut down. A lot of people are profiting from the health misery of others," Mari said.

Selah had to agree. She'd seen that same kind of sad behavior back home in Dominion. She trained her light stick into the dark space, disturbing some sort of animal that scurried away at the first shot of light. She jumped back. "Are we sure the woman is really in this area?"

Pasha walked up beside Selah. "The boy said she was sober when she beat the latest Joli challenger. She took the winnings and bought a lottery token and really won. The boy saw it."

"She's told us a half dozen times she won, and somebody stole it from her each time." Mari rolled her eyes and moved off in Brejian's direction. "You know that woman never won anything. She's too smashed most of the time to remember what's true."

Pasha flinched at Mari's words. "She once told me she stayed smashed to forget how many times she had won the right for her daughter to be well, only to have it stolen from her."

Selah stopped in the street and looked directly at her mother. "Do you believe her?"

Pasha smiled and nodded. "Yes, I do. She's very good at the game but gets taken advantage of on a regular basis. Someone's got to help her. We'll be leaving soon, and this might be my last chance to make a difference. So I have to try."

"She may be good at Joli because it's a game of skill, but the lottery is a game of chance, and when 'chance' finds the same person repeatedly, it's rigged," Brejian said.

"So is this woman being used as some kind of shill? They steal it back from her to raffle off again and keep all the money from everyone who entered." Mari moved up beside Pasha.

"I don't care about the lottery. I just want to find her and get out of here," Pasha said.

"Agreed," Selah said. "Which of these joints shall we start in? And remember, it doesn't matter if we find her in a Joli game or not, we're taking her."

"The boy from the shelter told me he knew where she went,

the man was hurting her, and she asked the boy to get help. So he came to me."

Selah hesitated. "Are you sure this is the real situation?" It had occurred to her that this could be another ruse to get at her.

"I know the sick child. I know her mother. The mother is missing," Pasha said. Mari nodded in agreement.

Selah looked up at the numbers on the buildings. "This is the six hundred block. Where's the Joli game in this section?"

"That third building over there." Brejian pointed at the building outlined in fluorescent rope lights that flashed off and on. "We could just wait for the game to be over in an hour and see if she comes out."

"No. The object is to find her now *before* anything else happens. I'll go in. You three stay right here." Selah started across the street.

"Wait, maybe this is a bad idea," Pasha said.

Selah smiled softly. "You're going to have to work on your timing." She continued across the street, still wearing her black and red aerodynamic training suit. She'd only stopped long enough to change from the combat rubber soles into her boots, and the forceful sound of her footfalls echoed in the street.

She approached the front of the building where several men sat around a barrel with a sheet of wood as a tabletop. They separated from the table and stood to face her. She scanned the table for weapons. None. The men were playing Joli. It was illegal to play in the streets.

She flashed them her most confident look, tossed her pony-tail, and strode past. Her heart felt like it was going to crawl out of her throat. The last guy grabbed her by the wrist with a large, meaty hand.

Selah jerked to a stop. Her demeanor never wavered. It was going to be all in her attitude. She stared into the man's bloodshot eyes, then slowly lowered her eyes to his hand. "It's not polite to restrain a lady you don't know." She breathed evenly though her brain wanted to scream at her stupidity. Doing a thrust would get her no closer to finding the woman, so she'd have to use her combat training when it came time.

"I think I've met you somewhere before." The beefy dock-worker turned to laugh with his friends. Selah saw the purple scar on his cheek. One of her previous attackers.

"I don't think so." Selah pulled three lightning-fast maneuvers and came up with the guy's thumb bent at a very uncomfortable angle.

She drew the man close so his friends couldn't see he was captive and whispered in his ear, "I won't pull off your thumb and ruin your occupation if you will consent to moving *away* from me when I release you."

A moment of recognition crossed his face. Selah smiled at him. Sweat broke out across his forehead as he nodded vigorously.

Selah kept her stony gaze fixed on the man and released him, pushing him far enough away that she'd have room for attack. He turned his back on her and sat down.

She blew out a few nervous huffs of air as she walked toward the doorway. She jumped out of the way as a man tumbled out of the opening. "I won and you're cheating me," he yelled over his shoulder.

"Keep going, ya bum. That's what all you losers say," a

rouster at the door said. He looked Selah over. "You come to play in my club?"

"Yes." She decided the less talk, the less she could mess up.

The rouster stared at her for a long moment. Finally he waved her in. Selah moved past him, and once out of his sight she added a little swagger to her newfound confidence. She climbed the wide landing and stepped into the Joli parlor. Her bravado faded when she surveyed the surroundings. She had never viewed any inside scene that compared. Something set off an internal alarm that bubbled to the surface as tangible fear. Her chest tightened and her arms surged with nervous energy. She glanced around, searching for the source of her undefined angst.

Her head throbbed. The club's wide and double-long room had been painted black, with multicolored rope lights traversing the ceiling at so many angles it made Selah dizzy to look up.

A pale wisp of some kind of mist hung over the darkened room. As she breathed it in, her throat grew dry. Light poles coming up through the center of each table provided the only ambient light for the games. Selah walked slowly among the booths and table groupings along the walls that weren't involved with the games. She had the description of the man she wanted to find. He would be wearing a knit beanie pulled down tight, with a foot of blond hair hanging from the back of the cap.

A hand rested on her shoulder. Selah spun around to see a woman carrying a tray.

"What can I help you with? Do you want to play Joli?" The woman grabbed a cup from the table next to her.

"No thank you. I'm just looking for someone," Selah said, relieved it was a woman.

"The boss is watching you, and he said to tell you if you ain't here to play, then you're gonna have to pay by sitting at his table."

Selah found herself wanting to give the man a few words about manners. "I don't want trouble. I'm just looking for a woman they call the Joli Woman because she plays so well."

The woman's face dissolved into a mask of fear. "Get out of here right now! Meet me in the alley."

A man grabbed Selah's left shoulder. She reached across with her right hand, grabbed the intruder's wrist, and spun herself around as she bent his arm and hand up his back. She whispered in his ear, "Didn't your mother ever teach you not to put your hands on a lady?"

He grunted.

"If I let you go, will you walk away?" She only wanted out of here at this point. The server girl might be the lead she needed.

He grunted again.

Relieved to have avoided a confrontation, Selah let go.

He spun to sweep her legs from under her. Selah's abilities put the speed of her reflexes between the strokes of a second. She sprang from the floor before his leg swept by and landed on her left foot. She planted her right boot in his back.

The guy flew forward across a Joli table, scattering the game and opponents. Fighting broke out at the table and spread like pollen to nearby tables.

Selah turned to flee. Purple Scar blocked her path and yelled over the fighting crowd, "Follow me if you want to get out of here alive."

"Why should I trust you?" She had a hard time reading people in the dome.

"It's follow me or go it alone back through that crowd."

Selah looked around him at the jumble of fighting men and quite a few women. They didn't have weapons, but more than one chair was sacrificed to become multiple clubs. Selah had no weapon and no scrambler. She figured she could take him one-on-one if she had to. "Okay, I'll follow—"

He snatched her by the wrist and elbowed his way through the crowd. His girth was such that Selah managed nicely with him as a shield. With no security agents that she could see, the fight grew louder. The chorus of breaking data glass and lighting elements added to the raging sound. They turned to the left and went through a passageway instead of to the front door she'd used.

Selah panicked. The corridor was too narrow for her to take a good hit at him. He charged forward, dragging her behind.

"No!" She pounded on his back with her free hand. "Let go of me!"

"Stop it, crazy woman!" Purple Scar edged around her so he was on the club side of the corridor. He continued to push her just by moving forward because he filled the space.

"Let me out. People know I'm here. You won't get away with this." Selah tried to push back at him, but she wasn't sure why. What was in the dark behind her?

No. She didn't want to go into the dark. She struggled against him but he pushed faster. With a jolt, her back hit a wall. She opened her mouth to scream. He slammed his hand against the wall, and it popped open outward. She tumbled into the alley.

Selah hopped to her feet. "Why didn't you kidnap me at the way station?" She was ready for a fight.

Purple Scar shrugged. "He didn't pay me. I don't collect his samples for free." He slammed the door shut. Selah peered around. She scrambled to pull her light stick from her pocket.

"Miss."

Selah swung around in a fighting stance.

"Wait! It's me, from inside." The woman came from the shadows with her hands raised. "The Joli Woman . . . I heard them talking about dumping her in the alley three buildings down that way." She pointed. "But they said she was dead." The woman ran away down the alley and turned back into the club.

Selah gathered the ladies, and Pasha counted off the buildings then pointed to an alleyway between two tall brick buildings. The light mounted on the building had been knocked off, and the air smelled ripe with intoxicating beverages and human waste.

Selah raised a hand. "Stay here. Let me look first." She was ready for this, but she hadn't told Pasha about the woman's possible fate.

She concentrated the light beam and passed over the alley the first time. Traveling back over it from the other side, Selah saw some waste packaging. She slid back the largest strip. The sight made her want to lose her last meal.

The poor woman lay among the corrugated package refuse. One leg was bent at an odd angle, and a dark crimson spot had spread across the front of her tunic. Dried blood had caked on the outside of her right ear and down the side of her neck, merging with the blood at the corner of her mouth.

Her face. A shiver crawled up Selah's back. The woman's face seemed familiar.

Selah bent close to the woman's ear. "Can you hear me? Pasha sent me to help you." She checked for a pulse. The woman was dead. "Mother, come here, please."

Pasha moved slowly into the lane, shuffling up behind Selah without looking down. "Is she . . . dead?"

"Yes. Is that her?" Selah pointed to the body.

Pasha looked over Selah's shoulder and shuddered. "Poor woman. Yes, that's her. Can you tell how she died?"

Selah grimaced as she knelt down beside the body. "It looks like she was hit in the head with something heavy." She looked around the immediate area. "But I don't think it happened here because there's too much blood on her and no splatter anywhere."

Tears slid down Pasha's cheeks. "So they just discarded her like trash. We can't leave her here."

"Brejian will call the proper authorities," Selah said as she rose. The copper smell of the drying blood made her stomach lurch.

A glint of light caught her attention. Selah hesitated but then gingerly used her foot to move the woman's bloodied hand.

Pasha had started to walk away but turned back. "What's the matter?"

"I don't know." Selah moved closer to the body. Congealing blood collected in the woman's hand, obscuring the object except where her fingers had closed over it.

Selah reached out. Her fingers hovered over the gelatinous

mess. She gagged, turned away, and grabbed a piece of packing material.

"What are you doing?" Pasha asked.

"I'm trying to see what's in her hand. The edge is shiny but it's mired in her drying blood," Selah said.

"Lottery tokens are gold!" Pasha moved closer.

Selah used the packing material to scrape away the blood, but it wasn't enough. The other fingers on the woman's hand would have to be pried open. Selah turned her head away from the body, sucked in a great gulp of relatively clean air, and turned back with a grimace. She swiftly pried the fingers open as her stomach flopped a couple times. She was rewarded with the nonbloodied face of a lottery token. Selah snatched it up, wiped the outer edges on the dead woman's tunic, and secured the token in one of her sealed pockets.

Selah quickly backed Pasha out to the entrance of the alley and gathered up the other two huddled against the building. The anxious women turned the corner for home.

Four beefy, broad-shouldered men stood in their way. One particularly ominous man wore a dark knit cap pulled down to his eyebrows. It pressed his long blond hair to his neck and covered his ears. The boss. Selah spread her arms to keep the other women behind her.

"We don't want any trouble, so just move aside and let us pass, please," Selah said calmly.

One of the men with a scarf tied around his short dark hair moved to stand in front of Selah. His bulging muscles showed the faint tattoo of an exotic bird. He looked down at Selah and then turned to a burly man with a green neck scarf. "Go check the body."

The man lumbered into the alley. Selah pressed her arm against her side, feeling the token in her pocket. She backed away a couple feet and checked her range. The man's growl of displeasure echoed the length of the alley.

Green Scarf trudged from the alley, ran to Bird Guy, and whispered in his ear. Bird Guy turned to look at Selah. "Give me the token."

Brejian and Mari tried to barge around Selah, talking at the same time. She held them back. "Stop!" They moved back behind her.

"If I did have the token, it still wouldn't be yours. It belongs to the woman's child."

"Leaving the token behind was a grave error on my part, and if it's not corrected there will be dire consequences," Bird Guy said.

Selah frowned. "I'm sorry, but our need to remain unharmed tops your need to reclaim the token." Calculating that the men were in the zone, she reared back and launched a wide thrust through the center of the four men. Two flew against the brick side of the building, while the other two were thrown into the center of the cobblestone street.

Selah and the ladies ran up the street until they reached the safety of the smooth rocrete and Brook Heights. Pasha stopped the group at the top of the road. Selah looked back, searching carefully to make sure they weren't being followed.

"Was it really the token?" Pasha's eyes were wide.

"Yes, I've got it." Selah produced the gold five-sided token.

Pasha gasped. "She actually won the lottery. Her daughter can be saved. We have to redeem it while the girl is strong enough to be cured. She only has a matter of weeks before she passes the point of a successful cure."

"Wait. How do we explain this?" Selah stuck the token back in her pocket. She remembered seeing a whole basket of this kind before. Why had they just been lying out?

17

December 15

Selah sat in the great room of her quarters. She'd grown to feel at home here, and in the next few weeks she'd be leaving forever. She floated the token between her fingers.

Pasha strode in from her clinic shift to begin the children's afternoon lessons. "Did you hear anything yet? It's been a month. The child is fading by the day, and I don't know how much longer she has before STORM won't cure her."

"Brejian is working on it, but she's gotten her permanent job now, and there's not much time to research the delays." Selah traced the design on the coin. She still didn't know who was safe to approach about the other tokens she'd seen lying on that desk.

"I don't understand why we can't redeem the coin in the name of the woman's daughter."

"Because they have some arcane law here about having possession of the death certificate or something. Brejian understands it, and we can't go to the lottery office without that certification." Selah flipped the token in the air and caught it. P8 stood out as the first two characters in the serial number.

The front door flew open, bounced against the wall, and almost closed again. "We got it." Brejian waved the certificate needed to claim STORM.

Pasha called Mari at the clinic. Selah's stomach fluttered. She could leave here having done something for the child that would restore her even in the event that she herself failed. The child would be one of the survivors for the next cycle of novarium.

Selah pulled Brejian to the side. "I can't stop thinking about this token. I've seen it before." She held out the token representing the lottery prize.

Brejian lifted it from Selah's hand. "This is official lottery property and the token for a full year's dose of STORM. I doubt you've seen more than one or two."

"I saw a basket full of them."

Brejian frowned and handed the token back. "That's impossible. For the lottery prize dose to be dispensed, the token must be inserted in the system, and the process destroys it. Every pill is coded to a single person and a single prize. No leftovers."

"I know what I saw." Selah gave a half shrug.

Brejian shook her head. "The lottery buys one dose. That one dose generates the token used to redeem it."

"Then with the ones I saw, either someone has a whole bunch of doses or they're counterfeiting tokens," Selah said.

"Where?" Brejian seemed a little more defensive than usual.

"I don't know." Selah grimaced. "When those men chased

me last month, I traveled the corridor on the other side of the lobby. I found my way outside on the other side of the complex."

Brejian rubbed her forehead. "Which corridor? Traveling straight across the lobby from here, or turning right at the lobby?"

Selah returned the token to her pocket. "Straight across from here."

Brejian seemed to pale. Selah was about to ask her if she felt all right when Mari blew in through the door, breathless.

"I ran all the way." She slumped dramatically onto the seat. "This is exciting. How long do we have to wait?"

"Let's go." Selah shoved her moist palms into her pockets, mostly to dry her hands but partially to finger the token. She had promised her mother this would work out for the child's benefit.

Selah strode to the counter in the lottery office with Mari, Pasha, and Brejian in tow. At first it had seemed like a great idea for all of them to go, but at this moment it seemed like they were a mob descending on the office. She dug the token from her pocket and placed it on the counter.

The clerk looked over his magnifying spectacles at Selah and picked up the token, turning it over in his hands. He spoke in a monotone, as though he'd repeated the words a thousand times. "Congratulations on winning the lottery. Our loss is your health gain."

He keyed the numbers on the token into the computer. His expression tightened. He appeared puzzled. "I'm not sure how this could happen, but there is no pill. It's already been assigned to this token number."

Selah furrowed her brow. "But this is the token with the number. How is it I have the token but you don't have the prize?"

The man fidgeted with the computer and several other systems. "Well, I don't know. But it's not here."

"I think we need someone with more authority," Brejian said. She keyed her communicator, and in five minutes Cinanji strolled into the lottery office, followed by four security agents.

Selah thought it odd that of all people Cinanji would be in charge of the lottery, but if this worked out to the child's benefit, she'd ignore her own questions—like why Brejian had never mentioned this before.

The agent behind the counter scurried out to talk with Cinanji in hushed tones. Cinanji glanced at Selah once or twice and made doe eyes at Brejian. Selah had figured out they were secret loves.

"Selah, Pasha, could you come over here?" Cinanji motioned with his hand. "We'll be glad to order you the winning pill for that token, just hand the token over—"

"I'll be glad to hand over the token when you're ready to trade it for a dose of STORM." Selah decided it was time to leave and come back with more people behind her like Bodhi, Mojica, and Taraji.

Cinanji wrung his hands and his dark eyes flashed. "That cannot be accomplished right away."

Selah balked. She couldn't read his body-speak. "Maybe I need to call the Keeper—"

"I'm sure we don't need to bother the Keepers with this." Cinanji's eyes darted back and forth.

"Then how do we take care of it?" Selah asked.

Cinanji angrily snapped his fingers at one of the agents. The man nodded and hurried away.

"We will have a dose of STORM for you right away." Cinanji walked away behind the guard, and the clerk followed.

Brejian tried to approach Cinanji but the agents turned her back. Selah frowned. Cinanji walked behind the counter and into the office. The rest of the agents blocked the doorway.

Selah leaned over to Mari. "Maybe I should call Bodhi or Mojica."

"I think you should call a Keeper. He'd be the only one to have more authority," Mari said.

Selah slid open the cover on her panic button and pushed it, waiting for the familiar heat wave and tingle, but nothing happened. She tried her comm on the scrambler—nothing.

She motioned to Mari. "Try calling Bodhi."

Mari tapped the comm link on her scrambler several times, then the earpiece. "No signal."

"We need to get out of here. They're blocking us." Selah motioned to Pasha and Brejian. "We have another problem."

As they approached the front door, two security agents stepped in front of them. Selah turned to Cinanji as he exited from the inner office. "Why are we being detained?"

Cinanji ran both hands through his dark hair. "You ladies are in possession of an illegal token. We've been trying to track down the source of these counterfeits, and you three seem to be a part of it."

His words sounded hollow to Selah. Something else was going on.

The shutters slid down across the front of the office with a resounding thud.

"The Keeper is going to be looking for me. He can track my whereabouts in the dome," Selah said. She should have told Bodhi where she was going.

"At the moment all signals from this location are being blocked so you can't alert your cohorts to destroy the plates that stamped those tokens," Cinanji said.

"You can't be serious." Brejian stood at the counter with her hand on her hip. "This is a joke, right? And there are *four* of us. I'm part of this too. We did nothing illegal. The Joli Woman's token was found in her possessions. Selah's just trying to redeem it so Pasha can help the woman's daughter get STORM."

Cinanji turned his back on her to confer with the clerk.

Brejian frowned. "Cinanji, don't you dare turn your back on me. Not after these last few months." She marched around the counter. A security agent physically stopped her.

Cinanji's eyes flashed. "Get your hands off her and don't ever touch her again." He rushed to Brejian's side and pushed the security agent away. He wrapped his arms around her and they talked in hushed voices as they moved toward the office.

Pasha sidled up to Selah. "What is *that* all about?"

"Not sure, but I'm hoping Brejian can work it to our advantage. We've got very little time to solve this problem." Selah leaned an elbow on the counter and drummed with her fingertips as she thought it through. It was a stretch to trust Brejian, but at this moment that's all she had to work with.

Brejian returned to the group. "We're free to leave, but we

have to keep this matter silent as the investigation continues. We can't tip off the perpetrators that they've been exposed."

Selah stared at her. "But Cinanji said ours is a counterfeit token. How can that be when it was a legal lottery?"

"How can you tell the token is a fake just by looking at it, especially since it has a real number?" Mari asked as she put her hand on Pasha's back and urged her forward.

Brejian pointed toward the door. "I don't know the answer to any of those questions, but I'd rather ask *after* we're away from this place."

Right now Selah didn't want answers. She just wanted out.

December 28

Selah walked the floor space of the great room, trying to decide how to break the news to Pasha that she was going to fail on her promise regarding the sick girl. Cinanji said the investigation was stalled and there wouldn't be any concrete evidence for several more weeks. She couldn't say anything to the Keeper because Brejian was pretty sure there was a rogue bunch of them involved in the operation. She would have to leave and never know, but it rubbed her the wrong way that Brejian had suddenly seemed so helpful and now she doubted the Keeper. She was too close to leaving to mess up now.

She fingered the token in her pocket. She'd have to ask Brejian to monitor the outcome of the investigation and redeem the token for the child when this was all over. She'd miss the token as a tangible reminder of how far a mother would go for her child and how precious good health could be when you didn't have it.

Unfortunately, repairing her own health wouldn't be as easy as redeeming a token. In the next couple days she would reach her six-month peak. Today she was as strong as she'd ever be, and then she would start to decline.

Selah glanced out at the garden. As usual, Rylla and Dane sat at the umbrella table situated among the purple rhododendrons with their only pastime—the Stone Braide Chronicles. She hadn't been able to sway their determination to read the book to the end, and they had missed most of the dome experiences other than a few outings, the flowers, and the food.

The two suddenly erupted in cheers. Rylla jumped in the air. "We did it! We finished the whole book. Now we can see the city."

"We made it to the end. The end." Dane skipped around Rylla in circles and into the kitchen, yelling to Mari that he'd made it to the end.

Selah laughed. "There's no time for you to do anything. We're leaving the day after tomorrow. I told you the book would be there later, but you wanted to read it first." Still, she was proud they had stuck to their determination to accomplish it.

"We had to. That was our job," Rylla said.

Selah stopped. "Who told you that?"

Rylla wrapped her arms around Selah's waist. "I love you."

"I love you too, but who told you to read the book?" Selah held the child at arm's length to see her expression.

"I don't know. I got told in a dream." Rylla smiled.

"Who told you in a dream?"

Rylla shrugged. "I don't know. I didn't see anyone, just heard them. If we're leaving we have to pack a lot of my new favorite snacks." She ran off toward the kitchen.

Selah watched her go. A dream. What an odd thing for her to say. Children were so innocent and unpredictable. Someday she would try to decipher their thought processes and the quick subject changes.

A sigh pushed its way from her chest. No sense putting it off any longer—she had to tell Pasha she couldn't get STORM for the child. Might as well tell her at the clinic, so she could calm some by the time she came back to the unit.

Selah yelled, "Mari, I'm going out. If Mother comes in tell her to wait for me, please."

She closed the door and walked toward the lobby. Turning the last curve in the hall, Selah saw Brejian in the distance, turning into the extension of the corridor on the other side of the lobby. If she caught Brejian now, she could give her the token and save a trip to her office on the other side of the building complex.

She hurried up the hall. Brejian turned from the corridor before Selah reached the lobby. She tried to not sprint through the lobby, because at times there were other visitors to the complex and she didn't want to appear rude or uncivilized.

A fast walk got her across the lobby in record time, and she turned down the hall where she thought Brejian had gone. In these narrow halls, Selah started to dash to the next hallway, sure that she'd see Brejian and be able to call out to her.

Selah stopped when she heard Brejian's and Cinanji's voices. Panic hit. *Easy—turn around and go back.*

"You've lied to me from the very beginning, and now you're

asking me to trust you." Brejian's voice was high and laced with sniffles.

Selah's eyes darted around. She rushed to try two other doors—both locked.

"These men know what they're doing. I don't condone their methods, but they've found the right composition," Cinanji said.

A skinny door next to the office where they were talking proved to be a utility closet. Selah squeezed herself in among the vacuums and cleaners. She pulled the door closed behind her. At the last second she realized there wasn't a handle on the inside. She tucked the hem of her tunic in the door where the magnetic latch should catch.

"I'm not here to bargain with you. You've made a fool out of me. This is over," Brejian said.

"My darling, listen to me. This will work. Things will change," Cinanji begged. It sounded like they were walking around.

"You're so stupid. This could have gone so differently, and corrupt Keepers are something I cannot believe you would endorse." Brejian's voice started to quiver.

"My darling—"

"Don't bother with flattery. I've turned the evidence over to a Keeper I trust," Brejian said.

"No, no! Tell me you didn't!"

Sounds of a scuffle and falling objects mixed together to create confusion. The door flew open, smashing against the wall. Selah heard the sound of sobbing and feet hurrying down the hall.

Selah pulled on the piece of tunic caught in the door. Nothing happened. She pulled again. Her shirt was stuck and the door wouldn't open. She could still hear the sobbing, so she gulped down her pride and yelled, "Help! Can somebody let me out of here?"

The sobbing stopped. "Hello?" a shaky voice said.

Selah leaned her head against the door. "Can you let me out? The door won't—"

The door opened and bright light streamed in the open doorway, framing Brejian's face.

"Selah? What are you doing in there?" Brejian held the door open wide.

Selah stepped out and straightened her clothes. "I'm sorry. I was trying to catch you to give you the token to redeem after we're gone. But then I heard you and I . . . I don't know why I got in the closet. I'm sorry." She lowered her gaze.

Brejian took her hands. "Selah, it's me who owes you an apology. Come with me. I have to show you." She led Selah through a series of corridors and side ramps until they passed a corridor with a sign saying *Lottery Office*.

Selah stopped. "What are we doing over here? Isn't this illegal?" She had a feeling trouble was about to rear its ugly head.

"What they're doing to you is illegal, but you've got to see why." Brejian dragged Selah across two more halls. She punched a code in the door. "Put your hand up here."

Selah pulled back. "Why?"

"Just do it."

Selah hesitated but laid her hand against the plate. The door buzzed open.

"How did that happen?" Selah followed behind Brejian as she palmed illuminators.

"Novarium is a universal handprint here. It will unlock a lot."

"And I'm learning this as I'm ready to leave? Why didn't you tell me before?" Selah turned to look directly at Brejian.

Brejian looked down. "I wasn't sure I could trust you after the way they treated me back in the transport, but when Cinanji came clean about the operation I knew I had to take a chance that you'd help."

Selah wanted to be offended, but she had done the same thing. They were more alike than different. "What did you mean when you said what they're doing to me is illegal?"

"Cinanji works for, or with—I don't know what his role is, but he is responsible for—"

"I heard part of your conversation," Selah said.

Brejian turned on the illuminators and the long laboratory grew brighter, revealing stations of equipment and tools that reminded Selah too much of the Mountain. She turned to run.

"Please stop. Please. You have to see this. I told you. It's illegal. It will all be destroyed very shortly. The high Keeper will not tolerate such an invasion," Brejian said.

Selah, still nervous in this environment, calmed herself with a few deep breaths. "What invasion?" Were they going to attack the East Coast?

"On you."

Selah tipped her head. "An invasion on me?" She jerked a glance around the room, looking for any attackers she might have missed. The room was clean.

Brejian motioned her to a light table. "The fast explanation is that every time someone attacked you they were only after DNA samples."

"But my DNA—novarium DNA—degrades fast. That's one of the things I learned in the Mountain. A sample is only good for an hour at most." Selah looked at the slide progressions on the table.

"They had to keep testing until your DNA got to the right strength. No one knew the date you were transitioned, so they didn't know when you'd reach the tap point. You reach your peak in forty-eight hours. They need a blood donation from you now."

Selah's mouth went slack. Her tongue stuck to the roof of her mouth. She had to move it a couple times before words would come. "You want blood from me?" Had she misjudged Brejian? Was she the enemy after all?

"I told you, this is illegal. No one can ask you."

"Then why am I here?"

Brejian held up the last slide. "Because you could offer."

Selah's head screamed *run*, but her feet and hands wouldn't cooperate. She looked at the slide Brejian swept in front of her. It estimated the plague would kill *all* dome inhabitants in the next five years. "Is this correct?"

"Yes, these are the true projections. The degraded strength in STORM has allowed the population to become infected with this plague. Not all of them at once. The weaker are going first," Brejian said.

"What will my blood do?"

"Create an inoculation for everyone in the dome and eradicate the plague."

Selah felt light-headed just thinking about it. "How much?"

Brejian perked up. "Platelets. I can create the inoculations faster with platelets. I need to hook you to a machine."

Selah shook her head. "No, I don't like that idea. I've been drained of blood before. There must be another way."

"There isn't."

"But there were dozens of other novarium here at different times. Why wasn't their blood used to create this inoculation?" Selah felt sick at the thought of needles draining her blood again.

"Before they didn't have the opportunity to test for strength, and they never found the optimum sample," Brejian said.

Selah wasn't sure about this, and if she asked Bodhi he'd say no under any circumstances, whether it was the right thing to do or not.

She sighed. No good choice. But after being here this long if she didn't trust Brejian now, in a few days there'd never be another opportunity. The woman had been a big help.

"Let's get it done before my brain catches up to my shaking head and I run away."

Brejian expertly guided Selah to the separator. "We'll do both arms and get it done faster. It will take out small amounts of blood, remove the platelets, and return the rest to you with a little saline."

"Both arms." Selah gulped. She leaned back on the table and closed her eyes.

The process was done much faster than she expected. Brejian directed the platelets into the vaccine chamber, and the injectors all across the line turned green.

Brejian turned to Selah. "In two days every bit of plague in this dome will be eradicated."

Selah felt accomplishment for the first time. She had directly helped someone by being a novarium. All these people would live. "I'm glad that little girl whose mother got the phony token at least won't have plague, but I wish you could help her." Selah pulled the token from her pocket.

"Yes! And that! Come here." Brejian dragged Selah across the room to a tall circular machine with plugs, tubes, and moving parts. She took the token from Selah, laid it in a slot, fingered in several different codes, and punched a square button.

The machine swallowed the token.

"Hey, wait," Selah said. "That's not—"

An insert popped into the receiving tray. A silver pill rolled around in a clear container.

"Grab that one," Brejian said. She used a couple different screens to set codes, then fingered in several different codes and punched the button.

Again, another insert and pill. Selah picked up the second container. "I don't understand."

"Oh, this? I'm using Cinanji's password. He's in league with the fringe group of Keepers running the corruption in this dome. That's how I caught on. It was a real token because they had access to the real numbers, and they made sure it was her number that won and then robbed her every time." Brejian pressed her lips tight. "Anyhow, they also cheated the woman out of her personal dose for the year. It was scheduled to be administered two days after she died. So I just gave you that dose for the girl too."

"What should Mother do, give one now and one later?" Selah put them in her pocket.

"No. Give her both now. Two doses for someone that small should cure her and restore her immunity instead of it needing to be built back up."

"I don't know how to thank you."

"You've saved my people. That's enough." Brejian smiled.

Selah and Brejian walked toward the lab exit. "Do you want to be there when Mother gives her the pills?" Selah asked.

The door flew open and Cinanji stormed in. "I was coming to destroy the evidence and you betray me even now. The Keepers have an alert out for me. Where can I go?"

Selah backed away. Brejian approached him with her hands out in surrender. "Cinanji, I will go with you and help explain."

"No. No. No." He put his hands up over his ears. "But it's all your fault." He pointed at Selah and charged forward. Selah stood her ground. She could thrust him.

Cinanji pulled an illegal laser from his jacket and fired at Selah.

"No!" Brejian threw herself in front of the charge. It hit her directly in the chest, exploding her tunic. She fell to the floor.

Selah knelt beside her and scooped Brejian's head into her lap. "What did you do that for? He was shooting at me!" Tears rolled from Selah's cheeks to the woman's blood-soaked shirt.

Brejian's eyes fluttered and she touched Selah's cheek with her finger. "You brought me home and saved my people. What's one life compared to that?" A smile flitted across her lips. Her eyes slid closed as the last breath escaped from her chest.

Selah laid her head down gently and rose. She stood there, stuck in time, her mind flashing back to Cleon getting hit in the chest with the laser his own father had fired.

Selah snapped back and looked at Cinanji. "What did you do? She loved you!" She turned, pointed at the machine, and screamed, "You're crazy! I gave the blood. I gave the blood!

You killed her for nothing and she loved you!" Tears blurred her vision but rage filled her. She concentrated on building a charge.

Cinanji stood rooted to the spot where he'd fired. "Brejian, sweetheart?" His voice wavered. "Get up, honey."

"She's not getting up. She's gone." Selah shook, blinking through tears, fearful of moving. She was not good at outrunning lasers, and it was taking longer than normal for a charge to build. The blood donation must have hampered her ability.

"The operation is exposed, and I've lost everything I've worked for." Cinanji's voice broke. His shoulders started to heave. "This is your fault." He aimed the weapon at Selah again.

She faced him square on. "I gave the blood. What more do you want?"

"Nothing!" His hand shook, and the weapon lowered. He grabbed his head. "It's all gone. The life I built for us is all gone." His eyes filled with rage and the weapon came back in line with Selah's chest. "And that is your fault! You had to wedge yourself between us." He charged at Selah.

She sidestepped his advance and pushed him as hard as she could. Cinanji threw out his hands to keep from falling into the laboratory counter. His chest smashed into the edge, knocking the air from him. The laser clattered to the floor as he gasped for breath.

Selah scrambled to beat him to the weapon.

"No!" he yelled. He grabbed her hair and jerked her back.

Selah screamed and twisted herself under his arms so he had to let go of her hair. She kicked at him. He backhanded her and she tumbled over a chair but regained her footing and came up swinging. They both scrambled for the laser. Selah got her fingers on the barrel.

Cinanji kicked it from her grasp. Her fingers stung but she clawed at the floor to get hold of it again. Her hand landed on the laser and Cinanji smashed his foot down on her fingers.

Selah cried out and pulled her hand away. When she looked up he was standing over her with the laser pointed at her head. She shut her eyes and lowered her head between her hands as she knelt on the floor, her breath coming in heavy gulps. "Why are you going to kill me now?"

He waved the laser haphazardly as he ranted. "Because Brejian is dead. I waited all these years for her to come back and now she's dead."

Selah pulled in a long breath to clear her head. "*You* killed her. You were trying to kill me for no reason, and you killed *her*." She forced herself from the floor in one swift movement and launched at the weapon. She got both hands around it. Cinanji grabbed at her hair again. Selah sunk her teeth into his hand. He howled in pain and punched her in the side of the head.

She slumped to the floor, dazed. She had no strength to fight back. After all she'd sacrificed, it was going to end here and no one would know why. She tried to rise up on all fours, but her strength failed her. She looked up at the man who was going to end her life. "I'm sorry for everything you want to blame on me, but I did not cause Brejian's death." Selah lowered her head to stop the swirling stars in her vision. She looked up at him and waited for the end.

His eyes glazed over like he had forgotten something, and

he shook his head as though he could no longer see Selah. "I have nothing left." He turned away.

Selah mustered up the last of her strength and grabbed for the weapon. They struggled hand over hand, back and forth. She pulled him down to the floor and they rolled over and over. Cinanji pointed the laser at her again. The weapon fired, the beam streaking the wall across from them. Selah tried to wrap her legs around him to get on top. He wrenched back and forth, their hands struggling for control of the deadly weapon. Cinanji ranted about his lost life. He pushed her over and pinned her down. She fought to keep the laser pointed away from her. It fired again, marking the ceiling. He mumbled words Selah didn't understand.

As they struggled, Cinanji suddenly put the laser to his chest and fired. His eyes rolled back and he spun away from Selah, coming to rest with his hand across Brejian's.

Selah blinked. A heat wave passed before her face and her upper lip tingled.

"Do you have any idea what's going on in this dome? There's a lottery stealing people's STORM, a plague about to wipe out the whole place, and the inoculations are ready to go." Selah marched toward the Keeper's desk and slumped in her regular seat.

"What in all the dome has happened? I had multiple alerts of weapons discharge in this building, and in the vicinity of *you*," the Keeper said.

"Brejian is—wait a minute. You said in *this* building. I know where I was at the time. So this is where you've been hiding the whole time. But it is still a fact that Healer Brejian is dead, and so is Healer Cinanji."

"Very unfortunate about Brejian. Her information blew the whole dirty operation into the light. It was very brave of her to take on members of her own family. She told me last night that they tried to coerce her to save the operation, but after being around you for so many months she had regained respect for the Protocols and the bravery you exhibited in the face of the struggle you were dealing with."

Selah rubbed a hand across her forehead. "I feel bad that I mistrusted her for so long. She gave her life to save me in the end. Cinanji was a real menace."

"Cinanji was headed to a life of squalor and disgrace, but after taking Brejian's life he would have been executed, so he took the faster route by about three days," the Keeper said.

"I keep telling myself she sacrificed herself to save me," Selah said. "I feel so unworthy of her sacrifice, especially after the way I thought of her."

The Keeper appeared distracted by a screen in front of him. "She saved you for rescuing her people."

"Just didn't feel equal. All I gave was a little blood, and not even whole blood."

"But there are long-range costs to you—decreased abilities, reduced recovery—and we're not at all sure if it will reduce your time leading up to the fracture." The Keeper had worry lines etched on his forehead that she hadn't noticed before.

"So are the Keepers going to let the people have the inoculations?" Selah slanted her eyes to look at him. He didn't seem uncomfortable, so either he was really good at acting or he was innocent of corruption. She hadn't decided which yet.

The Keeper sat back. "With Brejian's sacrifice, the Keepers couldn't let her die for nothing. And since there is a markedly short expiration on your DNA, inoculations began as soon as they saw the green light on the injectors. So yes, the citizens of this dome are becoming your direct descendants as we speak."

"Does that clean up the whole operation?"

The Keeper shook his head. "No. On the whole it will take years of testing to see what changes introducing your DNA brought about. There will always be those who find a way to capitalize on someone else's misfortune, either by ignorance or omission, so the black market will live on until the whole gang of them can be rounded up to face charges. Many of them are very powerful people here, and they will do everything to keep the status quo. Then again, if you succeed we will all be changed to the next level of Protocol, and that in itself will create new opportunities for mistakes."

"So it just keeps going forever and every solution creates more problems." She sighed. "Well, I have the cure for one very sick little girl, and I think my mother would like to give it to her. So I'll take my leave." Selah, disheveled and tired, stepped forward and the Keeper sent her to her quarters.

December 30

Selah stared out at the garden, then slowly ran her gaze around the great room, committing it to memory. This was the last time she would ever see this place. The family was waiting for her in the vehicle to take them back to the transport. Mojica,

Bodhi, and Taraji had taken turns going out with supply runs and checking systems. They were jabbering about new changes using the system tricks they had learned in the dome.

She wanted one last visit with the Keeper, but the technology had been reclaimed from her scrambler and she never did find out where he was located. Maybe she could leave a message for him.

Selah said goodbye to her garden and opened the front door. She jumped back. The Keeper stood there holding the hand of a young girl about eight or nine. Selah looked at the girl and did a double take. The child reminded her of Amaryllis. Selah looked up at the Keeper. "And who do we have here?"

"This is the child your mother saved with the pills," the Keeper said.

"She looks beautifully healthy. Why is she with you?"

The Keeper smiled. "Because she is my granddaughter. Her mother was my daughter."

Selah frowned. "Your daughter was living on the streets with a chronically ill child and you did nothing to help her?"

The Keeper stepped into the quarters and shut the door. "Have you ever met anyone who refused to listen to their parents when they were taking part in dangerous things?"

"Yes. Sometimes hard love is necessary to bring someone back to their senses."

"Well, that's what I was trying to do with my daughter. She had strayed so far from our value system and was involved with so many substances that there was just no talking to her. I lost track and hadn't spoken to her in more than a year, and I didn't realize that my grandchild's health was in jeopardy."

"How long was she involved with substances?"

The Keeper nudged the child out into the garden and turned back to face Selah. His head hung low, as though he were ashamed. "She became a user as a sort of protest to my involvement with the black market."

Selah backed away from the Keeper. "Excuse me? You were involved in the black market? Aren't those the people you said are ruining your society?"

The Keeper laced his fingers in front of him. "Sometimes it can take a hundred years to find some good sense."

"That's the easy way out." Selah's anger welled up. She didn't know if he meant her harm. But at least everyone else was conveniently out of his way.

"You don't know, until you've lived a life as long as I have, what you are capable of doing to fellow humans in the name of progress."

"Progress? A black market selling health for outrageous prices is *progress*?"

"It actually created a cottage industry in biometrics—"

"Don't try to legitimize something so evil," Selah said. "People are dying."

The muscles in the Keeper's jaw flexed. "Walk in my shoes for a couple decades and then give me your assessment."

"Fake!" Selah pointed a finger in his face. "You are a fake! You're supposed to protect and serve these people, and all you've done is use them for your profits." Her legs shook with anger. She started pacing so her whole body wouldn't tremble.

"I told you. My daughter made me see the error of my ways, but I couldn't convince her that I had changed because I didn't give up the profits I had amassed. She would never come back home. She said the walls were built with blood money." He choked up.

Selah wanted to lower her guard, seeing the man so vulnerable, but being slapped in the face with the reality that her trust in him had been sorely misplaced made her rethink the idea. "I am leaving today . . . " She hesitated. "Or at least I *think* I'm leaving today." She waited, expecting bars and force fields to capture her.

He nodded and closed his eyes.

Relief flooded over her, and the built-up tension faded away. "So whatever happens here will be up to you. It will be the legacy you leave for that sweet child out there." Selah nodded toward the child sitting on the garden bench, smelling the latticework roses.

"You have done a good thing to renew and save our world. I know you'll never be back, but I will know if you succeed next summer because we'll be changed."

Selah leaned against the doorjamb. "Do you know what it's like to never feel like you can trust any of the strangers you meet?"

The Keeper frowned. "I've never trusted any of the novarium who came through here. They never cared about any of us, only what we could do for them, but I have to admit you were different. It touched me when I found out how much danger you put your family in for my daughter's sake."

Selah decided this wasn't the time to admit that was all her mother's doing. "Those novarium were singular people. Have you ever had a whole society that you couldn't trust?"

"No, I guess not. I've always known the agenda of those around me, so trust wasn't an issue."

"Well, it's draining. It pulls at your soul, at your humanity, when you can't trust anyone. People smile at me and are nice, and I have to doubt every fiber of their sincerity. I'm tired." Selah moved closer to him. "And you know why I'm tired? Because I chose to distrust Brejian and trust you! And as it turns out, it was *you* I should have worried about." She could feel an outburst welling up.

"I'm sorry."

"You're sorry?" Selah threw up her hands. "Well, that's just great. Brejian died to save me and I didn't even trust—" She turned away. It made her physically ill to think how easily Brejian had given up her own life. "I have to go before I say something I will regret for the rest of my life."

The Keeper stepped back as she moved to the door. "I've never been allowed to tell the novarium what comes after the next dome, but I feel I must tell you. I owe that much to you after all you've done," he said.

"What do I need to know?"

"There is no more."

18

January 5

Selah hurried onto the command deck and grabbed a navigator seat behind Taraji. It felt strange to look out the sides and see grass and trees instead of snow or ash. They had steered clear of the last snow around Cleveland by veering south of the snow line.

As soon as the journey west began, recurring problems had cropped up with the transport's operational systems. Propulsion difficulties, specifically the magnetic components, slowed their travel to a crawl. After an hour of calmly creeping along at subpar speed to avoid an accident from control lapse, the ship pitched hard to the right for the second time in ten minutes.

Selah grabbed the console with one hand and strapped on her seat restraint with the other. "Magnetic calibration fluctuations?"

"Yes. A whole wave of them. I can't maintain the same

mix on each thruster. First they run in opposition, then they default to tandem. It's going to blow the system if I don't shut the whole thing down." Taraji wrestled with the controls.

Bodhi shifted his seat around to face Taraji and used the short console between them to stack control models. He connected them and reinserted the new unit in the panel. "The patterns on the operating parameters dampened the modulators. I've piggybacked to compensate for the voltage drop."

The transport shuddered and dropped five feet. Selah's stomach dropped as well, and queasiness flashed over her as she grabbed the console. "Do I need to check on the others or is this temporary?"

The ramp door to the right of the lift slid open and Mojica charged in. "What's going on up here? I've got all kinds of minor systems blowing out below." She swung into the seat at the tactical console behind Bodhi and strapped in.

"We were fine until we dropped below the snow line." Taraji's hands rose and fell over control beams, trying to compensate for the noticeable discrepancies on the VR console.

"In a snowstorm briefing at the dome there was reference to major magnetic disruption," Mojica said. "Selah, I installed several dome data modules of weather patterns. See what you can pull up."

"Most of what I learned in the dome was the effects of the super volcano. The land upheaval disrupted the earth's magnetic harmonics and changed the weather patterns for this whole side of the country." Selah worked to pull up the file. It took her a few tries to find the right set accompanying the snowstorm. "The data only extends to Chicago, but the magnetics show a ribbon effect. I'd say the variations seem to

follow the snow line—or could it be the other way around?"
She looked to Mojica. "Is it possible that intense magnetism
could melt snow?"

"Theoretically, yes. Mags produce electricity, and that can
generate heat," Mojica said. "But melting snow . . . I don't
know. That's reaching."

Bodhi and Taraji stared at each other. "Could it be that
easy?" Taraji asked.

"Go back above the snow line and see if it stops," Selah
said.

The transport jerked left. A stabilizer failed and the top of
the transport tipped right as Taraji tried to pull the vehicle
back on course. She righted the angle and steered a slow, wide
path around to the north. She cut the fusion to an idle and
punched the air generator thrusters. They would only creep
along, but it would maintain the forward motion.

"We've had to turn the magnetic shielding off, and the mag
confinement on the fusion thrusters is failing. They can only
be cycled down this far without turning them off," Bodhi said.

The transport shuddered then jerked—another loss of
power along with a five-foot dip that brought them danger-
ously close to the ground. Taraji and Bodhi wrestled to pull
it back to cruising altitude.

Selah gulped down the rising bile. "If you shut the thrusters
off, will this nauseating movement stop?" She could almost
define the moment she'd started the six-month decline, but she
hadn't expected symptoms to be this dramatic in the first week.

"Yes," Bodhi said. "But we'd have to set down to start them
back up. I'd rather not land and need a hard start with a magnetic problem like this." Taraji and Mojica agreed.

Several shudders, a shake, and another dip sent the transport careening for the tall tops of a snow-covered forest of pines. Taraji muttered and pulled on her VR appliance. Bodhi drew his VR console screen in from the side. The transport refused to rise fast enough. They worked together to swing the transport to the right through a narrow area where the treetops appeared to have been sheared off by recent lightning.

Selah glanced from Bodhi to Taraji then peered out the front shield at the fast-moving trees. "Aren't we going a little fast for the terrain?"

Taraji wrestled with the controls. "I've lost primary. Bodhi, hit command change!"

Bodhi two-handed the change and pulled the command panel forward.

Taraji pushed back from the panel and slid from her chair to the unit underneath her station holding the control modules. Sitting cross-legged, she pulled the top two units and replaced them with the bottom two. She scrambled back into her seat and helped Bodhi navigate the forest again. Selah watched them release a collective sigh of relief when they'd coaxed enough altitude from the air thrusters to avoid a crash.

Selah put her hand to her stomach. Her earlier meal didn't like being shaken around. "How much longer would the trip to Chicago take if we just used the air generator thrusters?"

"Air generators are supposed to be used only for maneuvering the transport into tight locations, not actual flight time. I don't want to burn them out this soon," Taraji said.

The transport bucked then pitched to the right. Selah clutched her station surface.

They limped along for five minutes before the vehicle gained equilibrium and leveled out. Mojica moved to sit beside Selah at the other navigation station. She pulled up the same data stream Selah viewed.

"Do you see how those surges coincide with the recorded magnetic disturbances on the sun?" Mojica pointed to each in turn.

Selah felt sick. "This data cube predicts the solar flares will last for six months. Where did this data come from?"

"I told you I brought it from the dome," Mojica said.

"No, I mean where did the *dome* get this information? We studied that old technology in school. In the dome I didn't see a telescope big enough to look at the surface of the sun," Selah said.

Mojica shook her head. "We probably won't ever go back to find out."

"Regardless of where they got it, we have it, so how do we get around the disturbances of the solar flares?" Selah looked around the room at each person.

Mojica stared at the projections. "This isn't going to be easy, but I think we could retrofit the system to harness the ambient magnetism of those streams to pump up our system."

"Do we have the parts?" Taraji turned from her console.

"I don't think so. We cut weight of all nonessentials, and at that time our magnetic pulse thrusters and shielding were at the optimum level, so we sidelined all upgradeables," Bodhi said.

"I'd feel a lot better if we procured parts from the Cleveland dome," Selah said.

"We can't go back there. We have less than an hour to go. If we return to Cleveland we risk getting caught by another storm," Bodhi said. "Do you really want to risk three more months in that dome?"

"No, I don't. I'm just a little homesick for our unit's garden," Selah said. "That's the longest I've stayed in one spot since I was transitioned last July."

Bodhi turned to her. "I'm sorry. It was a decent place. Other than a few bumps it could have been a nice life."

"I miss Brejian too." Selah looked down at her hands. She would forever remember the woman's sacrifice. So many things had happened and she'd never gotten to thoroughly investigate the Repository records to find help for Bodhi's condition. If she completed the Third Protocol he would be changed like everyone else, but she still feared failure.

"She gave me several data crystals before her death. I haven't had an opportunity the last couple days to see what they are," Taraji said.

Their focus shifted as the transport began to shudder again. "I don't understand. The shaking should have abated once we rose above the snow line," Bodhi said. He looked over at Taraji who had command control again.

"We need to get as close as we can to the Chicago dome," Taraji said.

Bodhi quickly glanced over his panels, his hands moving data onto his screen. "You're going to think I'm crazy, but my system said we were heading north."

Taraji looked at hers. "Mine says west."

"I know. Mine says west *now*," Bodhi said.

Taraji muttered under her breath and slapped the arm of her chair. "I just lost the dampener panel on the air generators."

"We're going to have to set it down. Maybe I can cobble

replacements together until we get to the Chicago dome," Mojica said.

"As soon as the failure notice came across, I started sliding south of the snow line. At least we won't have to walk around in snow while we're here," Taraji said.

Selah saw a glint of light reflected far to the west. The only thing big enough to be seen from this distance had to be the dome, and that was about twenty miles away. Her vision was decreasing. "We don't have to go south any farther. I can see the dome ahead."

The transport would travel several miles then buck and jerk. The dome had been growing in her sight, but not large enough for the others to see as they coaxed the transport along.

"Stabilizers just went critical. I have to set her down. Hang on to your seats," Taraji said.

Bodhi put down the landing struts just in time to avoid a crash. A resounding thud shuddered through the transport.

The hard landing jolted through Selah's spine, radiating down and out her arms and legs. She sat back and ran a hand across her forehead.

Taraji waved the systems off. "Cut everything to keep the damage from cascading."

Selah swiped off her panel, using both hands to hit different systems. Mojica swiped hers off and darted back to the tactical station.

Bodhi finished his systems. "Everybody okay?"

Selah blinked a couple times and stretched the muscles in her neck. "Yes, I think so. I'm going down to see if Mari, Mother, and the kids are all right." She charged toward the ramp to the family areas, passing the lift as it arrived. She skidded to a stop and backed up as it swished open.

The women and two frightened children spilled out into the command deck entrance. Dane ran to Selah, almost knocking her down with his hug.

"Easy. It's all right. We're down now." Selah stroked his hair. Rylla wrapped her arms around Selah from the other side.

Mari and Pasha continued onto the command deck. "Did we crash?" Mari peered out the front shield.

"We hope not," Bodhi said.

Pasha moved back and forth, looking out the two sides. "Was it enemy fire?"

"No, and that's especially disturbing to think about with the shielding down," Taraji said.

"No shielding?" Mari and Pasha said at the same time.

Selah disengaged from the two kids and entered the command deck. They scrambled to follow. "No, you two stay out here where you can't get in trouble," she said.

Taraji explained to Mari and Pasha about the magnetic problems.

"The scramblers I brought have the ability to depress magnetic interference. Maybe with amplification we can expand the technology to something that might work for the transport," Mari said.

"That's the best idea I've heard so far. Show me what you have." Taraji unbuckled and followed Mari below, leaving Pasha to peer out the side shields at the forest landscape.

Selah leaned on Bodhi's command chair. "You good?"

"Yeah, but you look a little pale," Bodhi said, reaching to touch Selah's cheek. "You feeling all right?"

Selah smiled softly and lied, "Sure, I was just thinking about damage outside. It sounded like we hit pretty hard." There wasn't time to let others worry about her when the whole family could be in peril. She knew Bodhi would be distracted by concern for the transport.

Bodhi tapped Taraji. "We need recon for exterior damage." Taraji nodded.

"Come on, suit up and we'll get some fresh air," Bodhi said to Selah. He unstrapped from his seat and started for the ramp.

Selah squeezed her eyes shut. That was her punishment for lying. She trudged behind him onto the ramp for the lower level.

"Yeah! Can we come outside?" Rylla and Dane scampered behind her.

"No!" Selah held up a hand. "Neither of you are going out there till we make contact at the dome and know if it's safe." She closed the ramp entrance and headed down to Bodhi. "Do we need bio-suits? Our regular tactical suits are temperature sensitive to zero. It's nowhere near that."

"Sounds good. Less trouble." Bodhi rehung the suit then handed her a laser dart and holster from the weapons locker before he strapped on his own.

Selah felt a shiver as she held the laser dart. "Will they work if there's magnetic interference?"

Bodhi's shoulders drooped. He unhitched the strap for his holster. "No, they won't. I think we've neglected manual protection in a bid to be less encumbered." A look of concern crossed his face.

"Mari has her bows," Selah said. "Should I get her?"

"No, it will only take us a few minutes. Let's rough it this time. Just keep your eyes open. We'll go out on the right mid-side, travel to the left all the way around and back in. Ten minutes tops. I'll inspect, you guard," Bodhi said.

"Sounds good. What do I use for a weapon?" Selah hit the release for the ramp.

"Your thrust," Bodhi said. Selah cringed. She hoped she wouldn't need to use it until she could test in private whether the ability was still there. The Keeper had said the last abilities to come would be the first to go.

"Everything is shut down," Bodhi said. "The ramp's not going to move, and neither are the magnetic stairs. We'll have to climb." He led her to an access next to the magnetic stairs and released the panel. The door swung out and a metal ladder slid down to ground level.

Selah scrutinized the landscape. It appeared benign. Snow sat higher up on the ridge to the north. The forest they passed over was mostly of the evergreen type with a few interspersed trees bared of leaves. They'd landed in a small west-facing valley, deep and narrow.

Something flashed in her peripheral vision to the right. Selah jerked her head in that direction, but it was gone—or had she imagined it? Was this another symptom?

"Let's get this done. It's been cloudy all morning, and I don't want to get caught in bad weather if we need repairs before we can take off." Bodhi turned and climbed down the ladder, hopping off to the left.

Selah stared out at where she thought she'd seen the movement in low leafy bushes—probably blueberries since the Keeper said they thrived in this volcanic soil. The bushes grew at the edge of a grassy swamp about fifty feet in front of her, off to the right. Selah moved quickly to the left—she'd let Bodhi get ahead by himself. She caught up.

"How's it looking on this end?" Selah tracked 180 degrees around them. Her head continued spinning even after she stopped moving.

Bodhi answered but she didn't catch what he said. Her stomach flopped, and she quickly covered her mouth as she burped. Bodhi crossed the bow and headed down the keel on the port side. Selah rushed to catch up, gazing at the countryside as she went.

"I feel a lot better about this. It looks like only one of the forward landing struts is a little bent." Bodhi turned to look at Selah and hurried back to her. "What's wrong? You look a little green, or gray—something's not right with your complexion."

Selah touched his arm. "Please don't say anything. I don't want anyone fawning over me."

Bodhi leaned against the keel. "Do you think it's right to hide what's happening?"

"Let's wait until we're out of the Chicago dome with the next destination." Selah leaned back beside him. "The Keeper said the weather would hold for at least a week from the time we left there—"

"The time ends tomorrow. We made horrible progress with the magnetics," Bodhi said.

"We're making even worse progress standing here for so long. Let's get done so this will be one less thing to worry about. Then we can hole up and fix the system." Selah followed Bodhi around the stern and back to the ladder.

Selah climbed up first, then Bodhi. He turned around to close up.

"That's okay. I can do it. I want the fresh air for a few more minutes." Her fingers were cold—probably because she was hanging them over the sill. But she didn't like when that look of pity came into his eyes, like she was helpless already.

Selah pulled up the ladder and reached out to close the door. As she did, movement in the brush caught her eye. She stopped and stared this time, not daring to breathe or move. A squeal then a laugh echoed in the valley. It sounded familiar.

Selah furrowed her brow, looking around at the rest of the landscape. There was someone out there. She lowered the ladder and yelled down the hall over her shoulder, "Bodhi! Come listen." No answer. Where'd he go?

Selah hit the wall comm, then remembered—all systems were down, and no one bothered to wear their clunky scramblers inside the transport. She hesitated to go outside alone. She leaned out and looked around again, trying to hear more.

Above an overgrown field that bordered on a small meadow, a section of underbrush rustled, then the commotion traveled along the underbrush. Squealing erupted from the crackling winter-dead brush, followed by staccato laughter—Dane!

Selah scrambled down the ladder and tried to run. Adrenaline trembled her legs as her pounding heart forced it through her system. "Dane, come out of there!" She ran down the field and crossed over to the low grass meadow. "Dane!"

Her brother broke into the upper meadow after catching a piglet tangled in the underbrush. Squealing with laughter as the piglet screamed, Dane's voice echoed across the valley.

"Put it down! Dane, let it go before—" A three-hundred-pound feral boar broke through the tree line, head down, hooves throwing up dirt as it charged from the woods.

Selah sprinted toward Dane, waving and yelling his name, but the piglet's screams and his own laughing were too loud. She calculated the boar would reach him five seconds before her. She called out again as the boar roared down on Dane.

Her screams were lost in her throat as the boar's jaws opened and aimed for Dane's leg.

The front hooves stumbled, taking the boar's snout to the ground and throwing up dead grass and dirt as the plowing nostrils dug a trench. An arrow pierced the boar above its front legs. Another arrow ripped through its chest.

The boar's hooved feet stretched out and shuddered. It fell silent. Selah ran to a stunned Dane standing over a dead pig four times his size. Selah snatched the piglet from him and sent it off in the direction the male had traveled.

"What were you thinking? You could have been killed." Selah glanced around for the bowman. No one appeared. Shaking, Selah dragged the pouting boy double time across meadow and field to the ladder. She didn't turn around until she had Dane's feet on the rungs of the ladder and her breath had returned.

A lanky boy in a sleeveless vest, with skin the color of a raw pecan, stood over the boar. Selah flinched. How could he be without cover in this cold weather? He pressed his heel to the carcass and bent to remove the arrows.

Selah could feel the adrenaline rush drain away. Her hands shook on the ladder, the tremor radiating through her shoulders. She watched the boy's swift work.

His curly black hair spread from beneath a sky-blue scarf

tied tightly around his head. Selah remembered a painting from a Dominion Borough building of workers laboring on railroad tracks in the Old West. This boy's scarf was the same vibrant blue as one in the painting. She raised a hand to acknowledge and thank him for saving her brother.

The boy paused from dressing the boar but didn't wave back. Selah climbed the ladder and watched from the safety of the transport. Another boy and two girls with long stringy hair and bundled in coats appeared from the woods to the left of the meadow, pulling a large sled with wooden runners. The first boy stood by as the others wrapped the pieces of meat and packed the sled. They headed off into the woods.

The boy looked back toward the transport once more before disappearing into the forest.

19

Selah stormed into the galley quarters where Mari and Pasha were preparing the meal, brushed past both of them, and headed for Dane cowering in the corner. He hadn't regained his breath from running from her. She grabbed him by the shirt and drew his face up to hers. "Do you have any idea how close you came to dying?"

He let out a howl. Both Mari and Pasha came running to his defense. Pasha snatched him from Selah's hands. "What's the matter with you? Why would you scare your brother like that?"

"So he hasn't told you what he's done?" Selah still shook with fear from the close call.

"Selah, what's the matter? Calm down and tell us what you think he did," Mari said.

"What I *think* he did?" Selah reached for him again but Pasha pulled him back. "He was outside alone trying to catch feral piglets."

"I was not! So there!" Dane yelled. He screwed up his face and crossed his arms over his chest.

"You were not what?" Pasha asked.

"I wasn't alone. Me and Rylla—"

Selah grabbed his shoulders. "Rylla was with you? Why didn't you tell me before I pulled up the ladder?" Panic overtook her. She had locked the girl outside in a hostile world of children with weapons and feral hogs and no way in.

Selah ran to the systems area at the front of the transport. She scrambled to the door and swung open the hatch. "Rylla!"

Her call echoed and returned. Nothing.

Selah screamed again and strained to hear beyond the echo. She descended the ladder and started across the overgrown field to the grazing meadow where she'd grabbed Dane. "Rylla, where are you? Rylla!" The cold weather and strain on her voice was making her hoarse.

She reached the spot. The boy's helpers had dug a hole and buried the entrails. All that remained was discolored dirt and plant matter, but it gave Selah a place to start. She moved toward where she'd first seen the undergrowth disturbed. "Rylla, are you in there?" Her call was answered with a deep grunt. Selah backed out of the tangled area.

Footsteps crunched behind her. Selah jumped and spun into a crouch, ready to fight.

"Whoa!" Mari held up both hands. "Easy, girl. Two are better than one, especially when one brings weapons." She held out her second bow and arm quiver.

Selah stood up and strapped them on. "You thought ahead. The only thing better would be—"

Mari handed Selah the leather pouch holding her beloved

kapos. She grinned. "You've been itching to use those again. No better time than the present. When Bodhi came back from the hull inspection he told me to unpack the bows, so I got everything out."

Selah took the throwing knives. "How does this keep happening?" She was beginning to notice a pattern of coincidences.

"How does what keep happening? Hey, hold that thought. Look." Mari walked over to where the kids had dragged the sled. Wide runner marks sliced deep through the brush. She pointed about five feet to the right. "Do you see the imprint beside that broken twig?"

Selah walked over and glanced around. "Sure, I see that one and those over there and the ones beyond."

"This one has the grooved pattern of our tactical boots. The children's are the same. The rest of these shoes are handmade and worn. No two prints are the same. We go this way." Mari pointed at the woods where the grooved pattern traveled.

Selah stopped. "Hey, wait. We have to tell—"

"Pasha will tell them. I got an idea of Rylla's direction from Dane," Mari said.

Selah strode beside her sister through the dense forest. She was feeling better again. Maybe it was just normal, or maybe her determination to find Rylla helped. Either way she forgot about herself. She watched Mari's tracking skills as she searched for clues of disturbed earth, boot marks, and broken greenery. Her skills seemed a practiced sense. One Selah was sure she didn't have time to learn, but it fascinated her.

She asked anyhow. "Teach me what you do." Anything to help find Rylla.

Mari smiled. "Be observant of disturbed or broken green-ery, and watch for signs on the ground. The rest is practice. The only thing I'm confused about is our direction. I can't see the sun, but this feels like north instead of west."

"Can you still see Rylla's shoes?"

"Her tracks follow theirs." She pointed to the sled marks.

As they picked their way through areas of overhanging branches and tangled aboveground roots, Selah lagged behind Mari so she wouldn't destroy evidence, but she noticed the difference in sled tracks. "Why are those sled tracks getting lighter?"

Mari stooped beside the tracks. She felt the ground and looked back down the line in the direction they'd traveled. A smile spread across her lips. "Good catch, little sister. You've found their curing station system. They're dropping off meat parts as they head home."

Selah pulled back. "I didn't see any meat back there. Besides, the animals would get it."

Mari pointed up. "They hoist them up in the trees."

Twice after that Selah tripped from not watching where she walked because she wanted to spot hanging meat. She recalled Mother's smoke-curing shed. One year rats had climbed the beam and navigated the rope to eat out a whole ham, leaving behind only the bone and skin covering.

Mari stopped and held up a hand for quiet. She motioned Selah to stay low, then she silently slid through the brush and disappeared. Selah hunched down in place and waited, listening to sounds that should have been clear but now seemed muffled.

Mari crept back and spoke in a whisper. "I hear talking up

ahead—sounds young, but not Rylla. We're going to observe, not engage, unless we see Rylla in trouble."

Selah nodded. They crept forward. They heard chatter then giggles. Mari signaled Selah to stay low. They peeked between the branches of a creeping evergreen spread over a boulder about twenty-five feet from the group.

The four children Selah had seen stood at the edge of the tree line where the woods opened into a long and wide meadow of grass and dirt tracks. They were talking to someone in the forest.

Selah watched as a girl with long black hair rode into view around the edge of the forest opening. She dismounted a sleek black stallion and held it by leather reins.

The horse apparently smelled Selah and Mari, and it continued snorting in their direction at random moments. It became restless, pulling on the reins and whinnying, but the girl drew the reins tighter in her hands.

Mari and Selah leaned forward to see the other person in the conversation. Rylla came into view as they leaned into the bush. The rustling caused the horse to snort and rear back on its hind legs.

Selah panicked. "Rylla, look out!"

Rylla turned to face her with wide eyes and open mouth. The kids scattered. The girl with the horse yanked the reins, grabbed the horse by its mane, and slung herself up on its bare back. She galloped away as Selah and Mari ran to Rylla.

"I was so frightened." Selah hugged Rylla close. "Why did you leave? What possessed you to come into the woods?"

"I was exploring. I thought I heard you yelling, but when I came out of the woods the access panel on the transport was closed. I talked to the kids and told them where we were going—"

"Rylla, you shouldn't be telling strangers our plans," Selah said.

"But they're right and we're going the wrong way," Rylla said.

"What makes you think we're going the wrong way?"

"Because Chicago is here."

"Here? Rylla, this is forest. We're looking for the dome," Selah said.

Rylla huffed her annoyance. She grabbed Selah by the hand and pulled her through the opening in the forest.

"The way we're heading is north *past* Chicago." She pointed up the hill. "Chicago is up there."

Selah paced in tactical, walking around the inoperable data cube layout for the tenth time. Lack of power had them scouring the paper documents, looking for written words on the string of pearl locations. All that remained were tiny image logos.

She rested her elbow on the counter while she tapped her fingertips. Mojica walked in.

Selah straightened. "Are we ready to go?"

"No, Bodhi and Taraji needed to recalibrate the compass. It took me an hour to coax the true settings from the memory files," Mojica said.

"But we can't go anywhere anyhow. Why do they need to do that right now?" Selah paced. She understood their position but she was anxious to see another dome.

Bodhi and Taraji took another two hours to reset all the systems that needed navigation integration, and with Mojica's help, the three rigged old-fashioned technology to thwart electromagnetic pulses to the compass system.

The three strolled into tactical. Selah swung around and slapped the doorway to the galley area. Pasha and Mari hurried into the room with the children right behind them.

"Mother, will you stay with the children?" Selah wanted them out of trouble's way.

"No, wait. Not fair," Rylla said. "I'm the one who found the dome, and I know those kids and you don't. They ran away from you."

Selah pressed her lips together and looked to Bodhi.

He shrugged. "I hate to agree with the kid, but she's right. She's pretty smart."

"If she gets to go, then I want to go," Dane said.

"Oh no you don't." Pasha pulled him back beside her. "You've gotten in enough trouble for one day." He struggled then gave up.

"Mari comes with her bow," Selah said, "I carry the other—"

"How do we know weapons are allowed?" Taraji asked.

"Baje said they carry their bows everywhere," Rylla said.

"Beige is a person's name?" Selah asked.

"Yes, Baje is the name of the girl riding the horse. I liked her brother's bow and wanted one." Rylla's cheeks reddened. "If they're old enough, I am too. So I asked where to get one and she said the marketplace."

"Do we believe a kid's opinion on the level of security in the dome, considering how tight it was at the last place?" Taraji leaned back against the hull.

"I thought of that. The dome kid was an expert shot. So weapons are familiar, and he ran toward the dome with his weapon. And if for some reason they get confiscated, it's only two bows and easy-to-replace technology," Selah said.

Taraji remained silent for a few seconds. "Okay. It's worth that risk. Selah, Mari, Bodhi, Rylla, Mojica, and I go visit Chicago. This place stays locked up tight, Pasha. You open for no one other than us."

Pasha nodded.

Bodhi navigated the overgrown field. Breathing fresh air was more enjoyable than being cooped up in the transport or a dome, but not having an adequate weapon made him nervous with the kind of situations they'd encountered lately. The advanced combat training in the last dome had prepared him for hand-to-hand but really had no effect when people were shooting pulse rifles at him.

An empty satchel for part collection flapped against his side, reminding him the trip back would be a lot more difficult if they found everything they needed. They traveled down the field for a half mile. Bodhi found a stick that would work for a fighting staff, and twice Mari had a shot at a deer but didn't take it because they weren't short on provisions.

Selah, with Rylla at her side, led the group to leave the field where the woods abruptly ended. The empty meadow to the left of the forest led up a meandering hill. As they passed the tangled opening to the forest, Bodhi peered in among the trees. Something felt a little off.

A young sow charged from the brush. It looked to be

veering away from the group, but at the last second it turned and charged. Mari and Taraji tried distraction as it headed for Rylla and Selah. Bodhi had a second of horror before Mari pegged the sow with an arrow planted right at the top of its front legs. Mari must have dialed up the poundage on her bow because the arrow flew through the pig and carried it along until both reached the earth.

"Too bad we don't need the meat. Maybe we can sell it to someone for a ride out this far from the dome," Rylla said.

"You'd have to be sure no other wild animal stole the carcass, or you'd still be liable for the ride if you arrived here and the carcass was gone," Selah said. She wrapped an arm around Rylla's shoulder and pulled her close while Mari retrieved her arrow from the carcass.

Bodhi looked around. He hoped Selah had really seen Chicago and not some mock-up to draw them out in the open. It just didn't look like the area could hide a dome that large. They trudged into the meadow, walked around the forest area, and headed for the top of the hill.

Bodhi and Selah crested the hill together and looked down over the huge valley. It contained a dome as large as Cleveland with roads going in and out of it! And no snow anywhere to be seen. He frowned. There had been snow at this latitude on the other side of the forest. Why not here?

The rest of the group reached the top.

Bodhi looked at Taraji. "I suspect this hill wasn't here before the volcano. That could be the source of our strange magnetics."

"Agreed. Looks like pedestrians travel in on foot. We may not appear suspicious," Taraji said.

"Taraji and Mojica, look for parts and weapons that will work in this environment," Bodhi said. "Selah and I will search for the Seekers. Mari and Rylla, keep your eyes out for anything we can use."

"I'm not happy with Selah being with neither Mojica nor me," Taraji said.

"I can be of no service searching for parts I've never seen, which would slow our progress considerably. I think we can make it for three hours," Bodhi said.

Taraji didn't appear convinced. "Since we need the parts to get going, I'll let it slide this one time."

"Glad you see it that way. Synchronize the timer on your scramblers. If we get separated, meet here by this gate in three hours."

Bodhi stayed close to Selah. He could tell she still wasn't feeling well. He feared what her decline would begin to look like. Maybe if they could get out of here soon enough they'd reach the end faster.

They joined the others walking the causeway into the dome. The inside was an immediate assault to the senses. He usually didn't smell much of anything, but this was strong and musky. He looked at the ladies before they separated to explore in multiple directions. They weren't enjoying it either.

It must be market day, but looking at the selections made Bodhi more uneasy. The streets were full of vendors of all kinds of weapons, beverages, and strange substances imaginable. Some vendors looked as though they'd sampled too much of their product. The loud, pounding beat of the music set a rhythmic tone that affected the mood of the crowd. Bodhi had never seen a crowd subjected to music. Each song seemed to affect the flow of traffic. He watched as the tension in the crowd grew with the intensity of the music and died accordingly.

Selah gravitated closer to him. From a booth about ten feet away, several guys jumped a railing and sauntered toward Selah. Bodhi stood his ground at her side.

A guy wearing a beat-up, torn hat approached. "Hey, pretty lady, I haven't seen you at our market before. Where you been hiding?"

Bodhi moved to step between them, but Selah edged him out. She smiled at the guy. "I'm trying to find the Seekers—"

The guy's eyes went wide and he disappeared like he'd been scared by a bear. Selah watched him then turned to Bodhi. "Well, that went well. Was it something I said?"

"Have you lost your good sense? That guy could be dangerous!" Bodhi said.

Selah turned to take in the noise and the crowd. "Why? Because his hat was beat up? Look around this place. All these people look that way. This obviously is the working man's part of town. At least now we know that mentioning the Seekers generates fear."

"Well, pick a better working man to talk to." Bodhi glanced over the stalls they passed as though he were in a military operation.

"Please. We don't have time for niceties. They're all strangers, and I don't have time to misjudge more people like I did Brejian and the Keeper." Selah turned to look in Bodhi's eyes. "Besides, I know you're always there to watch my back."

Bodhi put a hand on the small of her back to guide her through the crowd.

Someone grabbed Bodhi's hand from her back and spun him around. A fist came at his face. Bodhi's heightened reflexes saw it coming in slow motion. He caught the man's fist and twisted it to the left. The man's wrist responded with a resounding snap, followed by a howl. Bodhi let go.

The man swung at Bodhi with his other hand. Bodhi blocked it and punched him in the gut with his left. A right uppercut to the man's jaw sent him sprawling to the ground.

The music pounded. *Where's Selah?*

Someone jumped on Bodhi's back. Solid, sturdy, male. Bodhi spun to shake him off and look for Selah. He wanted to yell for her, but the music blared too loud.

From behind, another man tackled him at the knees, and Bodhi crumpled to the ground. He tried to move but he was pinned. He struggled to raise up on his knees and elbows. For the first time, he noticed the sting on the back of his hand where he was first grabbed. A bloody dot.

A commotion surrounded Bodhi. The weight on him rolled off amid a flurry of furious kicking and yelling, and multiple hands lifted him. He felt light-headed. His sight faded. The music weaved in and out, filling his head.

Selah, where are you?

20

Selah quickly navigated at least twenty feet through the rushing, pushing crowd, feeling Bodhi's hand on her back. He pushed her faster past several questionable stalls where people reached out with their product. She didn't recognize what they offered. How did Bodhi know?

"I wonder if some of this stuff is legal. What was that he just offered me?" Selah frowned. That was the second time Bodhi didn't answer her question. When they first came in he said the music was too loud, but it didn't seem loud to her. Would it be fair to ask if he heard her?

Selah turned. Panic hit her. She stumbled and tried to turn back, but to where? Selah fought off a girl trying to turn her back in the direction they were traveling.

The girl continued to push her forward with a singular focus. "Keep moving or they'll catch up. You're not safe out here."

"Who are you? Where is Bodhi?" Selah tried to look back.

Why didn't Bodhi yell? Confusion, loud music, and the bad smell assaulted her senses.

"No time. Keep moving."

Her eyes darted around the crowd and back to the girl. "Wait. I know you. Burgundy . . . no, brown . . . no, beige. That's it! Your name is Beige. You met my Amaryllis."

The girl looked at her oddly and screwed up her lip. "Yes, my name is Baje. I know you must be Selah, but I don't know nobody named Amaryllis. We need to keep moving if you want to stay free." With both hands she gripped the material of the tactical suit at the small of Selah's back.

"Her nickname is Rylla. Stop, I have to go back for Bodhi." Selah tried to dodge the girl, who artfully recovered her subject with several sweeping hand moves.

"My brother will bring him, but you can't go back there. They will kill you." Baje grabbed Selah's hand and pulled her between two colorful rug dealers and down a narrow brick alleyway. They traveled down wide stairs and turned left, then right. Selah ran a hand over the rough wall to maintain her balance at the dizzying pace. The structures reminded her of the adobe buildings in the back of the Mountain where Mojica had led them out—sunbaked mud and straw bricks.

"I have to go back," Selah said. A door to the right of her opened and the girl pushed Selah in, closing it behind them.

Selah blinked several times to adjust her eyes to the dimmer light. A little boy with curly blond hair who had opened the door ran away with a pronounced limp. It looked as though his lower leg was trying to separate at the knee.

"Sit down and I'll get you something to drink while we

wait for them to bring your friend." Baje gestured to an area of large bright-colored pillows piled on intricately patterned thin rugs in the corner.

Baje walked the length of the long narrow room and disappeared to wherever the boy went—perhaps a kitchen. That was the first time Selah noticed the young girl also had a decided limp.

She watched the girl walk back. Baje's right leg was deformed at the knee. She handed Selah a cup sweating from a cold liquid. She smelled then tasted the liquid. The water, probably spring fed like at home, was wonderfully refreshing. The dome had sucked her moisture away and she hadn't realized how thirsty she'd become.

"May I have more?" Selah held out the cup.

The young girl bowed her head. Her long black hair collected around her shoulders as she took the cup from Selah and hurried off for a refill. Her walk made Selah curious. She didn't mean to stare, but she had never seen anyone with a deformed body part.

"What happened to your leg and that other boy's leg?" Selah drank from the second cup. Two people with the same defect raised a multitude of questions.

"I was born this way, like all the kids here." Baje sat beside Selah, fingering the material of Selah's tactical suit. The girl's clothes appeared to be a coarse, thin fabric printed in earth tones.

"What did your mother say happened?" Selah drank the rest and handed back the cup.

"I don't have a mother. We're the Outcast," Baje said. She sounded bitter.

"Who cares for you?" Selah glanced around the clean and orderly room.

"Nobody cares about orphans. We watch out for each other. I have my brother Tuere, and he takes care of our little brothers. They're helping him steal Bodhi from the Hunters," Baje said.

"Tour? Is that the boy who killed the boar in the meadow this morning?" Selah said. The boy she remembered didn't appear related to this girl.

"Yes, Tuere is the best hunter among us. We have enough meat saved for everyone all the way into spring," Baje said. "Too bad he won't be here for the next generation. Good hunters are hard to find. Our group is the best fed in a long time."

"Next generation? Is this an orphanage?" Selah was enchanted by this girl. Her demeanor was gentle and tough at the same time, much like Rylla's.

Baje made a face. "I don't know what an orphanage is, but this settlement is the place of Outcasts. There's a lady who watches over us till each one dies, then carts away the body."

Selah frowned. "Body? Why are you dying? Someone should be giving you medical care." It grieved her that children were so resolved to dying young. She instantly thought of the disease at Cleveland, but that didn't cause a physical defect.

"We have a DNA defect that limits our lifespan to sixteen years and gives us this strange knee, usually on the right side," Baje said.

"Isn't there a yearly pill or something that citizens get to bolster their immune system?" Selah thought of STORM but didn't know if other domes used the technology.

"I don't know. I've never been into the city. Outcasts aren't allowed," Baje said.

A commotion filled the doorway as three boys hauled a groggy Bodhi in and dumped his limp form on a pile of pillows next to Selah. She noticed they each had some form of the limp, but the boys were all different. The lanky pecan-colored boy had thick curly hair, a younger boy had reddish short hair and freckles, and the last boy looked to be of Asian parentage with stringy black hair and almond eyes. Selah was confused. Brothers?

Selah checked Bodhi over. "What happened to him? Did they hurt him?"

Tuere held up Bodhi's hand. "That pinhole there is a sure sign they stuck him with Twilight. He'll sleep it off in an hour or so. They almost had him."

"We outsmarted them all! They were big guys, grown men," the other two boys chimed in.

"Can you go find Rylla and Mari, and my two security people?" Selah stayed beside Bodhi, rubbing his hand.

Baje shook her head. "I can get Rylla and the lady." She motioned to the boys. They scrambled out the door. "But I don't want *no* trouble from *no*body, and if I bring your two security people in here, the other kids will throw us out. So no, we're not rounding them up."

"We've been in the dome for less than an hour. How could anyone know we're here?" Selah figured the Seekers weren't aware of her or they'd have contacted her right away like the Keepers.

"That's funny. You stick out like a hairy tare in a wheat field," Baje said. "The Seekers know you're inside. Those were their Hunters trying to grab you two."

Bodhi stirred. Selah leaned down to him. He fell quiet again.

Baje moved to check Bodhi's pulse. She also looked at his eyes and hand. "He's clearing nicely. He'll be awake soon."

Selah settled a bit, allowing her to concentrate on the girl's conversation. A tremor traveled across her chest. "Why would you think Seekers want to hurt us?"

Baje looked directly into Selah's eyes. "Because you're a novarium."

Fists banged at the front door. "Baje, open now!"

Baje dropped her chin to her chest and sighed. "Stop it! Don't disrespect me." She stormed to the door and threw it open. Three kids about her age tromped into the room. They did seem to be related to each other, with the same widow's peak in the front of their thick dark hair and the same square chin. Selah had seen twins before but never triplets.

Selah backed up on the pillows, shielding Bodhi in case there was trouble. She couldn't thrust in such close quarters or Baje might be injured.

"Why did you bring them here? We saw you save her," the first boy said. "And then your brother brought the other one, heaping more trouble on us."

"Let them have her and be done with it. It's none of our business," the second boy said.

"They're not like the others. They don't see us as Outcasts. Someone has got to stop the Hunters," Baje said.

"Who cares what happens among the normals? We don't want trouble," the third boy said as he lunged toward Baje.

Baje stumbled back in surprise, but Selah was ready. She charged forward. The three separated and two backed off to the doorway. The one remaining squared off with Selah.

"So you're a novarium. Let's see what you're made of." He moved forward with arms spread.

Selah spun and swept his legs. The boy crashed to the floor. Selah heard his two brothers snickering in the background. He tried to scramble to his feet, but she jumped on his back with one hand full of his hair and the other at his throat.

"I think you need to let me get my business done here, and we'll be gone," she said.

"Let Selah and her friends alone. They haven't come to hurt us," Baje said.

"You lie!" The first boy's face contorted with a hatred Selah had never seen in someone so young.

Selah let go of the boy's throat and backed off him. "You don't even know me," she said. "How am I lying?"

He struggled to get away and rise at the same time. "Because you novarium always say you're going to help, and not one has ever helped any generation of Outcasts."

"How do you know none have helped?" Selah returned to Bodhi's side.

"Because there would be no more Outcasts. We'd all be cured," Baje said.

The door opened and Tuere announced with a flourish of his arm, "Well, at least they didn't get very far."

Rylla and Mari entered and rushed to the corner. The three boys slipped out the door. Mari looked over Bodhi and asked Baje about the drug he'd been given while Rylla stood nearby talking to Tuere.

"I think we need to get out of this dome as soon as Bodhi wakes. This is dangerous, and we're not prepared for this hostile an environment," Mari said.

"Then buy some of the weapons I saw. I have to find the Seekers. We're stuck here till I do." Selah went back to rubbing Bodhi's hand. The mark had receded to a dot.

"That's a bad idea. The Hunters who tried to grab you work for the Seekers." Tuere looked at Rylla.

"Thank you for saving Bodhi," Rylla said to him. "Do we have to worry about them following us back to the transport?"

"Yes, but they don't dare go in our woods, so we'll take you that way," Tuere said.

"Wait a minute, you two. I'm not ready to leave." Selah stood up. She didn't know what to do with Mari and Rylla against her plan.

"I think the kids are right," Mari said. "We need to get you back where it's safe."

"No, it's not going to get any better. They'll still be chasing us tomorrow," Selah said. She turned to Baje. "Do you know anyone who might know how to find an honest Seeker? Just one. All I need is one."

Tuere and Baje both broke into laughter. The sound startled Bodhi and he jerked awake. His arms flailed until he opened his eyes and saw Selah. She helped him to sit upright and hugged him.

"Baje, may I have some water for Bodhi, please?" Selah saw the look Tuere gave Baje as she went off to the kitchen but figured it was sibling angst. She'd had her share of it back in Dominion. "Tuere, do you know anyone who can get me to a Seeker?"

"What happened to me?" Bodhi stood to test his legs.

Baje handed the water to Bodhi. "Hunters drugged you and tried to capture you. They do the dirty work for the Seekers."

Bodhi rubbed the back of his hand. "This is a lot different from Cleveland. We need to go back to the transport and come up with another plan. We don't know who to trust."

"No!" Selah stood. "I'm not leaving. I just told them the same thing. They'll still be chasing me tomorrow whether we have a plan or not. I need to find just one honest Seeker and we can get out of here."

"Pasha will not like this, nor will Mojica and Taraji," Bodhi said. He still seemed unsteady as he punched the comm link on his scrambler. Nothing happened.

"I tried that when we first got separated. They must have frequency scramblers inside the dome," Selah said.

Bodhi muttered under his breath. He swayed a little before regaining his footing.

"I'm not giving them a choice. I want this done. We need to be on our way," Selah said. The excitement had tired her, or maybe she just felt crushed that the Seekers were less than the caretakers they were bred to be.

"Contressa would know," Tuere said. "She would know if there was an honest Seeker."

Selah looked from Baje to Tuere. "Who's Contressa? How do I find her?"

Baje slapped Tuere on the shoulder. "I think you're more trouble than you're worth, little brother. How can you be sure Contressa wouldn't turn us in for Hunter bounty?"

Tuere hung his head. "She wouldn't do that to us."

Baje pointed a finger at him. "This is going to be on you if they throw us out."

"Well, your time is up in six months, so you won't have to worry about being on the streets. It will be me alone." Tuere turned away from Baje. Selah saw his tears. So young to not have a future. Her heart ached for them.

Rylla stepped between them. "You don't have much time left. Stop being mean." Her lip trembled. Selah wrapped an arm around her.

Bodhi sat back on the pillows looking confused. His eyes drooped. Selah was sure the Twilight hadn't worn off completely.

Baje softly told Tuere to find Contressa and bring her to the house.

"Did anyone find Mojica and Taraji?" Mari sat on the pillows next to Bodhi.

"We can't bring them in here. It might be better to meet them at the three-hour limit," Selah said.

"Whose idea was it to keep your security away?" Mari said to Baje.

"Not so much to keep them away from me but to keep them away from this location," Selah said.

Rylla stared at Mari like she had dished out an insult to her new friend. She looped her arm through Baje's and they walked outside.

"I don't think we should get heavy-handed with a bunch of kids," Selah said.

"They're not that much younger than you," Mari said. "This could be a trap to sell you themselves, like thieves stealing from thieves."

"They went to a lot of trouble to help us and find you. I don't think they'd have brought us together if they wanted to sell me off. They'd have kept us separated so we'd be easier to manage."

Mari agreed. "I just get overcritical when people offer to help after all the resistance we've encountered. Are these kids really alone?"

Rylla and Baje charged back into the room. "Tuere found Contressa. She's coming."

A tall, slender woman, Contressa had black hair with a section of white-blonde highlights that cascaded almost to her waist. Side clips held her hair back from her face and her almond-shaped dark eyes. She stepped into the room like a graceful swan. Selah immediately liked her body-speak.

"I hear we've been unfortunate enough to have made contact with a novarium," Contressa said. She didn't look the least apologetic for the comment as she defiantly faced down Selah.

Baje wrung her hands. "Ma'am . . . Contressa, these people—this girl . . . her name is Selah—"

"Can someone translate for this girl so I don't age a whole year waiting for the explanation?" Contressa appeared bored.

"I'm sorry. I'm trying to find the Seekers," Selah said. "Tuere thought maybe you could lead me to an honest one, preferably one who won't turn me over to Hunters."

Contressa smiled. "How can you be sure *I* won't turn you over to Hunters?"

Selah followed behind Contressa as she wove her way through the kitchen area and out the back door into a small enclosed garden of scraggly weeds and a few hardy perennials. Contressa led her to a stone table and benches.

"I brought you out here because the children don't need

to be involved. They wouldn't understand," Contressa said. She sat on the opposite side of the table and leaned forward with her elbows resting on the smooth stone.

"I'm not sure *I* understand," Selah said. "To start with, what's wrong with these kids, and how are they sisters and brothers when they look . . . so different?"

Contressa leaned back and tipped her head to the side. "You're the first one to ever ask about the children. They are all brothers and sisters because they have no one but the others afflicted like them. Why do you care?"

"That's a dumb question. When I see children who appear neglected I want to know why."

"I would think your first thought should be about avoiding capture," Contressa said.

"Forgive me for being different, but I've been chased for six months now. I'm getting used to being the target, so I don't always put myself first," Selah said.

"Fair enough. The children here have a DNA defect in an area that controls longevity and specific cellular growth affecting the knee joint. Because they only live sixteen years, they are disposable to this society," Contressa said.

Selah tensed at the word *longevity*. Reminders of the Mountain sucked the breath from her. She inhaled sharply. "DNA always leads back to me and my blood. Do they use STORM here?"

Contressa smiled wryly. "Yes, we get STORM here once a year, but it's degraded over time, and these kinds of defects show up when two people of a specific abnormality have offspring."

"So what are novarium used for in this dome?" Selah knew it had to be related to blood.

"We don't ask, we just sell your kind."

Selah jumped to her feet and moved quickly away from the table. She poised for a thrust.

Contressa never flinched. "Relax. Sit back down. If I'd wanted you caught, the kids would never have gotten close to saving you. But they've never saved one of you from Hunters before. This makes me curious about you."

Selah stared at her. The woman's passive body-speak indicated she was being truthful. She was not a present threat. Selah relaxed but stood her ground. "What are you offering?"

21

January 10

Selah sat at her transport navigator station watching Taraji and Bodhi working on a system overhaul. Nothing was going as it should. The only plan Selah had at the moment was no plan.

Bodhi looked up at her from the parts he was fusing. "You look far away. Do you feel well today?"

"I'm fine, I guess, but it's frustrating. We have no idea how long it will take to find enough parts to rebuild these propulsion systems, and—"

Bodhi set his jaw. "We're working as fast as we can, but needing to manufacture our own replacement parts has slowed the process."

"But yesterday, nothing got done at all. Everyone went off in their own direction." Selah refused to tell them about the changes she could feel, but at the same time they couldn't know her need for urgency. This slide was happening too fast.

"We didn't have parts! The merchant didn't get the silica spacers. We can't finish the port system without the material. We'll cut it ourselves, but we have to wait until we get the parts."

Taraji poked her head out of the cabinet space. "But Mojica and I did spend the day on business. We took another of Glade's stones in to be cut down to tradeable value size. I have to say I thought it was foolish to bring that bag of stones since back home they're useless and plentiful, but on this side of the mountain range they'll allow us a comfortable life for many years to come."

Selah calmed. Father again. *Thank you.* "I'm sorry I'm being crazy, and I know it's not your fault, but I can't yell at their invisible political system as easily as I can yell at you guys."

"We do realize that even if you got answers today, we wouldn't be ready to leave, but what is the holdup? Not being able to be involved in the negotiations makes me very nervous," Taraji said.

"I don't think there should be negotiations without me there," Pasha said as she entered the command deck with a tray of sandwiches and drinks.

Selah's stomach had forgotten it was lunchtime, but she didn't want to hear any more of Mother's words. "I'm sorry, but you're not going to be involved in anything in that evil place, especially because Dane would act out if you went and he didn't. And there is nothing in that place that I want him to see. It's bad enough Rylla—"

"All right! I give up. Who's the mother here?" Pasha set the tray down on the navigation console and raised her hands in surrender.

Selah bit her lip. She needed some air. She grabbed a sand-wich and walked to the ramp toward systems.

"Selah, don't go away mad," Pasha said.

"I'm not," Selah said. She muttered the rest in her head.

Selah drove the Wheeler through the woods to the dome. The kids had showed her how to get closer, but it only worked if she borrowed a horse. This noisy, petrol-powered three-wheeler had to be left in the woods to be hidden.

She walked the rest of the way. She felt a little safer with the gun strapped to her side and the long knife across her back. It reminded her of the one she'd found at Rylla's.

Three men near the dome checkpoint alerted one another as they saw Selah coming. There should have been at least one of Contressa's people nearby as a safety, but she didn't see anyone.

Selah hadn't been feeling enough energy to use a thrust, so hand combat or the old-fashioned weapons not affected by magnetism were now her choices.

The three lined up close together in her path.

Selah stopped in front of them, but not close enough to be grabbed without a fight. "Do you want something?"

"We want to know why we shouldn't just grab you and sell you to the highest bidder." The first scruffy guy was short and dirty, maybe a mine worker.

Selah rested her hand on the Remington in her holster. "Because I'm under Contressa's protection."

The three men put their heads together. Selah caught their body-speak right away. They weren't ready to harm her, just shake her down for the stones they'd probably heard about.

The three faced her again. Off to the right, Baje came charging from the dome. Her bad leg slowed her steps, but her voice commanded attention. "You three need to go harass another entrance into the dome. Contressa will hear about this."

The men looked fearful of the declaration and scurried off, and Selah strode to the girl. "Thanks. You saved me again." Selah wrapped an arm around Baje, who blushed but clung to Selah's side.

"I'm late or this would never have happened. I was coming to your transport. Contressa has news." Baje headed back in toward the main area of Contressa's holdings.

Like Cleveland's, the Chicago dome was divided into degrees of territory. Contressa's holdings consisted of fifteen degrees of the outer commerce ring, including one of the twelve entrances into the dome and the market. Selah had resigned herself to dealing with this mobster, but only because the hardened woman had a soft spot for disabled children.

Tuere came scampering out of the entrance. "Where's Rylla? I promised her a bow lesson."

Selah offered him a hug. He allowed it but seemed as reluctant as Dane usually did.

"Not today. I may bring her in tomorrow. She's been behind in her studies." Rylla and Dane had spent so much time reading the Stone Braide Chronicles that very little other work was accomplished, and now real school needed its due.

"I'm glad we don't have to study," Tuere said. "But sometimes I wish I had time to use the stuff I do learn." His eyes held momentary sadness.

Selah was grateful Contressa gave the Outcast children a place to be sheltered for their short lifespans. She pulled her lips tight, trying not to cry. Wet eyes were never a positive negotiating point unless the object was sympathy, and today there would be none of that. These kids needed a chance to live. She hadn't discussed her decision with anyone because she couldn't take hearing any more voices giving her advice.

She walked casually with the children. Now that she was inside she had no fear of attack. The merchants knew her as someone under the boss's protection. No one tried to hawk their wares as they passed.

Selah knocked on the door and it opened. A young girl with a limp closed it and shuffled away to another room. Contressa sat off to the right of the door in a courtyard terrace that looked out on an impressive garden with a pond and waterfall.

Selah strolled over to the circular table. "You have news?"

Contressa looked up from her bowl of soup. "Well, hello to you too. Such a pleasant day—"

"Listen, you didn't call me here to wish me a good day. What news do you have?"

Contressa laid down her spoon. "Here's the way it works. The Outcasts are considered to be a blight on our society. Their plight has caught the attention of a group of do-gooders looking for a cause. They think these children should get better care through the dome government like other citizens. The group is an active and strong political voice in the Chicago dome, and any Seeker who gets their endorsement is a good contender to win the seat to run the dome government."

"I still don't see where I come in," Selah said.

"There is a particular Seeker who would covet the endorsement from this do-gooder group. The Seeker could be convinced to tell the novarium the truthful answers to her questions, including wherever you're supposed to go from here." Contressa picked up her spoon and resumed sipping the soup.

Selah hated when people talked around her questions. "You still didn't answer my question of where I come in."

"I told you the Seeker will give you any answer you're looking for."

Selah pounded her fist on the woman's table. The soup bowl jumped. "Stop playing with the needle and get to the point. What do you want from me?"

Contressa sat back in the fluffy cushion of her chair. "I don't want anything from you."

Selah's eyes narrowed. "I don't understand. How can you get a whole political group to endorse the Seeker? How does that happen? It must cost something."

Contressa looked bored. "I own the group."

Selah's mouth fell open. "I probably don't want to know anymore, except why you are doing this for me."

A smile crept across Contressa's mouth. "Because of the children. Even though they're not mine, I do love every one of them for their short lifespans, and my Tuere is infatuated with your Rylla. Baje thinks the sun rises in your eyes. So it's for my children. Besides, with a Seeker in my pocket I'll have more dome clout without needing to play the game."

"I haven't been to the interior of this dome. In the Cleveland dome we spent the majority of our time in the interior and took only a brief trip to the wharf, which was in this outer diameter. What's it like here? I mean, since you call politics a game."

"This dome went to the dark side so many generations ago that now it is the norm. That's why their moral code allows them to throw away these children."

"Why aren't you bargaining for my blood like everybody else?"

"Because my kids like you as you are. Excuse me for speaking so frankly, but the others captured were only bought and sold to profit the rich and elite in the dome. Any lasting effects would never be passed to the common masses. Besides, I think it is a rather ghoulish practice to drain a living person of their blood to make money or extend your own life." Contressa furrowed her brow. "I do have standards and that's not one of them."

That complicated any thought Selah had of giving plasma and the cure code to the dome for the STORM project, but she still ached for the children.

"Do you know how many novarium made it out of here?"

Contressa looked off toward a large red rhododendron bush that looked the size of a tree.

"Contressa?"

"Go to that tree next to the rhododendron and count the marks," Contressa said.

Selah, hesitant at first, approached faster as she saw the notches extended under the foliage. "Twenty-nine. There are twenty-nine marks."

"There have been a total of thirty-nine who have come through here during the life of the dome. Nine got to leave here, twenty-nine were captured," Contressa said.

"Where's the other one?"

"That's you and yet to be determined."

Selah's shoulders felt a little looser. "How soon can it happen?"

"I'll let you know. It may take a while, but I hear tell in the market that you've got a big job going on out there. You've been real lucky so far the snow has held off."

February 4

Selah had cabin crazies, the kids had cabin crazies, and in general the whole group was on edge. They'd been trapped by three snowstorms in two weeks' time that had left the transport surrounded by five feet of snow, and with the wind and cold weather it refused to melt. For hours Selah would sit staring out the front shield, willing the snow to melt . . . but it was still there.

"I wondered where you went," Taraji said. She slid into her command seat and swiveled to face Selah, who had taken up residence in Bodhi's chair.

Selah turned her eyes in Taraji's direction but didn't turn the seat. "Was there any question that I was still on board?" She had lost an incremental amount of energy since this time last month, and she was no longer able to thrust.

"Guess not. I was just wanting to talk with you. We haven't had a good discussion since . . . well, since Brejian died."

"I wanted to talk to you about her. Did you always trust her?" Selah swiveled to face Taraji.

Taraji furrowed her brow. "Yes, of course I did. We three originally came from the Cleveland dome together, but then we separated. Mojica went to the Mountain, I went to Tic-

City, and Brejian traveled with the Keepers of the Stone until the last died, then she came to TicCity also."

Selah sat up. "Keepers of the Stone? That's what Treva's parents were. They died less than twenty years ago."

"That's the time frame in which Brejian came to TicCity."

"It's funny how so many people can be interconnected and not even know it, and how so many can be directly connected to Brejian," Selah said. "Like the ones who will live on in Cleveland because she verified that breakthrough cure with my plasma."

"Well, that's what I wanted to discuss with you," Taraji said.

Selah smiled softly. "Good, two minds with one thought."

Taraji lowered her chin but raised her eyes, giving her a sinister look. "What are we talking about?"

"I want to give a plasma treatment to Contressa for the kids," Selah said.

Taraji bolted from her seat. "No! Absolutely not! You can't do that anymore."

Selah flinched. She had expected Taraji to be an ally. "What's the matter? It wouldn't be that much. I've gone over the data a dozen times since we've been snowed in. With the formula Brejian provided, we can create an inoculation that can cure the defect no matter the stage."

"Are they forcing you to do this? What are they holding over you?" Taraji was visibly upset. "Is this their price to find a Seeker?"

"No, I promise they're not asking for this. They don't even know about it. I was going to wait until we were ready to leave before giving it to Contressa. She's helping because she loves those kids and the kids have taken to us."

"I'm sorry I misjudged them, but it's still not a good idea for you to do this," Taraji said.

"I'm swearing you to secrecy. I'm going to do this, and you can't say a word about it to another person on this transport."

Taraji leaned forward in her seat and ran a hand across her forehead. "You can't give away any more samples of your blood."

"I think I'm the one who gets to decide that." Selah felt her anger rising.

Taraji looked out the front shield and sighed. "I finally had some free time to go through the data crystals Brejian gave me the morning before she died. One of them is a long letter of apology to me, Mojica, and you for deceiving us."

Selah frowned. "What did she lie about?"

"It was more a lie of omission. She 'forgot' to tell us that the large plasma sample, in addition to what they took from you in the Mountain, shortened your lifespan considerably. You're not going to make a year."

Selah felt adrenaline course through her body, then shakes that quivered even her fingers. "When will I die? How much time did it take?"

Taraji shook her head. "No one knows how much they took out of you in the Mountain. Brejian apologized for taking a month of your life, but she said she couldn't apologize for saving people who had dedicated their lives to you."

Selah gulped for air. She couldn't force her lungs open. She felt the life squeezing from her a breath at a time. "Is there anything we can measure, anything at all? I could drop over right here in the snow." Her mind raced.

"I only had time to go through the crystals once. We've

been full speed on the retrofit. We picked up supplies right before the snow started, so we've had plenty to do. We only need one more load of piping and parts, and we can be done in two weeks."

"The sooner, the better." Selah needed an answer from Contressa. Had the Seeker agreed? She needed that next station so they knew what direction to go.

Taraji stood to leave. "I'm glad you understand why you can't give any more of your blood away."

Selah understood. She just wasn't listening. "And you understand this whole conversation was just between you and me and no one else."

Taraji nodded and started to walk away. She stopped and turned back. "I do remember one thing Brejian was sure of. The length of time from the beginning that you picked up skills, you will lose them in reverse order." She walked down the ramp to systems.

Selah gripped the chair arms. She'd gained the thrust in September and lost it sometime in January.

When was it first gone?

22

Selah traveled across the bright white snow, wrapped in an animal skin coat, gloves, and dark goggles to prevent snow blindness. The snowshoes Baje brought out to the transport had caused her hesitation at first. It would take a lot of energy walking that far. Hopefully there'd be an easier way back like something drivable on snow.

"Are you feeling all right?" Baje walked close to Selah as they trudged the path she'd created on the way out to the transport.

Selah didn't feel well, but she knew Baje would tell Rylla at the first opportunity, so she pasted on a smile. "I'm using muscles that I really have no reason to need other than doing this in the winter." She laughed.

They plodded onto the entrance pad for the dome. It radiated heat, causing the snow to recede from the area, and allowed the market to be back in business. Whereas in Cleveland everyone lived inside the dome with no settlements around it, here at the Chicago dome there were small settlements spread around outside, and areas that outsiders could visit inside the dome, like Contressa's holdings. But there were no ways for them to enter the actual city.

Baje helped Selah from the snowshoes. She was happy to stand still for a few minutes and regain her breath. She slipped from the coat and felt a hundred pounds lighter. Her strength slowly returned. "Is there water to drink out here?" Selah felt her throat sticking.

Baje looked sheepish. "Not out here, but Contressa will have water for you." She pulled Selah by the hand to Contressa's and opened the door. "I'm back!" she yelled. "How's that for fast?"

No answer.

Baje started to yell again, but Contressa came around the corner from her garden. "Stop bellowing, child, I heard you the first time."

The room faded in and out. Contressa touched Selah's arm and spoke, but it was as though hands covered her ears. All that reached her were muffled noises, then the sounds all whooshed back.

"Baje, help Selah to the couch." Contressa hurried to put down her shears and flower bunch.

"She asked me for water when we first came inside," Baje said.

"I took my card from the flow. Here, put it back in and bring her a cup. She must have gotten dehydrated in the snow wind." Contressa sat beside Selah, rubbing her hand.

Selah understood and could see, but she could barely breathe.

Her chest rose and fell but her limbs refused to move. First her fingers twitched, then stretched. Next, the nerves tingled in her legs and sensation returned.

By the time Baje brought the water, Selah was able to hold it herself. She drank it down and asked for more. Contressa nodded and Baje rushed to get another cup.

Selah straightened. Her full senses returned. "I'm sorry. I don't know what happened." She feared these were probably symptoms of her winding down.

Baje returned with the cup.

"Thank you, Baje. You may leave now. I will call you when Selah would like to return to the outdoors," Contressa said. The girl nodded and hurried away.

"I have a couple developments for you," Contressa said to Selah as the front door closed.

"I've been hoping. The repairs are almost complete on the transport. We could leave in two weeks."

"Well, let's hope this Seeker has enough sense to help you. I will have you escorted to him, but first . . ." Contressa held up a small wafer. "I want to tag you for your own safety. I'm sure nothing will happen to you while you're away from my holdings, but just in case something unexpected comes up, I want to be able to find you."

"I agree," Selah said. She felt even more anxious at the thought that there could be trouble while she was with the Seeker. Visiting the Keeper had always made her feel safe.

Contressa tucked the wafer into the fold of Selah's top and pressed the spot flat with her fingers. "I've got another surprise for you. I think we've jammed the city signal to be able to communicate with your transport. Try your communicator."

Selah tapped the ComLink on her scrambler. Mari answered. "Hey, little sister. Are you still outside? What's taking you so long to get to the dome?"

Selah laughed. "I'm inside the dome. We have free line communications with Contressa's holdings. You can link with the merchants we need parts from. I'll pay them and they can snowshoe or sled the orders out to the transport. Just please don't let any of them inside. Talk later. Bye." Selah hung up before Mari could ask too many questions and find out that Selah was leaving the holdings without anyone or anything except a tracking device.

Selah walked in the bright daylight with Contressa through several back areas clogged with haphazard piles of barrels and stacked containers, always with an outside curve to their right . . . and a hum. There were physical barriers to prevent coming in contact with the dome, but Selah could feel the dome's vibration as though it were alive. "How far do we have to go?"

"The next holdings on this outer dome ring are the wharf areas of Lake Michigan. The entrance to the city ring is just up ahead," Contressa said.

Selah liked walking close to the static energy hum. It seemed to give her energy. "I find it odd that two domes were built on huge lakes. Is there much water commerce?"

"I stay away from the wharf area. Strange things are known to go on there." Contressa looked visibly shaken by the question. Her steps took on new urgency. Selah had to make an effort to keep up.

Selah grabbed her arm to slow her down. "Okay, I won't ask any more questions about the wharf." She tried to catch her breath, but the exertion coupled with the constant smell worked to keep her off balance. "How come there's no tele-port systems? Don't they use the technology in this dome?"

"There are in the city, but not out here on the fringe. It wouldn't matter anyhow. A Seeker would never transport a stranger to their chamber, not even a novarium."

"This is all contradictory to what I experienced in Cleve-land. Has a—"

Selah stopped. In front of them, a container system sat emblazoned with a sword and lightning bolt three feet tall. She had almost forgotten this was their original home.

"What's the matter? Are you feeling ill again?" Contressa slowed and returned to Selah's side.

"No, I'm fine. It's that symbol." Selah pointed a shaky finger.

Contressa made a face. "That was a long time ago. It means nothing now." She pushed up her sleeve, revealing the same tattoo extending to her shoulder.

Selah backed away. Fear churned in her stomach. The trap had finally showed up.

Contressa let her sleeve drop and chuckled. "You look like you've seen a ghost."

"I've been chased by Blood Hunters and that symbol for six months. How do you expect me to react?"

"That was your world, not mine. No one uses the term *Blood Hunters* anymore. It's derogatory. They're just Hunters now, and novarium are so few and far between that they've almost become a joke."

Selah tensed. "Killing novarium is *not* a joke."

"The novarium who've come through here are anything but docile. They've caused just as much death and confusion. There are Seekers who've survived their attacks."

Selah was trying to remember the directions they were turning in case she had to find her own way back. "Novarium have tried to hurt Seekers?"

"Yes, actually, there is recorded history in the dome of three different novarium who killed Seekers."

"Excuse me if I don't believe you, but what would cause something so outrageous? My father never gave me any reason to believe novarium were dangerous or combative."

"Maybe they didn't like the answers they got." Contressa stopped at a stone gate and ran her hand over a shiny black circle in the right side of the wall.

The gate shifted to the left, and a woman walked a flat stone path to the opening. She wore a long brown robe with a white sash and a wide hood that rested on the crown of her head, making her look mysterious. "I am an Oracle of the Seeker. You will accompany me to his chamber." The woman bowed at the waist and stepped back from the opening.

Selah looked into her eyes before the hood obscured them. She sensed nothing. The person in front of her was a black void. Selah backed up, arm out to move Contressa back with her.

"Selah, what's the matter? It's extremely rude to treat an Oracle in this manner," Contressa said, trying to push Selah's arm away.

"She's not being honest. I don't know if she's the real Oracle or just corrupt, but walking away with this woman would be a death sentence," Selah said.

The woman spoke. "You will accompany me—"

"Now hold on. Selah has some concerns and you're ignoring them." Contressa put her hand to her sidearm.

"You will stay out of this. You are not the novarium," the Oracle said.

"I don't like your attitude. Do you know who I am?" Contressa said.

Selah could feel danger building in the Oracle. She reached for Contressa's arm to pull her away. At the same moment the Oracle pulled a long sword from the folds of her robe and lashed out.

Selah dodged the flashing steel, and Contressa delivered a blow to the woman's head with the butt of her sidearm. The woman slumped to the ground.

Contressa stood over her. "Can you believe this? In my own holdings, I am attacked by a useless sword-wielding woman! In my own holdings!"

Selah looked down. "I don't think that's a woman." She felt a power surge building. It was close. It was . . . Selah grabbed Contressa's hand. "Run! Now!" She kept a grip on Contressa until she ran on her own. They stopped and turned.

"Why did I just run away from an unconscious woman?" Contressa looked back up the lane where the body was draped across the threshold to the other area.

Selah held up her hand. "Wait for it."

The body exploded. Smoke drifted up from the remaining pile of little gears, circuits, and petri dish slabs of skin littering the ground. A greenish film covered every surface for twenty feet around the blast.

"How did you know she wasn't real?" Contressa led Selah away. "Have you dealt with these before? We have a segment of society that thinks they'll be the next wave of domestic help."

"I've heard of them but never seen one. It was more in what

I couldn't feel. I couldn't feel its intentions, and every human being has intentions." She was right this time, but she still worried that her abilities were fading. It had been hard in the Cleveland dome to read the body-speak of those around her.

She hurried beside Contressa back to her quarters. They monitored everyone who passed, watchful of another prong to the attack. "Besides, it was really old technology and I could hear her gears grinding."

Contressa stopped and stared at Selah as she passed into the room. "Your take is so simplistic. You make me smile." She shut the door. "I'm going to hurt a Seeker if I find out I've been duped into presenting them with a novarium." She picked up a communicator, fingered a code, then turned away from Selah. She paced in fast circles and spoke loud enough for the whole dome to hear.

Selah lowered slowly to the couch to be sure she had at least that much control of her knees. The adrenaline had worn off and her body was having trouble processing the recuperation. She needed water. Her forehead started to sweat. She wiped it with the back of her hand and leaned back into the cushions. The room weaved in and out.

"Looks like a fight among Seekers or Oracles, or both," Contressa said to her. "Who knows. Anyhow, a real Oracle has been killed in addition to that robot. The Seeker has consented to allow me to bring you to him, then return to retrieve you at the end of your session. It will be all day tomorrow. This is your only chance to talk to him." She shook her head. "They've gotten all kinds of nervous, and I think this is the beginning of a new time of troubles in here. I want to get you in and out of this dome while you can still make it. We'll start early."

Selah's relief evaporated. If she had to make the trip to the transport and then back here in the morning, she might not be in any condition to meet the man. She couldn't mess up this one chance. "I think I should stay in the dome tonight so I can get an early start. Is there a place that can accommodate me? I'd be glad to pay. I came prepared to pay for any of our parts that arrived."

"Please be my guest here. This is only a symbol of my presence in my holdings. I actually live in the city. I'll leave my water card—"

"What's a water card? Are you denied basic drinking water?"

"No, we're not denied. Clean water costs money. People from the city used to come out here and steal the water so they didn't have to pay for usage there. Now water out here is measured by the cup. So you pay for exactly what you use."

"But the children? Surely they get free water. Can't you melt the snow for that?" Selah felt sick, remembering how much of their water she and Bodhi had drunk.

"No, melted snow has a very metallic taste. The children get cards for two cups a day for the week, and when it's gone they go outside the dome and drink from the stream or wait till the next week for a new card," Contressa said.

Selah was horrified. She'd cost the children two days' water. Tears pooled and she blinked them back. "Can Baje and Tuere spend time with me?"

"I think that would be fine. They both have rooms here because they help me often. You can take my room. There's bread and fruit in the kitchen, and some winter vegetables like carrots and potatoes in the pantry if you prefer."

Contressa talked to several people by comm, sent a message

to the children, then turned to Selah. "You'd better call the transport before we close the energy loop down for the night, and it would be a prudent idea if they ordered anything else you might need. I think this new diversion is going to shut down your parts pipeline. Merchants will take payment from anyone, but no one wants to get in the middle of another war. There's already talk that you're the ones responsible for the dead Oracle."

"We didn't have anything to do with a killing," Selah said.

"Do you think you could convince a raging, angry mob of that?"

Selah frowned. Their window of safety was rapidly closing, but she had to stay overnight. Her body couldn't make another trip through all that snow. She knew Bodhi was going to be leading a chorus of protests about that.

She fingered the scrambler and in her head begged her mother to be the one to pick up. The call connected. Bodhi's mellow, husky voice said hello. Selah tried to remain upbeat. "Hi, Bodhi, we ran into a little difficulty, and I'm going to stay overnight so I can hit the problem fresh in the morning." Selah squeezed her eyes shut, waiting for the explosion.

"Okay, if that's what it takes. What was the problem?" Bodhi asked calmly.

Selah's eyes opened. She stared at her scrambler.

"Selah?"

"Oh, I'm sorry, I was looking for something. The Oracle of the Seeker I was supposed to meet turned out to be a robot. It was programed to self-destruct and I'm assuming I was the target. But luckily, I heard the gears and got away in time."

"Be careful, Selah. You know I love you, right?"

Selah blinked a couple times. "Yes, I know you love me. Good night." She disconnected. What was that all about? No arguments. Not a single chastisement. Selah figured Taraji had told him about her shortened time as soon as she'd left.

The front door opened and the two laughing children poured in.

"Have a great night, you three. Baje, you know where the food is, and my card is in the flow," Contressa said. She waved and departed.

"We really get to spend the whole night having a party with you, and the other kids can't even say anything since it's at Contressa's," Baje said.

"Speaking of water cards, young lady," Selah said, "why didn't you tell me that each cup of water you gave us cost you?"

Baje looked at her innocently. "You're the novarium. We should give you our best. When you're changed, we all will be changed."

Tears fell from Selah's eyes. Baje wrapped her arms around Selah and laid her head on her shoulder. Tuere pretended reluctance but joined their hugging party. His lanky little body was underweight for thirteen years. And Baje at fifteen and a half had just six months of life before her heart would decide it was time to stop.

Selah hugged both kids and cried for herself and for them. She didn't believe she would make it now. She had to help them regardless of the cost.

February 11

Selah and Contressa walked the same cluttered road as yesterday. They weren't expecting more trouble, but both women remained highly aware and vigilant of their surroundings. This time when the gate slid open a wizened old man with soft eyes and a white beard like cotton greeted them. Selah wondered what made Seekers and Keepers the guardians of these domes.

With hands crossed in front of him and a nod of greeting, he led them along the trimmed path to a stone cottage. As they approached Selah saw a much larger building attached to the cottage, but it was hidden by a rolling fog bank.

"Are you the Seeker?" Selah asked as she strolled behind him, taking in the garden landscape. She saw an apple and a pear tree with full-sized fruit.

"You're not supposed to talk to him until spoken to," Contressa said. She looked fearful that Selah had spoken.

Curious. For all her bravado, Contressa seemed just as impressed with the Seeker's position as the ordinary people. Selah decided her own personal relationship with the Keeper had probably been beyond the norm for his position.

"It is acceptable for the novarium to speak directly to me," the Seeker said. He led them into the small cottage with a stone fireplace and two overstuffed chairs, then turned to address Contressa. "As you can see there is only room for two of us. I would ask if you would kindly sit outside so I may confer with the novarium in private."

Selah was embarrassed at Contressa's dismissal, but the woman readily accepted the fate and seemed to hear nothing but that a Seeker was addressing her. She quickly exited with a smile.

"You are nothing like the Keeper in the Cleveland dome." Selah took the chair on the right of the fireplace.

"Is that a good thing or a bad thing?" The Seeker lifted a tray from the side table and set it between them on the hearth. He sat in his chair and reached to pour the steaming drink into cups.

"Don't know and don't particularly care," Selah said. "Seekers have been hostile to me in this dome. I just want to be out of here and on my way. But where do I go? What is the next point to the Third Protocol? I must leave quickly because I've made several mistakes that have cost me time."

The Seeker lowered his head then looked at the fire. "Then you must leave as soon as I tell you because you can't linger here after that final revelation. But I suspect, unlike some of the more self-absorbed, you want answers to other questions as building blocks for your future. If you choose wisely, the answers I give could have long-reaching implications."

Selah tensed. Her eyes darted around the room, looking for listening or video devices. She understood his body-speak and it made her mind race. He was trying to give her more information than he was allowed to offer, but he was not prevented from answering truthfully when asked.

"Then let's save my destination until the end of the day." Selah sat back in the seat to get comfortable. "What am I? What *is* a novarium?"

The Seeker stared at her. She squirmed, then reached for the cup he'd poured her and smelled it. The same blend as the Keeper. She took a few sips. "You haven't answered me."

"I'm trying to decide what to say."

"How about the truth."

"It's not that easy."

Selah slammed the cup in its saucer and leaned forward, her eyes reduced to slits. "Do you think being me is easy?"

The Seeker recoiled, sitting up straight and pulling his feet under his chair.

She decided to ease off the mad eyes. Her head hurt and caused a throbbing behind her eyes. "I've been chased since the moment I transitioned. No peace, no happiness, and *no* choice!" Selah stared down the Seeker. "I deserve the truth. I've earned it." The throbbing subsided.

"Fair enough. What are you? I don't know. We were never deep enough in the project to get that level of information. I know it's something with your DNA, but in the dome we've never had the level of expertise or equipment development to go much further."

"You're lying!" Selah stood and paced in front of the fireplace. The roaring fire was beautiful and hypnotic, but there was no heat coming from it—just another dome illusion. "You have dome technology, which is highly advanced."

"Ah, but we didn't create or build the technology and have no way of replicating it. We can program fixes for any non-functioning systems from here. The system runs a diagnostic and repairs itself," the Seeker said.

"What do you mean 'from here'?"

The Seeker gave a half smile. "You saw the building when the fog bank glitched."

Selah smiled. Observant man. "If this is the control room, where's the room generating the dome?"

"We don't know, but it's not inside this dome."

Selah thought about that for a second. "The technology used to run these two domes is the same technology that runs the Mountain. Their generator was underground—maybe yours is also."

The Seeker's body-speak relaxed. "Thank you for that suggestion. I'm not sure we have the motivation to seek it out now. We all transferred from the Mountain, so it makes sense they used the technology at the home base. As you can see we're limited by circumstance on the knowledge we have available. New discoveries take time and resources we just don't have."

"Then tell me about STORM. You can't say you don't know about that. It extends the lives in both domes, and somehow both domes have succeeded in messing it up."

The Seeker sat back. "Nobody's asked about that relationship in a long time. STORM was never meant to be permanent. It was just supposed to be used for the first phase of the testing."

"What kind of testing?"

"They never told us. It was above our pay grades back in that day, but the whole thing was a need-to-know project for DARPA," the Seeker said.

"What is DARPA?"

The Seeker gave a grin that turned into a smile, then he broke out in real laughter. Selah felt uncomfortable watching the man laugh. It struck her as more scary than funny.

"I don't remember after all these years. We had acronyms for everything back then, a real alphabet soup of government offices. It had something to do with defense. None of us remember much." The Seeker stared at the crackling fire. "But that's what we signed on for."

"But STORM wasn't a defense project. It keeps people healthy, and that lets them live longer," Selah said.

The Seeker nodded. "Extreme health was the object of the testing. The longevity came as a bonus many have tried to duplicate. That's why so many fools have sought your blood."

Selah felt her temper rise. "So if they were fools, why didn't you tell them to stop killing novarium?"

"Because it was useful for the correct reason."

"Excuse me, the *correct* reason? There is a correct reason that you should be able to have me killed for my blood?"

The Seeker paled. "I didn't mean to sound callous, but when it's for the good of many people's health I consider it the correct reason—one sacrifice for the many."

"How about if the *many* meant every one of us everywhere? If this process had been completed, then all of us would have been changed instead of just the few in this dome benefiting."

"We only care about the dome. This is the world we are charged with protecting."

"Don't you understand how insane it sounds that you care only for *your* people? Your people are not the whole dome. They consist of the wealthy and elite who are willing to pay to be healthy—those who can pay your inflated prices. You leave the rest of the city to wither." Selah jumped to her feet. "Contressa's holdings are right below here. You and your rotten government throw away children who have broken DNA that you could fix, but you sentence them to death at sixteen years when they should be learning to live. You're evil!" Selah moved away from the heatless flames. It was no longer pleasant to sit with this man.

"Those defectives are a drain on society. All they'll do is breed more defects. Yet there are those who choose to help them and make their last days brighter. It's not my problem."

"But they are children! You adults made the problem. It shouldn't be the children who have to pay for your mistakes," Selah said. She couldn't get much angrier without ruining her chance of getting information about the next station. Would the Seeker hold back if he got angry?

"Are you novarium intentionally left this much in the dark? Or has that just developed over time? STORM was the first phase of the project, and you were the second phase. The Third Protocol is combining you with the original source of STORM."

Lightning stabbed at Selah's brain as his words bounced back and forth in her head. She squeezed her eyes shut and willed herself the strength to breathe. She had to answer or he'd notice. "So we're back to me. What am I?"

The Seeker shrugged. "A lot of the projects we worked on in those days had multiple applications, and we never knew what any of it was for. We just liked the money and notoriety. Our section won patents five years in a row. The excellence award became our brand." The Seeker pushed up the sleeve of his robe to expose the sword and lightning bolt.

Selah's breath returned in time for her to look at that symbol of hate. It pumped up her heart rate. "Why did the Blood Hunters come about? You've changed the name here to be more palatable, but on the other side of the mountains they're chasing novarium and draining their blood."

"It's such a stupid and wasteful quest. The DNA in your

blood remains alive outside your body for only one hour. From the reports of the first Blood Hunters to return through the Mountain pass, it appears that over time they lost the notation that novarium samples are only viable for an hour. Most of their facilities and those they sold blood to were far too inept to ever have anything but limited success. Now that they've been here, the next 150-year cycle will be different."

Selah looked at the floor. "I can see you expect me to fail also. Thank you for that gratifying lack of confidence, but this has got to end with me."

The Seeker shook his head. "It was never supposed to be this way. It was just a friendly rivalry between development teams, and then the Sorrows happened. I never dreamed I'd live to see the end of a complete cycle."

Selah straightened. "Have Blood Hunters from my side of the mountains been here?"

"Yes, they came in early December, another clan returning to their roots since the pass is open. These were Kingstons from Waterside, Virginia."

Selah forgot to breathe for a second. How was it even possible for them to get here? She stopped to think about Jericho and her almost wedding . . . for about two seconds. They had come through the pass. Others would too. "I'm ready to leave now. Tell me where I'm to go."

The Seeker raised an eyebrow. "Was it something I said?" He paused then raised his head. "Ah yes. Let's see. You are the last novarium in the cycle, so that makes you Glade Rishon's kid, and that set placement was in Dominion. The Kingstons are from Waterside. I get it. And I do wish you well, whatever happens."

Selah held up a hand. "Wait! What do you mean by 'set placement'?"

"The original plan had a protocol for specific groups of paintings to be distributed along predefined routes. We had them mass-produced in New Jersey. I even delivered some paintings personally, but I never got as far south as Dominion," the Seeker said.

Selah looked at him, waiting for more. Nothing came. "So what was the purpose of the paintings?"

"Don't know. I never got to ask, or if I did, it was part of the memory wipe before we were let go. About a hundred years ago I found documents I had left here on one of my trips back to Washington. It did give me a little info to add to the pile of what we discovered. All I remember about that group was that the titles were an anagram for the Space Needle."

"What's that?"

"Don't know that either." He pushed a lever on the arm of his chair, and three guards emerged from around the wall. One held the door open. Selah was glad she hadn't let her temper get away from her. They might have appeared and tackled her.

She raised her hands. "Well . . . next destination, please."

The Seeker stood up and straightened his robe. He crossed his hands in front of him.

The guards moved closer. The Seeker took a deep breath. "There is no more."

Selah tipped her head and looked at him. "I'm waiting for the punch line. This *is* a joke, right?" She shivered, remembering the Keeper had told her this exact thing when she was leaving his dome. After all they'd been through in Cleveland, she had been afraid to believe the Keeper, but now to hear the same thing from this new stranger . . . The reality stung.

"That is why the guards are here. Three of your novarium didn't take kindly to being told there was no more, and they killed the Seeker who delivered that message."

Selah moved toward him, but a guard blocked her way. She slumped to her seat. What was she supposed to tell her family?

"Why is there no more? How do the clues just stop?"

"Cleveland and Chicago were the only two domes to go with the new technology. The rest kept putting it off, and then the Sorrows happened. The dramatic upheaval of Yellowstone changed the magnetism in this part of the country, and the first time there were solar flares, the intense pressure and rapid polarity changes blew up the other domes like fireworks."

Selah rocked back and forth. There had to be something. "Give me anything. A place. A direction."

The Seeker looked her in the eyes. "North and Milwaukee were where I sent the other novarium. But there are no domes there anymore, and I have little on the indigent population."

The closest guard laughed. "Yes, *little* is the operative word."

The Seeker threw him a dirty look, and the guard straightened up.

Selah looked between them. "Is there something I'm missing?" They seemed to be sharing a secret.

The Seeker smirked. "You may run into some small problems once you leave this jurisdiction."

"Then why go north? What about traveling south?"

The Seeker sat back in his chair and shook his head. "There's nothing to the south, not even vegetation. It was all destroyed by the magnetic storms."

"But there is life to the north, correct?"

The Seeker shrugged. "Water, wastelands, or cities. You're on your own."

"Can you give me anything?" She looked at the guard who'd made the smart remark, hoping he'd have something to add, but he remained silent. "Anything I can use. Do you know what I'm looking for?"

"I heard tell there was an old lady who could help, but that was 150 years ago."

23

Selah choked from the billowing, acrid smoke as they worked their way back to Contressa's holdings. Alarms blared and people with buckets and hoses ran everywhere in the marketplace, trying to find available water. Black soot spread from the center of the marketplace.

Contressa grabbed a man hauling a length of hose. "Where?"

"Slito's stall," the man said and hurried off.

Contressa muttered under her breath, then turned to Selah. "There's no active water line anywhere near that part of the layout. Come help me. This could take out the whole market if not contained." She ran flat out to her dwelling in the holdings and threw open the door. Grabbing a cylinder from an inside closet, she thrust it at Selah then snatched up an identical one. Selah stopped her and reached back in the closet, snatching two scarves from a shelf. They wrapped their heads to cover their noses and bolted in the direction of the market.

Disoriented by the heavy smoke, Selah followed Contressa

as they wove through the rows of stalls covered in gray ash. Contressa stopped. Selah came around beside her, facing the raging inferno fed by a ruptured fuel line. Angry flames crawled along the walls and ceiling of the stall, licking around the conduits and communication networks above.

"Aim at the base of the flames. You take the right and I'll do the left." Contressa coughed from trying to yell over the siren. She pushed the guys with buckets of water out of the way so Selah could join her. Onlookers crowded around.

"Get back and let us use the chemicals!" Contressa sprayed from one direction and Selah sprayed from the other.

A huge yellow then blue flame accompanied by a loud whoosh shot fifteen feet high. The crowd moved away from the heat. Contressa changed her spray width for a wide burst. Selah matched the coverage. The flames retreated. Ten feet to the left another pipe that had been subjected to the flames glowed red.

Contressa saw it at the same moment Selah did, and they trained their chemicals on the spot, building a solidified layer that cushioned the explosion when the pipe ruptured. Additional chemicals were added when the fire team arrived, but by then the two women had saved the market.

The crowd assembled erupted in cheers. Contressa shook Selah's hand, grinning broadly as they both got slaps on the back for the swift job. "Are you sure I can't talk you into staying? With a right hand like you I could control the entire outer ring by summer."

"I suspect if I haven't found the Third Protocol long before summer, I will fracture."

Contressa's smile faded. "It's that bad? I didn't realize. What can we do to get you out of here faster?"

Selah looked at the burned-out shell of a shop. It had burned so hot any metal parts inside were a liquid mess. "This was where I was picking up our last order of parts. I'm going to need replacements."

"I'll find out what Slito was fabricating and we'll get it done for you," Contressa said.

Selah pressed her scrambler. Nothing happened. She pressed again then turned to Contressa. "No signal to the transport."

Contressa looked up and pointed. "The junction box for the fiber connections melted."

Selah's chest tightened. She'd have to go out there and come back. "What could I use to go out there? I need to know if there's anything else they need before we cut off communications."

"Are you coming back today?"

"Yes, I want as much done as I can. Could you ask Baje and Tuere to meet me at your place? I'd like to say goodbye," Selah said.

"Then take Slito's SnowRunner. It's his fault you need the extra trip." Contressa pointed to a closed-in box sitting atop two treads.

Selah scrambled up the ladder into the transport. Rylla and Dane met her at the entrance to the family quarters. They made faces at her smell, but she loved on both of them. She passed the galley, motioning to Pasha and Mari, then ran through the tactical areas and poked her head in the rear compartment where Bodhi, Mojica, and Taraji were retrofitting the last system. "Need you three in tactical right away. Bring a list of any missing parts. We have to leave today."

Selah darted back into tactical, but nervous energy kept her moving. Pasha and Mari took seats, and Selah shooed the kids to the family area to play. She couldn't risk having Rylla hear they were leaving and she wasn't going to be able to tell Tuere and Baje goodbye.

Pasha covered her nose. "Why are you covered with soot and smell like smoke?"

"After I saw the Seeker, I helped Contressa fight a fire in the marketplace."

"Why did you risk yourself like that?"

"Because I was the only one there, and I'm capable of pointing a chemical retarder," Selah said.

"So why do we have to leave? Please don't tell me there's more snow on the way," Pasha said. "I've had enough of being stuck indoors."

"No, it's worse than that. Wait till everyone's here so I only have to say it once." Selah tried to control the tremor in her hands. She wasn't sure if it was a Kingston-related fear or another symptom of her decline.

Bodhi, Mojica, and Taraji piled in the doorway. "Why do we need to leave here today?" Taraji asked.

Bodhi came closer and recoiled. "Why do you—"

"Fighting a fire in the marketplace," Selah said. "The Kingstons are in the dome."

"Jericho Kingston from Waterside?" Fear etched across Pasha's face.

Mari looked around. "Somebody fill me in. Who's Jericho Kingston?"

"He's the man my husband tried to sell Selah to in marriage, to unite our Borough with their petrol," Pasha said.

"Well, that's a mouthful. How did they get here so fast?" Mari asked.

"They're part of the bandit crew we fought at your place, and then I fought them at the transport depot after Wood-Haven," Taraji said. "I saw a regular transport in the depot for repairs. They must have hijacked it after we departed. They arrived before we could leave Cleveland because the snow receded from the lower part of the route first."

"The point is they're Blood Hunters, so they'll be after Selah," Bodhi said.

Selah held up a hand. "I'm under Contressa's protection while I'm in the dome. They've been in there since early December and we didn't know to be worried. I'd say it's too late to worry now, but we do need to leave."

Everyone tried to talk at once. Selah felt the familiar ebb and flow to their speech like an elastic band that stretched and then snapped, propelling her back to the center. They stopped talking and stared at her. Selah tried to pass it off as a long pause.

"And now that I have your attention I'll tell you the bad news. There is no more."

She said it the way the Seeker had and got the puzzled look she'd anticipated. But she had to remain upbeat for her family. "That's the same look I had when he told me there were no more domes. But he did tell me to go north to Milwaukee, Wisconsin. So I guess the fact we were going north by mistake was correct."

Pasha glanced at the model. "What happened to the mountain of pearls we digitized?"

"They were smaller and older technology. Magnetic storms blew them up," Selah said.

"Then I guess we've got work to do." Taraji left tactical with Mari, discussing map routes they needed to tag.

Selah noticed her mother staring at her and could only ignore it for so long. "What?"

Pasha touched her face. "You look tired. You're not getting enough rest."

Selah kissed her mother on the cheek. She couldn't stay near her too long or Pasha would know she was up to something. "Mojica, do we have all the parts we need? Slito's are being replaced."

"That's it. They brought the last load out this morning. We can be done in twenty-four to forty-eight hours if I go back to work now." Mojica waved and departed, taking Pasha with her.

Bodhi walked over and wrapped his arms around Selah's waist. She rested her head on his chest and listened to his heartbeat for at least ten seconds. It was funny how long that felt when she was anticipating the end.

"Taraji told you, didn't she?" Selah kept her head against his chest. She didn't want to see a storm cloud cross his face and ruin the moment.

"Yes, she did. Did you expect her to hold it from me?" Bodhi rested his chin on her head and stroked her hair.

"No, but I told her not to tell you."

"Well then, I'm glad she doesn't listen to you," Bodhi said as he released her.

That was a great note to leave the conversation on. "I have to pick up the last order of replacement parts, and Contressa will have Slito bring me out with the delivery," Selah said.

Bodhi stared at her, then smiled and shook his head. "I can't yell anymore. We're almost out of here, so just please be careful."

"I always am." Except when she wasn't . . .

"I know, but it makes me feel better saying it."

Selah kissed him on the cheek and left tactical. She walked down the hall to her quarters, where she had the data from Cleveland regarding the process used with her plasma. There were notations of several experiments where they had injected directly from the host. That didn't work for diseases, but it had dramatic effects for DNA defects that were physical. Selah grabbed a syringe and two canisters and hid them safely in the waist pocket on her tactical suit.

As Selah was copying the protocol notes, Taraji walked in.

"Glad we're almost out of here," Selah said. "Jericho Kingston is the last person I want to see." She turned back to the transfer. If she looked at Taraji for long it would be over.

"Yeah, you've been fortunate." Taraji glanced at the transfer. "What are you copying?"

"A file from Cleveland. I figured Contressa might find help for the kids." Selah's fingers were beginning to tremble again.

Taraji leaned back against Selah's desk. "You're giving them a sample of your blood, aren't you?"

"No, of course I'm not. I took heed of what you said." Selah tried to will the cube to hurry and finish the file. She started to sweat.

Taraji crossed her arms. "No, you didn't listen to me at all."

Selah closed her eyes. "Please, this time . . . don't tell anyone, not even Bodhi. I spent a lot of time finding my father

313

and then my family, but now I have to find myself. I can't do that with everyone scrutinizing my every move."

"But they deserve to know."

"If finding myself means losing myself, then so be it. There have been enough coincidences so far that I know my fate is already sealed. All I have to do is choose wisely," Selah said.

"You think weakening yourself even faster is the wise thing to do?" Taraji asked.

Selah turned to face her. "I think letting those kids have a life is the wise thing to do."

Selah parked the SnowRunner and hurried into the dome. The weather report at the entrance board inside showed a snowstorm coming in. Selah couldn't afford to waste time. She swung by Slito's to announce he could begin loading the parts and she'd be ready shortly.

She turned down the lane to Contressa's. Baje and Tuere vaulted the wide stairs two at a time, trying to be the first to reach Selah. She laughed at their game and corralled them inside, where Contressa sat in her garden drinking tea.

"Selah, I hope you've gotten everything you needed from the Seeker." Contressa motioned the children to come out and join them for goodbyes.

"Everything he had to give, but this is the end. There is no next place to go, so we'll wander and hope for the best," Selah said with a grimace. She looked at Contressa. "Unfortunately, my chances of finding the Third Protocol in the time I'm allotted are next to none." She turned to the children. "So I'm giving you an infusion of my blood." She pulled the syringe and canisters from her pocket and laid them on the table.

The children huddled together, whispering, then Baje spoke for them. "Is this going to hurt?"

"I don't know. The file didn't say anything about pain, just the instantaneous healing, and I figured we should give it a try on you."

"Does that mean we still die at sixteen?" Baje asked.

"No, that means you will be a permanently healthy person who can live very long, but your blood will only be able to cure people with the same defect."

Contressa sat up straight. "You're serious about this? You can cure them and they don't have to die?" Tears appeared in her eyes. She waved a hand. "You children go into the kitchen so that I can talk to Selah for a minute." She waited for them to go. Selah studied her body-speak. Contressa was clearly very conflicted.

"I forgot to get the tracker back from your uniform." Contressa reached over and untucked the patch. She held it out to Selah. "I'm sorry, but this is not just a tracker. It's an audio-vid with both voice recording and images of everything that happened while you were with the Seeker. Because you are doing this for my Outcast children, I want to give you the opportunity to destroy the patch."

Selah sat back. "No, I'm leaving. These Seekers are a mean bunch. Anything you can find to work against them is a positive thing. Keep it."

Contressa called the children back in. Selah motioned Baje to the seat beside her. "I'm going to extract a sample from me and pass it to you. Your leg should be healed instantly."

Selah put the cartridge to her forearm and extracted a sample, then injected it into Baje's arm. They sat back to watch. A minute went by with no change, then two.

Selah's shoulders slumped. "I'm sorry it didn't work. The procedural protocol may have been faulty—"

Baje screamed loud enough to shatter glass. They could see movement in her leg. Contressa and Selah urged her to get up and walk. As she marched away the pronounced limp was easy to see, but on her way back to them it disappeared. Baje noticed right away and began whooping and yelling, running circles in the garden.

Selah's hands shook and tears clouded her eyes as she changed the cylinder and they did the same thing with Tuere. He reacted like the original prediction had indicated, and his defect cleared in the first forty-five seconds. Selah could barely breathe. She'd never seen anything like it. Her heart pounded with exhilaration.

With much reluctance, she rose to leave. The children ran around the garden enjoying their new freedom. Joy filled Selah. Her sacrifice would save a whole world of children.

Contressa hugged her goodbye. "You've freely given of yourself, and I owe you more. So I have another admission." She hesitated. "I've been watching you for the Kingstons."

"Yeah, I sorta figured that when I found out Jericho was here all this time. I've had so many people after me that now I suspect everyone, and if they turn out to be friendly it's a plus. I have no more energy to be mad at anyone." She pulled the data cube from her tactical suit. "This is the data on the study and how to extract samples from Baje and Tuere to cure others. Remember, only the original two can ever be donors, and it will only work on this defect." She handed Contressa the cube.

The woman stood there staring at the clear cube in her hand. "You're still going to give me this much power after all I've done to you?"

Selah smiled. "You've really been quite helpful, and this is for the children. Besides, I didn't trust your motives to begin with. It's not all the things I've thought of that scare me, it's the single thing I *haven't* thought about that really worries me."

Contressa walked with Selah out to the entrance. Selah's gait wobbled. She was still trying to recover from the two extractions. Her body's response to losing two tablespoons of blood was beyond anything she'd have expected. A person could lose that much to a good cut from a farm tool. She wondered what made her different.

Selah stumbled and Contressa steadied her. "Are you all right?"

"I expected a slight dimming for a short period, but this is severe." Selah pitched forward.

Contressa caught her. "I can't send you with Slito while you're in this condition. He'll sell you to Jericho Kingston between here and the transport and you'd disappear forever."

Selah tried to focus on what Contressa was saying. She struggled to straighten, but her arms and legs felt strange—first stiff then rubbery. Her mind wouldn't focus. It seemed like little parts of her brain were running everywhere, refusing to stay together.

Contressa sat her on the step of the SnowRunner. She walked away and tapped her communicator, speaking in rapid tones. Her words ran together in Selah's mind. Too many vowel sounds.

Selah tried to shake it off. Her head bobbed, and when she looked up . . . Jericho Kingston stared back. She remembered his face from a recent picture that had replaced her childhood memory of him looking like a stick bug.

He grinned at her. "Selah, I finally have you again."

"No, get away from me." Selah put all her effort in trying to punch him. Her fingers splayed. Her hands didn't have the strength or coordination to ball into fists. She started to cry, slapping out in frustration. "Go away. Go away!"

Kingston threw back his head in laughter as he locked his large hand around her wrist. "Did you really think you'd get away from me? My father paid a hefty price for your hand in marriage, and I want my money's worth."

"I'll never marry you. I hate you!" Selah tried to yell, but it came out like a garbled whimper.

"I'll never marry you either. That would have worked back home, but now I just want your blood."

"My blood won't help you now. Can't you see how weak I am?"

Her fingers clawed at his hand, but she was too weak to loosen his grip. He lifted her off the ground and over his shoulder. She beat on his back with her fists, but there was no strength to her punches. She tried to kick, but Kingston had both arms wrapped around her legs.

She cried out as he carried her, but no one paid any attention.

Kingston plopped her down on a padded seat inside some kind of small conveyance. She could see out of windows on all sides. He laughed again. "These stupid hicks don't know what makes your blood so special. I thought we had solved this problem with the extraction in the Mountain, and then the whole place collapsed in on itself before I got there." He strapped her into the seat and moved up close, grinning with yellowed teeth. "But I do know what makes you special, and we're going to extract it for ourselves."

Selah shook her head to order her thoughts. He knew what made her blood special! She clawed at the seat to sit up straight. She had to focus on listening to him. Bursts of color swirled together. "Tell me! Tell me what it is!" She tried to grab his arm, but her hands fell to her sides like lead weights.

Selah's fingers grappled with the closure that held her prisoner. Her eyes were getting heavy. She had to stay awake.

Kingston winked at her. "I guess I can tell you because it won't do you any good here in this backwards society. They'd never be able to see—"

She heard noise and sounds she couldn't decipher. The conveyance jostled back and forth. Loud voices. *Help! Wait, tell me the secret!*

She jerked, and a familiar buzz overcame her, fading in and out . . .

February 14

Selah awoke on a cot with her arms flailing. Jericho Kingston had been close enough to touch. Where was he now? Did he drug her?

Her eyes stretched open. He had been about to tell her the secret of her blood!

Where was she? The only light she saw was what filtered under the door. She couldn't make out the walls. The resonance of her movements made it sound like she was in a small space with sparse furnishings. She tried to sit up but her head still buzzed. She didn't know if she should yell or not. Maybe Contressa had played her after all and slipped her something, but there was no way that could have happened because she hadn't eaten or drunk anything. She tried again to fight her way into a sitting position. She leaned back against the wall and let all the pieces go back into place before she attempted to stand.

She took a step and her right ankle gave way. She crashed to the floor. She lay there with her head swimming as memories flew through her mind, making her stomach wrench. Bright lights, cold tables, everyone dressed in white, but she couldn't see their faces. The scenes melted together like candle wax at the base of a sconce. *Stop! Tell me the secret!*

She found the strength to sit up again and used the cot to help her stand. She tried a leg without letting go. It held. She felt stable. Another foot in front of her and she reached the door. Her hand felt for a wall pad or door handle. Her hand flopped across a door panel several times before it hit the doorknob. She fumbled with getting all of her fingers to close around the cool metal. She had to find Jericho Kingston. *He knows.*

The doorknob felt cool to her touch. She stood for a minute with her forehead against the door. There was no way out of this darkness other than through the door. The light called to her from beyond it.

Selah took a deep breath. Her head didn't feel dizzy any longer. Her arms felt normal. Her legs felt normal. It was just the sparkles in her stomach that made her apprehensive.

She pushed on the handle and opened the door.

24

Selah burst into tears and ran into her mother's outstretched arms. "Jericho had me. I'm sorry, Mother. It's my fault. I gave an infusion to those two Outcast children Rylla met." Selah slowed down her confession, noticing that her mother was not responding with any level of horror. Selah leaned away from her mother's shoulder and looked into her eyes.

"I already knew what you were planning to do," Mother said.

"Taraji! I need to get better at figuring out how to keep her out of my secrets," Selah said.

"It's well that we knew. At least the Cleveland documents on the infusion protocol gave us enough supplemental material to help you recover," Pasha said. "We've never gotten into the chemistry that makes your blood a lifeline for other people."

Taraji walked into view off the common room. She poked her head in. "How are you feeling?"

"She's almost good as new. Those supplements helped," Pasha said as she hugged her again. Selah could feel the fear and tension in her arms. She hated that she scared her mother so often. Her level of fear hadn't registered with Selah until she had begun worrying for Rylla's safety.

Selah glanced over her mother's head at Taraji. Her facial expression said she hadn't told them these blood infusions were shortening Selah's lifespan. Taraji nodded, but her expression looked sad. Selah dismissed it. Her head hurt and she could only concentrate on one problem at a time, and right now that was a Blood Hunter.

"No!" Selah shouted. "I have to go back. He was going to tell me." She scrambled for the door.

Taraji stopped her and glanced at Pasha. "Is this a side effect?"

Pasha looked concerned. "Mental confusion is not a symptom from everything I've read."

Selah pushed her away and scrambled to leave. "You don't understand. Jericho was about to tell me what makes my blood special. We have to go back to the dome. I need to find him."

Pasha rushed to her side. "Honey, it would be useless to go back. It's been three days. He's long gone, and I doubt he'd tell you the answer even if you asked him from a distance, which would be the only safe way to talk to any Kingston."

Selah pressed her lips into a scowl and sat back down with a sigh. "I came so close. I was face-to-face with Jericho Kingston. How am I here without him?"

"Contressa said the poor man had an unfortunate accident."

Taraji smiled, and her eyes actually twinkled with laughter. "While he was securing you in a SnowRunner, a whole stack of pallets holding hoses became unstable and tipped over on him. It only knocked him out, but that was enough time for a getaway. You went unconscious from the infusion, but Contressa drove you and the parts out here."

"She's another person I had concerns about, but the one thing I've learned about human nature is that people are willing to raise their values when children are involved."

"She said to tell you it was a token for a debt she could never repay," Taraji said.

Selah looked at her and then Pasha. "I almost had the answer, but I can tell you one thing." She shrugged. "I'm not afraid anymore. If someone like Jericho Kingston can figure out the secret, we can surely find it."

"You've healed in time to be part of the festivities. We're ready to leave. For this special occasion the children have been allowed onto the command deck. Do you feel like going up? It would be wonderful for us all to be together," Pasha said.

Selah marveled at how easily Pasha changed gears, but she agreed and rode the lift up with them. When the door slid open at the command deck, the new atmosphere startled her. The refit system generated a new harmonic vibration that replaced the greens and reds of the former system and generated a purple and blue hue on the control panels. It calmed her and she felt refreshed. Maybe there was hope to slow her disintegration after all. She needed to scrutinize those injection protocols. Apparently Pasha had found notations for supplements that Selah had missed. There might be extenders for her condition hidden in the files. She had spent so much time hiding her decline she never thought to enlist aid in slowing the process.

Rylla and Dane ran to hug her. "I thought I would get to say goodbye to Tuere," Rylla said sadly. Selah fought the urge to smile as Rylla's lip poked out, remembering the same method of self-expression just a few short years ago.

Selah moved to sit at the navigator station next to Mari. "I'm sorry, but it became too dangerous. People who were chasing me at home have come here, and we must go."

The child ran the back of her hand down Selah's cheek like she was stroking a puppy. "That's all right, as long as you're safe. I'll say goodbye to him in my head."

Mojica sat at the tactical station. "I've got all systems integrated with online weapons and defense. Shields are at optimum. I'd say we're ready to go."

"We've been testing the fusion engines for about two hours. Not a single glitch under any of the extreme conditions. Let's go," Bodhi said, looking a little nervous.

Taraji turned to Bodhi and smiled. "You want to take her out?"

Bodhi nodded and ramped up the engines to break inertia. The transport lifted slowly then slid forward. The landing struts retracted with a solid thunk, and everyone clapped.

Selah relaxed. A new start. Not much of a destination with no more domes to seek, but they were together, safe, and putting distance between them and Jericho Kingston. That's all that mattered.

The sun shone brightly for the first time since the last storm. The snow melted under the brightness, and they watched out the windows as the woods passed by. Selah wondered if the

Outcast children were playing in there, where the canopy of evergreens kept a lot of the snow at bay. Rylla and Dane pressed past Selah's navigator station to look out the side shield.

Rylla yelled. Selah jumped. It took her a second to realize Baje and Tuere were standing at the end of the woods where the meadow sloped up the hill to Chicago. They waved furiously at Rylla and she waved back.

Selah felt bad Dane hadn't been able to meet them, but she feared exposing too much of her family to the Hunter way of life. Rylla ran down the side of the command deck until she was out of windows to wave through. The transport shot off to the north.

Rylla came back and put her head on Selah's shoulder. "You fixed them, didn't you?"

Selah looked at her. "How did you know?"

"They were wearing skis. They couldn't wear skis with their bad knees. So I guess they don't have bad knees anymore, and you're the only one I know who can do that. You know, after the plasma in Cleveland and all."

Selah smoothed the girl's curly hair. "You're a very smart young lady. I hope you put that to good use."

"I'm smart too," Dane said. "I memorized the whole storybook."

Selah smiled. "I'm very proud of you—"

A nasty screech burst from the right-side forward thruster. A thin wisp of smoke filtered from the vents. Selah released the children and hustled them from the command deck. Pasha joined them and the children clung to her sides.

"It's all right," Taraji said. She hit a series of relays and the sound stopped. "The new generator engines must need breaking in. I think the metal expansion should happen slowly so we don't blow any receptacles." She slapped a ventilation relay, and the noxious smell cleared from the air.

"Easy it is," Bodhi said. He reengaged the thrusters. "What's our track north?"

"Keep the water on the right and follow Lake Michigan to Milwaukee," Taraji said.

The transport shuddered. Pasha clutched the children. Selah turned to her console just as the transport bucked, sending her against the navigation console. She tightened her seat restraint.

"Mother, take the kids below and strap in. Mari, watch out for them, please. Don't use the lift," Selah said. The four of them streamed off the command deck to the family quarters.

"Somebody tell me why we have problems when these systems were tested?" Selah had a map of the route they could fly the fastest to avoid magnetic storms. It was only eighty miles to Milwaukee, but at this rate they'd be lucky to get there after a full day of travel.

Taraji replied, "You're not going to like it if I tell you there's no reason for—"

A vibrating growl worked its way through the transport. By the time it reached them at the front, it was accompanied by an ear-piercing connection of metal parts. Alarms went off along the console. Taraji slapped off some components and activated others, silencing the sounds.

"We went over everything brought into the transport from Chicago, but has anyone stopped to think we could've been sabotaged while we were trapped in the Cleveland dome? We don't know how soon the snow was actually manageable," Mojica said. "We've been so preoccupied with the refit, we really didn't investigate much."

"But that would mean we might not have fixed the actual problem that brought us down here in the first place," Bodhi said.

A banging sound pulsed through the transport. The right rear generator started to skip, and with the left side thrusters trying to move forward, the conflict caused a drag. The transport started to dip on the right side. Bodhi wrestled it straight again with Taraji's help.

"No! We replaced everything," Taraji said. "We need to set down and pull a thruster. The quality of the metals must be bad. Blades must be warping."

An explosion rocked the transport. The right rear fusion generator blew out, shooting debris fifty feet from the transport. Taraji struggled to keep control as the transport careened toward the ground on the right side.

Bodhi's panel flashed red warning lights. "I've got an aft generator going critical!"

The generator exploded. With the rear center stabilizer gone, the transport spun out of control, clipped the ground, and hurtled into the air. It smashed back to the ground and burst into flames.

Selah's world erupted in heat. Surrounded by flames and smoke, she struggled to free herself from the restraint. It was supposed to keep her safe, but at the moment it was holding her upside down from a seat that had been bolted to the floor and was now on a wall. A warm trickle inched down the side of her face. She reached up. Blood oozed from a cut in her scalp. *What happened?* She blinked several times. Nothing looked the same. The command deck was a pile of burning rubble, with ceiling and walls collapsed into a heap and broken, sparking conduits competing for brightness with the flames.

Her head started to get fuzzy. *Not now!* Her fingers fought with the clasps until they released. Selah fell to the burning wall that was now a floor. Flames licked between the panels. She couldn't breathe. The smoke burned her eyes. Selah closed them to wash it out.

A strange explosion happened as she opened her eyes. All the flames around her were sucked away in the same direction. The hairs on her arm rose. Her hearing faded as though hands had clamped over her ears, and then it returned like the rushing wind of a tornado.

She opened her mouth to yell. The transport exploded out at the front, and Selah was suddenly weightless. She slammed into an object that was carried along with her.

The air turned black.

Selah's eyes opened. A stinging sensation brought a flood of tears, obscuring her vision. She felt warmth from above. She closed her eyes, and warm tears slid down her cheeks and plopped on her cold hands. Did she have enough strength to open her eyes again?

She did and wiped away the fluid with the back of her hand. More stinging—the back of her hand was covered in grit. She didn't have the energy to open her eyes again, but it would be all right. It was always all right when she awoke.

Her eyes fluttered, cascading light to her brain like one of those kaleidoscopes her mother had bought her at the fair when she—

"Mother!" Selah's eyes flew open. She forced air into her lungs as she tried to push herself up. Confusion stopped her until she remembered the explosion and looked up at the transport twenty feet away. Billowing black smoke churned from the blown-out front and the gaping hole in the side where the transport had split behind the command area. Flames were consuming the broken outside panels and the lower portions where the family would be.

"Bodhi! Anybody!" Selah scrambled to her feet and ran toward the wreckage. She stumbled into the jagged side, and metal pierced her uniform at her left thigh. She yelped as it tore her skin. She fought her way inside. To add to her confusion, the transport was on its side.

The fire raged. "Mother!" Selah gulped in a mouthful of smoke and started coughing. She lurched forward anyway, crawling over debris and beams. The ramp door to the right of the lift was broken open with a space too small for her to squeeze through. She mustered her energy and kicked until it broke through, but the motion propelled her down the chute that had been a wall.

Selah clawed at the sides to slow her descent until she crashed into a beam blocking the path. She pressed a hand to her side, the hip she had injured in the Mountain. It had healed stronger from that incident, and now it saved her from another serious injury. Selah crawled over the smoldering beam and worked her way through the smoke and flames to the family area.

It was unrecognizable. Twisted panels, beams, and fire covered the area around her. She wanted to yell but doing so made her choke. She tried to cover her mouth but then her voice was muffled. She searched, pulling at easy things to clear a path. They'd be in the family room. The comfortable seats had restraints. But Selah couldn't recognize the areas lying on their sides, and she was already disoriented from the loss of blood from her head.

She reached up to touch the cut and her sleeve snagged on a jagged conduit. It jerked her into a pile of panels on her left. The fear of falling made her gasp, and she inhaled a good handful of smoke. She crawled off the pile, coughing.

A moan.

Selah froze. The only other sound was roaring flames. Selah glanced around the area in front of her, figuring out the order of the debris. She bent to her right and shoved a broken container under the edge of the panel to hold it up. She got down low to look under. Darkness.

"I'm here. Where are you?" Another moan.

The sound was too mild in the noise. The flames worked closer. The smoke billowed thicker. Selah crawled to the other side of the panel and tried to lift. A crosspiece rested on top, preventing her from moving it. Selah tried to force the piece off the panel, but it had broken at an angle that wedged it in place.

She angrily pounded on the crosspiece with both hands but only dislodged the debris above it, which rained down on her head. She was struck on the left shoulder by a loose transfer case that drove her to her knees. Selah cried out and tried to stretch the battered shoulder muscle.

The sound of another moan renewed her energy. Selah easily removed the debris now that most had fallen. She pulled over the transfer case and used it to prop up the other side of the panel. Crawling underneath, she pushed things to the side, creating a path that amplified the moan. It was much closer this time. Selah snaked her way through a pile of conduits. A hand!

She darted toward it, clearing the arm and shoulder. Dane! He was unconscious but alive. He would be all right. The rest of them had to be right here. She crawled around under the panel to be sure no one else was trapped, then went to the back wall.

Selah recoiled at the heat. The fire must be on the other side and ready to break through. She moved back to Dane and pulled him out. When they broke through the front of the panel, Selah stood and slung him over her sore shoulder. It wasn't good for much more.

Stumbling out to the opening, she carefully laid Dane out of danger and darted back in. Knowing where he had been made her confident she could find her mother. She began a search of the next collapsed panel using the transfer case and broken container. It took longer to search because there were numerous large objects underneath. She found nothing, but she couldn't get back to the wall because the heat was too oppressive. She had to go in the other direction to search. Her mother wouldn't have been that far from Dane, under the circumstances.

Selah crawled out from under the panel. The next one started to smolder and she fled. It would burst into flames soon and this whole section would go up. She rushed to the other side of where she found Dane, her coughs burning her lungs. She slowed a little, covering her nose with her arm.

"Mother!" Selah gagged. She couldn't get enough air to cough.

"Selah!"

"Mari! I'm coming." Selah clawed at the debris. Conduits and ceiling tiles, several wall panels, and everything from the opposite side of the transport's open area rested in a pile.

She barreled into it, throwing things in the direction of the fire so they could run the other way. Mari reached her. "Once I heard your voice I knew which way to dig."

Selah pulled Mari to her feet and hugged her. She put her head next to Mari's ear and said in a hoarse voice, "I have Dane."

Mari nodded. "Dane was at his seat at the table. I was going to strap him in. Rylla and your mom were at the seats right beside me. So they have to be under here." She bent over and coughed several times, gagging till she retched. Selah patted her on the back.

The fire broke through the panels at the back, roaring at the new fuel and sending darker, heavier smoke pouring into the area.

Selah grabbed at the pile, fighting the creeping heat and punishing smoke. Her lungs burned but she kept going. How could this have happened? They couldn't die. She wouldn't let them die.

Mari worked at her side, holding up pieces while Selah checked under them. The fire crept closer, but it was the heat that was the main problem. The floor that had originally been a wall had begun to melt. The surface was gummy to stand on.

They found Rylla first and pulled her out. She was choking and gagging but unharmed.

"Pasha is right beside me, but there's a case on her arm. I can't get her loose," Rylla said.

Selah and Mari scrambled into the opening she had come out. Mari used her back as leverage to hold up the case and Selah pulled her mother free. They each took an arm as they backed her out of the debris.

Selah grabbed Pasha's arms and Mari took her legs as they hurried out. The beams in the chute Selah had banged into served well as steps to move the unconscious Pasha. As they cleared the area, the fire blew through the last wall and sent an explosion of flames out the broken side right where they had run.

They laid Pasha next to Dane. Mari looked around. "Where's Bodhi, Mojica, and Taraji?"

"Still in there. I expected them to be out behind me. Rylla, watch Mother and Dane." Selah charged toward the flames licking out the left side of the hole and dodged in at the right. Mari ran right behind her. The rest of the area where they'd come up from was blocked by broken conduits and sidewall panels. Beyond that the command area was easier—not as many moveable parts as below, just the acrid smoke and approaching heat to hamper their rescue.

Selah reached them first. Mari gasped.

25

Selah screamed, then her knees gave out and she crumpled to the floor. The force of the blast that had propelled her out the front shield had sheared off the remaining command chairs about halfway up.

There was no question that Taraji and Mojica, still strapped in their seats, were dead.

Selah stared at Taraji's lifeless hand slumped over the side of the chair. Mari moved up beside her and helped her to her feet.

"They never knew what hit them," Mari said.

Tears streamed down Selah's face. "I don't know how to deal with this. Both of them at the same time." She waved a hand. "They don't have—" She slid back to the floor. Her stomach heaved and rolled in waves. She bent over and retched.

Mari held Selah's hair away from her face and rubbed her back as Selah emptied everything. Her heart ached for the mentor and friend she had lost.

"How do I tell the rest? I can't let them see this." Selah glanced around at the chaos. "They need to be covered."

"There's nothing here that we can use," Mari said. "This place isn't stable. We shouldn't stay here." She tried to help Selah to her feet.

"I can't leave them." Selah pulled herself from Mari's grasp.

Mari swung around. "Where's Bodhi's chair?" An explosion punctuated her question. The hull shuddered, and loose material fell from above.

Selah jumped to her feet. She searched the wreckage where his command chair should have been. "He's not here. What happened? One chair doesn't vaporize."

Another explosion and they had to grab onto debris to stay upright. Mari took a quick assessment. "Two chairs are gone. The blast came from behind your chair and out Bodhi's side of the front shield." Another explosion and the smoke turned jet black. "He's outside."

"You sure?" Selah panicked. Choosing wrong meant his death if he was still in here. There'd be no coming back in.

"Yes." They both dashed out the hull tear as the last explosion propelled flames thirty feet into the air.

Selah and Mari dove for safety, rolling away in the melting snow. Selah clawed to get her footing as she screamed, "Bodhi!"

She ran for the tracks leading to her abandoned seat. Mari caught up. They both looked for anything recently disturbed. Nothing.

The field had overgrown with tall, heavy bushes during the summer, and now winter's weight and deep pockets of snow made the areas of dried weeds look like sentries watching the landscape.

Mari methodically searched where Bodhi's chair would have traveled. Still nothing.

Selah ran in haphazard circles but forced her mind to calm and move in the logical search pattern sequences Mari had taught her. Ten . . . fifteen minutes passed. She grew anxious again.

Mari continued to search her grid pattern, ignoring Selah's jabbering. But Selah knew her sister was wrong. She had convinced Selah to leave the command deck, and now Bodhi was dead. Didn't matter that the girl was blood. Why had Selah trusted in Mari's skills instead of her own intuition?

Selah ran over to Mari and snatched her tactical uniform, turning her around. "Why did you make me leave the command deck? Bodhi is still in there. You killed him."

Mari stared in her eyes. "If you had stayed there you would be dead."

"You disregarded Bodhi's life." Selah shook her. "Did you do it to save me?"

Mari paused. She stared at Selah, then over Selah's shoulder. She grinned.

"Don't you dare laugh at me at a time like this. After all I've lost today, how can you be so callous?" Selah's lip quivered. She wanted to die.

Mari grabbed Selah by the shoulders and turned her around. Selah's gaze drifted out across the open field. About twenty feet away, an arm wearing a tactical uniform waved above the snow.

Selah ran across the field and dropped in front of Bodhi. Her chest heaved from running, but she managed to talk between gasps. "Are you okay?"

She was afraid to touch him in case he was injured. He

337

mumbled something. She took that to be a yes, he was okay. She disconnected his harness and helped him out of the chair.

"I remember being hit in the back of the head and that was it."

"I think that was me. The transport's gone," Selah said.

Bodhi glanced at her. "Your face says a lot more."

Tears welled in her eyes. "We lost Mojica and Taraji."

Bodhi moaned. "How?"

"The blast that blew us from the command deck cut—killed them," Selah said.

"Are you sure? Both of them?" Bodhi struggled to see where the transport burned.

Mari nodded. "I think we had two separate events going on—equipment failure because of bad parts and Blood Hunters firing a missile."

Selah and Mari helped Bodhi to his feet. He wobbled at first. "The parts failure I can believe, but what evidence do you have of a missile? How would they even know where Selah was in the transport?"

"Because five minutes before, Selah was peering out that exact window waving goodbye to the kids from Chicago." Mari led them back toward the burning hulk. "And because of this." She pointed at the hull. They could clearly see the blown-in effect behind where Selah's navigator station sat. The structure of her seat had protected her and forced the blast outward.

Rylla ran to Selah, grabbing her around the waist. "Pasha came to but Dane won't wake up."

They hurried to Pasha. She cradled Dane's head and shoulders in her lap. A gash from his head had bloodied Pasha's top. She looked up at Selah with tears filling her eyes. "He won't wake up."

"We have nothing, not even water to give him or a pot to put it in." Selah searched the landscape.

"Maybe we should search by the lake. There might be other people." Mari looked around. "Keep an eye out for signs of smoke or shelters."

"Bodhi, if there are people around, they might be attracted to the fire. Would you stay here to protect Pasha and Dane?" Mari asked.

Selah was glad Mari asked him that way. He had been unconscious for quite a while. Pasha needed to watch him and he needed to watch her.

Bodhi nodded. Mari gave him the heavy stick she had discovered while walking the field.

Pasha rocked back and forth, holding Dane close while she pressed the tail of her tunic against his gash. She lifted her head. "Where's Mojica and Taraji?"

Selah, Mari, and Bodhi exchanged glances. Pasha stopped rocking. "Where are they?"

Selah pursed her lips as she closed her eyes and shook her head. She didn't know how to say it with Rylla watching her. "They're gone," she said in almost a whisper.

"What do you mean gone? Gone where? Why would they leave us at a time like this?" Pasha looked like she was getting angry.

Selah didn't have any choice but to be honest. "They're dead."

Pasha's mouth fell open. "Are you sure? Maybe you missed a life sign."

Mari grimaced. "There's no chance we made a mistake. They—"

"Now is not the time for details." Selah nodded in Rylla's direction.

Pasha pressed her lips together and buried her face in Dane's chest to cry as she rocked him.

Rylla wrapped her arms around Selah's waist. "I didn't get to say goodbye to them."

"Neither did I," Selah said. She rubbed Rylla's back as the child cried.

"You'd better get going before we attract unwanted attention," Bodhi said.

Rylla tagged along with Selah and Mari to the lake. Selah found it hard to speak. Her emotions were drained but she had to keep going. She worried they wouldn't find anything usable in the transport after the raging fire. Chicago said there was snow coming. They were out in the elements and close enough to be affected by the same weather.

Selah's adrenaline rush from the crash had worn off after the first quarter mile. Her legs turned to weights, and Rylla complained her feet were cold. Selah refused to stop. She could see the frozen lake—maybe another half mile.

"What will we do if we can't find anyone?" After Taraji's and Mojica's deaths, Selah doubted whether they could make it. How would she ever be able to get the group to safety?

"We keep moving north to Milwaukee until we can't go anymore," Mari said.

"But we need—"

"We need nothing. We will live from the land like my people do. Remember, I'm the big sister here," Mari said. She smiled softly at Selah and put her arm around her shoulder.

That was the first time Selah understood the feeling of an older sister. It brought a measure of comfort that warmed her for the rest of the walk.

Rylla stood at the top of the hill, staring down at the sloping woods and open shore. Selah and Mari joined her and stared out over the frozen lake before looking up and down the shore. Off to the left about a half mile up the lake Selah spotted a short wooden dock in good shape. It didn't look abandoned. That meant there were people close by, but she saw no homes or shacks. Her heart sank.

"We should move up or down the shore a half mile looking for help," Selah said.

"I don't think we have to go that far," Mari said. "I've seen several familiar trail markings. I just won't know where the people live until we go down to the shore."

Selah looked at her like she was crazy, but she was too tired to muster much opposition. "Can you share your theory, please?"

Mari pointed to the lake and led them down the hill. "See those two perfectly round holes? Someone is ice fishing. I figure they have to live nearby because of how fast those holes would close in this weather . . . and because there are different addresses on the trees."

"What are you talking about?" Selah asked.

The three of them reached the bottom of the hill, and Mari turned to look up it. "And there they are."

Selah scanned the hill. At least six, maybe eight, homes

341

were built into the hillside at different levels, with the natural curved contour of the land serving as a roof covered with grass. To passersby at the top, there was nothing but the lake. Her hopes were once again bolstered—there could be a whole community around this lake.

Mari led the way to a door and knocked. Almost immediately the door swung open to reveal a short, stout man, maybe four feet six or seven, with a mustache and a tight round cap on his head. He showed no fear of strangers, unlike many of the people Selah had met.

"Why are you knocking on my door?" the gruff little man asked.

"Sir, we've been attacked—"

"No, she's mistaken. It was a propulsion problem. Bad refit parts caused a generator engine to blow," Selah said.

The man looked back and forth between them like he was unimpressed by either explanation. "So which is it?"

Selah started to answer but Mari stepped in front of her. "The evidence shows we were attacked."

The man still looked unimpressed. "Are you a Blood Hunter?"

Selah didn't know which answer would get them help.

"We are not Blood Hunters," Mari said. "We've got several injured people up in the field who we need care for, and we'd like to get them away from the burned transport before Blood Hunters *do* come by."

"What kind of wagon do you folks have that travels the field instead of the road?" the man asked.

"We don't have a wagon—ours is air travel." Selah was getting nervous saying too much, but the transport wasn't anyone's secret machine anymore.

"Well, that's fancy. You must be rich folks." The man didn't budge from his close hold on the doorknob.

"No, not rich, and with our ride still burning, we have nothing to offer you as compensation," Mari said.

"And you're not Blood Hunters?"

Selah shook her head. "No, we're not."

"Then good, come in. We will help you," the man said. He lifted a hand piece from the wall and spoke into it, then returned to the group. "Men will bring your people here for rest."

Selah sat on the floor against the wall. She could close her eyes right now. She was thankful just to have a wall to lean against and a warm fire. "Do you know Milwaukee, Wisconsin?"

"Yes, we know that place. What would your business be there? Not many people there do business with strangers," the man said.

Selah looked at Mari. She didn't know what to answer him, but finally said, "We're on a quest. We have something we're supposed to find."

The man had an equally tiny wife, who brought out a tray of cookies and crackers along with a pot of tea.

Selah glanced at Rylla, who had been remarkably quiet since coming into the house.

The little wife scurried over to Rylla. "I saw you limp when you came in. Are your feet cold, dear?"

Rylla bobbed her head up and down. The little woman took her by the hand.

"No!" Selah reached for Rylla. "I'd rather she stay with me." She was too tired to determine if it was safe for Rylla with these people.

The lady eyed Selah suspiciously and retreated to her kitchen.

Voices at the door preceded Bodhi carrying Dane, who was still unconscious. The little man directed Bodhi to lay him on a bed that Selah suspected was the man's own, but it barely fit Dane.

The lady came in with a bowl and rags. She looked at Selah. "May I treat him?"

Selah blushed. She hadn't meant to be rude before. "Yes. Please help my brother."

The woman went to work with the contents of her first aid basket and stitched the deep gash on Dane's head, then raised a bottle of vile-smelling liquid to his nose. He bolted upright and immediately began to cry and hold his head. But he was awake, and for that Selah was relieved.

Pasha and the woman took the children into another room while the man and the two who had retrieved the family gathered around the short, wide table. "We've got a proposition to offer you folks," the man said.

Bodhi looked at Selah, who looked at Mari. "What do you have in mind?" he asked.

"We have a shipment that needs to go to Milwaukee. We've been having problems the last few months with shipments being hijacked. If your family will act as guards for this one, we will give you a ride to Milwaukee."

"What kind of shipment is it?" Bodhi asked.

The three men talked among themselves, then turned as a group. "Let us see your right arms," one of them said.

"Didn't we just tell you we're not Blood Hunters?" Mari said. "Why should we show you our arms?"

"It will prove once and for all that you aren't Blood Hunters, and then we will tell you about the shipment," the little man said.

Bodhi, Selah, and Mari bared an arm to prove their innocence. The men scrutinized each arm.

"Do you want to check my mother's also?" Selah asked.

"No, no. If you three are fine, she would be also." The little man looked excited. "We are the master craftsmen of Lake Michigan when it comes to barreled weapons fabrication. We are also a continual target for the Blood Hunters because we will not fabricate their weapons."

Bodhi broke into a huge grin. "Do you mean 'barreled' as in using bullets?"

The little man nodded. "We are supplying the freedom fighters who battle the Blood Hunters trying to take over the northern part of the lake. We have more fighters than weapons because of the regular hijacking of our shipments."

"Blood Hunters have been a bane to my existence since the very beginning, so anything to thwart their cause is a good cause to me," Selah said.

February 15

Selah slept with Rylla and Dane cuddled up beside her on the floor, flanked by Pasha and Mari. Bodhi sat up in the corner to keep guard over all. He and Selah had decided he could sleep in the wagon to Milwaukee and Selah would wake him if necessary.

The perk of being a bodyguard for a weapons shipment was that they got weapons. The little man gladly gave each of the four adults one of his handcrafted rifles. At first Mari declined because she was a bow and arrow person. But the man told her that in a city like Milwaukee she could trade the rifle for a high-tech bow.

At daybreak, they piled in the two sleigh wagons pulled by teams of six draft horses. They wound up the trail to the fields above. The little men drove the sleighs to the burned-out hull of the transport. Selah was saddened by just how little was left. Slender tendrils of black smoke seeped from three areas along the skeleton hull. Everyone stayed in the sleighs while Bodhi and Selah walked around it.

"I'm glad the command deck completely disintegrated in the heat," Selah said as they walked down the side to the back.

"I thought about Taraji and Mojica. They'd like it this way," Bodhi said.

"So there's nothing left of them, but we also have nothing to salvage," Selah said with a flip of her hand. "Not a data cube or file or anything we worked so hard to collect. What does this mean? Why did we spend so much time collecting everything just to lose it?"

Bodhi shrugged then wrapped an arm around Selah's shoulders as they trudged back to the sleighs. "Maybe that means we don't need that stuff anymore."

"Maybe it just means I'm finished." Selah smiled wryly and climbed into the sleigh.

In a couple minutes they were gliding across the hard-packed snow headed north. Selah and Bodhi had Rylla with them while Pasha, Mari, and Dane rode in the other sleigh.

Selah could barely keep her eyes open. It was Bodhi's turn to sleep, but she kept nodding off. Rylla kept nudging her awake.

Even the constant bumping and jostling wasn't enough to keep her eyes open. The scenery just added to the monotony. Snow everywhere. The trees were mostly a form of gray except for the evergreens, which were the only splash of color on the boring landscape. Selah almost hoped for something exciting to keep her awake.

At lunchtime the men stopped for a meal and treated Selah and the family to fruit, crackers, and cheese. There hadn't been any signs of bandits, and Selah wanted to know if that was unusual. "Do they consistently attack you at a specific place or time?"

"Their new base is centered in Milwaukee," the little man said. "Blood Hunters don't usually stray too far from there since we had them charged with raiding once when they strayed into the next county. They'll attack in the last five miles. The old city of Milwaukee covered the whole area at one time, but now that it has shrunk, the area they attack us from is controlled by outlaws. I'd say it should be around dusk tonight, so when the sun starts to set, stay alert."

Once lunch was finished and the sleighs started moving, the constant hissing sound of the runners put Selah to sleep again.

Rylla nudged her again and she jerked awake. "The driver says we've passed into the hijacking sector. Do you want to sleep more or wake up?"

"I better wake up. Nudge Bodhi." Selah sat up and stretched her back and arms. She glanced at the empty winter landscape. Other than long shadows and the sun being in a downward slide toward night, the scenery looked the same as it had two hours ago.

Selah checked her weapon and the case of bullets next to

her, then she watched Bodhi wake up. He had this thing he did to shake his hair into an organized mess. It normally made her laugh, but today all she could muster was a slight smile.

Bodhi looked up at her and grinned, then his smile faded. "How long has that wagon been behind us?"

The driver of the sleigh yelled back, "I don't know. He wasn't there fifteen minutes ago."

"How close are we?" Bodhi straightened and checked his weapon.

"We have to stop long enough to raise the runners and let the wheels take over since the city area will be devoid of snow. We could travel on the runners if we had to, but they make a lot of noise on hard roads and slow us down," the man said.

"You'd better signal the other sleigh, hide the kids in the vaults, and get those runners up now so we don't have to stop again," Bodhi said.

Rylla and Dane hadn't been fond of the idea, but the impenetrable munitions vaults were the only safe place for the children if lead started flying. There was plenty of ventilation for a short time. Rylla reluctantly crawled in, and Selah saw Dane do the same.

Selah rose to the driver's level of the wagon so she could see ahead. The driver's seat sat several feet higher, giving a broad look at the approaching city of Milwaukee. She was confused about where to look. The Seeker hadn't been any help. So Selah just kept repeating to herself, *You'll know it when you see it.* She needed to will her mind to stay strong enough to find it, whatever *it* was.

They stopped, and the little men hopped down to raise the runner with hand cranks on each side of the sleigh. They worked perfectly in tune and the sleigh lowered evenly.

Selah turned toward the setting sun, and when she turned back to the east, she caught a bright glint in Milwaukee about three miles away. The few times she had spotted glints in the landscape they were reflections from domes, but that wasn't the case this time. The next dome had been much farther west, and it hadn't survived the beginning of the magnetic storms after the Sorrows.

The sleighs were now wagons with huge lumbering wheels and a decidedly bumpier ride. Rylla complained from inside the vault. Selah looked down at her. "The ride is almost over." When she looked up, she saw the glint again. She pointed at it. "Bodhi—"

A shot rang out. Selah ducked. The driver whipped the horses into a gallop and Selah lurched to the back. Bodhi caught her and put her back on her feet. She reached for her weapon and returned fire to the building on the right side of the road. Bodhi took the left.

The little man peered from beneath his seat and pointed as he yelled, "There's the city gates! We get inside and we've made it." He reached out and slapped the whip to the horses' backsides.

If they continued to go this fast they'd clear the gauntlet in another minute. A bullet ricocheted from the side of the munitions vault. Rylla yelped. It bit into the heavy wood side, chucking a splinter at Selah's face. The wood sliced her cheek, and red dripped on the back of her hand. She wiped it away with her sleeve and pulled the trigger.

"The first wagon made it!" the little man yelled as he put the whip to the horses again.

Gunfire from both sides of the street sent a hail of bullets into the wagon. The whip cracked and the horses pulled faster. Suddenly the wagon dipped in the front as it slammed into a wide and deep depression. The back end came up at Selah as if in slow motion. The weapon lockers slid forward in the cargo channel and reached the munitions vault. They stood up on end as the wagon bed flipped free of the sleigh base and sling-shotted the weapons case and munitions vault into the street, with the wagon bed tumbling behind.

Selah and Bodhi dangled by the framework of the sleigh as it flipped and rolled. The horses ran out of control toward the city gate. The harness was still connected to the sleigh frame, where it tangled when the wagon bed flipped off. The frame bumped and zigzagged, hopping on end. Selah thought of jumping, but she wanted to be closer to the gate and didn't want to leave Bodhi.

The frame disintegrated, releasing the horses and throwing Bodhi off to the left. Selah slid off to the right. She dug at the ground, getting her footing in the slippery dirt and snow mess. Shots grew closer from the dilapidated century-old buildings. The shooters were dialing in their aim so they didn't have to move any closer. They probably hadn't planned on chasing the wagon to the gate, but two people on foot must have looked like an easier target.

Bodhi lay near the final destination of a weapons crate that had rolled up the road and split. Selah scrambled to him, trying to find the munitions vault. She couldn't see it. It had to be in the wagon debris. A shot came closer, kicking up a wad of frozen mud about ten feet in front of them. Selah hauled Bodhi behind the split crate. The metal bottom would at least give visual protection.

Bodhi shook his head to clear himself. "How far to the gates?"

"About a hundred feet. I'm going to get guns and see if I can find Rylla," Selah said.

"Are you crazy? The guns are back where they're shooting at us. If Rylla's still in the vault, she's safe. We'll find her," Bodhi said.

"They're using a stationary gun and the person doesn't know how to shoot. If I run down there, they won't be able to dial in distance adjustments that fast. We learned tracking that way as kids," Selah said. She knew she wouldn't be able to do this kind of stuff much longer.

She didn't wait for an answer but took off running. She grabbed the first two weapons that weren't broken and glanced around for the vault. *Where did it go?*

The weapon fired at her three more times, but she ran back serpentine style so the shooter would have to work at tracking her. A bullet ripped into her right arm, spinning her around. White-hot pain bit into her arm as Selah slid feet first behind the crate.

Bodhi's eyes were wide. He shouted, "Why did you do that?"

"Because I could. I still don't see Rylla." She grabbed at her arm. Was she being reckless to save Bodhi and Rylla, or reckless because she knew she was dying anyhow? She glanced at the burned, streaked furrow cut through her coat near her shoulder.

Selah fished in her pockets for the extra magazine the little man had given her. Bodhi did the same. They barraged the stationary weapon location and it went silent. They ran toward the gate.

A new weapon started firing at them. One that fired a fast flurry of bullets. Selah and Bodhi worked their way down the street as a unit, hiding behind stationary objects and ducking in doorways, with one shooting and the other leading the way.

In front of them, another gun firing repeated bullets cut off their run to the gate.

Selah pulled back where Bodhi had stopped. "Why'd you stop?"

"I'm out of ammunition," Bodhi said.

Gunfire came from both directions. Selah returned fire until she met with a click.

She looked at Bodhi. "I'm out too. Got any ideas?" A shot ricocheted off a stone building behind them. They both flinched and ducked. More shots. One struck the doorway.

Bodhi smiled. "I love—"

The gate to the city burst open, and an angry mob of little people charged out with guns blazing.

Two of the little men fired rockets, blowing a hole that exposed most of the building's insides where the second set of repeating bullet guns had come from. Stone and brick rained down on the street, mixing with the gunfire smoke and rocket fire. One man was throwing hand bombs like they were baseballs. He easily took out the pocket of repeating bullet guns and caused several spot fires.

The gunfire aimed at Bodhi and Selah ceased. Bodhi started for the gate, but Selah still wanted to find Rylla.

Bodhi grabbed her by the arm. "You didn't see the vault. We don't know where to look."

She couldn't talk without shaking. She pushed him away and started down the street toward the fighting. Bodhi grabbed her around the waist and hauled her kicking and screaming to the gate.

He passed through the gate still holding her by the waist, and the opening closed behind him.

He put her down, and Selah stumbled to a plodding walk in a circle. "You stopped me from saving Rylla."

"You didn't know where she was. If you did, I'd have gone with you," Bodhi said.

She fisted a hand to her side to ease the pain cramping her stomach. She breathed hard and continued to circle by the gate. Pasha, Mari, and Dane ran forward to hug them.

Dane looked between everyone. "Where's Rylla?"

Selah chewed on her lip and pointed to the gate. "She's out there somewhere. I couldn't find her. I left her." She dissolved into tears.

"It will be all right," Dane said. He looked scared to see Selah crying, so she stemmed the tears.

The gates opened, and the cheering crowd welcomed the victorious little men, who carried the recovered weapons and an open munitions vault between them. Rylla rode in the center.

Selah ran to help her out of the vault and check her over.

"I'm okay, just a little bruised from rolling so many times," Rylla said.

The little man who had driven the first wagon and given them a place to stay overnight walked to the front of the vault.

"We found her under the liner from the sleigh, along with the driver. You were very brave to try to go back there."

"I'm so grateful to you for saving my Rylla," Selah said. She shook the man's hand.

"We want to thank *you* for giving us a renewed sense of confidence. You are the first high people who have ever fought for us, and that is why my people were willing to fight for you."

Selah hugged Rylla. "High people?"

A little woman with leather straps full of bullets crossing her chest strolled over. "That's what we call the people who tower over us. They do their best to intimidate us with their stature and are always talking down to us as though we're children."

"Generations ago we had our own community on the lake in Chicago. When they built the dome they deemed us defective and unfit participants for the project, so they used eminent domain and forced us to sell our land to the corporation," the first wagon driver said.

"I recognized your tree markings from the little wood people near my home," Mari said.

"We had kinfolk everywhere before the Sorrows. Living on the lake hillsides like we do now was the easiest way to keep them from running us off our land. We built under it instead of on it."

Selah turned to Mari. "If it weren't for you seeing the tree markings, we'd never have found these people or this help. I wonder how many others missed the help?"

"We've never known strangers that weren't the hated Blood Hunters, and that's why we didn't turn you away yesterday," the man said. "Maybe now my people will understand that all high people aren't like Blood Hunters."

Two little men came forward with an armful of weapons. The little man at the front pointed to the cache. "We owe you combat pay that goes above and beyond what you signed up to do."

Pasha started to tell him that it wasn't necessary, but the little man cut her off. "You are in the city now. To go anywhere or do anything you need funds. All you have are the clothes you're wearing. You may need others soon. Sell these at the market on Layton. It's in the park, that way." The little man pointed.

Selah's group thanked him and started to walk away.

"And don't sell to Red Crest. He will have you followed, beat up, and robbed to get his money back."

26

Selah walked between Dane and Rylla while Bodhi, Mari, and Pasha carried the weapons. She saw Bodhi wince at the cut on her face and the graze on her arm, neither of which had healed.

The weather in Milwaukee cooperated for about the first ten minutes into their walk. The snowflakes came down so fat and fluffy that in the still evening Selah could hear them plop. It was serene and peaceful in the snow even though Selah nursed aches in every part of her body. They turned left onto Twenty-Seventh Street. Selah lifted her head . . . and stopped.

Bodhi ran into her back and grabbed her around the waist to keep from knocking her over. "What's the matter? Are you okay? We can sit down if you need to."

Selah ignored him and started to chuckle, and the chuckle turned into a laugh. She laughed until she cried, and warm tears made cold trails down her face. Everyone stared at her like the world was ending.

Selah pointed. "Look!"

Off in the distance in the middle of a large open space sat three beehive-shaped domes. They were each approximately seven stories tall and only about 140 feet in diameter. The lighting made them appear as sparkling beams in the night. In the snow they almost looked magical.

"I guess that must be the market. Hope it's warm in there," Selah joked.

And it was. Each dome had a different tropical climate containing strange birds with loud screeching sounds and large plumage. One dome had a floor-to-ceiling waterfall and a forest where Selah wanted to stay forever. The domes were twenty-four-hour hubs of activity, and the warmth and food were welcome. It appeared the majority of people dealing in the marketplace were wealthy or were dealing illegal goods because they dressed well but acted shifty.

They hurried through the three marketplaces. They received enough money from one weapon to buy food and drink for all of them and had leftover currency for their travel fund.

As they sat eating cheese and fruit at a metal table bolted to the floor in an eating area, Mari pinned down the situation. "What do we want to do now?"

They came up with at least half a dozen things they needed, from sleep to clothes. Selah dozed between bites of the late-night meal, too tired to add suggestions.

"No," Mari said. "We're not focused. What do we want to *do*?"

Selah lifted her head. "Go to the West and find the Third Protocol." She let her head plunk back to the table for effect.

Mari smiled. "We have no transportation and only as much

money as we're going to get from these weapons. So we need suggestions."

"Why can't we go by train? And what's a train?" Dane asked.

The conversation stopped and everyone turned to look at Dane. He backed into the corner by Pasha. "I'm sorry. I won't talk again." His face turned red and he covered his head.

"No, honey, we're not mad at you. We just want to know where you got that idea," Selah said.

Dane pointed across the room. Selah turned. A sign said TRIPTIC—TRAINS TO PACIFIC NORTHWEST.

Pasha looked at the sign then turned to Dane. "A train is a vehicle that pulls cars of people and products. We never had any in Dominion because constant raiders made smaller personal craft easier to protect. Can it be that easy?"

Selah chuckled. "Nothing has been that easy."

Her hearing had started to go. She cupped a hand to her right ear to test it and brushed her hand across the cut on her cheek. It still hadn't closed, and neither had the cut on her arm. She was becoming fixated on watching them, because in the past cuts this minor would have healed by now, with no scar.

She mustered her effort and slowly walked to the sign to read the maps and schedules attached to it. Bodhi strolled up beside her, put his arm around her waist, and snuggled her ear as he talked. "Are you feeling okay? Your face hasn't healed."

Selah turned her head toward him and spoke in a hushed tone. "I just noticed my arm hasn't either. I'm so tired I can't stand up long. We need a long discussion so you know what to do with my family after I'm gone."

Bodhi pulled away from her. "You're talking crazy. We haven't come this far to fail."

"That attitude didn't serve Mojica or Taraji very well." Selah gulped back tears. Her emotions were starting to jump all over the place, and she hadn't had alone time yet to mourn her friends' passing.

"That's not fair." Bodhi looked hurt. He hesitated. "*We're going to make it.*"

"I don't think I will, but we'll talk later," Selah said, suddenly feeling overwhelming fatigue. She pulled four trifold maps from the sign stand and headed back to their table. "Okay, folks, we have four routes west. Each one has slightly different stations and they all end in different locations. Which one do we pick?" She spread the maps out on the table. Could getting there actually be this easy?

Selah nodded off a couple more times, and each time she awoke the others were still arguing routes. Rylla and Dane curled up together to sleep in a corner, and Selah went back to sleep, listening to the familiar drone of Bodhi's, Mari's, and Pasha's voices.

February 16

When Selah woke, the breaking light of the morning sky blistered red on the horizon outside the dome. Old farmers in Dominion used to say red sky in the morning was a warning sign, but Selah and her family had been subjected to so much danger they were desensitized by it. She thought it ironic that dangerous, chaotic days were a normal way of life.

She stretched and studied the three sets of bleary eyes staring back at her. Despite the uncertainty, they still needed a plan to have a purpose. "Did you figure out which route we're taking?" She was counting on them for the strength and mental clarity to figure that out.

"We each know several of the symbols but weren't able to narrow it down farther than three—Portland, Los Angeles, and Seattle." Pasha held up the three.

"Where do you remember the symbols from?" Selah looked at the tired group.

Mari shook her head. "We went through hundreds of documents. It could have been on anything."

Selah looked at the route maps and the destinations. Nothing about any of them stuck out. She'd failed to sit down and study Glade's data because she kept thinking there'd be more time.

A steam locomotive chugged into a station somewhere nearby. It shrilled a ten-second triple blast that vibrated the dome and created a strange whirring like a moan.

The noise jerked both children awake. Rylla, a morning grump, tried to hide her head behind Dane to block the noise, but Dane was an early-day bee in a bottle and couldn't sit still. With hair sticking out in all directions, he proceeded to flit from person to person, playing with the paper maps. He mumbled as he unfolded and refolded them, then tossed each map until only one remained.

Dane smiled confidently. "This is the map we need."

Once again he had silenced four adults. Sleep-deprived eyes stared back at him.

"Why is this one the right map?" Selah asked. He had been

so good through this whole ordeal that she couldn't just dismiss him outright.

"Because all the stories are in order—Tunnel, River, Dome, Devil, Wolf, Bear, Ice, Apple, and Needle. The nine stories are in order. I memorized them all."

Selah looked at him and pulled the route map over to look. "Mother?"

Pasha shrugged. "I read some of the Stone Braide Chronicles at the beginning, but the children went at it on their own in Cleveland while Mari and I were helping with the epidemic."

Rylla finally brought her grumpy self to the table.

Selah nudged her and wrapped an arm around her shoulders, trying to cajole a smile. "Wake up and tell us if Dane is right. Are the stations on this routing the nine stories in the Stone Braide Chronicles?"

Rylla rubbed her eyes with the heels of her hands, then pouted and leaned on the table, staring at the chart. She looked up as if she were deep in thought and counted a few times.

Dane bumped her. "Come on! Tell them I'm right." He bounced around like a nervous frog.

Rylla scrunched up her face. "He's right. They're all there in the correct order."

"What about these?" Selah scooped up the other three from the floor.

Rylla looked at the first discard. She puckered her lips. "Nope, this one only has four symbols." She tossed it and opened the second. A storm formed between her eyebrows. "This one is closer but it only has eight."

Selah looked at the map. The Needle was missing. This

route led to Spokane, Washington. She tried to remember where the state was. The routes weren't typical maps but a straight line with symbols at each dot, representing a station or detour.

"That sets our destination." Selah pointed at the sign. "When does the next train leave, and how much does it cost?"

Bodhi and Mari hurried to the sign and did some furious calculations. "The trip takes four days, and the cost for six of us is more than we can get with the remaining weapons," Bodhi said.

"By how much?" Selah asked.

"A whole ticket," Bodhi said.

"The Red Crest guy would give us enough."

"He'd also rob or kill us to take the money back." Bodhi leaned away from the table.

"Then somebody has to stay behind," Selah said. She didn't really mean it, but wanted Bodhi to see the futility of not taking a chance on getting the best price for the weapons.

"I'll stay here," Mari said. She pulled herself up tall. Her lips disappeared as she pressed them together, her brows furrowed. Selah saw Mari's hand tremble, but she quickly shoved it in her pocket.

"I'd be willing to stay as long as you promise to take care of Dane," Pasha said to Selah. Selah hugged her, waiting for Bodhi to speak up.

The look on Bodhi's face turned to horror. "No! No one is staying behind. We go together."

Selah smiled. "These people don't seem to know novarium

or Landers, so we may have an advantage with our fighting skills. I think we could devise a plan."

They walked the shortest route to the train station. After she saw the armed security, Selah felt better about leaving Pasha and the children sitting on a bench near the ticket counter for Seattle. Bodhi and Selah trudged back to the marketplace alone while Mari shadowed them, remaining at a location they'd agreed to about halfway between the market and the station. It was the longest direct sight Mari could have of the pair on their way back with the currency.

After talking to some of the marketers, Selah figured a daylight attack wouldn't happen in the open where there would be witnesses. She and Bodhi could control the situation by leading the bandits through the area of abandoned buildings west of the station—a dangerous shortcut that most people avoided. That would happen right after Mari secretly joined up with the group.

Bodhi carried all five of the weapons. Part of it was a mind game to give Red Crest the illusion Bodhi was a tough guy and could beat him in a fight. After Bodhi saw the man's physique, he whispered to Selah that he knew there'd be a problem but that the plan itself was foolproof.

Earlier they had worried about the plan because there was still a thin coating of snow on the ground and it would be hard to hide where Mari waited, but on the way back to the market the sun had gotten so warm the snow covering melted.

Now Selah wondered if there was an easier way than being targets walking out of the market with a pocketful of Milwaukee currency. They'd made the deal with Red Crest and received quite a bit more currency than they expected.

As they walked away, Selah held Bodhi's hand as part of their innocent couple façade. "Why did Red Crest give us so much more and make a big deal out of it to the people standing around?"

Bodhi squeezed her hand. "This way he just upped the price he'd pay for that model, and it will bring in better business because now he can sell the weapons for more. He doesn't intend to let the buyers keep the money. He'll take it back at his rigged gambling tables, or his thugs will get it back if people like us try to walk away with it."

They hung around at the marketplace, trying to throw off Red Crest's henchmen, but they finally had to leave. With the currency stashed in their tactical suits, Bodhi and Selah took off at a jog toward the shortcut to the train station.

Selah dreaded the need to expend her precious energy, but the train station was only about two miles away. Halfway there Mari signaled them with a piece of shiny metal, letting them know she'd follow along on the sideline.

Selah kept up, but she had to push herself a lot harder than she normally would. It was happening too fast. The two open wounds were glaring reminders that her novarium cycle was almost done. At this rate she would only last a matter of days instead of months.

She could hear Bodhi's breathing as they ran. They were so in tune. How would he be without her?

Bodhi's chest pounded like a fist. He felt every fiber in him ready for this fight. He could have no doubt. The men working for Red Crest were going to be big.

Two men ran from the other side of the first abandoned building and charged at them. Bodhi drew the bigger guy with the gray shirt around the corner of the building to separate the men and let Mari help Selah. The guy confronting Bodhi planted his feet and held up two fists on arms that looked like logs.

Bodhi put up his hands and jabbed. The guy dodged to his right and came around to hit Bodhi in the ribs, buckling him over. With a twist, Bodhi came back with an uppercut to the guy's jaw, and Gray Shirt staggered back.

He charged toward Bodhi, who stood his ground till the last second and then sidestepped. Gray Shirt spun to hit Bodhi again, and Mari appeared crouched behind him. Bodhi shoved the guy with two fists, and he flew over Mari's back. His head smashed into the ground, knocking him out.

Even with Bodhi and Selah at less than their optimum, they were still stronger than normal people their size, so surprise and speed were the advantage with these guys.

Bodhi and Mari ran to help Selah with Black Shirt Guy. They arrived just in time to see Selah sweep his legs and come down on his chest with the full weight of her body. Her elbow and then her fist smashed into his face.

Bodhi pulled Selah to her feet, and they ran. She was a little slower, but he held Mari back to help synchronize their steps as they worked their way through the crumbled stone and brick buildings of the ancient factory complex.

Around the last corner, the station came into view. The huge ten-wheeled steam locomotive sat on the track at the front of a six-car train. Running footsteps bore down on them. Bodhi turned to see another black-shirted guy roaring toward them. Mari also saw him.

"Keep running!" Bodhi yelled.

Mari grabbed Selah by the arm and spirited around a tall container and into the station. Bodhi ran around the container behind them, then spun and planted his fist in the guy's face as he caught up. The man crumpled into a stone barricade and slid to the ground. Bodhi sprinted into the station.

He hurried to the ticket counter where Pasha and the kids waited and laid out the currency for the six tickets with a sleeper car. Everyone piled on the train barely two minutes before the stairs were pulled up and the whistle was blown to push off from the station.

The kids ran down the aisle looking for the compartment number and excitedly announced to anyone listening that they were going to the West. Bodhi enjoyed hearing that. Despite his doubts at the beginning, he had been able to keep the family together. Glade could rest in peace now.

They filed into the six-person car, which had a wide window. Three people sat on each side, and overhead a sleeper bunk pulled down on each side so two could sleep and four could be awake and comfortable. Once cabin fever hit, there was a viewing car and dining facilities, their tickets said.

Bodhi helped Selah up into one of the overhead bunks. She protested that she wasn't all that tired, but she only uttered two sentences before she fell asleep. He was afraid to bring it to Pasha's and Mari's attention, but besides Selah's lack of healing, her skin had taken on a yellowish tinge. Bodhi wasn't sure if she'd notice the color of her skin because her eyes were covered in the same film.

He decided to make notes for Selah to read later, after she

connected to the Third Protocol and they began their lives together. They were so close to the end.

February 17

Selah awoke ravenously hungry. She sat up quickly, forgetting her surroundings, and whacked her head on the ceiling of the overhead bunk. She looked over the edge.

Bodhi looked up from the seat beneath her. "Good morning, firefly." He stood and helped her down.

Selah stretched. It felt good, but weakness had crept into her bones. She glanced around. "Where's everybody?"

"Pasha took the kids to the observation car," Mari said. "She's decided to turn this into a learning trip about the stories they remember from the Stone Braide Chronicles. We had a good bit of money left over from the tickets, so we have an account in the dining car. Help yourself."

"Leave it to Mother to get them to learn without knowing," Selah said. Her stomach growled.

Bodhi leaned forward. "Pasha did it to keep them from spending too much time around you."

Selah balked. "Why? What's the matter with me?"

"Sister, I love you dearly, but you're beginning to . . . well, not look so good, and the kids are getting concerned. Pasha just wanted to spare them some of it," Mari said.

Selah looked down at her arms. The color was off. Her hand went to her cheek. There was still moisture at the cut, and she could see the furrowed edge of the bullet graze on her upper arm. "Do I look that bad?"

Bodhi frowned.

"No, to an outsider you look normal. It's just to us who know you better that it's noticeable." Mari smiled then reached over to cuff Bodhi. "You never tell a woman she looks bad!"

He was so surprised he couldn't say anything. Selah had to leave before she burst into laughter. "My stomach is ready to revolt. I'm going to find something to eat for breakfast." She quickly exited and headed up the narrow aisle, thankful that the walls were close enough for her to balance on wobbly legs.

She looked at the sign ahead declaring "Dining Car." Selah stopped and glanced at her dusty, dirty tactical uniform. Everyone in there probably wore travel clothes, not a uniform run through fire. She had gotten used to the family smelling burned, but she noticed strangers seemed to pull away.

Selah reached for the handle. She wasn't going to worry about people's thoughts of her clothes, because there were bigger problems. She held her head up and walked in.

Most of the men in the car appeared to be miners probably going to gold fields that she had seen posters for in the train station. Selah smiled. Their clothes had years more dirt than hers. She sat at the service counter and requested an order of eggs, fruit, and bread, which was delivered quickly while she looked for a seat. Selah took the food to an outside table with a window view of the countryside.

Selah watched out the window for the longest time between bites of food. She enjoyed the peace and monotonous turning of the train wheels.

"Would you like some water to wash down that dry bread?" A black-haired man smiled and offered a cylinder of water and a cup.

Selah nodded and drank down two cups of the chilled liquid. She put down the cup and picked up her fruit.

The man sat at the next table with his hands crossed in front of him, staring at Selah. She stopped mid-bite and looked at him. "Is there a problem?" Was he one of these clothes-sniffer types?

The man pursed his lips and shook his head slowly. "Nope. No problem at all. I just wanted to get a good look at one of you."

Selah jerked to attention. "Excuse me?"

"A novarium. I wanted to get a good look even though you're no good no more," the man said.

Selah began to stand. "What makes you think I'm a novarium?" Now that she was paying attention she saw part of a lightning bolt under his rolled-up sleeve. She panicked and tried to scramble away, but her coordination failed and she fell forward.

The man caught her before she reached the floor and sat her back on the seat. "Relax. I told you that you're no good anymore."

Selah leaned back in the seat. It was stupid to be this close to him, but there'd be eleven other witnesses if he did anything. Her heart raced.

"Explain. Why am I not good anymore?" She felt crazy for asking such a question.

He gestured. "Your face. It's not healing. Your blood is soured now. No one will bother you anymore, not with that open cut on your face."

27

February 20

Bodhi helped Pasha bring Selah down the steps of the train. Her legs wobbled and her hands shook. One step was enough. Bodhi picked her up in his arms and felt her sigh against his chest. He pressed her tight against himself, never wanting to let her go. He held her longer than necessary, but he wanted to have the memory.

Mari came down the steps with both kids in tow. "Dane, Rylla, tell us the last story, the one about the needle."

Rylla and Dane looked at each other. Rylla spoke up. "It was mostly about her children, and how hard they worked to make a living, and how the old lady always made everything better with her needle."

"She mended all their problems," Dane said.

"That's the last thing we have. You said this place has the Space Needle?" Bodhi asked Mari. He watched Selah with Pasha.

On the train, Selah had quickly lost her mental abilities and wandered away from the cabin twice. Now Dane and Rylla crowded around her. They'd become protective as her senses waned.

Mari walked over to the station wall and ran her finger along the city map. "Here's where we want to go. It's two miles north."

Pasha looked around. "How much do we have left? If the currency was good at the other end of the line, it should be good here."

Bodhi walked with Pasha to find a way to the Space Needle that didn't involve Selah walking. They stepped out of the station and stopped to look around. The world outside the station had bright sunshine and a crisp blue sky with fluffy white clouds.

Looking north toward the looming ancient Space Needle, he saw the sky filled with multiple layers of air traffic, both personal craft and larger commercial craft similar to Air-Wagons. Heavy foot traffic clogged the streets, but he saw no visible commerce.

Bodhi looked at the different layers of traffic. "Do we just ask someone?"

Pasha looked around. "I remember something similar to this from when I was a child . . ."

"Really? Where were you to see technology this advanced?"

Pasha opened her mouth to answer then frowned. "I don't remember." She put her hands on her hips. "But I'm positive I knew it at one time. There are four layers of air traffic. Personal vehicles, mass transit, commerce, and a government layer for military and security."

Bodhi looked at the traffic. "Okay, if you know what you're doing, find us a ride to the Needle."

Pasha bit her lower lip and searched the area. She marched over to a red hologram sign that said "Services" projecting from the surface of the street and ran her hand through the beam. A pole rose from the street to waist height and blossomed open into several user screens for various services.

Bodhi watched as Pasha ordered a vehicle as easily as if she'd done it every day, and within three minutes a vehicle dropped from a traffic lane. It hovered two feet from the ground and the side lifted.

"How did you do that?" Bodhi peered in at the driverless conveyance.

Pasha shook her head. "I've got smells and sounds and images all swirling in my head right now. I feel like I'm waking from a dream."

"I'll get Selah," Bodhi said. Noting Pasha's abilities in this strange place would be a conversation for later. He turned to run inside, but Mari and Rylla were already helping Selah down the station steps. Bodhi scooped her up in his arms and brought her to the vehicle.

All six piled in, and Pasha told the conveyance to take them to the Needle. The auto-system asked for her handprint. Pasha looked around. Bodhi shrugged. "Go ahead. You seem to be the guide here."

Pasha hesitantly laid her hand on the surface. The machine cleared and geared up to leave.

Bodhi noted every new piece of scenery with surprise until they were close enough to see the Needle. An adrenaline rush traveled from the soles of his feet, out his arms, and up his neck, tingling the base of his hairline. He knew this building.

The conveyance deposited them at the base of the Needle. Mari and Pasha were holding Selah up when a girl dressed in white hurried out of the building and approached Bodhi.

"I'm sorry, but you are not allowed to have sick people outside among the population. Illness is to be quarantined until no longer viral."

Bodhi started to say Selah wasn't contagious, but by the time he opened his mouth two men with a wheeled stretcher had snatched Selah and were rushing her inside. Everyone followed, and Bodhi worked his way up front to the stretcher.

Selah looked up at him. She mouthed several words. Bodhi put his ear close to her mouth to hear. The attendants jostled the stretcher through a conveyance with a wavy blue light. By the time they came out the other side of the tube Selah was unconscious, which seemed to send the attendants into a panic. Bodhi rubbed her arm, trying to bring her around, but she remained unresponsive.

The attendants ran the stretcher through a second machine, and the reading said "Undetermined." They put her in yet another machine, with the same results.

Twice Pasha stopped Bodhi from yelling at attendants for not talking to him. "Let's wait and talk to a doctor."

"You mean tell them Selah is the novarium?" Bodhi wasn't ready to be that open with strangers.

"No, of course not. I don't think it's something they can detect, so we keep our mouths shut. I was talking to a woman while they were trying to diagnose Selah. Seattle is one of the plague cities. The Red Plague was eradicated over a year ago, but anyone who shows up with anything undetermined is held in confinement until they figure out what it is or the person gets better."

Bodhi grimaced. "Or the person dies."

Pasha lowered her head. "Well, that too, but I didn't want to say it. For the moment this place is a plus. They'll give Selah anything necessary to keep her comfortable as long as she stays undiagnosed and they fear she could start another plague."

"How do we find the Third Protocol?" Bodhi tried to remain calm, but his fear that Selah was becoming too weak kept bubbling up into a panic.

Pasha shook her head. "I've been asking everyone I think I can trust. Nobody has any idea what I'm talking about."

The attendants wheeled Selah down a long hall and into a side corridor that led to numerous solid white rooms. They moved her to the bed and shooed everyone out, but Pasha refused to leave. She moved to the corner and the door closed.

Bodhi paced. He didn't have Selah's advice to guide him. He took a deep breath. He had to stop overthinking. He loved Selah, and that should be enough to prove he wanted the best for her.

The door opened and the attendant let the rest of them in.

Selah lay like a small dot of long dark hair and sallow-colored skin amid a sea of white bedclothes, sheets, and walls. They approached the bed as though their footfalls might wake her. Bodhi pulled up a chair and sat beside the bed. Rylla and Dane moved in close on the other side of the bed to stroke Selah's hand. Mari came alongside the children, smoothed Selah's hair, and spoke softly in her ear. Pasha sat on a chair in the corner.

Bodhi felt his lip tremble. He had to get out of there before he cried. He bolted from his seat and stormed down the hall and out the doors into the open air. He walked in circles, inhaling deeply, and started to cry. This wasn't fair. She couldn't die.

The fierceness of his tears scared him. He ran around the side of the building where there was no traffic and paced again until he gained control, then walked back around front.

Mari ran out the door. "They're looking for you, hurry!"

Bodhi darted back inside. Two doctors and a nurse stood with Pasha near Selah's bed. Pasha looked relieved to see Bodhi.

"Now that he's here, please repeat what you told me," she said.

The doctor looked like he didn't appreciate being told what to do. "I said that the girl has an undiagnosed deficiency we can't say is not contagious—"

"Please just tell me what it means," Bodhi said.

"She has to stay here until we know what's wrong. And one other thing I'd suggest for all our well-being is that you find clothes that don't smell like forest fires." The doctors and nurse left the room, trying not to be obvious about holding their noses as they passed by.

The nurse stuck her head back through the door. "I heard you were strangers in town. We have family services that will give you a hot shower and a change of clothes. Take these cards down the end of the hall. Each will admit one." The woman handed Bodhi five plascine-looking cards.

Bodhi let Pasha and Mari take the kids first while he sat beside Selah. Her breathing grew so shallow at one point that Bodhi thought she had gone without telling him goodbye. His eyes moistened. An attendant came in with a cloth to clean and swab the cut on Selah's cheek.

"Tell me the truth. How long does she have?" Bodhi stared at the profile of the woman until she turned to face him.

The sadness on her face said it all. "This is hospice care. Her body function has dropped so low that the only measurement we get is her heartbeat. Hours now."

For the first time it sank in. There wasn't going to be a fix for this. They had failed.

He took Selah's hand. Her fingers were already feeling cool.

Bodhi relished the few minutes alone after such a revelation, to wash off the smell of defeat. He would try hard not to be bitter. But this wasn't fair. They had made it here.

The group poured back in the room with everyone smelling and looking clean in tan unisex outfits. Mari and Pasha stayed with Selah while Bodhi showered and changed. When he finished he headed outside to walk off the anxiety digging a hole in his heart. Rylla and Dane sat on the low stone wall in front of the medical unit. Bodhi sat across from them and looked up at the building. Curious. Was his anxiety about Selah or this building?

Bodhi's drifting thoughts were interrupted by the squabbling children. "Stop! Come over here and tell me what's bad enough you have to fight about it at a time like this," he said.

Rylla and Dane tromped over to him.

"Selah will be real mad when she finds out he stole her rocks!" Rylla stuck her lip out.

Dane crossed his arms tightly.

Bodhi looked at Dane. "What rocks?"

"The rocks he's been hiding in the compartment of his uniform till now," Rylla said. She pulled Dane's arms apart and a canvas bag dropped to the ground.

Bodhi recognized it right away. It held the precious stones Selah was trading in Chicago for parts, and it was still quite full. He pulled the strings and opened the bag.

Dane became irate. He grabbed at Rylla's neck and pulled off three slender chains, each holding a small silver angular pendant. Rylla tried to snatch them back. Dane jerked away, and the necklaces flew from his hand and skittered across the walkway in a tangled pile.

An older woman in a white coat bent and picked up the pile of jewelry. She straightened, holding the necklaces out in front of her. The three pendants spun in a slow circle and gravitated to each other to form a shape.

The woman's eyes widened. She grabbed Dane by the scruff of his neck. "Where did you get this?"

Dane cried out.

Bodhi ran to her and pulled Dane from her. "Leave him alone. He's just a kid. You shouldn't scare him like that."

"I don't care about the kid. I want to know where these necklaces came from. It could be a matter of life and death."

Bodhi tensed. Would there really be Blood Hunters this far west? He decided to detour her and get reinforcements to protect Selah. "Okay, she's on the second floor. I don't know the room number, but they'll know."

He hoped he'd been vague enough to give them a head start. As soon as she disappeared into the building, Bodhi grabbed the sobbing kids and ran for Selah's room on the first floor. They charged in.

Tears streamed down Pasha's face. Mari stood on the other side of the bed holding her hand over her mouth. Selah's skin had become waxy and translucent.

"I'm glad you got here. The doctor said she has but minutes. Children, come say goodbye." Pasha motioned them closer to the bed.

Rylla was still crying. Pasha looked at Bodhi. "Why is she crying?"

"Some crazy woman bullied Dane and stole her necklaces," Bodhi said.

"They were Selah's necklaces. She stole Selah's necklaces," Rylla wailed.

"Who stole them?" Pasha asked.

The door to the room flew open and the woman in the white coat raced in.

Rylla pointed. "She did."

Pasha turned toward the door. Her eyes widened as she gave a sharp intake of air. "Mother?"

The woman ran past Pasha and Mari and grabbed Selah's hands with both of hers.

Selah's mouth shot open in a long gasp. Her chest rose and fell deeply several times. She coughed long and hard. The woman put a hand behind her back and sat Selah up.

Bodhi pushed his way to her side and took her hand. "Selah, firefly, come back to me." He broke into a wide grin when her eyelids fluttered.

Selah's eyes opened and her color returned in mere seconds. Bodhi watched as the cut on her cheek closed and disappeared beneath the layer of salve.

"Did I make it?" Selah said in a weak voice that got stronger as she spoke. "How did it happen? I'm beginning to feel better."

Rylla squealed with delight while Dane whooped it up, spinning in circles.

"Hush, children. Let's celebrate a little quieter for the rest of the patients' sake." Pasha brushed the tears from her eyes and wrapped her shaking arms gently around Selah. She kissed her daughter on the cheek then moved past Bodhi. "Mother!" She hugged the woman fiercely.

"Pasha, how are you, my child? You and Glade should be so proud. You are the first to complete a Protocol."

Pasha hugged the woman again. A strangled sob came from her lips. "Glade didn't make it."

"Oh, how sad. I hope he was proud of this lovely granddaughter of mine," the woman said as she reached for Selah's hand again.

Pasha took Selah's other hand. "Darling, I'd like you to meet the person who completed your Protocol, your grandmother, Prudence."

"Hello, Grandmother. I'm very glad to meet you. It's been a long trip." Selah smiled softly and leaned back into the fluffy pillow surrounding her head.

Prudence turned to Pasha. "Are you ready to reintegrate or do you want to finish a log?"

"It's funny what I began to remember when I got here. I want to document things before I forget them," Pasha said.

"Let's do that then. I'm sure Bodhi's anxious to get his life back as a fighter pilot," Prudence said.

As she said that Bodhi felt a buzz. He stood and glanced around the room for the source. The air felt cleaner, he could breathe easier, and colors were brighter.

Do you feel better now?

Bodhi's glance darted around the room. Mind-speak! He could hear mind-speak again. His eyes came to rest on Selah. His heart pounded furiously. She winked.

He wrapped Selah in his arms. "I love you."

She looked up at him. "I love you too."

Their lips met.

February 29

Selah sat up in bed, eating a sweet frozen treat Rylla had found in a machine that kept things cold. Mari was appalled that they'd eat food that contained so much sugar, but Selah laughed. "After surviving all the other things that could kill me, I think sugar will be the least of my problems going forward."

Though relieved, she sometimes found it hard to believe that no one would ever chase her again. The Protocol cycle had been completed with a single moment of contact from her grandmother Prudence. She could see and feel the evidence of the change that instantaneously affected all Landers everywhere.

Her novarium mark was gone. Bodhi's head markings were gone. The marks on all Landers had disappeared. The process would never happen again. All people with Lander DNA—

they and their descendants—were biologically free of disease and able to regenerate after injury for as long as they lived.

Selah fingered the bare spot below her collarbone and looked at it in a mirror. When the cycle completed, the cells forming the marks had returned to their regular function in the body and the markings were reabsorbed.

The old lady Selah had heard about turned out to be her grandma Pru. She literally *was* the Third Protocol. She had carried and protected the coding for 150 years, waiting for this time. Transferred by the moisture of a touch, as soon as the Second and Third Protocol merged, the cycle completed and the self-directed systems began.

She looked out the window at the view of the Pacific. As the first completed Protocol, Selah was relegated to this room, at least until her grandmother finished taking samples. Pasha and Bodhi had been given a reversal series to restore memories that would have jeopardized their missions if they'd had total recall all this time.

The door opened. Pasha and Prudence strolled in, laughing.

"Well, you two look happy enough," Selah said.

"I've talked your grandmother into giving you some of the answers you want, but there's a catch. You'll have to join the Project." Pasha held up both hands. "I promise this will be exciting and different from anything you've ever imagined."

Selah smiled. "I have to get used to you as a scientist. This is a huge change from being a mother and running a flax-cloth business."

"The possibilities are endless," Pasha said.

Selah squinted at them. "Who would we work for and what do we do?"

"You'd work for me, but as to what you'd do, that's need to know, and you don't need to know right now." Grandma Pru winked.

"Then how about things that I do need—well, *want*—to know? If you've been here all this time, what was the Landers coming by sea thing all about?" She remembered the Landers her stepfather had killed and how many others had died for the Project.

Pasha frowned. "Funny you should ask. Now that I remember the process, sending people by sea created quite a debacle."

Selah looked between the two women. She didn't think anything about this process was funny. "Funny ha-ha or funny sad?"

"Funny sad in the long run. When you're designing a bio-mechanical project, the separate parts are designed to learn and mature before they're combined," Pasha said.

Selah grinned. "You mean the cells have to grow up first."

Her mother nodded. "That's a basic and reasonable explanation. We created biological machinery on a subatomic level smaller than most human cells. The individual assemblies perform over a million processes a second, but each phase of the program needed to mature before the next phase."

Selah frowned. "Subatomic?"

"In the twenty-first century they called them nanites, but we perfected the machines on a scale a hundred times smaller."

"That's where the problems started," Prudence said. "By the time the original cells were mature enough for the next Protocol, the East Coast had been declared a dead zone. Our best uncontaminated source of First Protocol cells was in the south. So we gave a certain South American country large monetary payments to drop off specially prepared people like Bodhi. We tried to protect them by placing a bio-film over the boat to filter out impurities, but sometimes the cells went rogue and the bio-film disintegrated. That left the person vulnerable before their body could handle the environment, which resulted in their death."

Selah gasped. "Just like the clones."

Prudence and Pasha looked at each other, then at Selah. Pru's eyes clouded with worry. "Clones? What happened?"

Selah waved a hand. "They said they were an abomination and just dissolved into dust that blew away in a whirlwind."

Prudence huffed out a great sigh and slapped her hand to her chest. "Then thankfully the nanos performed exactly as planned. In case of unauthorized replication, they were programmed to lose cohesion to prevent pilfering of our technology."

The door opened and Bodhi strolled in. "You look great, firefly!" He kissed Selah on the forehead.

Selah chuckled. "I feel great. What do you think of me joining this Project?"

"If they work you half as hard as they're working me now that I've gotten my memories back, I'd say run," Bodhi said with a grin.

Selah shook her head and leaned back against the bed, looking at her grandmother. "I could think of at least a dozen ways this Project could have been done easier."

"When you're better and if you join us, we'll let you see how many different things we tried and failed in getting to this day," Grandma Pru said. "Some of our latest attempts had gotten pretty silly, but hey, I'm the one who said this particular scenario with the clues from the Stone Braide Chronicles and the domes wouldn't work. So what do I know?"

"Okay, one of you tell me what *Lander* means." Selah crossed her arms.

Pasha bit her bottom lip to keep from laughing and lifted her mother's lapel. "Meet your grandmother, Dr. Prudence Flanders, the foremost authority on nano-cellular biotechnology."

Selah looked at Bodhi then at Pasha. "What am I missing?"

Bodhi smiled. "You're missing that the word *Lander* was just an anagram of your grandmother's company name, Flanders BioTech. They may have started by dropping BioTech, then the *F* was lost, and instead of being employees of the company, over time they became Landers."

"Why was it a 150-year project?" Selah asked.

"That was the original termination date on this set of nano-biologicals. After that we'd have had to reprogram a new set and start the cycle over again, but then we'd lose so many of the advances we've made," Grandma Pru said.

"What is the purpose of all this?" Selah looked between her mother and grandmother.

Pasha and Prudence glanced at one another but remained silent.

"I came very close to losing my life for this Project. I think I get to know that answer." Selah sat forward.

"When a thousand years have passed after the Sorrows, this world will endure a great battle of good and evil. Our goal by redesign has always been to have the strongest fighting force possible to combat the coming evil. We have 850 years left to get prepared," Pasha said.

"So if I join this organization, am I going to have to get my memory wiped and live incognito for a hundred years?" Selah didn't think Rylla would like that at all.

"No, the Protocol part of the Project is complete. But we have a lot of hot zones in the safe areas of this country and a couple places overseas we still need to secure. And here on the West Coast we're working on programming the biomechanical cells to eat the volcanic ash and produce bio-fuel. So there's lots for you to do," Grandma Pru said.

"Will I get any assignments with Bodhi?" Selah asked. "You know, Grandmother, he promised to marry me someday." Her grin spread as Bodhi blushed.

"Yes, there may be a need for a team approach. I've had an interesting development beneath one of my old stomping grounds in the East, and I might need to send a team in there," Grandma Pru said.

Selah perked up. "I left behind a very dear friend named Treva in the East when we crossed the mountains, and I'm wondering if there's a chance we might be able to find her. Where would the assignment be?"

Pru smiled. "A place outside Washington DC that we used to call the Mountain."

Bonnie S. Calhoun is the author of *Thunder* and *Lightning*, the first two books in the Stone Braide Chronicles. She loves to write, but it doesn't make her happy unless there are the three Bs: body count, blood, and blowing things up. She also has mad skills at coding HTML and website design.

Bonnie lives in a log cabin in the woods with fifteen acres and a pond full of bass, though she'd rather buy fish at the grocery store. She shares her domain with a husband, a dog, and two cats, all of whom think she is waitstaff. Learn more at www.bonniescalhoun.com.

Get to know

BONNIE S. CALHOUN!

• • •

BonnieSCalhoun.com

Join Selah on the journey that will
change her destiny . . . **AND HER WORLD**

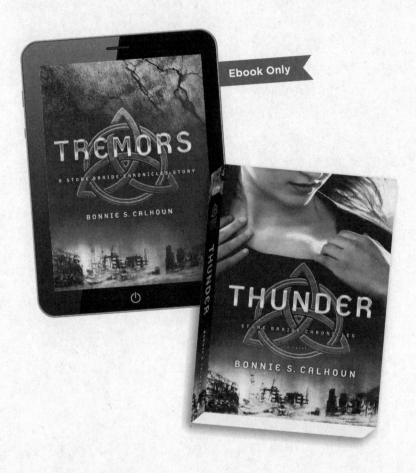

Ebook Only

"Calhoun paints an evocative picture of post-apocalyptic
America and its inhabitants in her first Stone Braide
Chronicles title. . . . Heroine Selah is wonderful, smart, and strong,
and you'll finish this title looking forward to the next."
—*RT Book Reviews*

Selah is DODGING ATTACKS
on every side . . . but time may be
HER GREATEST ENEMY

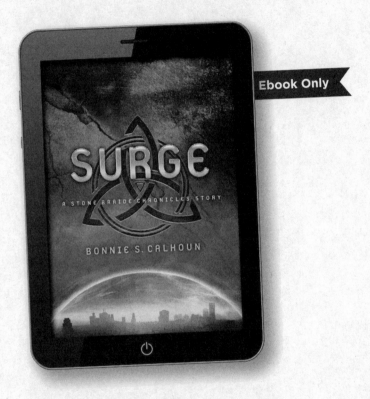

The Mountain is destroyed, the way to the
West has been opened, and Selah's quest must
continue. Her very life depends on it. But how
many casualties will she leave in her wake?